TALES OUT OF LEGEND . . .

Novice priestess Morgaine questions the teachings of the Druids in **Marion Zimmer Bradley** and **Diana L. Paxson**'s *The Heart of the Hill*. . . .

Diana Gabaldon and **Samuel Watkins**'s *The Castellan* must conquer a shape-shifting blue dragon before he succumbs to the wyrm's love spell. . . .

Merlin confesses the sins that led to Camelot's downfall in **Eric van Lustbader**'s *Marwysgafn (Deathbed Song)*. . . .

In **Nina Kiriki Hoffman**'s *The Mouse's Soul*, a meek creature learns what life would be like as a dragon. . . .

And eleven more stories of magic and myth born . . .

Out of Avalon

OUT OF AVALON

Tales of Old Magic and
New Myths

Featuring stories by bestselling authors
Marion Zimmer Bradley, Diana Gabaldon,
Eric Van Lustbader, and others

Edited by

Jennifer Roberson

Ypsilanti District Library
5577 Whittaker Rd.
Ypsilanti, MI 48197-9752

A ROC BOOK

ROC
Published by New American Library, a division of
Penguin Putnam Inc., 375 Hudson Street,
New York, New York 10014, U.S.A.
Penguin Books Ltd, 27 Wrights Lane,
London W8 5TZ, England
Penguin Books Australia Ltd, Ringwood,
Victoria, Australia
Penguin Books Canada Ltd, 10 Alcorn Avenue,
Toronto, Ontario, Canada M4V 3B2
Penguin Books (N.Z.) Ltd, 182–190 Wairau Road,
Auckland 10, New Zealand

Penguin Books Ltd, Registered Offices:
Harmondsworth, Middlesex, England

First published by Roc, an imprint of New American Library,
a division of Penguin Putnam Inc.

First Printing, May 2001
10 9 8 7 6 5 4 3 2 1

Copyright © Tekno-Books and Jennifer Roberson, 2001
All rights reserved

Authors' copyrights for these stories can be found on p. 338.

Cover art by Jeff Barson

 REGISTERED TRADEMARK—MARCA REGISTRADA

Printed in the United States of America

Without limiting the rights under copyright reserved above, no part of this
publication may be reproduced, stored in or introduced into a retrieval system, or
transmitted, in any form, or by any means (electronic, mechanical, photocopying,
recording, or otherwise), without the prior written permission of both the copyright
owner and the above publisher of this book.

PUBLISHER'S NOTE
These are works of fiction. Names, characters, places, and incidents either are the
products of the authors' imagination or are used fictitiously, and any resemblance to
actual persons, living or dead, business establishments, events, or locales is entirely
coincidental.

BOOKS ARE AVAILABLE AT QUANTITY DISCOUNTS WHEN USED TO PROMOTE PRODUCTS OR
SERVICES. FOR INFORMATION PLEASE WRITE TO PREMIUM MARKETING DIVISION, PENGUIN
PUTNAM INC., 375 HUDSON STREET, NEW YORK, NEW YORK 10014.

If you purchased this book without a cover you should be aware that this book is
stolen property. It was reported as "unsold and destroyed" to the publisher and
neither the author nor the publisher has received any payment for this "stripped
book."

CONTENTS

Introduction

There are few "universals" in literature: the story that becomes so popular, so entrenched in a given culture's mind that no explanation beyond the title—or a character's name—is necessary for an individual to grasp the entirety of the universe and its concepts in one fell Gestaltian swoop. Robin Hood is a literary universal; throughout history and countless cultures the tale of an outlaw-hero who supports the oppressed against the predations of the wealthy and powerful thrives. But the hero's name is often changed to suit the cultural context—Zorro, for instance—to make it more user-friendly, more marketable to the target audience.

There is only one King Arthur.

Many books have debated and discussed all aspects of the Arthurian mythos. Some scholars claim Arthur actually existed; some insist "Arthur" was merely a concept representative of certain ideals; others believe the man who has come to be "Arthur" is a composite of several lesser historical personages. We very likely will never know the truth; despite ongoing investigations, excavations, and interpretations, as yet nothing has been accepted as hard evidence that Arthur the King actually lived. The wishful thinking of certain pundits and politicos with regard to the JFK White House notwithstanding, the search for Camelot continues.

And the fact that it does continue, that it exists at all, is part of the fascination.

How many *stories and legends*, merely the constructs and conventions of "professional liars"—bards, poets, minstrels, playwrights, novelists, screenwriters, etc.—have inspired archaeologists and layman scholars to play detective? How many authors, readers, and students have gone off on pilgrimage to pay tribute to, and to soak up the atmosphere of, surroundings that have not yet been proved to be anything but supposition and speculation? Lastly, why do so many people feel Arthur *should* be real? Is it that we embrace his warrior-king image? His Everymanness? The triumphs and tragedies of his reign? The classic rags-to-riches story of his magical begetting, ordinary upbringing, and rite of passage into a perfection of manhood?

Ah, but his manhood wasn't perfect. One aspect of the Arthurian legend claims that he demanded the infant sons of a certain season be killed in an attempt to avoid the foretold doom of his death at Mordred's hands, Arthur's incest-begotton bastard son. Not precisely a heroic act. And, too, there is his apparent neglect of his wife, Guinevere; why else would she turn to Lancelot?

And yet Arthur's reputation survives such sins. He remains the King for All Seasons, Britain's someday savior, for legend claims he will return in England's darkest hour.

Of course, legend also claims England shall survive as long as the ravens inhabit the Tower of London; and so their wings are clipped.

Nonetheless Arthur remains the idealized concept of a good and true hero, a man who accepts all challenges, all responsibilities, all sacrifices, to safeguard his realm and her people. His world fascinates and inspires. It is a wellspring of ideas for countless authors; and many of them have devised fresh and compelling interpretations of the accepted legend. T. H. White gave us Arthur-as-child in *The Once and Future King*, discovering the magics of the world, which in turn inspired Disney's animated film *The Sword in the Stone*. Mary Stewart transformed Merlin, heretofore accepted as a rather androgynous and eccentric old wizard, into a young and vital hero in his own right, sacrificing his own future as king to prepare Arthur for the world—and the world for Arthur. Marion Zimmer Bradley, author of *The Mists of Avalon*, presented us with a more feminist angle, a worldview predicated on the women integral to Arthur's life. Other authors continue to mine the legend, seeking and creating variations on a theme.

With that in mind, the goal of this anthology was not merely to present stories retelling those that have been told many times before. This isn't a collection of tales strictly about Arthur and his doings, though some are included, but also about people other than the famous and infamous, about the ordinary folk who become heroes and heroines because of the choices they make. Small choices often lead to great change, and all too often the beginnings of legend are lost in the endings.

I am very pleased to present a new look at old imaginings, to welcome the intriguing and varied interpretations of gifted storytellers—some household names, some new to all of us—who understand the wonder of the times, the tales, the people who made Arthur's deeds worth doing.

And there is magic afoot.

©—Jennifer Roberson

The Heart of the Hill

Marion Zimmer Bradley
and Diana L. Paxson

Morgaine speaks . . .

Time runs strangely in Avalon, but I no longer look into the Mirror to see what passes beyond the mists that separate it from the world. Arthur is dead, and Lancelet as well, and on the other isle, Christian nuns pray for Viviane's soul. Saxons have overrun the land, and the priestesses here are fewer than they were when first I came here as a little girl, but from time to time the little dark people of the marsh still send to tell us that a daughter of the old blood has come.

One such was brought to me this morning. Ildierna, they call her, and she is the daughter of a chieftain from the Welsh hills where they keep the old ways still. I do not remember what I said to her—and no doubt she was too awestruck to really hear me. She was too amazed to see one whom all in the outside world think must be long dead to pay proper attention. But there was strength in her, and it came to me that she was just such a child as I might have had if I had borne a daughter to Accolon, and I wondered if I were looking at the maiden who will one day follow me.

But I think now that it is not Accolon that she reminds me of, but another maiden whom I knew long, long ago when my breasts were scarcely grown. These days I find it hard to remember the young priestesses who serve me, and call them sometimes by each other's names or by the names of maidens long dead or grown, but I remember quite clearly the girls who were being trained on Avalon when I first came.

There was one called Gwenlian whom I remember very well. I do not know why she should come to mind just now, except that this new girl has the look of her, with her strong bones and bright brown hair, and because she taught me a lesson I had great need to learn.

"This is work for servants, or slaves!" exclaimed Gwenlian, lifting the crude straw brush from the lime-wash and watching the white drops fall back into the pail. "Most assuredly it is not a task for a princess, or a priestess of Avalon!" Grimacing, she let the brush fall.

Morgaine reached swiftly to catch it, jumping back to avoid the spattering droplets, for even diluted, the stuff could burn.

"But we are neither," she answered tartly. "Only novice priestesses who will be very glad next winter to have watertight walls."

Whitening the daub and wattle walls of the House of Maidens was a yearly task. The mixture of burnt lime shell and fat repelled water, but it did need to be renewed on a regular basis or it would wear away. It had never occurred to Morgaine to resent the task, any more than she did the spinning, which was the constant occupation of all the young priestesses when indoors. As Viviane had once warned her, the life of a priestess could be hard and bitter, but she did not include among its hardships this work, which at least got her out in the sun and air.

"You are so very good!" exclaimed Gwenlian mockingly. "The perfect little priestess, afraid to take a breath that Viviane does not allow. But I was brought up to make my own choices."

"She who is slave to her own will has a fool for a master . . ." Viviane had often said, and yet they were also taught that a priestess had to be willing to bear the responsibility for her own deeds. Soon Morgaine would begin her year of silence, and after that face the ordeal of initiation. She was almost a woman—and almost a priestess—already. Was it perhaps time for her to begin thinking like one?

She dipped her brush into the whitewash and slathered the stuff over another section of wall. "And what, princess, would you choose?" Her tone was tart, but not, quite, mocking.

Gwenlian was tall and fair skinned, one of the sun people. Beside her, Morgaine was once more reminded of her own lack of height and small bones, and the skin that so readily darkened when she spent time out of doors. "Morgaine of the Fairies" they called her, but it was a brownie she felt most like just now. And yet when the younger girl had first been brought to the House of Maidens, Morgaine had been made her guardian, and despite their differences—perhaps, even because of them—Gwenlian was the closest Morgaine had to a friend.

Rather absentmindedly, Gwenlian dipped her brush into the pail as well. "To learn . . ." she said in a whisper. "To use the abilities that the Goddess has given me, instead of sitting and chanting lists from the old lore with the little girls."

"By learning the old lore we train and discipline our minds . . ." Morgaine began, then realized that in this, too, she was merely repeating what she had heard from Viviane. To commit vast quantities of information to memory was the ancient way of the Druids, but it did not encourage creative thinking. Viviane spoke often of the necessity that bound her—had the traditional ways of training constrained her thinking so much that she could not change it even if she desired?

With a shock, Morgaine realized that she was on the verge of criticizing the Lady of Avalon. She stopped short, biting her lip, the brush dripping milky drops onto the ground, but words came from some part of her mind she did not control.

"What would you do?"

"Whitewash the stones of the Processional Way so that we do not trip when we ascend the sacred hill in the dark?" Gwenlian shook her head and laughed. "No— that would be a child's trick. I want something *real*. In meditation, I have had visions. The egg-stone, the *omphalos*, is calling me. If I could touch it, join with it, I would touch the power at the heart of the hill, and then, I would know. . . ."

"Know what?" Morgaine asked faintly.

"What I truly am . . . what I was meant to be. . . ."

Gwenlian was wrong, of course. There were no short-cuts, no magic beyond simple patient hard work and discipline in the making of a priestess. So Morgaine told herself, but she could not help thinking about what the other girl had said to her. Her head told her that Gwenlian's impatience with the training was the petulance of a child, but her heart kept wondering, at the oddest moments, if what she had said might just be true.

And if even she had doubts, then what was Gwenlian thinking about now? In the days that followed, Morgaine contrived, whenever she could do so without being obvious, to keep an eye on her. She told herself that she watched her so that she could put a stop to it if Gwenlian tried something foolish, that she would feel responsible if the other girl came to harm. She never questioned her own motivations until the night when she awakened to glimpse a white form slipping through the doorway of the House of Maidens, and felt a pulse of excitement flare through her veins.

And then there was no time to wonder, only a moment to find her own shawl and her sandals and in the same ghostly silence, to follow. Clouds covered most of the sky, but those stars she could see told her that the time was a little past midnight. The Druids, whose task it was to salute the hidden sun, would by now have finished prayers in their temple and sought their rest. It was not one of the great festivals when most of the community watched through the night; any of the priestesses whose own work required them to be wakeful would be doing so hidden and in solitude.

Otherwise, the isle of Avalon was wrapped in slumber. *If I can catch up with Gwenlian swiftly, no one will ever know!* thought Morgaine as she hurried down the path.

The columns of the Temple of the Sun were a pale blur in the gloom, but something paler still was disappearing between them. What could Gwenlian be seeking there? Then, between one step and another, Morgaine remembered that the Temple of the Sun was where they kept the *omphalos* stone. The Druids preferred to worship beneath the open sky, but the Temple had been built by the wizards from the drowned lands across the sea, and was still the setting for those rituals the Druids had learned from them.

Nothing will happen, she told herself. *Without the proper rites, without the touch of the priest to awaken it, the* omphalos *will be no more than an egg-shaped stone.* But nonetheless, she forced herself to move more swiftly.

The hinges of the heavy wooden door were kept oiled so as not to squeak during the rituals, and they made no sound as Morgaine slipped through. The oil lamp that was always kept burning in the sanctuary cast a faint, flickering illumination. Its light gleamed from the colored stone set into the granite floor, and highlighted the textured images in tapestries so ancient their colors had faded away.

Morgaine stopped short, her head whirling. She had been here only a few times, when they needed a maiden to serve in the rites, and then she had been so intent on playing her part correctly she had not had much attention to spare for the setting. But her most recent training had addressed the art of reading information from one's surroundings, and now she was nearly overwhelmed by the hard, bright masculine identity that radiated from every stone.

As a novice priestess, she was an initiate of the mysteries of the darkness, of the cool radiance of the moon. Here, all things spoke of the Sun, and the Son, the northern Apollo of the Apple Isle, and even in the depths of night, she was dazzled. She controlled her breathing, rooting her awareness in the earth—at least that was still the same—until she could see once more.

A grunt of effort brought her back to attention. In the center of the mosaic star set into the stone of the floor lay the *omphalos,* a flattened egg-shaped stone about the length of her arm. Gwenlian knelt beside it, pressing her hands against the stone. Swiftly Morgaine hurried to her side.

"For a moment I felt it, Morgaine!" Gwenlian whispered. "The stone tingled against my palms!" Her eyes were alight with mingled frustration and fear.

Morgaine tugged at the other girl's shoulders. "You found the egg-stone—come away now, before we're found."

"But I haven't!" wailed Gwenlian. "The power is gone."

In the next moment her resistance abruptly eased and Morgaine staggered backward, but it was not Gwenlian, but the stone that had moved. The slab on which it lay had shifted to reveal an opening and a flight of steps, which led down into darkness.

"A passageway . . ." breathed Gwenlian. "It is true then. There are tunnels that lead into the hill."

"Or somewhere . . ." objected Morgaine. But her heart was pounding too. "Now you know—come *away*!"

Gwenlian got to her feet, and Morgaine released her grip, but instead of turning, the girl flung herself forward, into the opening. For a moment Morgaine stood with her mouth open, staring. *She has no light—in a few moments she'll come back,* she thought, but Gwenlian did not return. With a sinking heart, Morgaine realized she was going to have to follow her.

She took an unlit torch from its holder on one of the columns and, trembling, lit it from the altar lamp. No blast from the heavens punished her impiety. With a last look over her shoulder, she followed the other girl into the passageway.

The air in the tunnel was damp, but that was not what set the shiver in Morgaine's bones. The Druids were masters of wood, not stone. As she looked at the mighty blocks that formed it, she knew that this passageway had been old when the first of the British-speaking tribes came over the sea. The ancient wizards who built the Temple of the Sun had made this passage into the hill. Morgaine trembled with wonder and with fear, for she was not an initiate of these mysteries.

She half expected to find Gwenlian huddled at the first turn of the passageway, whimpering in the dark, but she continued for some time without finding her, and when the tunnel forked she realized this might be more difficult than she had expected. Symbols were graven into the stones to mark the turnings. Which way had Gwenlian gone?

The other girl had moved so quickly—something must be drawing her. If there really was an *omphalos* in the heart of the hill, perhaps she had been sensitized by touching its image. But Morgaine had no such connection with the stone—only with Gwenlian. She closed her eyes and let her breath move in and out in a steady rhythm as she had been taught, sending awareness inward.

Gwenlian, where are you? Gwenlian, think of me and I will come to you. . . . She built up the image of her friend's strong-boned face and brown hair and launched her will toward that goal.

At first her mind bubbled with a confusion of impressions: Gwenlian winning a footrace, slapping limewash on the wall, eating porridge, lifting her hands in ritual. Morgaine allowed each picture to take shape, to add its essence to the whole, then sent it bobbing away, while her awareness sank deeper and deeper, until all the images merged in the powerful current that was Gwenlian's true identity. It drew her, and Morgaine started to move again, slitting her eyes so that her upper mind could note the turnings and mark them.

Her superficial senses noted that the blocks were giving way to solid stone—she must be moving under the Tor itself! Presently the marks of the chisel became fewer, and she realized that this tunnel was a natural one, carved by running water. Indeed, the walls were shiny with moisture, and a trickle of water was wearing a new channel into the roughly leveled floor. Now the torch-light showed her wet footprints, but she hardly needed them. She could *feel* Gwenlian ahead of her, and some-thing else, that pulsed in the air and throbbed in the very stone.

"Goddess, defend me!" she whispered, understanding with her very soul, as her mind had already accepted, that what Gwenlian had believed was true.

A change in the air warned her that she was approach-ing a larger chamber a moment before the last turn in the tunnel. She took another step and stopped, blinking as the torchlight caught, corruscating, on a thousand crystal flecks in the rock walls that surrounded her. And then, as if those flecks were mirrors, all the refracted light fo-cused in the center of the chamber and kindled an an-swering light deep in the center of the egg-shaped stone.

Morgaine gazed in amazement, for the stone was translucent as curdled crystal. She could not imagine from what distant place it had been brought to lie here in the heart of the hill, if indeed it had come from any-where in the world of humankind.

And her magic had not misled her, for here was Gwen-lian, curled around the egg-stone with her arms clasped around it. Her eyes were closed, but there was tension in her arms; Morgaine did not think she was dreaming, but rather in the throes of a vision. Here also iron sockets for torches were set into the wall. Morgaine fixed her torch into one of them and moved gently to kneel beside her friend.

"Gwenlian . . ." she whispered, "Gwenlian, come back to me—"

There was no response. Frowning, Morgaine snapped her fingers around the other girl's head and blew in her ears. Gwenlian stirred a little at that, but her eyes did not open. If there had been water, Morgaine would have poured it over her, or even plunged her into it—that method could break even the deepest trance.

Clearly, Gwenlian could not be brought back to consciousness so long as she was touching the stone. In general, people in trance should not be touched, but she had no choice now. Taking a deep breath, Morgaine put her arms around her friend to pull her away.

The first thing she realized was that although Gwenlian's body moved, her arms remained fixed around the stone. The second was that the power that pulsed in the *omphalos* was passing through Gwenlian's body, and now Morgaine could feel it in her own limbs. At least she could still let go, but physical contact would make it much easier to establish a psychic bond. She was too small and slight to pick up Gwenlian, and even a full-grown warrior would have found it difficult to carry both the girl *and* the stone. The only way in which she could rescue Gwenlian would be to go into the Otherworld in which Gwenlian's spirit was wandering and find her.

Beneath the surface of her thoughts another voice was nagging.

"Foolish child, this task is beyond both your strength and your skill. Leave the girl and go to the Druids. They will know how to set her free."

It sounded like Viviane. Had the Lady of Avalon somehow linked with her in her dreams? Surely not, for if that were so, the Druids would have been here already. No, this was only that part of her that had been Viviane's most faithful pupil, speaking in the Lady's voice to keep her in line. If the Merlin had been there she might have called to him, for he had always been kind to her, like the grandfather she had never known, but he was away, with the king.

No wonder Viviane lets me go about without her supervision! I carry her inside me, doing her will even when she is not here!

Suddenly that seemed to Morgaine intolerable, that her own mind should have enslaved her to the Lady's will without anyone asking her yea or nay. If the Druids came, at the very least, Gwenlian would be sent home in disgrace, if they didn't think of something worse to do to her. Morgaine was almost a priestess; if Viviane had trained her well, she should be able to find her friend's wandering soul and wrest it free. She closed her mind against that inner voice and gripped Gwenlian's arms once more.

She could feel the power of the Stone, pulsing against her awareness, but she repeated the verses with which she had been trained to keep control, holding Gwenlian in her arms, listening to the other girl breathe until her own rhythm was the same. Then she set herself to follow the path to the Overworld, one image succeeding another as she walked the Sacred Way. A swirling radiance blurred the edges of her mental pictures, and she knew it was the power of the Stone, but she continued until she came to the grey expanse where only the occasional shadow of some half-remembered hill or standing stone marked the way.

And even these mists were shot with roiling colors. But still she searched, calling her friend by her secret name, and was rewarded at last by the sight of a sturdy figure around which lightnings played. Morgaine hurried toward her.

The image of Gwenlian stretched out her hand. Morgaine knew there was some reason why she should not take it, but the other girl looked so happy, so eager for her friend to share her joy. As Morgaine touched her, linking on the inner planes as they were in the flesh, awareness of the Overworld vanished, and she stood with Gwenlian in her vision and saw with her eyes.

Two minds in one, male, body, they stood on a parapet above a mighty city built of white stone. The sky was blue as it only is in southern climes, and the bittersweet cries of gulls rang in the air. Beyond the harbor rose a pointed mountain, from whose summit a trail of smoke twined lazily into the air.

"Behold the Isle of Atlantis, how mighty its works, how resplendent its wisdom," came an inner voice, or perhaps it was memory. But as the words faded, the man whose body they inhabited felt beneath his feet a faint vibration. When it ended, from the streets below came a babble of question. He looked up once more and saw the smoke from the mountaintop thicken, billowing upward in dense grey clouds.

Another tremor, much stronger, shook the tower. Now he could hear screaming. He staggered toward the stairway. "To the Temple"—came a cry from below, "we must save the hallows! We must save the Stone!"

He realized then that this was the trust that had been laid upon him. The vision began to fragment as he struggled downward, or perhaps it was the island, tearing itself apart as the mountain cracked open in ash and flame. Somehow he reached the shambles that had been the Temple of the Sun. The Stone lay among the rubble, glowing through the dust that filled the air. A few others had managed to join him—together, they lifted it into a chest and dragged it from the disintegrating city.

The harbor was a confusion of tossing ships and maddened men. Some of the closely moored boats had smashed into each other; others capsized beneath the weight of the men who tried to board them. But he knew a hidden cove—drawing his mantle over his face to filter out the ash that was falling, he helped to carry the heavy chest to the place where his own pleasure craft lay at anchor.

The images were even more chaotic now. They were clambering aboard, struggling to get out of the cove, flailing with the oars at the choppy sea. They had reached the ocean, and the sea heaved beneath them. Fire from the mountain filled the sky.

Fire . . . darkness . . . the glassy, flame-shot curve of the sea . . . A tiny voice yammered at the edge of Morgaine's awareness—*This is not happening, this is not my memory, this is not me!* And with more strength than she imagined she possessed, she pulled free as with a roar that transcended all other sound, the mountain blew.

Morgaine opened her eyes and flinched from the flicker of flame. The volcano's blast still echoed in memory—her head ached, and it took a few moments for her to realize that here, all was still.

Or very nearly. A faint, eerie groaning vibrated from the masses of rock that surrounded her. Then a tremor shook the Tor. For a moment terror froze her limbs. Then a glimmer of moving light showed her the *omphalos* rocking on its slab and Gwenlian lying sprawled just beyond it.

Morgaine breathed a prayer of thanks that whatever force had wrenched her out of the vision had enabled her to pull Gwenlian free as well. She grabbed the torch and then, with a strength she had not suspected she possessed, heaved Gwenlian's limp body across her back and staggered from the chamber.

As she struggled back through the tunnels, more

tremors shook the hill, one of them strong enough to knock her down. For several minutes she and Gwenlian lay in a tangle of limbs as she waited for falling rock to crush them. But by then they were in the last straight passage that led to the Temple, and although she was peppered by falling pebbles, the ancients had built well, and the great stones did not fall.

The torch had gone out when she fell, but now Morgaine could make her way by the feel of the stones, and soon the faint glimmer of the lamp in the Temple shining through the opening showed her the steps, and she hauled her burden up onto the polished floor. The earth had ceased to quake, but from outside she could hear shouting. Shaking with reaction, she shoved the slab back over the opening, then grabbed Gwenlian beneath the arms and dragged her to the door.

Morgaine would have told all to Viviane immediately, but in the aftermath of the earthquake, the Lady of Avalon was surrounded by priestesses and Druids alike, wanting instructions, and there was no way she could be heard. The young priest who helped her carry Gwenlian to the healers assumed that the girl had been hurt in the quake. In a sense, thought Morgaine, it was true.

But as she sat by her friend, watching her twitch and mutter as she made the long journey back toward consciousness, she wondered whether the tremors that had shaken the hill had caused Gwenlian's vision to fix on the drowning of Atlantis, or whether by awakening the memories recorded in the Stone, they had created a sympathetic vibration in the Tor.

When Gwenlian regained consciousness at last, she forbade Morgaine to speak of it. Viviane's implacable calm had restored order quickly, and although the quake had shaken some things down in the dwellings, the stone halls were too sturdy, and the daub and wattle round-houses too flexible, for the tremors to do them much harm. And the priests who kept the Temple of the Sun did not appear to have found anything wrong with their stone.

Morgaine told herself that no harm had been done. It was only gradually that she realized that although Gwenlian was recovered in body, she had changed. When at last Morgaine ventured to ask what she remembered of her vision, the other girl refused to speak of it. Nor did she come to her studies with the joy she had shown before. It was as if that part of her that had craved the things of the spirit had burned out. Now, Gwenlian's responses were as halting as if she were one of the Once-born, and after the feast of Midwinter, she asked to leave Avalon.

But by then, Morgaine had begun her year of silence. When the time came for Gwenlian to go, she embraced her friend, weeping. But she could not even say good-bye.

I never saw Gwenlian again, though I heard eventually that she had been married. It may be that this girl, Ildierna, is a child of her line. If that is so, it will be as if Gwenlian herself has come back to pardon me. In my life I have known diffidence and rebellion, pride and fury and despair. Now, when I am near its ending, forgiveness is a gift that I have great need to give, and receive.

For a long time after Gwenlian left us, guilt made me even more obedient to Viviane's will than I had been be-fore. If I had told her and the Druid priests what had happened, could they have restored Gwenlian's soul? Hindsight assures me that Viviane would have consid-ered what happened to my friend a fit punishment, and assured me that those who are priestess-born will find the way back to their powers, as indeed I did myself, in the end.

Now, when I reflect on Gwenlian's tragedy, I wonder what it was I should have learned. What lack in our training drove her to dare a deed beyond her strength, and laid on me the guilt for it, and thus, deprived me of the will to question Viviane? If I had not allowed the Lady of Avalon to meddle in my life, would Arthur rule still?

I have played my part in that story, and given over meddling in the affairs of the outer world. If I have something to teach this child who has come to me, it is that each soul must bear the burden of its own fate and make the best choices it may. My vision does not show me what dangers this girl will face, or even if Avalon will survive. But I will teach her as best I may to use whatever abilities the Goddess has given her.

The Fourth Concealment of the Island of Britain

Katharine Kerr

They are standing around a long table made of polished wood. In the dream he cannot count them, cannot see their faces; they are stiff figures wrapped in gray-like corpsecloth. The table he can see.

On the table lies a flat sheet of Roman papyrus. He has only seen ancient scrolls and never realized a sheet could be so large, covering half the table, nor so white. Upon it there are lines, marks—a map.

Myrddin wakes with cold sweat soaking into the blanket that covers his straw-stuffed mattress. His other blanket lies upon the stone floor next to his bed. He sits up, stretching his arms out in front of him, surprised as always by the wrinkles bitten deep into his hands and the brown mottles of old age. In his dreams he sees himself as a young man still. From his troubled night his back hurts, and when he stands up, his knees complain aloud. He puts on a pair of sandals and a linen tunic, then crosses to the window of his round tower room and pulls aside the leather curtain.

Morning sun floods over him and eases his flesh. He sits on the wide stone sill and turns his face to the sky, where rain clouds are breaking apart and scudding away to the east. From the hill-fort below him, the smell of wood smoke and baking bread, the stink of pigs and horse manure, rise up like incense from an altar, dragging his attention down to the busy ward. Slip-sliding in the fresh mud, servants are hurrying back and forth with firewood and buckets of water. Grooms are leading horses to the water trough.

Dressed in shirts without sleeves and loose breeches, a handful of men from Arthur's warband stand in front of the stone keep; they are arguing about something so loudly that he can almost pick out their words. Two of them face off, raise fists, scream in such rage that they are no longer using words at all. With a shout Cei, the seneschal, comes running and thrusts himself in between the pair. Over the winter Cei has grown stout, and gray streaks his hair, but when one of the young cubs snarls at him, Cei grabs his arm, twists, and drops him to his knees to wallow in the mud. Howling with laughter the rest of the men disperse, and Cei walks off to the stables. The shamed man gets to his feet and slinks away.

This summer the army will patrol the border and raid into Saison territory, but it will fight no battles. Peace hangs heavy on Camulodd. How long, Myrddin wonders, will it be before Arthur's men start feuding among themselves? The horsemen in his warband may grumble at Cei's orders, but they obey him in the end, will step apart and make their apologies, then go about their day as friends.

The noble lords, Arthur's vassals and his comites both, listen to no one when honor cracks its bloodstained whip. In time, of course, the problem will solve itself.

The demoralized Saison will find a new leader, mount a new army, and come ravaging once again into what is left of the province of Prydain. In the end, they will win. Years hence, certainly, but they will win. Myrddin would rather die tortured with hot irons than tell this truth to Arthur, but it weighs daily upon his soul.

The dream. When Myrddin shuts his eyes, he can see the image of the white map, floating on the red field of his sunstruck eyelids. Did the dream indicate Saison, then, by those doll figures who studied the map? He opens his eyes and looks out over the stone walls of Camulodd. On this side, the east, the hill slopes sharply away to fields, pale gold with the ripening of the winter wheat, bound by the silver ribbon of the river. On the dream map lies a line shaped like the river's turnings, but the rest of the marks mean little to him. Even as he tries to study them, the vision fades.

With a shrug Myrddin leaves the window. If the dream carries a message, it will repeat itself. His long years of living on the border of the unseen world have taught him that. Dreams, visions, omens, the voices that at times speak to him from fires—he can only invite them into the seen world, not command them. At the moment, like any ordinary man, he is hungry, and the dream will have to wait until he has eaten breakfast.

The year past, Arthur ordered a banqueting hall built at Camulodd, 'round the back of the stone keep near the kitchen huts. Sunny with windows and bright with tapestries and banners, the long wooden room has proved so pleasant, especially in contrast to the dank chambers of the keep, that with spring, the daily life of the hill-fort has moved into it. On this particular morning, when Myrddin walks into the hall he finds the warleader himself lingering at the head of a long table. Unlike his men

Arthur affects Roman dress in these days of victory: a simple tunic, sandals bound up his legs with thongs. A red, short cloak drapes casually on the back of his chair. At his right hand sits Paulus, the priest who serves the chapel in the fort, dressed in drab brown. A gaunt little man, Paulus has a bald stripe shaved out of his hair from ear to ear.

"Behold!" Paulus calls out. "Our last pagan!"

Smiling at the familiar jest, Myrddin walks down the length of the hall to join them. From the windows near the beamed ceiling sunlight falls across the pale new wood of the walls and shimmers on the polished tables as if it were *flames racing down the planks. The beams catch and burn like logs in a hearth as the roof gives way, crashing down in a spray of red cinders. Over the roar of fire there is screaming* and Arthur's familiar dark voice, saying, "What is it? What happened?"

Myrddin realizes that he is lying on the floor of the banqueting hall with Arthur kneeling beside him. Ordinary sunlight streams in and picks out the grey in Arthur's brown hair. His pale grey eyes are narrow with concern. When Myrddin raises a shaking hand to his own face, he touches something wet, slimy—his beard, soaked with spittle from the fit. Over Arthur's shoulder Myrddin can see Paulus, watching him *as the others are watching. He cannot see them, but he can feel their gaze.*

"Fetch me some mead!" Arthur calls to someone beyond Myrddin's sight. "Don't just stand around like dolts!"

A servant appears with a goblet and stands holding it out as if he's serving mass for some new god. Myrddin sets his elbows against the floor and tries to sit up, but he cannot move until Arthur slips a broad arm under his back and lifts him. *The watchers persist. Eyes grow on the walls, faces form in the banners that hang over-head.*

"Saison magic," Myrddin whispers. "Spying."

As if they have heard him, the eyes disappear. Myrddin smiles to himself. He has guessed correctly, and naming the threat has dragged it out of the shadows. He will be able to examine it rationally now, using the knowledge gained from working his own magic over the long years.

The fainting fit, however, has left his body weak. Myrddin allows Arthur to fuss over him, suffers Paulus to pray over him, drinks a little mead, and eats a little bread to soothe the fears of those who depend upon him to postpone their inevitable doom. Because Arthur wants so badly to help, Myrddin allows him and Cei to carry him up the long twisting stairs to his tower room, even though he would feel much safer on his own two feet. Servants follow with a pitcher of watered-down ale and a round loaf of bread in a basket. They mill around in his chamber until he loses patience.

"I need not one thing more," Myrddin snaps. "Now leave me! I can't rest in all this noise."

The servants flee, and Cei follows. Myrddin can hear their clogs pounding like hooves all the way down the stone stairs. Arthur lingers for a moment in the door-way.

"I truly am alive and all in one piece," Myrddin says.

"You gave me quite a scare."

"Did I? No need to worry. It was just a long message from Annwn."

As Arthur leaves, he pulls the heavy plank door shut behind him. Silence washes over Myrddin and carries him on a long wave out to the sea where his visions float, drifting on the tides of the unseen world.

*   *   *

They are searching all over Prydain. In mists he sees them, men walking green meadows, searching for something. They are binding the earth with spells. He can see them pacing off distances with their heads bent, one arm raised, each step as slow and careful as if they picked their way through a bog. They are binding the earth with wires. He sees them driving in pegs all around the edges of a field, then lacing wires between them to mark off squares. What lies underneath? he wonders. Treasure, perhaps. Off to one side stands a man holding a long flat staff, banded black and white. Every now and then he shouts orders to those stringing the wires.

When Myrddin wakes, sunlight streams in from the west window, telling him that he has lain in trance for half the day. He can feel their gaze still, the searchers, even though no more visions of eyes appear on the walls or ceiling. He sits up, slumping on the edge of the bed, his spotted hands dangling between his stick-thin legs. Had he ever been young? At times he wonders, simply because his youth lay so long ago. With a shake of his head for his own nonsense, he gets up and goes to his table to drink the ale-splashed water and eat some of the bread left there for him.

Food steadies his mind. His knowledge that the fort is being watched becomes merely that, knowledge, no longer a cold prickling of the skin or a shudder between his shoulder blades. The Saison have magic of their own, though Paulus insists they derive its power from evil spirits. If Paulus is correct, at some point the spirits will turn upon the sorcerers and enslave them, but until then, the magic feels dangerous enough. What, he wonders, are they searching for? Everyone knows where Arthur built his fortress. The warleader may prefer to call it a castrum, just as he likes to style

himself dux bellorum instead of cadvridoc, but its
doors stand as open as any Prydain lord's squat dun for
servants and flies, visitors and dogs, to wander freely
in and out. If these searchers want to see Arthur, they
can ride up like any other man.

But their evil spirits, those daemones, as Paulus calls
them. Traveling any distance in the seen world lies beyond their powers, because they cannot cross running
water, whether the mighty Tamesis or a trickling stream.
They must follow paths in the unseen world, if their
Saxon masters wish to send them upon errands of mal-
ice. This might well be what the map showed and what
the silver wires mark out, a guide for the daemones
through the unseen world, a secret road by which they
may enter the heart of Camulodd and burst out upon
Arthur.

Myrddin tears the loaf of bread into chunks and takes
one to the west window. He sits upon the sill and looks
out. Here, on the gentle side of the hill, a little town has
grown up outside the walls of Arthur's dun, straggling
down to the flat. Beyond it lie wheat fields, as gold as
honey in the late afternoon light, stretching west to a
sunset-tinged mist and far Dumnonia.

*In the gray cold fog blond men with woad-blue
trousers are walking through fields. Cattle lift their
heads as they pass, then return to their grazing. On top
of a hill the men find a carved stone lying on its side.
He can see them laughing as they kneel down beside it.
With the side of his hand one man brushes away moss
and dirt. These carved letters are plain enough: Drustan.*

So! Saison magic worked the curse against Arthur's
cousin that brought him and March to their doom. Myrddin returns to the seen world and realizes that he is leaning dangerously far out of the window, as if while in

trance he craned his neck to see farther. Slowly, cautiously, he shifts his weight back, leans into the chamber, then stands up in safety. When he was young, the second sight never took him like this, wiping away the seen world and leading him into risk. In one hand he still holds the chunk of bread. He puts it back in the basket. Tonight he will need to travel into the unseen world, and food will only hinder his journey.

Not long after sunset the moon rises past its full. Myrddin lies down on his bed and crosses his arms over his chest. In the silvery light upon his wall he can see the visions of the day parade past him: the papyrus map, the flames, the eyes, the wire-bound fields, Drustan's stone. The mists and the moonlight blend together in his sight, then brighten.

The figure kneels on bare ground in front of the stump of a broken stone wall. Myrddin knows immediately that he is a Sais, because his long blond hair hangs in two braids on either side of his face. He wears almost no clothing—a pair of torn woad-blue breeches, common among the Saison, and a dirty tunic, cut so short that it barely reaches past his waist. He is digging with some sort of tool like a tiny spade to make a trench along the base of the wall. In the hot sun the Sais pauses, laying down the tool and raising an arm to wipe his sweaty face on his sleeve. No—her face. In the vision the figure looks straight at him, and Myrddin realizes with cold shock that she is a woman.

He lies awake again on his narrow bed in the tower room. The moon has risen past his window, the room is dark, but he has seen everything he needs to see. So, then, the rumors are true, that among the Saison, women too know lore and work spells. And what could she have been doing but setting in motion forces that would some day undermine Camulodd's walls?

As above, so below. As this, so that. As this wall, Camulodd's wall. Water flows downhill in Lloegr just as it does in Prydain, and Saison magic will flow through the unseen world in an equally dependable fashion. The trench tells him everything he needs to know about this woman's spell. First she made a little wall to stand in the place of Camulodd's high wall. No doubt she has already walked 'round her stones three times by moonlight, this Wicca woman, chanting the name of Arthur's dun as she went. Perhaps she brought in a priest of their strange gods to kill an ox and let the blood drip over the wall while she called out Camulodd's name. Now she digs under it to weaken the very souls of the rocks that anchor it to the earth.

As this, so that. The eyes of her evil spirits are seeking Camulodd out. He has seen them peering from the banners in Arthur's high hall; he has felt them watching him, Camulodd's shield. Myrddin rises from his bed and smiles. He knows what he must do to thwart her magic. He will work spells of his own to blind those eyes. He will weave a shield to hide Camulodd forever from such treachery. *As this, so that.* In the wild forest he will rename himself Camulodd. He will take upon himself Camulodd's very essence. He will become Camulodd. And in an ancient oak he will bind himself and Camulodd away, both hidden from the unseen world of spirits and daemones. Once Arthur dies, once the fort falls to its inevitable destiny, they will join him there, forever hidden from both worlds, the unseen and the seen.

It will be a mighty spell, and his last.

"Damn!" Margaret Gruener sits back on her heels and throws her trowel to the ground. "That's blown it."

In the sun her tee-shirt is sticking to her back with

sweat. Her long blond braids have fallen forward to dangle close to her face. She tosses them over her shoulders and stands up with a shake of her head and a swat at flies. England isn't supposed to get so damned hot, she thinks. Scattered across the dig in this Somerset field, graduate students turn to look at her, and her colleague, Bob Harris, comes trotting over.

"What's wrong?"

"Maybe I am. Paleography isn't my specialty after all, so let's hope I'm misjudging its age. But I've cleared the dirt in front of the first tier of stonework, and I've found an inscription. Look."

With the toe of her heavy hiking boots she points at the culprit stone. Harris squats and pulls a camel's hair brush out of his pocket. He wipes dirt from the long-buried words, squints at them sideways, then looks up at her. His eyes swim behind the thick lenses of his glasses, but she can read disappointment in the set of his shoulders. He gets up, shaking his head, and reaches into the pocket of his khaki shorts for his cigarettes.

"It's seventh century at the absolute earliest," Harris says. "As you so cleverly remarked, damn! Whoever built this wall must have scavenged it from some Saxon relic."

Margaret swears, briefly, and walks a few steps away to get upwind of his smoke. He struggles with a box of matches, strikes one, and lights the cigarette with a couple of vigorous puffs.

"I begin to think Alcock was right," Harris goes on. "Maybe Cadbury Castle is the site, after all."

"I doubt it. To be honest, I'm beginning to doubt that Camelot ever really existed. If it did, it wouldn't be so damned hard to find. For crying out loud, the man was famous even in his own time."

Harris shrugs and lets out a long exhalation of white smoke, curling upward in the sun and dissipating into the wind. Like the glory of men, Margaret thinks. Like the glory of King Arthur, gone forever into the empty sky. All at once she shudders, oddly cold, and rubs the back of her neck.

"What's wrong?" Harris says, spewing more smoke. "Geese walking on your grave?"

"Maybe. It's the oddest damn thing, but I feel like we're being watched."

Prince of Exiles

Rosemary Edghill

My mother was a queen over the Wall, daughter to the same mother as the Southern King's wife, and so, by every proper reckoning, his born sister. Had her sister remembered that they were foreigners in the south, all filled with the lies of the Dead God's wandering priests, it would have gone better for us all.

The king—then no more but War King—had claimed her in their youth, when he first had it in his mind to drive Rome from the land. She was the Owl Priestess, just as her uncle was Horse King, and her mother, his sister, was Corn Mother. The War King was called Ator, which means "wheel" in the Old Tongue, and carried always on his shield the Silver Wheel of the Goddess, in token he was Her Champion.

In those days, the black horses we had stolen from Rome and bred up were our pride, strong and sleek and large. And if the southern warlord wanted them, then he must have the *Guen-hwyfar* as well, to seal the bargain with ties of kinship. The People did not know then that the men of the South were mad.

So the Ator got his horses and a wife and went away. Her sister, my mother, became Owl Priestess in turn, to see the future with owl-sight and to advise the Horse King on the best way of remaining in favor with the Corn Mother, by whose grace the meadows and valleys grew thick with succulent pasturage. And in time we heard that the young warlord called himself king, but—as my mother's sister had foretold when she was *Guenhwyfar*—he did not trouble us over the Wall.

We had news from the Priests of the Dead God— called by his followers The White—who would come among us to tell of their strange foreign god. We did not kill them, for it is unlucky to harm the mad, and so we heard also that the Corn Mother's eldest daughter was now Queen in the South; called Janiffer for the title she had once borne among us.

There had been White Priests in Logres almost for longer than there had been legions, and it seemed in these days that for every legion Rome had withdrawn, she had sent us a hundred priests. Every one of them was mad, and their insistence upon a god who had no mother proved it. Worse, they said their god was a mortal man who had been murdered, and for that cause they worshipped him in hope that he would come back.

Though the Horse King is a great power among the People, he dies at the pleasure of the Corn Mother, and I have never heard of any of the Kings Under Hill coming back. Who would come back from hall-feasting and night-riding and the fortune to sleep on the knees of the Mother? If the Dead God has a hill to go to, you may be sure that his mad priests will not bring him out of it with all their magic. And know, too, that he is no god, for he has neither sister nor mother that I have ever heard tell

of, only a father. They say it is the Dead God's father
who killed him, and that is the only thing the White
Priests ever have said that made any sense at all.

The years passed, and my sisters were born. In the
north we say that the North Wind is stallion to every
mare, and so it was with my mother, and her mother
before her. No one living knew the father of any of
Grainne-my mother's-children, save one.

But the Southern Queen had no children, which was
not an amazing thing, as perhaps the North Wind did not
blow so far below the Wall. And the Southern King had
no sisters, so there was no nephew Ator might call upon
to be War King, and Ator was growing old.

At length a message came to my mother from her sister. It came in the mouth of one of the Dead God's
priests, and so it made little sense, but my mother was
the Long-Sight of the People and did not need a madman's words to tell her what she must do. She caught up
the North Wind in a cup and tied the cup in a shawl, and
went to see her sister.

Now I must tell you of this cup, which was a great marvel and a treasure to our people long before it passed (as
you will see) into the hands of the Dead God and his
priests. It was, of a certainty, magic, for how else was a
cup to hold even a fraction of the North Wind for all that
long journey into the South? And the way of it was this:

Long ago the People lived behind the rising sun, in a
land far distant in a great city beside a mighty river
where they were treated as slaves. That land had one
great treasure, a stone, which had fallen from the sky—
some say, stolen by the son of the Great Mother, who
wished to give it to men so that they might have power.
This stone was green as water and bright as glass, and
upon it was written all of the wisdom that ever there

might be in the world. It was the great treasure in the
land, and without its magic the River would not answer
the calls of the priests and the corn would wither, or perhaps it would leap from its banks and drown them all—
they were not certain which it might choose, though
either was bad.

And the People, who did not wish to be slaves, knew
all these things, so one night they took away the Stone
and struck it so that it shattered into three parts. And of
one part they made a sword-blade, and of one part a
necklet, and of the third part they made a cup. And each
piece had as much magic as the Stone itself, but none of
them was the Stone, so when the priests came among the
People seeking the Stone, each man could answer: "No.
Your Stone is not here."

And when the priests had finished searching, the people took up the sword, the cup, and the necklet and
called the River so that it would drown all the land. And
then they came away, following the track of the Setting
Sun. But they were too many to travel together, lest their
beasts find no good grazing, so each part of the People
took one part of the Stone, and one went north, and one
went south, and one went into the uttermost west bearing
the cup.

I have good cause to know this cup well, and so I may
tell you this: its bowl is of the shape, as it were, of two
cupped hands together, and it is green like the sea, clear
like water, and bright like glass. Between its making and
today it has been set in fine red gold studded with agates
and pearls, so that it is grand and rich and fine. But most
of all, it is magic. Magic enough to carry the North Wind
in it even to the South.

I was not yet born in that time, but I know all the tale
well. How Queen Janiffer met and embraced Grainne

her sister with joy, and how Grainne gave to Janiffer the cup, and took Janiffer's place in the king's bed so that the cup might not be thwarted. But after a year and a day, through the sorcery of the Dead God's priests, Ator discovered the truth and called Grainne the false Janiffer, and demanded the return of his true wife.

Grainne went to her sister to take back the cup and found that her sister refused to give it, though the North Wind had made her great with child. She had been too long in the South and the cup had frightened her, and so she had given it over to one of the Dead God's priests to carry far away.

And so my mother placed a great curse on her sister, that she should work toward her own end in full knowledge and yet be powerless to prevent it. She cursed the child in her sister's womb, saying that it would be her doom and naming it Ancel, a servant. And then, because she could not do more, my mother fled for the Wall like a roebuck fleeing from the wolves, and not all the King's men could find or hinder her.

And when she found herself with child in turn, there was only one way she could have gotten it, and that was from the man Ator, who had been War King in the South.

My birth had severed the ties of clan and kin which bound her to the People so that Grainne was no longer Owl Priestess, for my father lay like an iron knife in the web of kinship. Though still a queen, my mother lived alone all the year in the great house where the People and the herds came to eke out life in the Great Dark that each year spun Arianrhod's Silver Wheel. I, her child late and last, had ensured with my birth that there would be no more, and—since my father was known—I had no claim in the lives of the woman-children who had left her womb before me, who were true daughters to the North Wind.

In the South, the King did penance for his sin and the Queen did also, for the King sent her to live among the priests of the Dead God upon the Isle of Glass, and said that the child in her womb was no child to him. And when the magi went to the king my father to tell him of my birth—revealed to those who watched the stars, so I was later told, by the bright winter stars that hung fixed at mid-heaven—he sent his army into the North, across the lands he held so uneasily in the shadow of Rome, to slay all the suckling children that they could find.

It is a hard thing to be a son with only a mortal father of flesh, and worse yet to know that this father has raised his hand to his sister's child—though not to me alone, for every child who was born from Samhain to Midwinter and lay within the shadow of the Wall was to be slaughtered by his decree.

I escaped that doom because my mother hid me in a basket of rushes down by the riverside, where I slept drugged with poppy while the soldiers burned our house and raped my sisters. It was an evil thing my father did, a thing that lay upon his reign as his fatherhood lay upon my life, and for it they called him the Herod of the North.

I called him otherwise.

I called him Saul, and to every Saul there is sent a David.

In the fullness of my young manhood I went to his southern court.

By then it was the center of all the world that Rome was not, for the Eternal City now looked Eastward and inward, as the old do, and her legions no longer came into the West.

The Southern King's city lay upon the bank of a great river, and even I, who had more cause to hate him than any other, must call it a marvel. Its walls stood higher than any work of Man I had ever seen: they were lime-washed brick, and the whole city glittered in the sun like the High Hills at Midwinter. Its gates stood open dawn to dusk, and on the High Holy Days it was said that any man might approach the King and stand before his face to speak.

I did not have it in me to do such a thing, though it was certain Ator would not have known me. He had never seen me, and had only rumor that I had ever lived. In certainty, he thought me dead now, with all the other children his soldiers had killed, and thought himself safe from the People because of it.

I cared not what the People thought, for by his father-hood Ator had cut me from them, as the death-child is cut from its mother's belly, and I had grown to manhood a creature apart. My mother's death finished that work of cutting that my birth had begun, and upon my mother's last breath I went to the herds and carried away the Bride Mare and all who would follow her, and so it was that I had wealth—and must find my life below the Wall, for if I went ever again into the North, the Horse King and all the People would have my death.

I sold all but the Bride as I went south. She was old and strong and wise, and the herd would miss her coun-sel sorely, but I had already learned that here in the South, men saw only with their eyes, and all that men would see was that she was no longer young.

I was a long time making my way to the South, for I had in me no mind to go as a mooncalf, with no mother-wit to sustain me. I learned the language of the south-men, and washed the paint from my skin and the clay from my hair and changed the deerskins dyed green with woad and lime for spun and woven cloth. By the time I came within sight of the River City I could pass as one of them, and I had learned many things.

Ator had taken back Janiffer, his queen, after she had done seven years' penance among the Dead God's priests upon the Isle of Glass. He must, that he might hold the North, for though the Horse King who had sworn to him was dead—slain by the Corn Mother in a famine year, and her youngest son set in his place—the bargain still held, and Ator would not try the bargain further than he had in the year that I was born.

Of the Queen's child, gotten of the North Wind, no one spoke, and it was thought that if it had been born alive, and a boy, she must have quickly overlain it. Perhaps she had not told the king of the words Grainne my mother had said over her belly, but my mother had told them to me in sun and moon and firelight, and I knew that whatever the queen might say and the people believe, the child Ancel lived.

There was one thing more that my mother had told me, the reason by which I was here, and which might yet lead me back into the true world north of the Wall.

There was the Cup.

Janiffer had given it to the White Priests. The White Priests had taken it away out of the sight of men, so that its magic could serve their strange foreign god who died. But it did not belong to him, and in the People's name I would have it back . . . though I must find it first.

I went first to the Isle of Glass, which Ator had given for the White Priests' home. It was a bad bargain, for in summer it is no island at all, but lies within that part of Logres called in the South the Summer Country, for that it cannot be seen three seasons of the year. In winter and spring and fall the meadows around the hill are under water and cannot be traveled, for the water that lies there is too shallow for a boat and the mud beneath it is too deep for a horse. So it is the worst of both island and field, and the best of neither, being neither. But the priests of the White Man were not clever enough to know that, and flattered by the attentions of a king.

I think the King my father hoped his gift would keep the mad priests in one place and away from the people—and in truth it was in one way a generous gift, for in high summer when the land is dry enough to ride across the grazing is as splendid as any that may be found in all Logres—but the White Priests were great ones for reckless and uncomfortable travel, and went out from the Glass Isle winter and summer to tell their endless tales of their unchancy god.

The year I went to see them they had a new tale.

They told of a cup.

It was a great marvel, was this cup, and could do many marvels beside. Of course it belonged to The White, for he was as greedy for magic as any true god. For myself, I thought only that the queen had carried that tale here as well, and so the priests must embroider upon it. For that my mother birthed no fools, it had been in my mind since first I heard rumors of these tales that the White Priests might have the cup that Janiffer had given into their hands and be claiming it now for their own.

But though I asked many of them while I stopped in the Glass Isle, each one said the same thing: that the Dead God's Cup lay under hill with The White, first buried with his dead body in a rich cave over sea and then taken by his father along with all his whole body into the land no living man might enter.

So wherever this cup was, it was not here on the Isle of Glass, but the priests said one thing more: they said

that their cup had been set in a place that mortal man
might reach, did he only desire the cup passionately
enough, for it would appear to show him the way. This
was the thing that convinced me that they did not speak
of the cup that was once a stone, for no mortal man had
ever desired to see that cup again more than I whose
mother it had been stolen from, and never had it appeared to me.

Later I understood that the priests had forged this marvel with their own tongues, and when I went to the River
City to see the king I understood why. But in that time I
was merely puzzled.

I had not gone to the Isle of Glass seeking the cup, but
to find my brother, but though there were many acolytes
among the White Priests, Ancel was not among the
acolytes.

In the South there were unwanted children, a thing I
had not known could ever be until I had come here.
Those that were boys the White Priests took in and
reared, for they would not have girls, in token of that the
Dead God had been betrayed to his death by a woman.
There were not so many of my age there, for the King's
Red Harvest had been thorough enough to make even
peasant boys a scarce and valuable thing for some years
thereafter, and among the shaven-headed acolytes I saw
none of my blood. A young boy with whom I shared my
food told me that the Queen's child was buried beneath
the holy altar of their church. He was willing enough to
show me the place, and I to see it, but I found that I
could not enter.

It was a round stone tower such as the Romans had
built upon the Wall to watch over us, but when I stood in
the doorway and looked where the lamps burned above a
wooden table, I felt such a dread take hold of the roots of
my heart as stilled me on the spot. Not to save my own

life could I have entered that dim chamber, so much like the cave wherein someday we all must lie. I felt as if my own shoulders bore up the roof, and that its weight crushed me. I had to go away, though the boy looked at me strangely, but it did not matter. Whatever pitiful bones were buried beneath that altar, they were not my brother's. My mother's curse was a stronger thing than that.

It had taken me all the summer to learn what I had, and before I and the Bride could be trapped here over winter, I made away from this haunted place, and turned her head toward the White City.

To Caliburn, and the King.

Fourteen years it had been since Ator had called his queen back from the Isle of Glass, twenty-one since he had sent her there, and these are all the years it takes for a man to grow old. And never in all that time did the queen quicken with child again.

Ator might have made another marriage, but after he had sent out his men with swords to slaughter children at the breast none of the kings below the High King would give him their sisters to wed lest such a Red Harvest should come again. They lay quiet beneath him all those years for fear of Rome, and because Ator had a tight grip on their throats. And now in the years of his age the king failed, and his queen was childless, and there was no War King in the land, though there were many hungry for the honor to choose from.

The king, when he was first come to the High Seat, had taken the firstborn sons of all of his princes and raised them in Caliburn, the River City. He did not let them from him while their fathers lived, but each went home to his kingdom upon his father's death with the king's army at his back to put him in his seat. In the

South men now were kings in their own right after the fashion of things in the White Priests' lands—Ator had encouraged this, so that the sisters of his princes would not speak against him.

And while they awaited that day there was hunting and hall-feasting, and the kings' sons sat about a great table in the shape of the King's Luck, the Silver Wheel. It will tell you all of what you need to know about my father that he wore his Lady's badge even as he schemed to overthrow Her service and slaughter Her children. It was for this quality of his heart as much as for any treaty that he had summoned back Janiffer after Grainne had shamed him: what Ator took was his, and never did he give it up.

But in the end I would make him give up everything that he had. And so I came to Caliburn, the White City on the River Tame.

It was a Feast Day: such I had intended. I do not know which of the Dead God's many feasts it was, but it was near to the day on which the Stag Lord and the Bull Son change places, and the Sun stands still in the sky to watch it. I did not go to the Great Hall where the king held court for all who would come, but to the kitchens that served the feast, and there I humbly asked to be put to work.

You might ask why a prince and the son of a queen, with the good red gold in his pocket and murder in his heart, would go to the middens of his great enemy to beg his bread, but you would not have been raised among the People, to understand how vengeance might be woven like fine wool on the loom. I went to labor in Ator's kitchens, and soon men began to speak of the great wickedness which lay in the King's heart, and kept him from getting the child that would make the land safe in afteryears. They spoke of the cup, which belonged to the White Man, the cup, which could heal any sin and they began to say that the King must gain it to show it forth, so that the people of his land could be eased.

And so it was that come the Spring, at the king's feast nearest to that day when the Corn Mother leaves her cave to walk among men once more, Ator's knights, proud princes all, rode forth from Caliburn to seek for Grainne's Cup, for glory and for the King.

If one should find it, I would take it from him, but none did. Spring became Summer, and the tales returned as the knights did not: tales of failure every one. And they died, or forwent the quest, and each who did was an arrow in Ator's side, for it had been his plan from always to keep the young kings under his hand. And now he could not—and further, all men could see that he had sent them on a fool's errand, trying to bring into the world of Men that which the White Priests said plainly belonged forever in the realm of gods. In the West and on the Borders, men took such lessons to heart and prepared for war.

It was then that I, from the kitchens, set wings to another tale: that only a man conceived in virtue rare could bring the cup into the world. This tale I set in Janiffer's ear, for I knew she was still her mother's daughter. It had come to me when I first thought upon my brother that Ator's queen was too much of the People to give a child of her body over to the White Priests, and that her gift of the cup would have brought silence upon that matter and more from those who held the Isle of Glass. And I watched, and was ready when her messenger rode forth beneath the cloak of night, and I put my saddlepad upon the Bride and followed him.

We rode deep into the West Country, where the land is bordered upon three sides by the sea, and all men die young. The southerners call the people who live there "foreigners," though they have more right to the land than their supplanters. They live there by cattle and raiding, so that every man is enemy to every other. Where better to hide a child who has no friends than in a land of enemies?

I crept upon the messenger by night and stole from him the queen's tokens and gold that he carried, and rode to the hill-fort in his place. I do not know what happened to him afterward; if he had sense he took himself back to his mother's fire, and meddled no more in the affairs of queens.

The Queen's child was a true son of the People, gotten of the North Wind. And so he was dark where I was redhaired, dark-eyed where mine were grey. They were dark after another fashion in the Western hills, and so he had been marked out always as a stranger, kept as a hostage to a unknown fortune. They called him Dubvh, which means The Black in their tongue, and did not let a day go by that they did not remind him that he did not belong among them.

It was an easy thing to gain his friendship and his love, for I, too, was an outsider. I kept hidden the message that I had stolen, which begged that the queen's child be returned to her, and bided with him in Strangerland through the long winter. There was a task I had set myself, which needed the Turning of the Year to complete.

On that night the world, like a door which is neither open nor closed, is many things at once, and the spirits that see everything ride through the world freely. And the son of the Owl Priestess can do many a thing, with a willing instrument and does he set his mind to it.

Dubvh was such a one, for he loved me and I had sworn to him that I would see him into his rightful name.

He knew nothing of his birth save that he was of royal blood, and had spent his life as I had, knowing there was a rightful place for him in the world and unable to reach it.

But if blood calls to blood, then so calls craft to craft, and I knew him to be begotten of the cup. And on this night I put him into deep sleep and made him tell me of the cup of his begetting. And I saw what Ator's knights had searched for all in vain, that magic that was a third part of the green heaven-stone.

Ancel-called-Dubvh showed me that it lay within a well at the Isle of Glass, where the priest who had been sent to convey it to his masters had thrown it in his fright. He had died raving in madness before the moon had grown great again, and so the Queen did not know that her gift had failed, nor the White Priests that they had been granted it. The tale of the cup had spread nevertheless, and the priests had capped it with a tale of their own to explain how it was that he did not have it: that the cup had gone of its own will back to the other-world. Yet the power of the Cup remained in the world, for the well in which it was drowned had come to be called Holy, and in fact I had drunk from it when I had gone there.

Winter followed the great darkness and then the spring, and I brought Ancel back to Caliburn with me to toil in the kitchens, for he had only his own word that his blood was proud, and there were many who might say the same and have more proof of it. So I told him—and this much was the clear truth—that in beginning in the kitchens he could hide the shame and strangeness of his origin and find great favor with the King.

And when the Wheel turned to bring in the May, I sent my brother to Ator at the High Table to beg of him the boon of knighthood and acknowledgment of his noble estate. And it was granted without demur, for Ator dared not seem false in any of his vows. The court looked to call its new knight Ancel, for that he had once served in the kitchens, and no one gave any more thought to his naming than that, for the days of the False Janiffer were long passed. And only I knew who he was and whence he had come—not even Ancel knew all the tale.

The queen loved him at once, but did not know why she loved. She only knew that Ancel called to her soul to soul and skin to skin. She had labored long beneath her husband's displeasure, and longed for a mirror that showed her only desire. And Ancel did desire her, his heart shaped in all ignorance to long for a woman's love.

Through the long summer days their love ripened, for the Court was empty of knights who might have prevented it and the king was often away to war, as he had no other to wage it for him. I saw them sotted with each other and reckless, until the Queen talked of making Ancel War King, and meant a different crown entirely.

And in time, as I knew she would, she sent to the North for allies, and to remind them of what they had sworn, long and long ago.

Now came my revenge full round, as the People, angry with the neglect of the King and the trouble on their borders—for Ator's rebellious princes raided north as well as south—made their mind to break with the southern king, for they had always and ever followed the Queen and sworn to her, not the King. They brought their black horses south to join with the Queen and those princes who had rallied to her standard, and then, when I saw that the Queen and Ancel were truly set upon this course, I rode to where the King lay camped.

I needed no good tale to gain me entrance to his tent, only the knack of moving with the shadow that Grainne had left me. To Ator it seemed that I had appeared out of air and darkness, and thus he was minded to heed my words.

There in that night I told Ator that the Horse King had broken his treaty and had risen against him at the Queen's behest. I told him that she had taken Ancel to be King in his place, and I told him that Ancel was the Queen's own child, begotten of the cup which had been brought to her out of the North. Because this is a custom of the People, it is held a great evil by the White Priests, and Ator would never now take her back again, nor hold off battle through any respect of the bed they two had shared. I told him that I had come to him for the vision I had been granted: of the cup for which his knights had sought so fruitlessly held in his own two hands. I told him that I wished no more reward than to see him achieve this wonder, and to ride with him when he rode against his traitor queen.

And he believed, for he was angry, and reckless, and old.

And because they are all mad in the South.

I knew that the People would not fight when they saw the Cup in Ator's hands, and when they do not there will be a Red Harvest indeed, for the King's troops will not spare them, blaming the northerners for all their misfortune. The People will die in the south, whether from being harried in retreat by the King's army, or of seeing their great treasure in the hands of a southerner—I do not care which—and the king's army will ride down those who stand with Ancel and Janiffer.

In that affray no one will look at me if I strike to cut Ator from life just as he cut Grainne my mother from all her kindred to leave me a rootless wanderer upon the earth. I have worked long and long to spin the threads of

Grainne's curse into a strong thread, and with this great fashioning, my spinning and weaving shall be complete.

The morning sun rose as I spoke to him, and for the first time Ator looked upon my face. He was wonderstruck—no doubt seeing something of himself in me and calling it a miracle—and asked me at last who I was, and for what purpose I had come. And with the words I had carried in my heart for many months, I answered him:

"I am called Parsifal, my Lord, and I am sent to show you to the Grail."

The Secret Leaves

Tricia Sullivan

On the night I decided to capture you the leaves were whispering their secrets in the forest outside your house. You were writing and I was—to use the words with which you were wont to instruct me at every opportunity—*practicing being quiet.* I remember holding a burning stick of incense while you scribed, wishing that you would look up from your work, see me, know me— feel something for me. I was nothing but desire; I turned the incense against the air currents and watched the smoke spiral and blur in the dark air between us. I never wanted anything before or since the way I wanted you then.

My cousin Morgen used to say magic is just a form of sex; I don't know. I do know that watching you write, trying to pour your art into words that could never hold one fingernail of your power, it brought on a leaping inside me. You bent over the page with total absorption, the quill shivering in your hand as you scratched out the words at speed. You reminded me of a small boy though your hair was streaked with gray and I knew I could cover you like a cloak, take you into my pores; I could hold what the parchment couldn't hold, whether it was you I wanted or your power I'll never know because the two are, and were, inseparable.

They will say you were my victim. It will seem as if I stole from you. Those who speak this way weren't there when you burned yourself into me like a sword being forged in my body. They weren't there to see you slide into animal form and flee from me. They weren't there when I laid myself into the hollow left by you in the dirt, when I lay in your impression and shivered until I was unconscious.

As I stand here on the hill in the snow the afternoon sun is like a candle illumining a stained glass sky streaked with waxen clouds: a forever sky. Your bark is rough and beautiful against my cold fingers. My tears fly bitter in the wind. I miss you.

It was spring the first time I came here. I could scarcely see through the rain, the monthly curse was on me, I had drunk too much hot wine in the saddle and needed to pass water, and I was sniffling. I was fourteen. The rains were especially severe that year, and I was renowned neither for patience nor for the ability to bear my troubles in silence. In the endless hours on horseback with rain dripping off my hood and steam rising from Gemma's neck as she plodded through the mud I conceived the notion that my journey to my cousin in the north was cursed in some way. We had been forced to detour into the Welsh border country where there are dense forests and the mountains brood in the west like robed figures, and everywhere there are crows. I complained incessantly.

"You would do well to curb your tongue," said Madeleine. She was hunched beneath her cloak so that all I could see of her was the tip of her red nose and her slim white hands on the reins, but I already knew what she was going to say next and I mouthed the words to myself even as she spoke them: "You will never be married if you do not learn the art of silence."

"Someone should tell the crows to be silent," I remarked, pushing back my hood and tipping my head up to see what had set the birds off. We were riding through a forest of holly and ash, ostensibly on a road but in truth it did not even qualify as a path by the standards of the Romans. Cator kept turning in his saddle to try to hold branches aside for us, which proved a useless exercise as they merely sprang back at the last instant, flinging water over our heads. I found it amusing but Madeleine did not. Apparently it does not rain this way in Brittany; I don't remember, being only three when we came to Lancelot's house in England, where I spent the next eleven years under the yoke of Elaine.

"Mistress Nina is too much of a crow herself," Cator said. "You devil-child, you had better watch out a raven doesn't come down and mistake those shiny black eyes for coins and pluck them out."

I resented being called a devil-child, even though at that very moment I was engaged in tickling his mount's rump with a willow switch at the end of which I'd secured a very large and prickly burr. Every time Cator turned his back I teased the horse, who reacted by shifting unpredictably from side to side and swishing his tail. Madeleine was too deeply hid beneath her cloak to notice my antics.

"My eyes are worth more than yours," I answered, "which the crows will mistake for fox spoor or dead toads unless—"

Madeleine shrieked and her horse shied, and mine and Cator's reacted sympathetically as horses will, skidding sideways in the mud.

"What is it, you foolish woman!" Cator demanded, exercised. A screaming murder of crows exploded from the trees, spiralled over our heads, and settled again not far ahead.

"I saw a wolf," said Madeleine. "There, in the trees. I knew it was true. Wales is a land of evil spirits."

"The horses don't smell anything," Cator said. "Ride on, and don't be so fanciful. Elaine and her magic have turned your head."

"Elaine's love potions and youth charms are nothing more than a sham," I declared. "It's only because of Morgen's spell that Elaine got her husband; she has never done one single act of power in her own right."

"Close your mouth, you horrid witchlet," Cator snarled. "Lancelot should have sent you to a nunnery where you would be forced to be silent as befits a girl. Sending you to your cousin is too good for you."

"Cator is right," Madeleine added. "You are lucky they didn't kill you for your crimes."

I said nothing. I was trying to think of a way to get them both back for their meanness to me, but I was as bereft of magic as Elaine and had no way to work vengeance on them. It was grossly unfair, I thought, that I was being called a witch even though I had been told by my cousin Morgen herself that I had no powers. When Morgen came to visit Elaine's house, she explained to me how Elaine's so-called spells work by deception and wishful thinking, and I was disgusted at the weakness that would let someone fall under a spell that was so transparent, so dependent on their own belief.

"I want to learn true magic," I said to Morgen, but she shook her head.

"You are too old," she said. "If you had talent, it would have shown by now. Besides, Elaine says you are a wayward child, always up to mischief, and my art requires discipline and self-deprivation."

I was angry at Morgen for rejecting me, but after she left I decided to learn magic anyway, so I took the few principles she had explained to me and began to explore them. That was how I came to make the poison that almost killed Elaine's nephew; it was an accident, of course. I had carelessly left out the goblet with the poison, intending to return to it later to thin it somewhat, and the boy had drunk it thinking it mead. That was why I was banished from Elaine's house and sent to the only other relative I had, Morgen.

I felt badly that the boy had become so ill, but he was only a year younger than myself and he might not have been so stupid as to drink something down without first knowing what it was. I could not bring myself to give up magic on those grounds, and even while we rode I was scheming for some way to avoid the unpleasant marriage that I was sure would be made for me within the year. I had visions of being burned at the stake for the murder of my husband because some idiot man had accidentally drunk another of my experimental concoctions. It was not inconceivable. People can be so stupid.

For no reason I could see, Gemma jerked beneath me and leaped to one side; I grabbed at her neck for balance but I could not control her. She was in a blind panic. Ahead I saw Cator's horse rear and paw the air. He spun and charged into the trees, and Gemma followed. Still clinging to her neck, I tucked my chin into my chest for protection against the assault of branches. Cator was shouting and I thought I saw something gray fly past his horse as it raged through the ferns. The horse reared and

Cator was airborne. Then Gemma started bucking. I lost my hold.

I landed in the mud, rolled, and curled myself into a ball as hooves passed over me. Both horses had plunged on into the vegetation, leaving snapped and crushed branches in their wake. I got to my feet, employing the swear words I had heard the kitchen staff use when Lancelot's dogs stole a suckling pig from the spit. In the distance I could hear Madeleine screaming her head off.

"Cator? Cator?" I was bruised and covered with mud, but exhilarated if the truth be told. I could see a bit of red, which must be Cator's cloak, so I picked my way toward him. He had landed halfway across a fallen log. His head was twisted into an unnatural position, and his eyes were open. His body was still twitching.

I turned and ran. Once out of sight of Cator, I squatted in the bushes and urinated. I stood up, shaking.

"Madeleine?" I listened, but I could hear neither horse nor human. The rain fell steadily. I went back to the body and looked at Cator again, hoping for a miracle. His neck was broken; even I could see that. I turned aside and spewed wine and tea cakes. Then I went after the horses.

At first their trail was easy to follow, and I hoped to soon find them standing and waiting for me, for they were on the whole sensible beasts. But though I trudged and trudged, I couldn't seem to catch up with them. Then the woods gave way to an open field. The wind blew rain hard into my face as I set out across it, hopeful of finding them at last; but there were now many tracks cut in the long grass by deer as well as horse, and the wind had blown whole sections flat. I didn't know which way they had broken, and I could not see any sign of them.

To my right there was a hill crowned with massive

oak trees. I decided to climb it in hope of getting a vantage on the horses. I set off up the slope, gritting my teeth against the cramps and praying that Madeleine had not done anything stupid, like riding back to the last village out of fear of evil spirits.

A voice stopped me. Just above me a dark-clad man stood on the rocks. He said something in Welsh which I could not understand; then, impatiently, in English:

"You're running the wrong way. Quick, back to your keeper."

I could not place his accent exactly, but he was no commoner, I was sure. His clothes were worn and had been many times repaired, but the boots had been well made and the knife at his belt had silver in its handle. His black hair had a few strands of gray in it but his face was no older than Arthur's.

"His neck was broken," I blurted. "It is only Madeleine and me. We shall be quite helpless."

"Your road is that way," he said, pointing. "Hurry or you will miss each other. Do not tarry in this wood, but ride on to the next village before it grows dark. You will be safe enough once on the main road; the brat Arthur has at least made the highways safe for ladies unescorted."

"You should not call the king names," I remonstrated, shocked.

"I'll call him what I damn well please, the little bastard," said the stranger. "When you see him you can tell him that."

"I most certainly will not," I snapped. "I am tempted to tell him to send men to teach you some manners, lout."

"Yes." He laughed. "Tell Arthur you met a lout in the woods who insulted him and then disappeared in a puff of smoke."

With that he vanished. Oh, there was no smoke; but one minute he was there and the next he was gone, only the slight swinging of a tiny branch betraying the fact that anyone had ever been there.

What had made him think I was going to see Arthur? All three of us were plainly attired so as not to draw attention to ourselves, and though I am sure I looked like no commoner, there was nothing about me to show that I was acquainted with the king personally. Anyway, we had been riding the other way.

Reflexively, I started to cross myself, and then stopped. I was angry. I had seen Cator fall dead, I had lost Gemma, and the pains were getting stronger all the time, as if someone were squeezing my womb in a fist to force the blood out. I bent double as the spasm came on, gasping until it subsided. I had never had pain such as this in other months.

I began to stumble in the direction he'd indicated, shaking with fear and uncertainty. I was on the point of panic. I had never been alone in the woods and they seemed hostile and terrible, their silence and my ignorance conspiring to make me believe the trees were willing me to be lost—laughing at my indecision and helplessness. I felt like someone was watching me, but when I called out to Madeleine there was no answer. I wasn't sure how far from the road I had come.

I turned, and turned again, and then I realized someone *was* watching me. Only a few yards away, a gray wolf was moving slowly through the bracken, all the while staring at me with such eyes as I'd never seen. Until that moment whenever I'd thought of wolves I thought of great teeth and slavering jaws dripping with blood, but when I swam in those silvery eyes I could feel *mind*. I could detect the calculations, tiny adjustments inside the creature as the nose trembled, receiving my

scent, and the wolf stopped and subtly aligned her body
with respect to me. Her gaze was unwavering and deep,
her head dropped low and ears forward, the body curving slightly to one side where she stood as if she were
about to approach me on a diagonal. I couldn't move.
The moments slid by but I didn't let myself think; I just
held myself still and let her read me. In my short but rebellious life I had stared down nursemaids and teachers
and nuns and duchesses but now I was already feeling
myself inside her jaws, inside her body, devoured: I belonged to the wolf and we both knew it.

She sprang at me. I ran, fell, ran again; she followed
me. I hurled myself forward, momentarily encouraged
because I didn't immediately feel her teeth on me; and
some hot ghost of strength came into me and drove me
on. I knew then that terror is not an abstract thing: it is as
physical as the stones and the dirt. It possessed me. I ran
mindlessly, driven by fear. I didn't look back; I didn't
dare form one thought. It wasn't until I tripped and fell
that I realized she was no longer behind me, for when I
scrambled to my feet I was alone, I knew not where,
winded, shaking all over, almost sick with emotion.
The rain hammered down. My knees went suddenly
weak and I seized hold of a sapling to keep my feet beneath me.

I tried to take my bearings but I wasn't even sure
which direction I'd come from, as if my memory of the
past hour wandering in the forest had been stolen from
me. I remembered pushing through underbrush and ferns
and ducking under branches, but I could not orient myself. I began to feel hysterical. I was convinced it was
my blood that had attracted the wolf; my blood for
which Cator had died and maybe now Madeleine too;
my blood by which I was lost, and I could now feel it
flowing harder, unchecked.

Something big was moving in the trees. I heard a high, gasping sound come from my own mouth. I clung to the sapling, desperate even for its pathetic protection. The rain got louder, and the animal moved closer. It was Gemma! She was nosing about, looking for grass. I spoke to her quietly. She let out a gusty sigh and stood still.

"Ah, Gemma," I murmured. "I'm so glad to see you. Come here, my sweet. Come to me."

Obligingly, Gemma started toward me, but her reins had caught in the branches and when she moved the tree struck at her like a snake. She stiffened on all four legs and tried to back away, but she was stuck. Her eyes rolled white.

"Shh, Gemma! All is well, there's a good—"

But Gemma had had too much excitement already. She danced in a half-circle around the tree, which shook violently when she moved. There was a peal of thunder. Gemma jerked her head and the branch snapped. She reared and came down running. Clods of earth and leaves shot from her hooves as she bolted. She flew over a log and went crashing off among the trees. Soon she was out of sight in the driving rain.

I started to follow but my legs gave way and I was on my knees in the mud. I had lost all hold of myself; I flung my arms on the ground in futile prostration. I could smell the green and the decay, and my shivers added to my sobs. The blood leaked down my legs, accompanied by a wrenching in my gut. I bared my teeth at the pain. I could see everything in unbearably fine detail, and it seemed to me then that I could put my hand through the world like a spiderweb and it would stick to me in the same way, and I would have broken something exquisite and there would be nothing on the other side.

I heard his boots squelching through the mud and I

was too far gone to react. He was talking to me in a low voice, the way you talk to a skittish horse. He put his hands on my back.

"Come and stand up if you can," he murmured. "The cold will do you no good."

He tried to draw me off the ground and I twisted and thrashed. He put his arms around me and I bit him as he picked me up; yet no matter how I struggled he contained me with what seemed no great effort.

"Do you think it will be tasty, Wolf?" he was saying. "Shall we boil it? No? Roast it on a spit? Remember those priests we fried last year? They were tough, weren't they."

I struggled, but I had nothing left.

"Ah, you're right, Wolf—we'll never get a proper fire going in this rain. But I'm in a very bad mood, and the rain suits me. I think I shall make it rain for a year at least."

My mind had glazed over. I closed my eyes and went limp in his arms. He carried me like an errant sheep, with an easy, matter-of-fact air. I couldn't think, but I was aware of the scratch of damp wool against my cheek and the hot blood sticking to the insides of my thighs and the smell of his skin and the rise and fall and shake of his legs as his feet met the ground. He possessed less bulk than any of Arthur's knights yet he didn't seem much put out to be carrying me up the steep hillside. I could hear the tread of the wolf beside us, passing through brambles and fern and dead wood and finally into the darkness of a grove. I could hear acorns thudding against the ground, loosened by wind and rain. He ducked and I opened my eyes inside a cave.

The cave was not perfectly symmetrical, but the natural fall of this hill cut the stone in split rectangular blocks like stairs, and as a result the cave had a natural chimney as well as shelves and furnishings. There were herbs hanging in bunches, and cured meats, and bottles of all sizes and shapes tucked into recesses in the stone. In the shadows were stacked boxes upon boxes, which I later learned contained pages of his writing. Lying on top of them were loose leaves of parchment and carefully rolled scrolls. Quills made from pigeon feathers littered the floor. On ledges about the cave were skulls of various animals, and hanging on a length of gut along one wall was a gigantic snake skeleton.

I was deposited in a wet heap near the entrance, and he threw wood on the fire.

"Here's a blanket," he said, and tossed it at me. "I don't think it has too many fleas. Use the water in the bucket to wash." My skirts had hiked up to my knees, and his eyes flickered to the bloodstains that had made their way down my legs. He pointed to the hearth. "It will be cold tonight. You had better sleep close to the fire."

Then he left. Outside, the sun had come out and the hellish day was turning into a perfect spring evening with water falling musically from the trees.

I was accustomed to having Madeleine assist me with my dress and hair. I was accustomed to hot water for washing. And I was hungry. Full of self-pity, I saw to myself as best as I could, finally curling up naked inside the rough blanket. It was still light outside when sleep hit me like a thunderclap.

In the morning he came in with eggs, which he said I should cook; he rummaged about among his papers while I did so, nervous because there was a glamour about him and it caught me immediately. I felt witless. When I gave him the bowl of badly scrambled eggs he dumped half of them onto a second dish and handed it to me. Then he stood looking out of the cave and eating. He said nothing about the poor quality of the cooking, but he could not have been enjoying the food very much. When I shovelled my portion down it was half burnt, half runny.

I heard myself stammer, "You aren't . . . you're Myrddin, aren't you?"

He didn't say anything, but something flashed in his eyes that said, *Yes, obviously.*

He put down his bowl. "Who sent you here and what is your purpose?"

I started talking too fast, in a high voice, like a foolish maid. "We're trying to get to my cousin Morgen's house. The roads are terrible, and then the wolf—"

"Ah," he exclaimed. I stopped talking, gazing into his eyes. They were an unusual color: brown in certain lights, green in others and, at the moment in this slanting morning sun, amber. "Morgen. Did she tell you she is my enemy?"

"No! She thinks very highly of you."

"Yet she drove Arthur away from me when she seduced him to conceive Mordred. Now Arthur fears his own nature, and he turns to the priests and he will ruin himself with this asinine Grail of his. Morgen! Are you really her cousin?"

"Yes," I said miserably. I am an excellent liar but it failed me with him.

"Well," he said in a slightly kinder tone. "You had better come with me. I don't trust you here alone. My book is here and Morgen has sent you to steal it."

He took a bow and arrow and led me out of the cave. The wolf was nowhere to be seen; when I asked him about her, he said, "She is her own creature. She comes and goes, as do I, which is a peaceable arrangement for us both. She will get ideas from time to time, though."

He glanced back at me then, curiosity glinting in his eyes.

"You must be the same age as Arthur when he took the sword," he said. "Too young, in other words, to be of any use."

He stopped and nocked an arrow.

"But he became king when he took the sword!"

"*Shh!* Be quiet." Birds broke from the tree overhead; he released the first arrow and shot a second one in quick succession, and a moment later, two wood pigeons dropped to the ground just ahead of us. Myrddin went to them and removed the arrows. He picked up the birds and stroked their feathers as if petting a cat. "You should not talk so much," he said to me. "I wanted to shoot them without frightening them, so they would die softly."

"What difference does it make? They are going to die anyway," I said callously. I was thinking of Cator; even if I hadn't liked him, I was upset by what had happened.

I was surprised by the sorrow in his face. "If you had been a bird, you would know how it feels to fly."

Before I could ask what this was supposed to mean he had moved on again through the wood, forcing me to follow. He continued talking about Arthur as if nothing had interrupted us.

"He was a boy king only because I *made* him king. I trained in him the strength that let him take the sword where others twice his size could not; I taught him the craft of disguise and the ways of mastering the mind known only to those who have made an art of living by their wits. I showed him the power of perception and I awakened his courage. This is as far from any fool magic of charms and potions as The Wolf is from Guinevere's damned lap dog."

"I remember that dog." I laughed. "I kept wishing it

would choke on a chicken bone, for it ate better than we did sometimes, and it bit everyone's fingers, besides."

"Arthur has put about too many legends," Myrddin said. "They make it impossible for me. No one would now see me as I am; everyone expects the ethereal being that Arthur decided I must be when he failed to grasp what I was trying to teach him. Men think me unable to use weapons; they think I cannot fight because they have never seen it happen. You saw my arrows: do you agree?"

"You seem earthly enough to me," I said. I was behind him, looking at his legs, which evoked thoughts of an earthly nature. I was breathing hard as I tried to keep his pace up a steep, rocky hillside.

"I could have thrashed Uther like a wet rag and he knew it," Myrddin declared, flashing a smile over his shoulder. "But kingship is not about fighting; it is all politics, and for that I have precious little talent. I thought Uther Pendragon my friend. Not only did I get him Ygrane, I agreed to help his boy get the throne—and what was my reward? To be called mad, and to be ignored. Yet Arthur was like a son to me. I would have taught him everything I know."

"Why didn't you?"

"I tried, and that was my mistake. I made it too easy for him, and he didn't see the value of what I offered. I should have made him figure it out for himself: then he would be something to reckon with. He could have become a great man—better than me in every way, if only he would have listened. If only he would have seen beyond himself. But he turned out to be like all men. He only wants to increase his land, and bed his wife who bears him no children."

"He ought to acknowledge Mordred," I said, repeating the sentiment spoken by Morgen.

"Mordred will be his downfall," Myrddin replied. "Now Arthur's death walks and talks, and waits for him to falter. He should have curbed himself. Bedding his own half-sister—it was perverse."

I was angry: again he had denounced Morgen. "They call you a neuter in Arthur's court," I blurted, and my face went hot. I was still behind and below him, and I was still staring at his body; there could be no doubt that he was a man.

But Myrddin only laughed. "Yes, and I am demon-spawned, they say. It is the secret of my youth."

"What do you mean?" I asked sharply, for I had been wondering how he could be Arthur's teacher when he and Arthur looked the same age. His reply was cryptic.

"Whatever it was that gave birth to me was not a soft thing, it was a demon with a woman's face, full of cruelty and power. To escape it I had to become strong of will and body—too strong to be tamed. My power is in my isolation. And there is also my doom to be considered."

"Your doom?"

"Arthur is not the only one whose death walks the earth in human form. Long ago it was prophesied that my end will come in the form of a woman who imprisons me in an oak for all eternity. So it is that I avoid women." He vaulted up a steep part of the rock face, and then turned and pointed off to his left. Lightly he said, "Try that way, it will be easier for you."

All this was spoken without irony, as if he were unaware that *I* was a woman. Well . . . I'd *thought* I was, until now. My bleeding had ceased overnight. And that was to be only the beginning. Every moment I spent in his presence I was disoriented and baffled, for he warped the very air with his heat until I felt that I myself had become a mirage.

At the top of the hill the forest broke. There was a line of enormous, old oaks at its edge, and then the land fell away and rolled down to an open meadow, which I recognized from our first meeting yesterday. In the deep grass, grazing, were three horses: Cator's gray; a heavy black warhorse that must belong to Myrddin; and my Gemma, who looked like a pony by comparison.

"There is your steed, safe and sound and with a full belly," Myrddin said.

"Do we ride to find Madeleine, then?" I asked. I was trying to think of a way to make sure Madeleine was safe without actually having to make the rest of the journey in her company. "I have money and can hire an escort in the nearest town."

He laughed. "You can do as you like. I'm not going anywhere."

"But how am I to get to Morgen's house with no escort?"

Myrddin shrugged. "I don't know, but believe me— you do not wish to be seen with me! Ah, look, there is Wolf with a rabbit she's caught."

With that, the subject of my leaving was closed. We never spoke about what I was doing there, or how long I would stay, or what was expected of me. As the days passed, he taught me to do things, and I did them—not very well at first. I chopped wood; I caught fish and killed them and cleaned them and cooked them; I made candles and gathered greens and medicinal herbs and mushrooms from which I was expected to make various tinctures; I learned to make arrows, and, in time, to shoot them. As I was busy doing these things Myrddin wandered about humming, or endlessly rewrote sections of his book, or lay in the sun by the streambank, twirling a blade of grass between his lips and posing silly questions, like, "How does the spider know what the web she's spinning looks like if she's too small to ever stand back from it? And how does she measure the angles so precisely? Does she have a compass in her backside?"

When I tried to discuss these problems with him seriously, as I thought an apprentice should, he only became more and more absurd. When Wolf was around they engaged in mock fights in which they growled and cuffed each other and rolled in last year's leaves. If I was engaged in a task demanding particular concentration, I could count on being sung to, or distracted by tiny missiles spat from somewhere under cover with a blowgun. He capered and play-acted: Camelot was the usual subject of his ridicule, and Guinevere his favorite target. I nearly fainted with laughter at his skits in which he played both the sinful queen and her Father Confessor. He was uncanny; I couldn't take my eyes off him.

I thought he was beautiful. The more ridiculous he acted, the more attractive he became. Maybe this, I thought, was his spell. For I kept waiting for him to show signs of being a great magician, but the only thing he seemed to be great at was being bone-idle while I worked. I intimated at this once and in a mysterious tone he said, "If you look too hard, you'll never find anything," and then glanced sidelong at me to see whether or not I believed him.

He had his foul moods, too. Lightning was his favorite thing, and some days after he had been talking about Arthur and the priests and the knights and their stupidity in searching for the Grail when—Myrddin said—they could instead devote themselves to learning something real about the world—after he had worked himself up into a fine rage, he would go out into the forest. Infected by his ire, I would find myself unable to concentrate on anything through the hot, brooding afternoon. Then would come the evening thunderstorm, and in its aftermath I'd hear Wolf and Myrddin howling at each other across the hills.

As strange as the situation was, it did not take very long for me to come to the conclusion that I was better off here than married off to somebody's youngest son. Myrddin didn't seem to mind that I was a girl; he didn't even notice as far as I could tell. As the summer progressed, he took me walking in the woods and told me all kinds of things about plants and the behavior of wild creatures: how to know which ones were where, not by magic, but by observing the directions that birds flew; which ones were singing and which not; the time of day; the weather; the proximity of deer to water; the behavior of insects; the height of swallows and the quality of silence—he said—in the trees.

"They see everything," he told me wistfully. "I wish I could talk to them. Imagine what they must know."

"Talking to trees?" It wasn't sensible. "Do you worship them? Like the Druids? Do you believe they have spirits?"

"I dunno." He took a maple seed pod, the kind that spin like wings when they fall, and, splitting it, stuck it on the end of his nose. "If they do, I doubt their spirits are interested in us. They have better things to do."

"Like what?"

"Like what? Why, they are bridges to the sun. And in their branches on a winter night you can see they make a reseau about the stars. They are star catchers."

"After they catch them, what do they do with them?"

The dreaminess in his eyes had been replaced by mischief. "Catch *me*," he said, and leaped away. Dropping the bluebells I had been gathering, I chased him through the trees, around brakes of thorns and over a brook—then I lost him. I stopped, panting, and listened. Something large was moving in the brush nearby. I picked up a stick, which I was planning to hit him with when I found him.

Suddenly there was a flash of brown hide through the brambles, and a doe crashed through and passed right by me as if I wasn't there. She ran a few strides upwind of the place where I stood, and stopped. I didn't move. A moment later a three-pointed stag leaped over the thorn-brake after her and she was off again. I expected them to vanish into the forest as quickly as they had come, but it was not like that. The doe did not go far before she turned and doubled back, and the stag followed at a little distance. He made no attempt to *catch* her, only to not lose her. For her part the doe seemed to be in no hurry to get away. She jumped lightly over a fallen branch, turned, went back the other way, turned again, trotted on . . . When a noise or smell alerted her she would freeze and the stag would stop also, wait for her to get her confidence back, and then move again when she moved, with his head always extended slightly forward on his neck, questing. It was as if an invisible thread connected her hindparts to his nose, and they made a game out of tightening and then slackening the string.

As for Myrddin's game, he didn't seem to be playing anymore. He was nowhere to be found, and as soon as the deer had moved off, I began to run back toward home. I crossed the meadow below the cave where the deer sleep in the sun among the wildflowers, and a hawk passed overhead. I turned to follow its flight path and Myrddin was standing behind me.

"I got bored waiting for you to catch me," he said. "So I went home and put the fire up for soup and came back. You're going to have to get quicker if we're to have any fun at all."

"Very funny," I said. There was no way he could have gotten back to the cave ahead of me and then circled around again and caught up to me from behind without being seen. I had only been watching the deer for a few minutes, and anyway I was out of breath and he wasn't even perspiring. "Where have you been?"

"I changed." He set off up the hill by the oaks, whistling.

"What do you mean?"

"Think about it."

I scrambled after him. We went into the cave and just as he said, the fire was burning and a pot of mushroom soup bubbled gently.

"How did you do that?"

Singing to himself, he dished up the soup into two bowls and gave me mine. I looked at it suspiciously. There was simply no way he could have had time! When I put my lips to it, the liquid was scalding.

"I can Change. I can share space with other animals," Myrddin stated. "Didn't you guess?"

He sat down cross-legged and blew on his soup. Wolf came in and sat beside him; he offered her the bowl and she put her nose to it and then jumped back, burned, just as I had done. Myrddin apologized to her. She sat on her haunches and looked at me.

I started to ask questions but Myrddin was having none of it.

"Will you be quiet," he said. "There is no way you will ever learn to do the Changes if you are always talking. Listen! Watch, and absorb everything you can. You have more empty space inside you than you know."

I wanted to listen but I was distracted. It was his eyes, and the creatures and people who lived in them all looking out at me at once: his eyes were wide and eager and they seemed always to be hunting for some understanding, some kinship. I told myself I was a fool for thinking they would find it in me, and yet my loins were heavy and alive in the field of his glance, and I found myself leaning toward him.

"What are you looking at?" he said impatiently, for I was staring. "I told you: *listen*, Nina."

To this day I do not understand how I could have felt as I did. Girls only play at desire; they flirt with pretty blond boys and then run away to giggle with each other. Men they scarcely perceive. And Myrddin was more than a man—he was older than the stones and he could see into every corner of me and I was beginning to guess that he was dangerous. Myrddin I should have feared. I *did* fear him. Yet I hungered also, and I have never been as good at fear as I ought.

"*What* are you looking at?" he said again.

"You," I said in a soft voice.

"Yes, and what is the matter?" he sighed, exasperated. "Did you not have enough soup? I am poorly equipped to care for you."

"Do you think me ugly?"

He blinked rapidly several times, gave his head a little shake as though trying to come to grips with the question. Then he shrugged.

"Not particularly."

I burst into tears.

"What is it? Why are you crying? Damned female thing, I cannot understand you. Why are you crying?"

I cried harder.

"What's wrong? Nina!"

"Nothing." I sniffled. "Nothing. Leave me alone."

He tried to teach me his magic, which he called the Changes, but I was not a very good student. For all the noise I had made about it in Elaine's house, now that I was faced with the prospect of real power, I was ambivalent about touching it. I wished there were someone else besides me, someone with real talent, or someone with a prophecy in his favor, like Arthur and the stone. For it burned me that Arthur had not taken up Myrddin's challenge to pursue this knowledge. If he had done so, then I wouldn't be the one on whom all Myrddin's energy devolved.

Yet in the end I had no choice. I knew it would be wrong not to try to take what Myrddin was giving, even if I had deep misgivings about what would come of it. And I wanted him. With my body I wanted him, and I would have done anything for that.

As time passed I seemed to get less and less work done. He would interrupt me and we would walk in the forest around his house, sometimes accompanied by Wolf, sometimes alone. I liked it better when Wolf was there because she made Myrddin happy.

"If you want to do the Changes then you have to understand what's going on in all life," he said. "It comes down to the sun. Do you understand?"

"No." I was hoping he would give up on trying to teach me, but he never did.

"The leaves transform the sunlight into matter, but only so they can grow back toward it. The sun is having a conversation with itself through the leaves, through the air itself, through us. Don't you perceive it, Nina? Those leaves hold all the secrets there ever were. Listen."

I listened. It was true that there was a constant sound, like the sea, up on that hill where Myrddin had his house in the cave. I don't believe the wind ever really stopped. The leaves that shook the stars, sleepless creatures, they gossiped all night and sighed all day.

"Let's sit here," he said. We settled side by side in the meadow below the cave, looking up at the ridge with the oak trees all in a line on its crest. They must have been a hundred years old, and each one had a different personality, it seemed to me.

"I like that one the best," I said, pointing to an enormous oak whose branches had been twisted as if it were whirling. It leaned over recklessly, limbs extended, as if seizing chances out of the very sky: movement masquerading as stillness. "It reminds me of you."

"Falling," mused Myrddin. "Always falling."

I smiled. "But never caught."

"Now, be quiet, and watch me," he instructed, suddenly serious. "I'll do the Change first. I'll be one of the rabbits. When you see me, follow me."

"I am no good at magic," I told him. "Morgen said so."

"Never mind that. Just try. Try."

"But—"

"Shh!"

I watched the rabbits. The hill beneath the oaks was riddled with their holes, and they seemed to tumble down the hillside when they came out to feed. I watched for a long time until I noticed one among the babies that looked . . . familiar. I glanced aside toward Myrddin and he was gone.

How was I to follow? I fixed my eyes on another of the rabbits and tried to become it, but I couldn't seem to meld with it—I was too caught up in my own head. It was frustrating. Myrddin continued to potter about in the grass, enjoying himself. I kept trying, to no avail.

Something was wrong. I could taste it on the air.

Still trapped in my human body, I studied the scene. From the underbrush at the top of the hill Wolf appeared. She began to creep among the tree roots, in the deep shade where nothing grew. On the hillside Myrddin froze in a round huddle, folding his ears back against his body so that he seemed nothing more than a stone. Wolf kept coming, intent on the kill.

Did she know it was him? She couldn't know. Wolf was only hunting as she always did, and Myrddin was a small round ball of fluff asking to be eaten. I could feel Myrddin and I wanted to stand up and scream, to do something to distract Wolf, but as in all nightmares I couldn't make myself move.

Wolf made a dash. As one, the rabbits broke for cover. Head forward, tail stiff, she gamboled among them, scattering the rabbits in every direction as they made for their holes. With the horrible inevitability that characterized the whole scene, she selected Myrddin.

Where effort fails, necessity succeeds: fear arrowed me into the tiny form, and then it was me and Myrddin and the rabbit as one, flying from the jaws of the wolf. We moved like lightning in a jagged line across the slope. There was a terrible smell, and the realization of death, and then the darkness of the earth was all around. Squeezing in among the bitten roots and the cool worms, with the vibration and stench of the wolf passing by above, I *was* the rabbit. Why I had managed to do the Change only when I was going *toward* danger, I can't say. It seems backward. But I couldn't hold on after the fear had passed. I couldn't stay. I couldn't become invisible like Myrddin, and the rabbit quickly forced me out. I felt myself pass through it, left behind as it continued down the burrow after the others.

Then I panicked. I had nowhere to go; I had nothing to be. The first thing I touched was a scraped section of root—so that is what I became, and that is how I lost myself inside the tree. It was a complete accident.

There are absolutely no words for what it was. I don't even think I remember—*yes, I do, but I won't look, not at that*—no, I can't remember anything except Myrddin shaking me so hard my head hurt.

Somehow he must have got me back into the cave, where the fire was burning. My fingers were blue. Myrddin was chafing my hands in between shaking me, and I was curled up in his lap like a hedgehog. I couldn't work out what was going on.

"You *are* some kind of demon," he said in a low voice.

"Why are you looking at me like that? All I did was what you said," I sobbed. "It's what you said, it's what you said." I kept repeating it; I was incoherent but it was true. Why did he tell me to do the Change if he didn't know the outcome? I knew now that going into the tree must have been almost the end of me. I could tell by his behavior, by the way he had turned ashen white and how he held me in his lap as if I'd disappear otherwise, and I began to cry in self-righteousness and delayed shock, I guess. He put his hands on my head and held me against him.

"I never thought it was possible." His voice was reverberating through my body. "You actually went into the tree. I felt you there. I never dared do such a thing; I never even imagined it."

"It was an accident." I gulped. "I was confused. I was afraid. I didn't mean to do it."

"If you could go in the tree, I could too, perhaps. What else might I become? What beyond the animals? I could Change into the trees, I could feel the sun translated in their leaves, I might understand the meaning of the sun. It would be the next best thing to Changing to the sun itself."

Incredulous, I stopped crying. I'd thought I'd done something wrong, broken a rule, when in fact for the first time I had actually done something right. I didn't care what it was or what it meant. I only cared that he was holding me; I was filled with blind happiness.

My lips were travelling along his neck, my fingers in his hair. I could feel his heat against my thighs, and my belly seemed to drop and expand, to flex like a bow being drawn. He was oblivious to me; he kept talking about our discovery. I slid my hands inside his clothes and found the shape of the muscles and bones. I smelled his skin. One of his hands rested on the back of my head and the other stroked my flank unhurriedly, almost as if he wasn't aware of doing it. Wherever I was in contact with him my body went quiet and listened. His hand cradling my head was warm and soft and certain, and large enough to grip my whole skull. I closed my eyes.

His voice trailed off. Our heartbeats chased each other like wood pigeons' wings, syncopating against one another, accelerating. Through the touch of his fingertips I could sense his slow realization of what was happening. Yet I was surprised when I suddenly felt his breath against my face and then his lips against mine and he opened my mouth with his tongue.

For the first time in my life I didn't have one single thought in my head.

He pushed me away. "No. I must not." Dazed, I tried to hold on to him but I found myself clutching air. He was on his feet, pacing, not staying in one place long enough to be seen, much less touched.

"You are trying to trap me," he said. "You are trying to define me. You with your words and your endless questions, and now this. I don't blame you; you can't help yourself. But I will not be contained."

"I'm not trying to trap you," I protested, but he didn't seem to hear me.

"If I make you with child, I will have been captured in your body. I must remain free. To go into another thing;

to become an animal, I must have no shape of my own, so as to acquire the shape of that other thing. I am nobody; I'm nothing. I cannot love you and I cannot be bound."

"But I—"

"*No,* Nina! Be quiet. A man who suffers himself to be repeated in the next generation then feels obliged to move over and die. I do not wish to die. I know the secret of how things are made and unmade; it allows me to move between things, but I can only do so because I have no attachments. I deposit no trace. The secret leaves with me."

"What about your book?"

"That's different." He scowled. I could not see how it was different.

"I don't want to study anymore," I cried. "I don't want the power. All I want is to be yours. I only want to be with you."

"You can't. I can't. It can't be both. It doesn't work that way."

"But I don't want it. Myrddin! Please. Let's not do the Changes anymore, I won't study, I'll be quiet, I'll be very quiet, I promise. Just come here, just for a minute. I can't stand it; Myrddin! Look at me."

He turned away.

"If you want a man, if you want a child, you must return to your own world."

"This is my world," I said. "You are my world."

"I'm nobody," he said again. "I thought you understood that. I thought you wanted to become the same. I thought you wanted to *learn.*"

He looked so puzzled, so betrayed, that I felt guilty for wanting him. I knew he was thinking of Arthur who had let him down, and I felt I had violated a trust.

"I don't know," I said. "I don't know. I'm sorry."

And I looked at him again, remembering the kiss and
the substance of him wrapped around me just for those
few moments, and I saw the lifelong wound in him that
made him fear enclosure, and that I was the very embod-
iment of enclosure. The wild thing that had taken seeds
from my hand now perceived the cage, and it was me.

He was outside before I could draw another breath,
and Wolf followed on his heels. I stumbled after them
into the heavy summer darkness but they were not there.
The trees had caught Cassiopeia reclining in the sky and
I could smell my own arousal, and I didn't understand
that, either. I sat down and covered my ears against the
sound of the leaves.

I really thought I'd lost him then. For days on end I was
alone, and being left in that cave surrounded by all his
materials and notes and his smell and the imprint of his
body still present in his bed it was almost too much for
me. I told myself I would do anything, if only he would
come back. I never would touch him; never would I look
in his eyes; I would be like a little nun. He didn't return.
But on the second day Wolf came to visit me, and I
could sense her nearby after that, watching me; guarding
me. On the fourth night she came and slept beside me
and the smell of her fur filled my dreamtime. On the
fifth day I came in from the spring with my bucket and
he was there, writing. He glanced up, smiled as if nothing had happened. I was overjoyed to see him.

"The tree," he said. "If only I could make it last! It's a
whole new dimension. You can see so much more."

"Is that where you've been?" I was angry. I'd thought
he had run from me; I'd been blaming myself and feeling guilty and all this time he'd been romping around
practicing the Changes, and now he gave me that sly

smile as if there were nothing in the world but his search for truth.

"I sent Wolf to watch over you," he said defensively, sensing my wrath. "I would not have left you unprotected."

"I wasn't afraid," I snapped, annoyed that he treated me like the child I was. I opened my mouth to say more and then closed it, remembering that I was not supposed to speak. He saw this, nodded his approval and went on with his work, whistling cheerily. I sulked. I had forgotten my promises to think only chaste thoughts. I lit incense and curled up by the fire, willing myself to become beautiful even though he had eyes only for the paper in front of him. Consumed with frustration, I watched him write down everything that was in his mind about the tree; it took hours. The smoke slithered around him while he worked, and I sat numb by the fire feeling overwhelmed. Myrddin could think of nothing but eternity, and I could think of nothing but Myrddin.

To hold myself back from him was torture, for I loved him and I wanted him; but to seduce him would have meant breaking his power, and what satisfaction could there be in that? Anyway, I wasn't sure that I could seduce him: he had resisted me so far. He might step out of the forest and eat out of my hand when it pleased him, but he would never be tamed and probably I wouldn't want him to be. The bitter conclusion was that if I really loved him then I mustn't try to have him.

There must be something else going on, though. He said he wanted no part of me nor any woman, yet I burned white-hot, undeterred by his rejection. I was fourteen, and he was an old man, black hair and lithe body notwithstanding. Was he casting a spell? Was I? Maybe it belonged to neither of us. Maybe we were both simply caught in something.

As I had this thought, I noticed Wolf staring at me. How those silvery eyes made me shiver. I felt her gaze all the way down at the bottom of my spine. Suddenly she rose and shot out of the house, tail stiff, ears back. Myrddin glanced up, alarmed. He gave a nervous laugh. "What's got into her?"

"She was reading my mind," I said.

"What were you thinking about?" he asked. "Ghosts and goblins?"

"Death," I said, which I thought sounded more sophisticated than *love*.

"Close enough! Go to sleep, devil-child," he said affectionately.

I lay down, but I couldn't sleep. I listened to the trees all night.

"The first day I was here you told me I didn't know what it meant to fly," I said to Myrddin the next morning. I had learned to choose my words carefully, for he meant for me to rely not so much on speech. "I want to fly."

"Ho!" Myrddin exclaimed. "What's this? I thought you didn't want to do the Changes anymore."

I said nothing.

"Why don't you answer me? Ah-ha, I get it! Practicing being quiet, is that it? Well."

He turned and stalked off, pretending to be angry. I followed, recognizing the game for what it was. We walked for a time.

"I'm hunting," Myrddin said in a conspiratorial whisper. Then he pointed up. I saw several gray wood pigeons in the leaves above. I turned to see what he would do but he was already gone.

I tried to follow. *We will mate in animal form*, I thought. Thus motivated, I directed all my energies toward the pigeons. I flowed with them; I felt them. Yet I

was earthbound. So I ran; it was the best I could do.
They outpaced me. I reached the fringe of the wood and
they were soaring over the meadow and back, striped
wings extended, and then one by one they cleaved to the
great oaks. I could hear them overhead, and my heart
was full but I was still only myself.

Myrddin came out of the sky and fell against the trunk
of the tree in human form, clutching his side, winded
and laughing.

"Ah, it's good!" he enthused, and his bright eyes
teased me. "Why can't you do it, my dumb one? No,
don't speak!"

He put a finger on my lips and for a second I looked
up at him, mute. I don't remember making a decision. I
just threw myself on him.

My great advantage was that he didn't know what to
do when this happened, not really. Neither did I, as I
soon discovered. But it was too late by then to go back.
We were all over each other.

The bark bit into the soft flesh to either side of my
spine, and I smelled moss and the dust left by ants where
they had travelled, and our bodies crushed the vines as
we slithered together into the place where the roots met
the ground. I looked up and the leaves were shattering
the sun, which rained its light in a thousand pieces; there
were spiderwebs in the branches and light-pierced insects drizzling through the summer air, and when he
penetrated me it hurt and it was strange. I wrapped my
legs around his back and pulled him closer. It was not
what I hoped it would be. It was not the same as two
deer darting through the trees in a spontaneous dance. It
was not like anything I knew, and I was afraid of it. I bit
my lip so as not to sob, and I put my hands on his head,
seeking reassurance but he didn't see me anymore; he
was too far gone. What he saw or felt of me was some-

thing deep in my body, something I didn't know and couldn't control, and it was speaking to him without my even realizing it. There was a kind of helplessness in his face when he climaxed and I knew he had surrendered, not to me although it seemed that way—but to *it*.

Afterward he looked sleepy and slightly weak and I took the license to kiss him and run my hands over his body and hold his head against my breasts and belly as I had yearned to do all this time but never dared, only now he seemed smaller and more real and what I thought was complex and difficult was really so simple: our hands exchanging caresses and our breathing running down to earth; we were clouds settling after a storm. Some of the hairs on his chest were white where I put my lips, and I ached for him, I ached all over just when I should have been feeling most fulfilled. This is how I know I really loved him.

We lay on the hill beneath the tree that was falling but never caught, and after a little while Myrddin's mind resumed its indefatigable activity.

"This tree, it's a negotiation between heaven and earth. Look how it keeps trying to reach the sky! This branch fails, so it sends two more in its place. It contends with winds and obstacles, and it harbors birds, and it keeps climbing. You can read its story in the shape of its wood."

"It must be a very old tree," I murmured.

Myrddin said, "It doesn't matter. The old, they are like the young only they have made more decisions, more pathways to the sky."

"But they never get there!"

"How do you know that?" He propped himself up on one elbow and directed darkly golden eyes at me. "Have you tried to find out?"

"No," I said. "And I don't want to. Not today, anyway."

He folded his arms around me and stroked my back. He always had a smell about him, a metallic smell like steel mingled with some essence of fire, and then twice combined with the familiar oils and scents of the body. It intoxicated me.

"Come on," he said. "Just let's go a little way. I'm curious. Just for a moment."

I could not deny him when he wanted to play, and he knew it. I squinted up at the tree. It *was* my favorite tree . . .

"You're good at it. You go first," he urged.

I sighed, stretched a languid arm over my head, and touched the bole. Myrddin was holding the fingertips of my other hand, and through his touch I could sense him leaning into the tree. There was no thought in me. I surged up the tree like water drawn to the sun.

Inside the tree we were of the same substance. We coursed upward, elemental, reduced to something at once more basic and more sublime, and in this moment of no identity he used me to pull himself along. Because I was not aware of myself, I didn't feel him slip by me and let go. I have no memory of the parting of our fingertips, and since we were not present to our bodies when it happened, to this day I hold the image of us lying under the tree, making fingerprints on each other's fingerprints, never to be parted.

Yet we were parted. Inside the tree I tried to catch at him as he passed me by. But it was his game we played; it always had been. He was gone.

I fell out of the tree. I was naked on the ground, looking up at the branches in astonishment. Alone.

"Myrddin!" I screamed. "No fair! Come back. Come back!"

There was no answer from the oak, nor from the indentation left by his body in the earth. I threw myself on it in disbelief, pressing my lips against the soil I wished could be him.

When I went through his things I opened the book he had gone to such pains to protect. Its many leaves were covered with Myrddin's impossible hand, the lines written from left to right and then over again, and then crossed from top to bottom, so that thrice the usual number of words could fit on a single sheet.

The text was completely indecipherable.

I picked it up and pressed it to my breast, bowed my head over it. It smelled like him.

I never saw Wolf again. I bitterly wished for her to come to me, for at least that way I would have someone to talk to, a witness to what had happened between Myrddin and me. But I suppose whatever sadness she felt was not of the same kind as mine, and she must be allowed her own way of mourning.

So it was that Gemma and I left Wales knowing too well what loneliness is. And instead of going to Morgen, I went to Arthur's court and I told him the story and showed him Myrddin's book, which no one could read, and Arthur said, "But is he dead or alive? Where has he gone?"

"He has gone where no one can catch him," I said. "He is not dead."

Guinevere turned to Arthur and remarked, "She is the one they used to call the devil-child, the one Elaine banished from Lancelot's house."

"She is like Myrddin, then," Arthur replied, and I thought he looked rather pleased. "He was never made of the same stuff as us. Probably he was not a mortal man. Tell me, did he teach you his art?"

"He was my lover."

Guinevere and I looked at each other. I could read the suspicion and the hate in her glance; but above all, the fear of me for I was an unknown. She must have sensed that Myrddin and I *had* been the same; that our kinship made us more alike than our opposite genders made us different—so in one sense I was no longer a woman at all.

"You foolish chit," Arthur accused me, darkening with anger. "It is well known that Myrddin was forbidden concourse with women lest his powers leave him. You have ruined the greatest man in the land with your wiles! He always withstood temptation, until now. You stole his power. It is plain to see. Ah, the longer I look at you the more I perceive that you have his way about you. You stole Myrddin's power, you witch."

I said, "It was worth stealing! Better that I should take it, and so honor him, than let him disappear as you would have done."

"He was an impossible man! If you knew him, then you must know the demands he made, the difficulties he caused."

I thrust my chin in the air to make it clear that I was not impressed.

"You will serve me," Arthur commanded. "Or I will have you killed, girl or no girl—do you understand? I loved Myrddin, God is my witness."

"He called you a brat and a little bastard," I remarked.

Arthur raised his hand as if to strike me, and then suddenly began to laugh. He laughed until his eyes streamed.

"Yes," he gasped. "That sounds like something he would say."

I wanted to distrust Arthur as I knew Myrddin had come to do, but I could not bring myself to completely dislike someone who had once also been close to Myrddin; Arthur alone, maybe, could understand what the wizard had meant to me.

What Arthur did not know was that I never did succeed in stealing Myrddin's power. Any power I had was my own, and I had got it only through the pain of finding him and then losing him again. But I would not expose my tragedy to the king, and it was more useful to be equated with the devil than to be a mere jilted lover, which I in truth was.

After that no one gainsaid me. I did not wish to find myself in the role of Myrddin's replacement, for all the propaganda were against me. Before long the dark and dangerous Myrddin had become a good and helpful wizard, and I had been painted the vicious usurper who had seduced and betrayed him and imprisoned him in an oak forever. The perception that I was evil gave me status, and although I could not read one single word of the book, I saved it and pretended to consult it when pressed by Arthur. Over the years I have tried to advise the king as I thought Myrddin would have done, save perhaps I am gentler, and do not call him a bastard, or threaten to tan his hide—at least not to his face. But I have never been happy in his court—not the way I was happy among the oaks or in the meadow. And I never married. So my episode of the story ends, and it is no great tale.

It is winter and even the oak trees are sleeping. Are you? I want to talk to you. The conversation goes on, and you are in the sun now and the leaves and the dirt and the water; also you are in none of these things, but only in the patterns they make that are scribed in the ethereal stuff of some other world; and maybe you are the folded potentials of the eggs in the nests made by the birds among your branches; and maybe you are in the birds themselves and the paths *they* make in the sky; or maybe even you are the thread of light unravelling itself endlessly, cycling through changes seen and unseen, turning over from night to day forever.

I am not comforted. I would trade all the knowledge and all the power of this oak, all things transcendent and all things divine, for an afternoon tramping through the mud and thorns, with you.

Yes, I want to talk to you but when I put my hands on the oak, you do not speak. It's late. The shadows stretch the snow and your branches are shaking under the weight of the boy who plays in them. He is ten now and his hair is black and his eyes are amber and when he climbs in the oak he doesn't think of the metaphysics of sunlight. He simply swings and stretches and grabs and pulls, and dirties his clothes, and disobeys me when I command him to come down. I crane my head to see him, a wild thing among the stark, whirling branches. I call him again and he heeds me not. He will fall. He will get hurt. Raising my voice, I begin to lecture.

Be quiet. I can almost feel your breath tickling my ear. *For once in your life, Nina, will you be quiet and listen.*

I will.

The Castellan

Diana Gabaldon and Samuel Watkins

The wind from the north smelled of rain and brimstone. Trusellas raised his head from the pages of the record book and breathed deep. Early in the year for serious rain, but this smelled like a major storm; the reek of lightning stung his nose, but . . .

"Why don't I hear thunder?" The harsh mutter echoed his thought, and he glanced down. Ivoire shuffled sideways along the desk, squinting as she pointed her beak into the wind from the open window. A sudden gust ruffled her into a blotch of white feathers, and she said something very crude in raven—a good tongue for curses, given as it is to gutturalities.

"Rude bird."

Ivoire's beak darted sideways and ripped a couple of hairs from his forearm. Trusellas swore in his own tongue, and swatted at her. Adept at this kind of game, she hopped nimbly out of the way, spread her wings and sailed out over the broad stone sill, swooping low over the heads of the men-at-arms playing dice and shove-ha'penny in the courtyard.

One of them, startled by the *whoosh* past his ear, shook his fist at the raven, then transferred his black look to the window where Trusellas stood. The soldier glared, but slowly lowered the fist. Trusellas was not popular, but he was protected.

The castellan stood in the window a moment longer— long enough to establish his indifference to the scowls and muttering below—then stepped back into the shadows of his chamber.

Son of a human father and a mother from the ancient race men called the Aelf, he was possessed of rather keener hearing than most men, but he didn't need it to tell what was being said below—he'd heard such things too many times.

It didn't matter that they viewed him with a mixture of jealousy and fear; didn't matter that the women of the castle drew their skirts aside as he passed. He was the castellan. It didn't matter that he was no warrior, that he blinked weak-eyed in the sun, that he held his office by cleverness and guile, rather than force of arms; he held it, nonetheless, and would do so, so long as the grace of the king was with him.

He took a deep breath of the storm-scented air, and sat down to his work.

He was deep in the aggravations of ill-kept records, when a *whish* and a small, feathery thud announced Ivoire's return. He didn't look up, but gently pushed her splayed pink foot off the page he was reading. She resisted, and dug a talon into the book, tearing a small hole in the parchment.

"Would you like to know why you don't hear thunder?" she asked, in a voice as sweet as a raven could manage. Hopping forward, she plucked the quill from his hand and stood on it.

"No. Take your foot off my pen."

She poked scornfully at the ragged quill with her beak.

"Brrawx, where'd you get this filthy stick—from a vulture?"

Trusellas ignored her. He plucked a fresh swan's quill from the jar and set about trimming a new point.

"I could shove it up your nose," Ivoire suggested helpfully.

Trusellas laid down the new quill and looked at her. The wind from the sea rustled among the sheets of parchment, and the brimstone smell was stronger.

"All right," he said. "Why don't I hear thunder?"

"Because," said the raven happily, "it isn't a thunderstorm. It's a dragon."

"Be calm," Trusellas said to the horse. "We aren't going too close—not yet."

The horse made a noise through its nose and laid back its ears, indicating that this statement was not sufficiently reassuring.

"Don't worry," said Ivoire, digging her claws into Trusellas's shoulder to keep her balance. "It's a blue dragon; they use lightning—that's a real quick death. *Zap!* and you're fried. You won't feel a thing."

The horse shied, and Trusellas nearly lost his balance.

The cave was visible only as a dark crack in the heap of boulders that topped the hill. It occurred to Trusellas that the arrangement of the rock seemed rather symmetrical for a natural occurrence. He squinted, peering upward through the light blue haze that hung like clouds over the top of the hill. Yes, he was right!

"A hill-fort!" he exclaimed. "It's the remains of an ancient hill-fort!"

"Oh, goody," said Ivoire, in a very sarcastic tone.

Trusellas paid no heed. He had made a private study of these; the remnants of fortifications left by a people more ancient even than his own, folk who did not even speak the language of metal, but left their mark only in the stones of their tools and habitations. He had a collection of these ancient stones, dark blades and rounded axe-heads, primitive, but graceful in their unschooled ferocity.

A distant rumble, as of warning thunder, was accompanied by a sinister puff of blue smoke from the crack in the rocks. A stone axe wouldn't be much help against whatever was in there. Or at least he didn't think so. What had the ancient hill-fort builders sought to guard against? The clawing hands of avaricious neighbors—or something else more sinister?

"Ivoire," said Trusellas thoughtfully, "how old are dragons?"

The bird cocked a head in his direction. Her eyes were dark red, but looked black in some lights.

"How would I know? I haven't even seen it yet."

"Not *that* dragon; dragons in general."

Ivoire clacked her bill a few times, though he couldn't tell whether it was with irritation or thoughtfulness.

"Older than you or me," she said at last, and shrugged. She meant older than human, Aelf, or even raven-kind—though the kitchen-boys and squires she tormented insisted that Ivoire was no mere raven, but a demon in disguise.

"Thanks," he said dryly, but she was paying no attention. Perched precariously on the horse's head, she gripped its mane with her claws and peered behind Trusellas.

"What are *they* doing here?" she asked.

Trusellas swung round in his saddle. Banners fluttered in the wind, and the sound of trumpets cut through the turbulent air.

"Nothing like sneaking up on it without warning," the bird remarked. "Of course, I don't suppose you can really sneak up on anything very well with two hundred men, can you?"

Trusellas said something rather coarse and wheeled his horse abruptly, causing Ivoire to lose her grip. She fell off, but spread her wings and flapped upward to catch a rising current of air.

The troops came out of a narrow defile, marching up the valley toward the hill where the dragon lay. Lancers, cavalry; nearly the whole garrison from the castle, Trusellas noted, as he rode grimly down the line. A few soldiers saluted him; a few more stared, with expressions between curiosity and contempt. Most ignored him, their eyes fastened on the wisps of blue smoke that rose to join the clouded sky.

Having seen what he needed to see, Trusellas wheeled again and galloped back to the head of the line.

"Halt!" he shouted, and rode across the line of march. The column halted, obediently enough, and the men stood, steaming in their armor. Trusellas backed and turned the horse until he once more faced the hill—and waited. Ivoire floated down from the sky, buzzing low over the line of men and making several duck for cover. She settled on the horse's head again, chuckling in her throat.

"What does a dragon want?" Trusellas narrowed his eyes, squinting at the floating mist that circled the hill.

"Three square sheep a day, a mattress stuffed with jewels, and enough gold to keep its blood cooled down," Ivoire suggested.

"Who cares what it wants?" Rathen, the captain of the Guard, had ridden up beside Trusellas at last. He looked warily at the castellan, who was known for talking to himself.

"Do dragons observe flags of truce?" Trusellas asked mildly. "I thought perhaps I should go and talk to it."

"You don't talk to dragons," said the captain, speaking carefully. He might be addressing an idiot, but it was the king's personal idiot. "You kill them."

"That's what *you* think, muscle-head." Ivoire rocked to and fro, chortling softly. The captain looked at her with dislike, but was, like most men, fortunately deaf to her speech. He understood her attitude clearly enough, though. If he had been able to translate the insults she was tossing at him, even his grudging respect for Trusellas's office wouldn't have kept him from trying to wring her neck.

"Have you ever killed a dragon?" Trusellas inquired. He didn't intend to be insulting; he was only curious. Captain Rathen seemed to take the query amiss, though. A large man already, he swelled noticeably, and went slightly red in the face.

"I've been a soldier all my life," he said, through gritted teeth.

"Yes, of course. I only—"

"I've killed lions and bears, and boars and serpents, wolves, foxes . . . why, even a Questing Beast!"

"Yes, yes, but this . . ."

The captain was still talking, but he had lowered the visor of his helm, and his voice was muffled. That was probably a good thing. Rathen turned his head sharply, and the rubies that studded his casque flashed fire. He flung up a mailed gauntlet, and the lancers began to jockey their horses into position.

Trusellas's horse, alarmed by the stamping and whinnying of the destriers, snorted and backed away into the woods, despite his attempts to stop it. When he at length got his mount under control and managed to fight his way back out of the tangle of larch and blackberry, Trusellas found at least two-thirds of the royal army poised with several different weapons in hand: lances, swords, bows, lassos, and other such arms. Each man gazed intently at the edge of the forest towering close to them, though eyes flicked up toward the distant crest of the hill, where blue smoke rose in the morning sky.

The castellan jumped off his horse, nearly tripping on his red robe. Captain Rathen had gone ahead and stood calmly, his hand on the hilt of his eagle sword. Trusellas strode slowly to the captain.

"Look at the little bitty weapons they're holding; enough to make a bird laugh," Ivoire cackled in his ear.

"You think they may not be effective?" Trusellas whispered to his companion.

"Maybe they'll tickle it, if they're lucky," Ivoire muttered. "Dragon's scales are harder than steel; a dinky little sword would just rebound off them."

"You mean dragons are completely invulnerable?" Trusellas asked. He swallowed, his throat feeling dry.

"No, not completely," the pesky white raven said. "The only spot I've heard of that *is* vulnerable on a dragon is its eyes, though—and I've never met anybody who got close enough to look a dragon in the eye."

"Stand steady, men!" Rathen cried, interrupting Ivoire's lecture. "The dragon approaches!"

The dragon did. Trusellas looked upward toward the ruined hill-fort, but the soldiers had been right. A loud thud emanated from the forest, followed by several more thuds. The dragon was definitely approaching.

"Dragons *walk*?" Trusellas hissed to Ivoire.

"They got feet." The raven huddled next to the trunk of an aspen, trying to blend in with the paper-white bark.

A vicious roar echoed throughout the woods, and birds flew out of the trees in panic.

Then the dragon came, with a rending screech of shattered trees and a shaking of the ground in its path. It was huge, and it was blue. Towering over forty feet tall at least, and the color of seas and clouded sapphires. A long silver horn protruded from its blue snout and two more horns, sharp as spears, stuck from its head.

It opened its jaws wide to roar, revealing pearl-white teeth. Dragons have very good hygiene, Trusellas thought abstractedly. Even for a flesh-eating beast, none could deny it was a glorious sight, with the sunlight reflecting off its scales.

Glorious or not, Captain Rathen was going to kill it.

"Spearmen!" The captain drew his sword and pointed it forward. "Attack!"

The soldiers hurled spears at the blue behemoth, not knowing that their spears would only be wasted. And they were; the spears rebounded off the azure scales.

"Its eyes!" Trusellas screamed above the soldiers' cries. "Aim for its eyes!"

The soldiers looked at Rathen for approval. He nodded, they heeded. Unfortunately, that moment of hesitation gave the dragon all the time it needed. The huge blue tail swept two spearmen away from their fellows, into reach of the dragon's claws. It clapped together two large paws, crushing the soldiers. It was barely audible, but the castellan swore he heard laughter from the dragon—a sound like ringing metal.

The rest of the thirteen spearmen stood aghast. Their two comrades-in-arms had just been slain by a dragon— would the same happen to them?

No time to think; the blue dragon inhaled a breath and

let loose a shaft of blue lightning, leaving charred bodies in its wake. With a lolling tongue, it scooped up the thirteen bodies and swallowed them like so many pickled nutmeats.

A few swordsmen vomited at the sight; the lance-knights' horses reared and screamed. The dragon bent over and delicately spewed the crumpled skeletons of the soldiers onto the meadow.

Distracted by the plunging horses and reeking bones, the soldiers milled in confusion, scarcely noticing as the dragon suddenly spread its wings.

Trusellas noticed. Its wings were huge, impossibly graceful. Terrified as he was, still he gaped at the sheer beauty of the dragon, sun shining on its gorgeous wings, long scaled body twisting as it drove itself up into the heavens. And then it plummeted upon the army.

The castle had no more than five bowmen; most of these had hung back, thinking arrows would be of little avail. One bowman, though, had heard Trusellas's cry. He plucked up his courage and sent an arrow directly toward the amber eyes, followed by another, and another, whirring in their flight like angry bees.

Knee-deep in its bloodbath, the dragon was distracted. But it did notice the arrows in time to roar out the word "Khachikiny!"

Trusellas didn't recognize the word, but he divined its intent: a spell!

"Duck!" Trusellas cried, as he dived toward the ground. The men still standing copied him, as an enormous fireball glided overhead, burning the arrows that would have driven straight into the dragon's brain.

"Wowzer," said Ivoire, cowering under the inadequate shelter of a burdock leaf.

"This isn't working," the castellan said to his comrade. "Don't dragons have any other weaknesses?"

"If I remember correctly . . . yes. Now what was it?" The wind from the dragon's wings stung Trusellas's face with a rain of gravel. Ivoire was no more than a smear of white feathers, but she cawed directly into his ear. "Wings! Their wings are soft as leather. If you pierce them while they're flying, they'll fall to the ground."

"It's not flying anymore." Still, Trusellas struggled to his feet and fought his way through the fallen trees and scattered bodies, to reach Captain Rathen's side.

"Captain!" he shouted. "Listen!"

But Rathen ignored him. Eyes gleaming through the slits of his visor, he lowered his lance and charged with a war cry. His destrier charged at high speed and the captain bent forward, his lance snugly braced.

The dragon saw him and dropped the soldier it was devouring. It waited calmly until the horse and rider had nearly reached it. Then the dragon reached out one slender arm. A long, sharp talon shot out and pierced the captain's heart. The dragon plucked the dangling knight from his saddle, delicately removed his helm, and ate him, headfirst.

Trusellas threw himself behind a rock and was violently sick.

He picked his way up the hillside, grateful for once for the weak sight that made it impossible to tell whether the charred columns that lay by the trail had once been tree or human. The reek of smoke and the stinging smell of lightning grew stronger as he climbed, until the breath burned in his chest. He had discarded both robe and armor—his sight had been good enough to tell him just how pointless wearing it would be—but even in shirt and chausses, he was gasping and sweat drenched by the time he reached the crest of the hill.

The cool, dark opening of the cavern came almost as a

relief—almost. He stopped just inside, feeling the sweat turn cold as it trickled down his back. He looked back at the world outside; he might never see it again.

"Oh, there's one thing about blue dragons," Ivoire muttered softly in his ear.

"What's that?" All his senses were alert, but nothing stirred in the blackness of the cavern beyond.

"They're shape-shifters." The raven lifted lightly from his shoulder, and vanished over the brow of the hill, leaving him to go on alone.

Shape-shifter, he thought. Fine. Just fine. So the tiny blue salamander that skittered across his path might really be a lightning-breathing monster; the bluebird singing over there in the bush could suddenly open its mouth a little wider and toast him into cinders.

He ran a sweating hand through his hair, undecided.

Normally, he wore his thick black hair loose, covering the ears whose pointed tips revealed his mixed blood. Would a dragon care what he was, or simply view him as a meal? So far as he knew, dragons viewed Aelf as edible, too—but that was only so far as he knew. Why didn't people write down their experiences with dragons, for the guidance of others?

Possibly because no one survived a face-to-face encounter with a dragon long enough to write about it. There was a cold thought.

Ivoire's claws closed on his shoulder, and he felt the brush of her feathers under his chin as she ducked her head toward the neck of his shirt. Something round ran down his belly, tickling. He slapped at it, thinking it a beetle, and bruised a rib with the hard little object.

"Heard of those little flies?" Ivoire asked. She spread her wings and flapped up to a singed branch, where she balanced, white as a cloud against the blackened bark.

"What flies?" He had succeeded in extricating the object from the folds of his shirt. A dull, lumpy stone, the size of a peach pit. He was about to fling it away in disgust when a shaft of sun through the rocks lit blue fires inside it. He breathed in slowly; he'd never seen a bigger sapphire.

"And where did you get *this*?"

"Stole it," the bird said cheerfully. "A magpie I know; he'll never miss it. About those flies . . ."

"What about them?"

"The male catches a tasty bug, and wraps it up in silk like a fancy present, then he gives it to the lady fly he's got his eye on. While she's busy unwrapping it, he slips behind her, and"—one dark-red eye gave a lewd wink—"does the deed. If he doesn't take her a gift-wrapped morsel, though, she eats *him*." Ivoire wagged her head from side to side. "Noooo baby flies if that happens, no sir."

Trusellas made a noise through his teeth.

"I suppose you're implying something with this indelicate anecdote?"

"Dragons don't eat bugs."

"I know that! But—"

"They, um, *do* eat Aelf," Ivoire said delicately. She twisted her head like a wine cork and peered over her shoulder toward the depths of the cave, where coils of soft blue smoke rolled slowly along the floor. "But that bauble there might keep her busy long enough for you to get a word in edgewise."

Trusellas found that his hand had clenched hard on the sapphire. He swallowed.

"Ah . . . thank you," he said.

"My pleasure," the raven said politely. Her eyes were still fixed on the cave. "I'd go now, if I were you—while she's still full."

*   *   *

It was dark in the cavern, but the air wasn't cool and dank, as it ought to be. It was warm and dry, and smelled powerfully of sulfur and ozone. Trusellas glanced up at the shadowy roof, and hoped she wouldn't think of shooting lightning bolts inside; the whole hill could fall in on them.

She? He was well inside before it occurred to him to wonder how in the name of St. Michael the bird had known the dragon was female. He hadn't seen anything indicating gender, though under the circumstances, his observations had necessarily not been prolonged. But perhaps . . . then he rounded a curve in the stony passage, and there was no more time for speculation.

He felt his heart beating in his throat. Not a salamander, still less a bluebird. The woman stood a few feet away, skin and hair glowing with a faint blue radiance that made her clearly visible, dark as it was. Her eyes were not blue. Slightly slanted, and a deep, luminous gold, they turned on him like rising moons, blank and pupilless—but not sightless, by any means.

"Ah . . ." he said.

"How met, worm?" she said, and her voice had the chime of metal.

"I am not a worm," Trusellas said, a trifle huffy. "I am the castellan."

Full lips curved; he saw no teeth—thank God!—but could tell she was laughing.

"And I am Lunaris," she said. "Lunaris, and a wyrm of no mean repute."

"Oh," he said, belatedly realizing that she had not been insulting him by calling him *wyrm* as well. "Ah. Yes. Well met, Madame." Remembering the stone—and Ivoire's story of the flies—he thrust his open hand out toward her. "I brought . . . er . . . a small token of . . . respect."

Her fingers slid down his arm, across his wrist, across his palm, taking their time and taking his measure. Suddenly, she closed her hand on his, the sapphire trapped between their palms.

"Oh," she said softly. "A fine stone, this. A lovely voice. Do you hear it?"

"Hear it?" Trusellas echoed faintly. He heard nothing but the thunder of blood in his ears. Her skin under his fingers was like oiled leather, cool and supple.

Her hand slid away, cupping the stone. She held it to her ear, a look of distant dreaming on her face that held him with its magic. What did she see, what did she hear in that dream, to make her look so?

"Listen, then." She held the stone out, close to his own ear. "Close your eyes. Hear." Obediently, he shut his eyes, and with the distraction of that cool blue face removed, he thought perhaps . . . yes. Yes, just barely. A deep, rich sound, more vibration than song, and so faint that he strained to catch its voice.

"So you *can* hear it. What are you then, castellan? No man has heard stones sing, that I have met."

"I am . . . half. Half man, half Aelf. I live between two worlds, and in that space, lady, I hear many things." Perhaps it was not so strange, after all. He could hear the voices of birds and of beasts, where men were deaf to them. He had not thought of it, but why should stones not speak as well? As well as dragons, surely.

Lunaris was speaking now, gold eyes wide, unblinking.

"As a gift, castellan, it is a pleasant toy. As ransom or as bribe . . ." She opened her hand, and the stone fell.

He caught it before it struck the rocky floor, cradling it to his bosom as though the jewel might be bruised by such rough treatment.

"A gift," he said, and held it out once more. "Tribute,

call it. A small homage to your . . . beauty." To your bloodthirstiness, he might have said; he thought she would still have found it a compliment. But she laughed, that odd chiming sound, and took the stone from him.

"It is accepted," she said.

"Good," he said. He hesitated, but after all, what had he come for? "You spoke of ransom," he said awkwardly. "What . . . ?"

"I don't know," she said. She stretched voluptuously, and yawned. "My belly is full; I need no more for now." She rubbed her back against the wall, scratching herself slowly, sinuous as a cat. He thought he heard the rasp of scales against the rock.

"Can you sing, castellan?"

"Yes." He had a good voice and knew many songs; it was his only real talent. Even so, he rarely sang; no one sings for their own enjoyment.

"Come, then," she said, and turned away. "Come and sing me to my rest. I am exceedingly fond of music."

He ducked his head beneath a low sill, found himself in a tunnel, and realized why she had changed her shape; the great beast he had seen in rampage on the hill would never fit through such narrow passageways.

The cave opened out quite suddenly, and he stood in a vast cavern, lit by random shafts of light from cracks in the ceiling above, and by the gleam of metal. There was not much; no great heaps of hoarded treasure, as he had heard of—but then, she had but recently come to this place. She hadn't had time to collect much—yet. He caught sight of Rathen's jeweled helm, lying empty by his foot, its rubies glinting in a shaft of light. He looked away, swallowing.

His eyes watered from the sudden light, and when he looked back, he didn't see her. He feared at first that Lunaris had transformed again and stood above him, leather-winged and freshly ravenous, but no—she stood quite still, a little distance away, beside a couch made of gold.

Trusellas swallowed, and looked furtively for Ivoire. Surely Lunaris had not been naked in the outer cavern? Was it only dragon-magic that had made him imagine flowing draperies, or the caution of his own mind? He heard a harsh, rasping caw of disapproval from somewhere aboveground; he found it comforting that Ivoire was keeping an eye on him—though if he were destroyed, she could tell no one of his fate; no one at the castle shared his gift of tongues.

Lunaris looked at him, and he moved without willing to. She smiled, lay down, and took his hand in hers.

"Sing to me, Aelf," she said.

"What will you hear, my lady?" His heart beat in his ears.

"What you will." The great golden eyes rested on him, and he saw they were not empty. Small currents moved in them, swirls that eddied, drifted, and broke to form new patterns. It was like looking into a goldsmith's crucible, watching the ineffable alchemy of metal turned liquid; a fascination that had its roots in the apparent violation of natural order—and recognizing the wild beauty of solidity set free, of order turned to chaos.

He sat beside her, and he sang. Light airs and simple lieder. A child's counting song. Soft lullabies. And then the bards' songs, ballads learned on the nights when the traveling singers lifted their voices in the courtyard, when love rose like a mist in the darkness and the murmur of couples in the alcoves was like the sound of doves in the trees—nights when he himself sat still and quiet in his tower, hidden, heart burning like a coal.

The lady's hand grew heavy on his knee; without thinking, he held it, to save it slipping off. The golden eyes glowed steady, though, and did not close. Their glow seemed strangely clouded, and it dawned on him at last that she slept as snakes do, a transparent membrane coming down across the open eye. The notion that she watched him even in her sleep should have disturbed him, but did not; no woman had ever watched him with such raptness.

He did not feel the trance come over him, nor hear the hoarsening of his own voice; he sat enchanted, and sang on.

A persistent pain behind one ear aroused him finally. His hair was caught, being pulled by something. He brushed at his hair, trying to free it, and was rewarded with a sharp stab of pain in his hand. He stopped singing with a gasp, and whirled, to see a pale blob perched on the rock behind him.

"Will you shut up and get out of here?" demanded a low-rasping voice. "Don't you know better than to look a sleeping dragon in the eye?"

It was a struggle not to turn back; he could feel the golden sea behind him, lapping at his feet with the promise of bliss. Even the thought of it . . . wings beat fiercely in his face, and he raised his hands to shield his eyes.

"Come *on*!" said an agitated croak in one ear, and sharp claws sank through the cloth of his shirt.

She rocked back and forth on his shoulder, urging him on by force of will as he stumbled down the rocky corridor, half-blind. He would have turned back at the entrance, but Ivoire drove him on with fierce pecks and harsh cawing. He stumbled over rocks and slipped and half-slid down the hill, but by the time he reached the spot where his tethered horse waited, the spell had faded. Hands trembling, he mounted and rode away, toward the castle.

It was well past nightfall when he reached the wall, alone. Torches blazed, and white faces rose from the dark all round him, terrified, tearful, reproachful, beseeching.

"I'm sorry," was all he could say to them. "I'm sorry. I'm sorry." He was still repeating it, though more softly, when he barred the door of his chamber, shucked off his boots in a shower of dirt and pebbles, and fell upon his bed.

He opened the cabinet that held his collections—not because there was anything of value there to tempt a dragon, but only for the comfort that the objects gave him. The bright shed feathers of birds, the cast-off skins of serpents, trivial things that had caught his curiosity, in his ridings to and fro across his demesne.

He picked up a stone axe, the helf smooth and heavy in his palm. There was a hole bored through the middle; it was soothing to stick his thumb through this hole and think of the maker, spending patient day after patient day, boring away with a stick of oak and a little sand. It was an approach Trusellas had always admired—but he thought it would not do now. He put the axe-head gently back, and began to pick things up and set them down, searching.

His eye lighted on an ornamental knife, made from the antler of a giant elk. The blade was shattered, and the whole of it stained with time and weather, but the pattern of carving on the handle was still clear; a sinuous form, the scales indicated by a faint cross-hatching. Not a serpent; this thing had claws, in which it grasped something—a man? a beast?—that time had reduced to no more than a lump of discolored ivory. The dragon's jaws gaped, and the eyes were open, smooth, and rounded as the opals set in Captain Rathen's dagger-hilt.

Trusellas ran his thumb across the surface of one blank eye, thinking of deep pools of gold, and the songs of stones.

Ivoire stood on the windowsill, hunched against the wind that blew from the sea, bitter with the scent of burning.

"What will you do?" she said, not turning. "Will you go back?"

"Do I have a choice?" He moved to stand behind the raven, looking out. The hill itself was too far away to see, but he knew it was there; he could see every stone of it in his mind's eye.

Ivoire turned and flicked a wing against his hand, impatient.

"You always have a choice," she said. "Shut the gates, stay inside. Even a dragon can't get in this place."

"And what of the countryside?"

"What of 'em?"

"You aren't a help, you know," he said, glancing down at her. The raven's eyes were black and round as beads of jet.

"Excuse *me*!" she said, and was gone, swooping low over the courtyard. She seized a loaf of bread from a baker's tray as she passed, and vanished over the battlements, leaving the baker startled and cursing below.

He slept at last, worn out with futile plans and speculations. He dreamed, small things at first of an ordinary kind—but gradually, the dream altered. He swam, it seemed, in a sea of gold. He was bare limbed; his arm and hand dripped and shone when he raised it, each joint gilded in glowing fire. The current took him, bearing him up, carrying him to the song of stones, along paths of shining radiance, to a place of love.

She treasured him.

He woke suddenly, to find himself out of his bed. He

was on the floor, on his hands and knees, crawling mindlessly toward the window. Something hard was under his hand, hurting the palm. He sat, head whirling, the hard thing clasped in his hand. It was a tiny pebble from the dragon's hill. He swallowed hard, shook his head to dismiss the dream, and threw the pebble hard against the wall.

"What are you looking for?" Ivoire stood atop his cabinet. She ducked her head and turned it, upside down, the better to peer at the things within.

"I have no idea." Actually, he hadn't thought he *was* looking for anything. It was his habit to look at his collections, to handle the objects, only as a way to soothe his mind and encourage thought. But Ivoire had known better than he, he realized; he *was* looking for something. He didn't know what it was, but something had taken shape in his dreaming, and he was looking for its mate, somewhere in the array of things before him.

But what was it? He sighed and began to go through the cabinet again, one shelf at a time, picking up each object and discarding it in turn, as it failed to trigger any sense of discovery. Beads on the top shelf—wood, bone, stone, and ivory; broken, whole, single, strung. Nothing there.

Carvings on the second shelf; some of great antiquity, some so old as to have been carved on river stones, the lines so blurred that the image was uncertain. He looked at these with great attention, hoping perhaps for something else like the elk-bone knife—but there were no more dragons. Bears, wolves, hares, horses, dogs, mice . . . even one piece of ancient silver carved with the likeness of a greenman, those fearful creatures half-man, half-tree. He had met a greenman in the forest once, and he put the piece down, shuddering at the memory.

"Oh, him." Ivoire shoved at the medallion contemptuously with her beak. She hadn't liked the greenman, either. She made a chuckling noise deep in her throat, turned around and cocked her tail over the piece, intending to make her opinion abundantly clear. Trusellas swatted her away with the back of his hand and she fell off the table with a shriek of surprise.

"Shoo," said Trusellas, and went back to his work.

The third shelf held natural artifacts—the shed skins of snakes, mummified toads, seedpods and dried roots. His hand hovered over these, but . . . no. Whatever he was looking for, it was not here.

He squatted to look again at the bottom shelf, where the heavier things were kept—the ancient tools and things of stone. Axes, scrapers, grinders, blades . . . one at a time, he picked them up, holding them, hoping.

A clacking noise behind distracted him.

Ivoire had abandoned the cabinet, and was on the floor near the window, playing a game that involved batting one round stone against another, so that the second shot away, rebounding from wall or table leg. She looked up at him, and he could see the look of calculation in her eye. He lifted a foot, meaning to set it on one stone, but she was too fast—her beak swung back and forward, and the stone shot up, hit the wall, ricocheted, and struck Trusellas right between the eyes.

"Goooooooooal!" gurgled the raven, staggering around the floor in a ruffle of feathers, helpless with mirth.

Teeth clenched on an epithet unbecoming to his office, Trusellas bent and snatched up the stone. It was one of the pebbles he had brought back inadvertently from the dragon's cave, caught in the folds of his high leather boot. It was an ordinary enough rock, no gemstone. And yet there were small veins of greenish stone crisscrossing the pebble—serpentine perhaps, or marble? The veins of green gleamed faintly in the light, and the niggling thought in the back of his mind dropped softly into place.

It lay at the back of the bottom shelf, out of sight. It was a thing he had picked up because it was unusual, but an object he didn't know the use of—a sliver of stone, too flimsy to be a tool, but showing the marks of careful knapping and shaping—it had been made for something, but what? Not an ornament, not a ceremonial object; it was plain stone, not carved—but with the same small veins of green marble running through it.

Long and thin, fragile—but very sharp. His hand closed carefully around it, this gift from some ancient castellan. He saw in memory the swirling seas of Lunaris's eyes, and his heart went cold within him.

It was nearly dark when he reached the hill. He began to sing at the bottom of the slope, his voice damped by dripping mist and the scent of ashes from the half-charred forest. As he came out of the last of the trees, though, his voice rang from the stones of the ancient fort. He stopped then, and waited.

"Come," said the dragon's voice in his mind, and his breast filled with warmth and longing. As he took a step toward the cavern's entrance, he felt a sudden sting and clapped a hand to his head.

Ivoire fluttered down on an alder branch and sat staring at him, the strand of hair she had plucked from his head dangling from her strong pink bill.

"What did you do that for?" he demanded.

She laid the strand down and put a pale pink foot on it, then looked up at him. Her eyes were black as the soot on his shoes.

"A keepsake to remember you by," she said. "I'll take it back to the castle and weave it into my nest on the tower. You'll be a part of the castle, then."

"I'm coming back," he said, and hoped he sounded much more confident than he felt.

"Sure you are," she said. Evidently he didn't sound all that confident.

"Come," said Lunaris, and her voice struck his mind like the clapper of a bell. He turned and walked into the cave.

He wondered, dimly, whether dragons could read thoughts, but he had forgotten to ask Ivoire—if she knew. It didn't matter, though. There was nothing else to do.

Lunaris awaited him, in her inner chamber. Words froze in his throat, but he didn't need them. It wasn't song she wanted, this time. She stood beside her couch and smiled.

"Come," she said, and he came to her.

"Why do you close your eyes?" she asked him, later.

"Your beauty blinds me, Mistress," he said, and kept his eyes tight shut. She laughed and the soft embrace of great wings enclosed him.

When he opened his eyes at last, the chamber was quiet, and Lunaris slept. Above him, one star shone silent in the velvet sky, visible through a chink in the roof.

He slid carefully off the couch, but she didn't stir. In the dark, he could see the faint blue gleam of scales, the graceful line where one wing swept the floor. Her face was still a woman's, though; golden eyes alive and dreaming.

He took from his boot the ancient tool, that needle-sharp sliver too long and too fragile for any use but one. The edge of it cut his palm as he plunged the tip into her eye, but it was not the pain of his hand that made him cry aloud in anguish.

The blood of a blue dragon is green, he thought, when he could think again. *I must . . . remember to write that . . . down.*

He leaned against the stone at the mouth of the cave, and the rising sun lit the sopping patches on his clothes, the stinking smears upon his hands. He stared out into the rising sun, not caring that its brilliance seared his eyes. His eyes watered and his sight blurred; he did not see her, but felt strong claws grip the flesh of his shoulder.

"Come home," she said, and he stumbled down the trail, drenched in stinking blood and desolation, so far gone that Ivoire had to direct the horse, standing on its head and pecking one ear, then the other, to turn it toward the castle.

It was the last thing that he wanted to do, but it was his duty. Some other castellan might one day face a dragon. Trusellas must put down what had happened, must pass on what he knew. He had slept for two days and two nights, yet his bones still ached with weariness. He went with dragging step to his desk, where he slowly sharpened a fresh new quill and then reached for his book.

The ink was newly mixed, the parchment scraped and chalked, the ponce-bag stuffed and ready. No excuse for delay. He dipped his quill and began, very slowly, to write of Lunaris. Lunaris the terrible, Lunaris the lovely. It was of the wyrm he wrote, but of the woman that he thought.

"She would have eaten you, you know."

"Don't bother me," he said. He stared sightlessly through the window, toward the invisible hill. Below, the courtyard seethed with unrest and ingratitude, a sea of uncrossable strife between him and that point of vanished bliss. He didn't need to hear the words to know what was said down there. Why had he taken troops? Why had he let them be killed? He should have acted sooner, he should have waited, he should, he should not . . .

"Maybe not your body, but certainly your soul. Dragons are greedy for more than gold."

"Be quiet, bird," he said.

And yet the unreasonable and ungrateful were his, by decree of the king. If they wanted him or not, whether or not he wanted them—the castle and its folk were his to defend, whatever the cost of that defense might be. He dipped his pen and wrote a word, two, not seeing the careful letters he formed. He didn't know that he had spoken, until he heard the words.

"Why me?" he said.

There was a rustle of feathers in the gloom behind him, but no answer, and he went on writing, one word, one letter at a time. Slowly, he realized that there was a feeling of warmth at his back, as though someone stood behind him, dispelling the chill of cold stone. Yet the door was bolted; he had fastened it himself, wanting no intrusions. The hair rose on his nape.

He sat still, not daring to turn. Something brushed his cheek, and a strand of silk-white hair fell over his shoulder, across his breast. A pale pink hand, its nails the delicate color of dawn, spread flat across the page of his book. The fresh ink smeared.

Then a voice spoke in his ear, hoarse and husky as a raven's laugh.

"Castellan," she said, "did anyone ever tell you that you ask too many questions?"

Lady of the Lake

Michelle Sagara West

The screaming could be heard across the lake, but it was not the screams that put up walls between the women who heard and the woman who uttered them; it was the laughter, the guttural, visceral enjoyment in it, a thing of power. At a safe distance, they bore witness with a grimness and a hardening of heart that the weak acknowledge: only death waits those who attempt to interfere.

They knew how it would end, although they had no benefit of vision in the darkening and paling of the even sky; they understood the fear, and the pain, and the humiliation that they heard. They had, after all, fallen in just such a fashion, like so much wheat before a careless scythe.

They knew that terror would give way to exhaustion, and that when exhaustion gave way to rest and healing, humiliation would return, and they knew—they *knew*—the anger that would follow. Knew it intimately. Knew it so well that they could only listen, transfixed, because they were rooted, hearing it, in the tenor of their *own* cries, their own voices, their own past.

They numbered nine, these women, and they had been gathered, one by one, by hands that were infinitely gentle compared to those that had destroyed their maidens' lives. Gathered and brought to the isle, upon which no man's feet might walk, save one.

In the darkness, they prepared; they came with torches, with blankets, with salves and a rich, herb-thickened mead that would both quicken and quiet the blood. They spoke, one to the other, in this terrible flurry of activity, this quiet torment, and at a distance, a careless eavesdropper might have thought they were praying.

In a fashion they were.

Elyssa was the first of the fallen, as they sometimes privately called one another; she had been young and beautiful, impatient with youth and youth's imperative. She had lived in a village ninety miles from the wide, still waters of the hidden lake, and in that place of sun and farm and home, she had grown from child to woman while the boys of her acquaintance grew gape jawed and shy and bullish by turns. She was, although she did not remember it herself, not clearly, astonished by their attention, and then captivated by it; it gave her a power that she didn't understand. Power. Her mother understood it, and her father—he was frightened by it and angered by it in his turn.

And then the lord had come, with his fine, armoured knights, his retinue of women, his pages and his maidservants and his personal squires: And he was a fine, handsome man, newly married. His wife she thought cold and distant, but he was a friendly man, with eyes the color of the sky during the harvest summer.

This was their story, and Elyssa, first, was not the last.

She was taken in by him, and then taken by him, and then passed, as a toy, to the knights at his back. Let them come after him, in all manner of the word, let them sully the earth once he had first turned it. He was not a kind man; he did the deed where all of the village might hear it if she screamed—and she screamed, and wept, and pleaded because she was not—not yet—out of a childhood where weeping might do good.

His wife, his cold, cold wife, had come to her in the darkness after the darkness had finally ended. She had thought that the lady might be harsh and terrible; she had scrabbled back, like an unhinged animal, pulling the shreds of clothing around her breasts, covering parts of her bleeding body that had never felt exposed before other women.

But his wife brought a blanket in the silence, and a lamp, and she led the girl home.

His act had changed home irrevocably. It was days, scant days, before Elyssa realized the truth of it; her mother withdrawn and terrified, her father wrathful—at her mother and the lord and anyone who came near, *especially* Elyssa, especially her.

And the boys, the boys over whom she had had that odd power, they changed as well. Some shunned her, and that hurt, but it eased the fear that had become so much a part of her she couldn't bear to stand in their shadows. The others . . . the others thought they might have—and she knew it now, by the look in their faces— what the knights had had: the sullied, the fallen, terrain over which the lord had passed so contemptuously.

And it might have come to that.

But *he* came, and although she was afraid of strange men in a way that she couldn't begin to speak of, he invoked no fear at all. He was, she thought, like an angel.

"I am," he told her, having driven off two of the farm boys, "a hunter. I have, perhaps, lost my way."

She did not believe him then, and she knew for a fact he was lying now, and she took comfort from both.

"Who are you? Are you with a large party?"

"I? No. A true hunter travels in isolation." He lifted a hand, let it drop almost immediately to his side. His face was gaunt, and a scar whitened the skin from jaw to brow, passing around the eye, marking him. She hadn't known what a map was, then—but she knew now, and she knew it was, in its way, a map of his past: visible, where her scars were hidden.

"I'm Elyssa," she said quietly.

"And I? You may call me . . . Merlin. After the bird of prey."

Years later, she would ask him, "Why Merlin? Why not Hawk or Eagle or even Falcon?" And he would smile, half genially and half bitterly, as he did in all ways. "Because, I am a small bird, a thing of danger that is often overlooked precisely because of the birds you otherwise name.

"But death is death, Little Elyssa, and vengeance is vengeance, and if mine is a long time in the crafting, I am still a hunter."

She took him home, and that night, she said her good-byes. Oh, they weren't meant to be good- byes, not then, but her father's harsh words and ugly dictate lingered between her past and her present, the blade that cut. Her mother had said nothing, and she had hoped for more, expected no less. She was left alone, with this stranger.

He said, "Aline sent me to you," and it made no sense, no sense at all—until she remembered that Aline had been the name of the lord's wife. "And if you allow it, child, I will take you to safety."

What other choice had she? She followed—as the others would follow, one by one—and he led her across the miles of country, during both daylight hours and moon-lit, brilliant night, until they reached the paths that led to the marsh and the boat, that wondrous white boat that seemed uncured, unoiled, untouched by water or time or any labor of man's.

"This is the Lake," he said, "of Sorrows. This boat is a boat of the lake's making. Here, we might cross and there, there in the night that you cannot clearly see, you will find your home. I will not keep you captive; I can-not. The lake will give and the lake will take, as it de-sires. I am its guardian. No, I am less than that.

"But I have been wronged, Elyssa, and I will right that wrong. I prayed, to the lake, and this was the vision granted me."

He led her to the boat. Helped her up and over the lip of its perfect edge.

"I will join you," he said quietly, "if the lake permits."

He settled into the boat beside her, and after a silent moment, the boat began to glide across water so still it seemed made of glass—and she had seen very little glass in her humble life. The silence should have frightened her, but she felt a peace to it, and a promise.

The boat stopped once, in the center of the lake.

"Give it," he said quietly, "your name."

But he needn't have spoken; she heard the lake weep, and she understood that it was giving her its own name, in a fashion, just as Merlin had done. She stood—and the boat did not tip or capsize, or even founder at all. "I am Elyssa," she replied.

After a moment, it accepted the name, and the boat began to move again. But she saw it: a flash of disap-pointment cross the features of her savior.

He said nothing; she, afraid now of his disapproval, afraid of their destination, said nothing as well. The water passed beneath them, smooth and black except where it caught moon and star; the small craft passed rushes, and then, gliding almost above the water's surface it left so little wake to disturb it, the boat came to a dock.

"Here," he said. He rose and very gently stepped out of the boat, turning to offer her his hand. She hesitated for just a moment, and then took it.

He led her, by turns, to the castle. "It is not so easy a home as all that," he said softly, "but no one will cross the waters who means you harm. That is the law of the lake, and the promise. You are safe here."

"But—"

"I know. But you will not live here alone for long. I have brought things that will ease your life, and the grounds around the castle are the most fertile grounds that exist in these lands; more so, in that they have seen no war, no fire, no burning." He bowed. "I will come to visit, as I may, and I will teach you what I am permitted to teach you, but these lands do not willingly tolerate the touch of man, and if I am lessened, if I am injured, if I, too, have known . . . humiliation, the lake and the island still count me as Man." He bowed, bitterly. "I will return, Elyssa."

He kept his promise.

Less than two months later, the summer months almost tapering into fall, the harvest so close she could smell it from the gardens with which she had—painstakingly, and alone—surrounded the castle to the east and the south, she heard a set of steps, two sets, and she looked up, her hair in her eyes, her eyes squinted near-shut against sunlight.

A young girl traveled by his side, her face replete with dark bruises, her clothing identical to the heavy traveling cloak that he himself wore. She did not touch him; he did not touch her; but he led and she followed, her eyes as skittish as the eyes of a wild creature.

"This," she heard him say, from a distance, "will be your home, if you desire a home."

She had brushed the dirt off her hands, rising to greet this newcomer and the hunter who brought her home. She saw the shadows in the girl's face; knew they were the same as the shadows across her own. But she offered the girl what the hunter was too wise to offer: her hand.

"I'm Elyssa," she said quietly. "I was the first."

He stayed until night. He inspected her gardens. He brought her seeds, which would, he said, keep until the following year. The night fell, and with the fall of night, the new girl, Anna, vanished into the hold. Elyssa understood it well, but she waited a moment, to see what the hunter would do. He smiled bitterly. There was always that bitterness about him; she wondered if it was anything like her own.

He bowed. "We have our work, Elyssa."

She wondered what that work was—but she was the first; she went back to the castle to introduce Anna to their new life.

Lady, they came.

The third one came at the end of the harvest season, battered and bruised, arm broken. She was older than Elyssa or Anna, and perhaps that was harder on her; she remained silent and withdrawn for six months; for long past the arrival of the next young girl.

During the winter there was only one newcomer, and she not so badly injured; she had been caught by the lord and two men, and they were loath to stay and play in the wild of frost and snow. But news came with the girl: Aline, the lord's wife, had passed away. She was his third wife, and she had died, as had the two before her, childless. The lord had no heir.

Heirless, his land might be claimed by a liege-lord he did not desire, or so Merlin said; it was the first time that she had seen the fullness of a smile cross his face, and truthfully, Elyssa did not like it. It reminded her of other, predatory smiles, and she saw the death in it, the desire for pain, the power. She wondered if her face would twist in the same way should that lord ever be in her power for a few minutes.

Was certain it would.

The winter turned. The spring came, and with it, another young woman, and another; their faces so similar, their pain so much like her own, they might have been sisters if such experience could force such a bond. The isle was a quiet place, and the planting of the seeds, the tending and watering, the pruning and weeding—and the vigilant guard against wildlife that would otherwise eat far more than they could afford to lose—gave them purpose, and even some pleasure, they who no longer dreamed of husbands, of families of their own, of children to cherish.

Some dreams had been taken from them, and some given, and the lake's waters were quiet and peaceful. No one who came to Elyssa and her isle ever desired to leave it.

Eventually, there came to them a young woman who knew how to read and write. She had been left for dead, the worst of the victims, because she might indeed cause the lord trouble should she remain alive to bear witness against him. But she had no desire to risk her life in that world; this world, like the cloisters for which she had been destined, was a world that suited her. It was only a matter of time before she began to teach them all—during the winter months, of course, when the cold and the snow kept them huddled together for warmth and company—how to read and write. How to sing, together and separately.

She was the seventh of the young women.

The eighth was different.

Her name was Gwyneth, and she was lovely; her face unmarred and unbruised, although her arms and legs were covered with long welts. She had spent not one evening in the company of the lord, but two long months, and was turned out in the end for her failure. The servants had helped her escape what might have otherwise been unpleasant exposure to the jackals that served just beneath the lord's table, but they could provide her with little else, and she could not go home to her family.

In pain, and in fear, she had been discovered—as they had all been discovered—by Merlin. She came to them, and Elyssa discovered that the lord himself had grown so desperate for an heir that he had taken no wife—had vowed to take no wife until he'd gotten a woman with child.

This was not to the liking of the nobility among whom he'd chosen before; not to the liking of the merchants who could otherwise afford to buy themselves a connection with a nobility that birth alone would never provide them. The wives that might have been vanished; he was left with his choice of the young women his villages could produce, and he used them with contempt. They all came to him, and those he deemed suitable he kept for his own uses. They had to be untouched, of course, and they had to be untouched after his initial encounter—but even so he was not a gentle man, and those that failed to "catch" were given to his men through the castle's back doors.

And so it went.

The pattern was different, the violence the same, the anger—the anger of a frustrated man, a powerful man—a growing darkness that only the lake kept them safe from. Sometimes, Elyssa would wake in a cold sweat, a dream of an army encamped, spears readied, swords and armor gleaming, at the edge of the marshes. But other times, she would wake from a dream in which all those women, all those young girls, all those broken dreams, had been gathered from across the water and brought to where safety and shelter and food might be provided in a harbor that allowed for no man, save one.

But the night that the Lady of the Lake came to them, they woke as one, their dreams a shattered mirror of the nightmare that had broken their lives and brought them here. They rose, some as new to the isle as Viviane, and some as old as Elyssa, and they met in the great hall that housed their winter lessons.

It was Elyssa who said, "She is coming."

They nodded. But they knew what would happen before, and they left, as one woman, to stand by the marsh edges, to hear what the lake gave them leave to hear: the cries of the helpless, the laughter of the powerful—an echo of the things they were not permitted to forget.

They gathered by the shore.

Elyssa often waited there when a newcomer arrived; the others came and went as they were able. But tonight was different; the air was warm and wind-heavy, and although the skies were clear, there was storm there for any who cared enough to look for it. They looked; they looked long.

" 'Lyssa, look—the boat."

She nodded; caught Anna's hand and held it as still as she possibly could; she felt trembling, palm to palm, and could not have said later whose it was. The boat was the same boat that had carried her, the first night she had arrived at the edge of the blessed marsh; unoiled, unstained, untrammeled by things like weather or reality, it passed almost above the water carrying its two passengers: Merlin and the newcomer.

She was wrapped in a cloak, and it was too broad in shoulder, too long in length, for her slender form. They knew it well, those who had come in the winter—it was his. She looked, Elyssa thought, as if she were cold; she was trembling.

The night air was barely cool.

Too soon, she thought. *We had to travel; we had to learn to walk in the world of men again.* But she said nothing. The hand that gripped hers gripped more and more tightly, until her fingers went numb and then she felt them tingle. She almost appreciated the sensation; it reminded her that breath needed taking.

The boat stopped.

As it had stopped for Elyssa, as it had stopped for each of them.

The figure cloaked in what appeared to be black—night colors, not true ones—stood shakily. She reached out for the side of the boat and then almost snarled. They all heard it; it carried across the water like a declaration of war.

Merlin offered the woman no aid; he sank back, to the farthest end of the boat, the end that did not contain her. It came to Elyssa then that the trembling she witnessed was not shock, not chill; it was *anger.* He had brought them a newcomer full of rage.

Had she been such a one? Had any of them?

She barely had time to wonder.

The woman spoke, and her voice uttered a word, a single word. "Morganne."

But the boat did not move.

She had offered her name; there was no question of it. There was a truth to names, especially here by the water's edge, that denied all pretense and all mask. But the boat was completely still; the water traveled outward from it in a wide, moving ring, as if it had finally touched down enough to disturb the lake's surface.

They watched; they waited. Elyssa's hair began to stand on end, rising in goose bumps across her arms, reaching up for the back of her neck.

"Why isn't she coming?"

"'Lyssa, what's wrong?"

"Hush," she said, more harshly than she'd intended.

"But 'Lyssa—"

Elyssa turned to the youngest. "She hasn't answered the question."

"But you *heard* her—she said—"

"She spoke a single name," Elyssa said. "A single word."

"That's all we ever spoke."

Aye, Elyssa thought, *that's all we ever spoke.* She felt it keenly, sharply, a gratitude for herself mixed with a pity so profound it was almost horror. Gently, as gently as she could force herself to respond, she said, "That girl is already with child."

That girl—the unseen girl, the cursed girl—spoke her name again, spoke it loudly; it echoed and resounded in the thick air like a clap of thunder. The lightning must surely follow; Elyssa had heard such a rumble before, such a heaving of heaven's own.

And the light did come, but it was all dark, a thing of knowledge and not a thing of nature. Or perhaps a thing of bitter nature, of an uglier god than the lake had ever shown itself to be. She cursed; they could hear the words, succinct and terrible. But the boat did not move.

Elyssa said, quietly, "The boat will be still a long time."

"But why—"

"She understands what it is that she carries, but she will not own it; she will not grant it a name."

"I wouldn't own it either," Viviane said coldly.

"If you had no choice?"

"What choice has *she*? What choice had any of us?"

"None. None at all," Elyssa replied. The night was cold, cold, cold.

"I'd bear it—because I had no choice. But I'd take it up after it was born, the vile thing, and I'd cut off its head and its genitals—"

"If it were a boy."

"What else could it be? I'd cut them both off, and I'd send them to—"

"Not here." Elyssa's voice was sharp. "Do not mention his name here."

"So he'd know," the girl continued. "So he'd know that he'd finally gotten his heir." She laughed, and the laughter was low and bitter and terrible, as ugly a sound as laughter had ever been. Elyssa had heard ugly laughter. They all had.

And *she* heard it. Morganne.

She heard it; she heard the words that Viviane had spoken.

She rose, then, rose and cried out a single word: "Yes!" And then, grim and terrible, she pulled the hood of the hunter's cloak away from her swollen, bloodied face, her tangled, bramble-torn hair; pulled it away from exposed flesh, bruised skin. She stood exposed to the night and the lake and the gathering, and she said the second word, and it was taken by the wind, whipped past their ears so quickly it might not have been said at all. Save for this: The boat moved.

Lightning came, then. Bright, white, a streak of pure brilliance that transformed the sky. The boat lurched forward, and she with it, stumbling in its prow. But the hunter did not offer her his aid; the lake did not smooth the boat's passage; she came to them, her anger complete, her vow still smoldering in the night air like a hanging echo of something that will never quite be forgotten.

Thus it was that the Lady of the Lake came to them all, a mere seventeen years of age, the hunter behind her, and before her the future that they had all been waiting for.

His eyes were bright and shiny, hard like glass, full of a light that she had never seen there before. He lingered longer at the castle than he had ever done, and he could not—could *not*—stand still for more than five minutes at a time.

"Merlin?" she said, and he spun on his feet at the sound of her voice, as if voice at all was something wondrous and dangerous, as if the words could catch him, hood him, bind him with jesses.

She stepped back as he whirled; he stepped forward.

Then he caught himself, stilled himself.

This, she thought, *is what you look like when you hunt.* But no, that wasn't quite true. She had seen him hunt for years; had seen him, consciously biding his time. This was new. This was different.

Bird of prey? She had learned much in her years at the castle, but she had never seen this: This was the hunter *before* the kill, circling above its prey, waiting for the right wind, the right movement, the right moment. Talons extended, blood a scant second's dive away, this was where the bird met the wind, and parted it, and rose triumphant.

"Merlin," she said, and he turned to her, and she was reminded that she had never asked him—that none of them had ever asked him—what had been done to him in the winter before her own ruin.

He came often during Morganne's confinement, although he never stayed the night. There was something within the castle that denied him an evening's rest—but they were used to that. What they were not used to was his shadow upon the shoreline, or the cadence of his voice at all times that the sunlight, deft in its ability to seek out nook and cranny, came into the courtyards and towers.

Were they jealous?

Perhaps. There were times when Elyssa looked over her shoulder to see them huddled together, he the attentive and intent keeper, and she the wild anger. At such times, the first of the isle's inhabitants wondered if all he had ever sought was this: a pregnancy, a certain physical remnant of the man who had destroyed all their lives.

He had always left the newcomers to Elyssa before.

One night she waited by the marshes.

"Elyssa," he said, although he did not seem terribly surprised.

"You have always left the newcomers to me," she replied, assuming a question although he was graceless enough not to offer that opening.

"Yes," he said. "I have."

"And this one?"

"I had hoped to spare you her anger."

She was not the girl that she had once been; she knew a lie when she heard it. The night closed in on them both, but the moon silvered the water. Her silence was all the accusation she needed.

His silence was all the reply she thought he would offer, and in the end, she turned away, toward the path that led to the castle. But he surprised her, as he often did.

"You heal too much, Elyssa."

"Pardon?"

"The others—you take them, and you offer them the isle, and you teach them how to heal themselves. They work in your gardens and in your great hall and in your kitchen, they toil in your castle and at your looms, they read in front of your fire after they've struggled with the words, with the concept of words. The newcomers— they hold their anger for as long as they can, but in the face of what you offer them, that isn't long at all."

"I am not depriving them of their anger," she told him softly, evenly. "I am helping them to let go of their pain."

He turned on her then, as if the physical act would force her to flee the conversation. She was not the girl that she had been, no; she held her ground.

Or perhaps she was very much that girl, but the isle itself promised her a safety she would find nowhere else in the land of man.

"What," he said, grinding the words through teeth that would barely open, "do you think anger *is*? Take away the pain, and you have destroyed it.

"The others did not matter. In the end, even you do not matter. But Morganne—she *is* the one. She is the vessel. She carries our salvation." He was shaking with certainty. "And I will not have you ruin her before our work is done.

"Don't you understand? You have been shortsighted here, and in the end, I have allowed it. But there is too much at risk now. We are almost where we must be. We are within striking distance. The word—the word of the child has already gone forth, and it will fill the land with its truth before it reaches his ears. He will hope, Elyssa. He will hope—and we will destroy all hope, bit by bit, before he is done.

"He will weep.

"He will scream.

"He will watch his sole heir perish.

"His rule, and his 'stewardship' over these lands—they will pass to someone who bears no taint of his blood."

He stopped speaking; the fervor of the words seemed to drain him, to calm him, to bleed him. "This is what we are owed, but we have not left it to the gods to give us our due; we have taken what is rightfully ours." He paused a long time; the boat was slow to make its way through the rushes. "Or we will," he said softly. "We will."

The boat bore him swiftly away after his silence had descended. She stared a long time at the wake across the water.

The following day, Merlin did not come at all.

His absence surprised Elyssa; it seemed to surprise the newcomer as well. The sun was out, but this one day it seemed to cast no shadow. She was heavy with child, and she found the heat uncomfortable—or so it seemed; not a single one of them had borne child before, and not a single one of them was likely to do so. They had been marked for life by the events that had brought them here.

They pitied her; they all did. And it was clear that she had no use for their pity. No use, in fact, for any of them at all.

But the next day, Merlin again did not come, nor the day after; the late summer seemed to have swallowed him in preparation for the harvest. By slow degree the newcomer's anger gave way to a bitter restlessness.

Elyssa had seen this before, in different ways; had seen it eight times. But she labored under no illusion; not a single one of them had had the bitter, bitter reminder of a child growing, like a demon's seed, in her belly. And yet.

They had all seen children grow; they had all held children. They had all been forced to watch over them, at one time or the other, in field or in town. The days became shorter; the nights longer.

Merlin did not come.

But the baby did.

Elyssa had been old enough to attend birthings. Neve was older; had actually aided in the delivery of the young. Between them all, with Gwyneth as patient as any knowledge-monger can be who is about to be put to the ultimate test, they tended Morganne.

She was not a screamer. It was almost as if the screams she had uttered that first night were the only ones she would offer; she fell into her pain and would not allow it to dislodge so much as a whisper from her throat. Her breath became quicker and sharper; they brought water for her cracked lips and parched throat, and sponged her face and body as often as she would allow it. She was not comfortable with their hands until the very end—but at the end, she reached out, as if in darkness, her fingers blindly curling and shaking in the air.

Elyssa caught them, almost by instinct; the others let her. This was her task, after all; she was as much the isle's steward as Merlin, she the firstcomer.

The baby came, wet and slick with fluid; the afterbirth followed.

"A boy," Viviane said. She, the newest, the one whose anger had only begun to slumber. Her hands were fists; she clenched them, unclenched them, clenched them, unclenched them, as if they were her heart, and they were beating.

Gwyneth caught him, held him up. Neve cut and tied the cord that had bound his life to his reluctant mother's; she held him up by the ankles until his face had purpled and he drew breath.

His cries were weak but distinct.

"What do we do with him now?" Gwyneth said quietly to Neve.

"We—if he were . . ." She took the baby from Gwyneth's shaking hands. Looked at him, scrunched up and reddened. Looked beyond him to his mother's face. "I'm sorry," she said softly.

Morganne said nothing.

"But if you want this child to serve as your weapon, one way or the other, he'll have to be alive some small time to do it. We none of us can wet-nurse him." She held the child out, hand coming up to cradle his tiny head.

They were silent, all of them. The night had fallen heavily; they were governed by lamp and torch, by moon and star, a cabal of the fallen; winter might have come at that moment, and it would not have chilled them any further than the birth of a boy and the utter stillness of his new mother.

Night was in her eyes when Morganne slowly untwined her hands from Elyssa's. She held them out, at the end of stiff, hard arms. No words passed thinned lips, but her meaning was clear. Neve did not hesitate. She placed the infant in his mother's arms.

His mother's arms were not welcoming, not soft, not yielding. But she took the babe, and she began to nurse it, biting her lip to endure the touch and the closeness. Her eyes were very, very cold.

His first weeks were lived in a world of silences and stiff movements. There was a cradle for him—one put together, grimly but quickly, by Neve, the ever-practical—and they placed him in it, in a room that was within hearing distance of his loudest cries. Such cries would rouse them, and they would take him to his mother.

She was listless and silent almost all of the time; the child did not sleep well. She would take him, arms and body stiff, eyes fixed on the floor or the wall or the garden's greenery—on anything at all but the child. When he was done, they would take him; they would clean him, swaddle him, put him back into the tiny walls of his home: the coarse cradle. No one spoke.

Who was it, Elyssa wondered, although she knew the answer. Who was it who had first betrayed that silence and those shadows, that terrible anger?

Had it been Anna, she might have spoken; had it been Morganne herself, she would have said nothing at all. Neve, she might have left on her own, for Neve was the eldest, and in many ways deemed wisest. Even Gwyneth, with her book learning and her scholarship, might have a justifiable reason for her lapse.

But it was the newest girl, Viviane. It was Viviane who offered the first act of betrayal. Elyssa remembered it clearly: The babe, weeks' old now—almost two months—had woken them all in a rage of hunger. They took turns fetching the little monster, and it was Neve's turn. She went to the cradle room, came back with the child, gave him to his unresisting mother. And then she tended fire; it was cold now, and likely to get colder before it got warmer. *The baby,* they said among themselves, *can't die before it serves its purpose.*

But after suckling, the infant was in no better a state, and it wailed and wailed and wailed until it was surrounded by Morganne and her nine attendants. Viviane at last, in an angry rage, carried the child off to his cradle. "Let him cry himself to sleep—what concern is it of ours? He's been fed, he's been changed, his fire is burning." They did not argue with her anger; they could not.

She took the child. She left the room. The nine remaining women fell into their habitual silence where the baby was concerned; he was a wall come between them, a thing they did not know how to look over or around.

And a strange thing happened: The night was suddenly filled with silence. Just that: silence. The screaming rage had stopped. They froze, as puddles do in winter, becoming hard and glassy in their place. "Elyssa . . ." Neve said, and Elyssa shook her head, thinking then what they all must have thought: *Viviane has killed the child.*

No one spoke.

But Morganne rose. Stiffly, quickly, her eyes wide and round, she rose and made her way to the door, her feet gaining speed, her steps distance. She was their signal— Elyssa would remember it later—for only when she moved were the others free of the terrible compulsion to give in to their . . .

Name it. Name it, Elyssa, and have done. Name it. . . . To their horror.

They reached the room running, eighteen feet; Morganne stood in the door like a warden. But beyond her, Elyssa could hear the sound of weeping. It was quiet, where the boy's had been loud. "Morganne," Elyssa said, and Morganne stepped into the room, leading them now.

She walked over to where Viviane sat, legs curled beneath her on the cold stone floor, long hair rippling down her shoulders in the light that Neve—only Neve of all of them—had thought to bring into the room itself. Morganne put a hand, a shaking, slender hand, a gentle one, on Viviane's shoulder, and Viviane looked up.

Elyssa thought she had never seen a face so beautiful as Viviane's at that moment; tears caught the lamp's glow and shone across the length of her face from eyes to chin, trails of light. The baby—the boy—was pressed so tightly to her chest they might have thought him dead were it not for the fact that his face crested her shoulder; he was staring at them all, his face so serene and so calm he might have been waiting for just this moment all of his short life.

She had been, Elyssa thought, she *must* have been, a gentle girl. It was hard to tell what the person beneath the tragedy was like until they had lifted enough of tragedy's veil to step clear.

"I'm sorry," Viviane said, still weeping. "I'm sorry, Elyssa. I'm sorry, Morganne. I thought—I thought I could kill him. I thought *we* could kill him."

"And we can't?" Anna's question, Anna, also young.

"*I* can't," Viviane replied. "I can't even hate him, and I've tried, I've tried. But he's—I can't—he's *so* alone—"

They turned, then, to look at Morganne, ringing her in a circle, nine women and an infant. And Morganne said, quietly, "Give me my child." There was a moment of hesitation; Elyssa saw Viviane's arms tighten involuntarily. But she did as Morganne ordered; the child passed from her to his mother. His mother held him a moment in stiff, stiff arms. And then, wrapped in their silence, blanketed by it, she said, "I thought you had killed him." And she brought the child as close as she might, as close as Viviane had done. She did not, however, weep.

They did, the nine.

*   *   *

He was not an angel. He was not a perfect little creature. He was not, as some would say later, a child who knew no taint; raised by ten mothers, how could he be? They argued constantly about how he might best be preserved, about how he might best be taught, about *what* he should be taught, on an island where men were not permitted to set foot, save this one. And each of them did what all mothers do: their best, as they saw fit.

But they also spoke, hesitantly at first, of his first smile. They spoke of the first day he rolled over, of his first attempt to crawl, of his first encounter with water and the rushes at the lake's edge. That edge fascinated him; he was called along path and beneath bramble to play by the water's side, to watch the red-winged blackbirds take flight, to stare fascinated at the passage of dragonfly.

It was by the water's edge that he first met Merlin. He was four years old, not yet five; five years, in the tradition of Morganne's people, was the age at which the child would be given his name. To name a child earlier was to tempt the gods, to invite the death that took most small children from their mothers, and she had already named him once.

But he was close enough to five that he came running up the path, well ahead of this stranger, this very oddly shaped, oddly spoken newcomer. "Mother!" Then, louder, "Gwyn! Neve! There's someone strange at the marsh!"

The hunter was ragged; his eyes were gleaming like steel in the sun's light until he lifted a hand to shade them. Morganne, first called, looked to Elyssa for silent advice, and then reached out for her hand—as she had at the birth of the boy they each all privately thought of as her own. They rose from the afternoon shade together and stood, waiting for the boy to reach their skirts. Only when he was safely within arms' reach did Neve move to gather him—and quickly—into her arms. He struggled there a moment until her grip tightened, then he turned to look at her face. He stilled at once, and Elyssa was sorry for frightening him, for she saw the stillness and watchfulness come full to his expression, and she knew that he was suddenly aware that they were, to a woman, afraid.

Merlin knew it, too. He stopped not five yards from where Morganne stood, and his bow, when it came, was shallow. "So," he said.

"You never came back," she replied, answering the accusation before it could be made. To spare their son.

He laughed; the laugh, like his face, was fey and wild. "Do you think that was *my* choice?" His arms, he threw wide, the gesture a bold, an angry, one. "It seems the lake decided. Or the isle. The boat would not carry me, nor the water support my weight. I have been trapped these five years and more by water, by water's curse; it will be my fate," he added bitterly.

"But you are here today." Elyssa stepped into the light. "And if you understood better the nature of the isle, you would know why you could not cross the waters. You meant harm to one of us."

"Do not lecture me, Elyssa. I understand the lake well enough."

They exchanged a glance, these women who had built a home and a life and a peace that the lands beyond the waters rarely saw. Morganne said, "You've returned. The lake has allowed it. Why?"

"Because, my dear ladies, you will shortly be under siege. Word of your child has finally reached the ears of the lord who claims him. He has come for what is rightfully his, and I have come as the vanguard, to warn you." He turned, then. Looked at the boy that Neve held in her arms, the still, quiet child. The child who met the hatred and the anger in Merlin's face without once turning away or flinching. He took a step forward, turned a pleading face—and that was the worst of it, the plea, the terribly angry yearning, the helpless frustration—to all of them in his turn. "It's not too late. Don't you see? He's coming. It's *not too late*. Turn back, turn back from this sentiment."

Morganne met his face; her own hardened. She opened her lips to speak, and the sound of horns echoed, like storm, across the autumn stillness. "It is time," she said. "Come, Neve. Bring the child. Let us see the armies of the enemy."

This was her nightmare. She remembered it; it had haunted her for the first month she'd slept alone within the safety of the castle walls. It had haunted them all: Men on horseback, in armor that gleamed with sun's light; spears. Lances. Shields. Swords. Men with less armor, no horses, and weapons that were wood and iron stood among them like small bushes. From one end of the lake to the other, they stretched as far as the eye could see.

In spite of her best intentions, Elyssa flinched; she found strength only when she was forced to offer Anna comfort. Viviane said nothing, but her lips were white; Gwyneth gained two inches, and Neve, carrying the boy, seemed to lose them. They stood, humbled by the banner and crest they recognized: the Dragon Lord.

Only Morganne did not flinch. She drew breath, stood taller, threw her scarf up and across her shoulders as if it were a mantle. They watched as she strode to the dock that was so seldom used it had always seemed superfluous. Silly, to think the lake provided anything without cause.

"Who are you," she said, her voice filling the silence, "and why have you risked your lives to come to the isle?"

And a man rode out, in the finest armor of all, wearing a surcoat with the colors of the Dragon. "I come," he said, "to claim my flesh and blood, as is my right."

"Upon these lands, you have no rights, and you have no claim to flesh or blood."

"You have a boy. The entire land speaks of him."

"We have a child, yes. And that child we took, unsullied, from the lands men know; we brought him here that we might raise him without your taint. We are the Ladies of the Isle, and the Ladies of the Lake, and we deny you. Turn back, turn back, Dragon Lord, and you may yet survive your folly. I will not warn you again."

He laughed. He laughed, but the men who did not sit astride the beasts of war were silent, uncomfortable.

"Go," he said, to the unhorsed farmers that he had gathered for use as weapons. "Go and get my son."

Neve looked askance at Morganne. She nodded, and Neve turned to hurry him away through the marshes, to take him to safety. But he reached out, instead, for his mother, and his face was very grave.

"No," his mother said, her voice hard and cold, "you *must* go." He shook his head; he was stubborn, and perhaps they'd all played their part in that, the spoiling and indulging of a child. But in the end, hard and cold as his father's armor, she allowed him to stay, to bear witness.

And so it was that he saw his first death, for some of the farmers attempted to flee, and six were cut down, their heads raised on pikes for the rest to see. The others came, then, to the water, and made their way into its marshy shallows—and they, too, screamed, and died. For the first time, the lake set as grand an example as the lord. They brought flat barges next, and at that, Merlin, silent until that moment, laughed; there was mirth and cruelty, and the boy turned to look at Merlin's face, to shrink from what he saw there.

The beasts escaped the marshes; they were grateful for that. The men who rose did not. And in a fashion, to begin with, they were viciously glad of it, but after a while, the screaming and gurgling was just too much for them—for all of them but Morganne, who watched in stony, icy silence. Her son looked over her shoulder, at the pale faces of his nine other mothers, and Elyssa saw that he was weeping, as if he had somehow absorbed the tears that his mother would not cry, and shed them for her.

"I meant him harm," she said, when the last of the knights had vanished beneath the still surface, and the lord would spend no more. "I meant him harm because I wished to harm you.

"But he is more than that; he is more than you will ever be, could ever have dreamed of being. *I* am Morganne, of the Isle, and the Lake, and I bid you and yours begone. Your son will never take what you have taken for yourself; he will never claim the lands that you have claimed. He will never rule what you have ruled, and in the fashion you have ruled. *I swear it.*

"This day, he has seen blood, and he has seen battle." She lifted him, then, lifted him high—and from the folds of her robe, she pulled out a long, slender dagger.

Elyssa screamed, and Neve, but Gwyneth and Viviane and Anna were silent; they trusted.

And she said, "You, child, are the son of the Isle, and this place will succor and strengthen you while life remains. You have seen bloodshed, and in your time, you

will shed it. Let the first blood be here, and now." And
the boy in her arms, rather than shrinking from the terrible feyness in her voice, her eyes, her face, unfurled his
clenched fists, offering her the white, white skin of his
palms. She lifted the dagger, and slashed the skin, and it
bled, a sudden, crimson streak.

The lord cried out in rage; the child, not at all.

But his blood fell onto the dock, and as she held him,
it fell into the water that surrounded the Isle. "You are,
this day, of the first age, and I name you: Arturus. Let
legend make of you what it will.

"You will never know him," she said to the lord, "and
you will never understand what you have lost in your ignorance. I would have suffered the same loss, in the
same ignorance and rage, but I was offered the choice
and I have chosen between your ways and my son. As I
choose, the land will choose." She held her child.

"As we choose," she added softly, "the land *must*
choose." Her eyes were misty, then. Hope or death; hope
or vengeance; nobility or brutality.

The sun set upon them, lady and lord, lake and child;
the dead lay between them almost as heavily as the
words that Morganne had spoken.

And Elyssa, the first to come to the isle's shores, was
the last to leave the docks, the still water, the graves. She
spoke her prayers for the spirits of the watery world, and
then, when the boat came for her, she crossed the river to
gather the horses that had somehow become trapped in
marshes that men could not cross.

She was practical in her fashion after all, and they
would be needed.

The Mooncalfe

David Farland

It was late evening on a sultry summer's day when three riders appeared at the edge of the woods on the road southwest of Tintagel Castle. The sentries did not see them riding up the muddy track that led from Berons-glade. The knights merely appeared, just as the sun dipped below the sea, as if they'd coalesced from mist near a line of beech trees.

The manner of their appearance did not seem odd, on that day of oddities. The tide was very low, and the whole ocean lay as placid as a mountain pool. To the castle's residents, who were used to the constant pounding of the surf upon the craggy rocks outside the castle walls, the silence seemed thunderous. Even the gulls had given up their incessant screeching and now huddled low on the rocks, making an easy dinner of cockles and green kelp crabs.

All around the castle, the air was somber. Smoke from cooking fires and from the candlers hung in a blue haze all about Tintagel's four towers. The air seemed leaden.

So it was that the sentries, when they spotted the three knights, frowned and studied the men's unfamiliar garb. The leader of the trio wore a fantastical helm shaped like a dragon's head, and his enameled mail glimmered red like a dragon's scales. He rode a huge black destrier, and as for the device on his shield, he carried only blank iron strapped to a pack on a palfrey.

Beside him rode a big fellow in oiled ringmail, while the third knight wore nothing but a cuirass of boiled leather, yet carried himself with a calmness and certainty that made him more frightening than if he rode at the head of a Saxon horde.

"'Tis Uther Pendragon!" one of the boys at the castle walls cried at first. The lad hefted his halberd as if he would take a swing, but stepped back in fright.

Pendragon was of course the guards' worst nightmare. At the Easter feast, King Uther Pendragon had made advances on the Duke Gorlois's wife, the Lady Igraine. He had courted her in her husband's company with all the grace and courtesy of a bull trying to mount a heifer. At last the duke felt constrained to flee the king's presence. The king demanded that Gorlois return with his wife, but Gorlois knew that if he ever set foot in the king's palace again, he'd lose his head. So he locked his wife safely in Tintagel, began fortifying his castles, and prayed that he could hire enough Irish mercenaries to back him before the king could bring him down.

Last anyone had heard, Duke Gorlois was holed up like a badger at his fortress in Dimilioc, where Uther Pendragon had lain siege. It was said that Pendragon had employed Welsh miners as sappers, vowing to dig down the castle walls and skin Gorlois for his pelt within forty days.

So when the lad atop the castle wall thought he saw Pendragon, immediately someone raised a horn and began to blow wildly, calling for reinforcements, though none would likely be needed. Tintagel was a small keep, situated by the sea on a pile of rocks that could only be reached over a narrow causeway. It was said that three men could hold it from an army of any size, and no fewer than two dozen guards now manned the wall.

The captain of the guard, a stout old knight named Sir Ventias who could no longer ride due to a game leg, squinted through the smoke that clung around the castle. Something seemed afoul. He knew fat king Pendragon's features well, and as he peered through the gloom and the smoke that burned his eyes, he saw immediately that it was not Pendragon on the mount. It was a young man with a flaxen beard and a hatchet face.

Ventias squinted, trying to pierce the haze until he felt sure: it was Duke Gorlois. He rode in company with his true friends: Sir Jordans and the stout knight Sir Brastias.

Ventias smiled. "Tell the duchess that her husband is home."

The celebration that night was remarkable. The duke's pennant was hoisted on the wall, and everywhere the people made merry. Sir Brastias himself told the miraculous tale of their escape—how they had spied Pendragon leave the siege and the duke had issued out from the castle with his knights. After a brief battle, Gorlois had broken Pendragon's lines and had hurried toward Tintagel, only to discover Pendragon himself a few miles up the road, frolicking with some maiden in a pool. Since King Pendragon was naked and unarmed, it became an easy matter to capture the lecher, both arms and armor, and force his surrender.

Thus Gorlois rode home in Pendragon's suit of mail.

So it was that the celebration began at Tintagel. Suckling pigs were spitted and cooked over a bonfire in the lower bailey, while every lad who had a hand with the pipe or the tambor made music as best he could. New ale flowed into mugs like golden honey. Young squires fought mock combats to impress their lord and entertain the audience. And everywhere the people began to dance.

But Duke Gorlois could not relish it. Instead, he went to his great hall before the festivities began and gazed upon his glorious young bride with a sultry stare. He never even took his seat at the head of the table. Instead, he studied her for less than a minute before he grabbed one of her breasts as if it were a third hand and began to lead her to the bedchamber.

This he did in front of some eighty people. The priest quietly complained about this impropriety to the duke. Gorlois, who was normally a very reserved fellow, merely said, "Let the people frolic as they see fit, and I will frolic as I see fit."

Though everyone was astonished at this crude display, no one other than the priest dared speak against it. Even Sir Jordans, a man who could normally be counted on to pass judgment fairly on any matter, merely sat in the great hall and did not eat. Instead, he played with his heavy serpent-handled dagger, stabbing it over and over again into the wooden table beside his trencher.

Then Duke Gorlois dragged his wife up the stairs against her will, stripping off his armor as he went.

Or at least that is the way that my mother tells the tale, and she should know, for she was a young woman who served tables there at Tintagel.

It seems surprising that no one found it odd.

The evening star that night shone as red as a bloodstone, and all the dogs somehow quietly slipped from the castle gates.

There was a new horned moon, and though the people danced, they did not do so for long. Somehow their feet felt heavy and the celebration seemed more trouble than it was worth, and so the crowds began to break off early.

Some went home, while most seemed more eager to drink themselves into a stupor. Yet no one at the time remarked about the queer mood at Castle Tintagel.

Late that night, my mother found Sir Jordans still on his bench, where he'd sat quietly for hours. He was letting the flame of a candle lick his left forefinger in a display that left my mother horrified and set her heart to hammering.

Dozens of knights lay drunk and snoring on the floor around him, while a pair of cats on the table gnawed the bones of a roast swan.

My mother wondered if Sir Jordans performed this remarkable feat for her benefit, as young men often will when trying to impress a young woman.

If so, he'd gone too far. She feared for Sir Jordans's health, so she quietly scurried to the long oaken table. She could not smell burning flesh above the scents of ale and grease and fresh loaves, though Sir Jordans had been holding his finger under the flame for a long minute.

"What are you doing?" my mother asked in astonishment. "If it's cooking yourself that you're after, there's a bonfire still burning out in the bailey!"

Sir Jordans merely sat at the table, a hooded traveling robe pulled low over his head, and held his finger beneath the flickering flame. Candlelight reflected in his eyes. My mother thought the silence odd, for in the past Sir Jordans had always been such a garrulous fellow, a man whose laugh sounded like the winter's surf booming on the escarpment at the base of the castle walls.

"Do you hear me? You'll lose the finger," my mother warned. "Are you drunk, or fey?" she asked, and she thought of rousing some besotted knight from the floor to help her restrain the man.

Sir Jordans looked up at her with a dreamy smile. "I'll not lose my finger, nor burn it," he said. "I could hold it thus all night. It is a simple trick, really. I could teach you—if you like?"

Something about his manner unnerved my mother. She was beautiful then. Though she was but a scullery maid, at the age of fourteen she was lovely—with long raven hair, eyes of smoke, and a full figure that drew appreciative gazes from men. Sir Jordans studied her now with open admiration, and she grew frightened.

She crossed herself. "This is no trick, this is sorcery!" my mother accused. "It's evil! If the priest found out, he'd make you do penance."

But Sir Jordans merely smiled as if she were a child. He had a broad, pleasant face that could give no insult. "It's *not* evil," he affirmed reasonably. "Did not God save the three righteous Israelites when the infidels threw them into the fire?"

My mother wondered then. He was right, of course. Sir Jordans was a virtuous man, she knew, and if God could save men who were thrown whole into a fire, then surely Sir Jordans was upright enough so that God could spare his finger.

"Let me teach you," Sir Jordans whispered.

My mother nodded, still frightened, but enticed by his gentle manner.

"The trick," Sir Jordans said, withdrawing his finger

from the candle flame, "is to learn to take the fire into yourself without getting burned."

He held up his finger for her inspection, and my mother drew close, trying to see it in the dim light, to make sure that it was not oozing or blistered.

"Once you learn how to hold the fire within," Sir Jordans whispered, "you must then learn to release the flames when—and how—you will. Like this . . ."

He reached out his finger then and touched between my mother's ample breasts. His finger itself was cold to the touch, so cold that it startled her. Yet after he drew it away, she felt as if flames began to build inside her, pulsing through her breasts in waves, sending cinders of pleasure to burn hot in the back of her brain. Unimaginable embers, as hot as coals from a blacksmith's forge, flared to life in her groin.

As the flames took her, she gasped in astonishment, so thoroughly inflamed by lust that she dropped to her knees in agony, barely able to suppress her screams.

Sir Jordans smiled at her and asked playfully, "You're a virgin, aren't you?"

Numb with pain, my mother nodded, and knelt before him, sweating and panting with desire. *This is hell,* she thought. *This is how it will be, me burning with desires so staggering that they can never be sated. This is my destiny now and hereafter.*

"I could teach you more," Sir Jordans whispered, leaning close. "I could teach you how to make love, how to satisfy every sensual desire. There are arts to be learned—pleasurable beyond your keenest imagining. Only when *I* teach you can the flames inside you be quenched."

My mother merely nodded, struck dumb with fear and lust. She would have given anything for one moment of

release, for any degree of satisfaction. Sir Jordans smiled
and leaned forward, until his lips met hers.

*   *   *

At dawn, my mother woke outside the castle. She found
herself sprawled dazed and naked like some human sacrifice upon a black rock on the ocean's shore.

The whole world was silent with a silence so profound
that it seemed to weigh like an ingot of lead on her chest.
The only noise came from the cries of gulls that winged
about the castle towers, as if afraid to land.

She searched for a long while until she found her
clothes, then made her way back to the castle.

Two hours later, riders came charging hard from Dimilioc. They bore the ill tidings that Duke Gorlois had
been slain in battle the day before. Among the dead were
found Sir Brastias and Sir Jordans.

Everyone at Tintagel took the news in awe, speaking
well only because they feared to speak ill.

" 'Twas a shade," they said. "Duke Gorlois so loved
his wife, that he came at sunset to see her one last time."

Even the Lady Igraine repeated this tale of shades as
if it were true, for her husband had slipped from her bed
before dawn, as if he were indeed a shade, as had the
other dead men who walked in his retinue.

But my mother did not believe the tale. The man she'd
slept with the night before had been clothed in flesh, and
she felt his living seed burning her womb. She knew that
she had been seduced by sorcery, under the horned
moon.

Two children were conceived on that fell night. I was
one of them, the girl.

You have surely heard of the boy.

King Uther Pendragon soon forced the widowed
Igraine to be his wife and removed her to Canterbury.
When the boy was born, Pendragon ripped the newborn

son from his mother's breast and gave it to a pale-eyed
Welsh sorcerer who slung it over his back and carried it
like a bundle of firewood into the forest.

I have heard it said that Igraine feared that the sorcerer would bury the infant alive, so she prayed cease-
lessly that God would soften the sorcerer's heart, so that
he would abandon him rather than do him harm.

Some say that in time Igraine became deluded into be-
lieving that her son was being raised by peasants or
wolves. She was often seen wandering the fairs, looking
deep into the eyes of boy children, as if trying to find
something of herself or Duke Gorlois there.

As for my mother, she fled Tintagel well before her
stomach began to bulge. She loved a stableboy in Tintagel, and had even promised herself to him in marriage,
so it was a hard thing for her to leave, and she slunk
away one night without saying any goodbyes.

For she constantly feared that the false Sir Jordans
would return. It is well known, after all, that devils cannot leave their own offspring alone.

My mother went into labor three hundred and thirty-
three days later, after a term so long that she knew there
would be something wrong with me.

My mother took no midwife, for she rightly feared
what I would look like. I would have a tail, she thought,
and a goat's pelt, and cloven hooves for feet. She feared
that I might even be born with horns that would rip her
as I came through the birth canal.

No priest would have baptized a bastard and a mon-
strosity, she knew, and she hoped that I would be born
dead, or would die soon, so that she could rid herself of
the evidence of her sin.

So she went into the forest while the labor pains
wracked her, and she gouged a little hole to bury me in,

and she laid a huge rock beside it to crush me with, if it came to that.

Then she squatted in the ferns beneath an oak. Thus I dropped into the world, and the only cries to ring from the woods that day came from my mother.

For when I touched the soil, I merely lay quietly gazing about. My mother looked down between her legs in trepidation and saw at once that I was no common girl. I was not as homely as her sin. I was not born with a pelt or a twisted visage.

Instead, she said that I was radiant, with skin that smelled of honeysuckle and eyes as pale as ice. I did not have the cheesy covering of a newborn, and my mother's blood did not cling to me.

I looked out at her, as if I were very old and wise and knowing, and I did not cry. Instead, I reached out and grasped her bloody heel, as if to comfort her, and I smiled.

When my mother was a little girl herself, she said that she told me that she had often tried to visualize angels who were so pure and good, wise and beautiful, so innocent and powerful that the mind revolted from trying to imagine them. Now a newborn angel grasped her heel, and it broke my mother's heart.

No human child had ever had a skin so pale, or hair that so nearly matched the blush of a rose.

Thus my mother knew that I was fairy child as well as a bastard born under the horned moon, and though she loved me, she dared not name me. Instead, though I bore no lump like a hunchback or no disfigurement of any kind that made me seem monstrous or ill favored, she merely called me Mooncalfe.

If beauty and wisdom can be said to be curses, no one was more accursed than I.

My mother feared for me. She feared what lusty men might do to me if ever I were found.

So she fled from villages and castles into an abandoned cottage deep in the wooded hills, and perhaps that was for the best. The Saxons were moving north, and on her rare trips to the nearest village, she came back distressed by the news.

At nights I could hear her lying awake, the beads of her rosary clacking as she muttered prayers to her vengeful god, hoping that he would heal me. I knew even then that she prayed in vain, that her god had nothing to do with me.

Mother raised me alone. Time and again she would plead, "Don't wander from the cottage. Never let your face be seen, and never let any man touch you!"

She loved me fiercely, and well. She taught me games and fed me as best she could. She punished me when I did wrong, and she slept with me wrapped in her arms at night.

But if she let me outside to play at all, she did so only briefly, and even then I was forced to cover myself with a robe and a shawl, so that I might hide my face.

Sometimes, at night, she would kneel beneath a cross she had planted in front of the cottage and raise her voice, pleading with her god and his mother. She begged forgiveness, and asked him that I might be healed and made like any other child. She would sometimes cut herself, or pull out her own hair, or beat herself mercilessly, hoping that her god would show pity on her for such self-abuse.

I admit that at times, I too prayed to the Blessed Virgin, but never for myself—only for my mother's comfort.

She sought to cure me of my affliction. She rubbed

me with healing leaves, like evening star and wizard's violet.

When I was three, my mother took a long journey of several days, the first and only one she ever took with me. She had learned in the village that a holy man had died, a bishop who was everywhere named a man of good report, and she badly wanted to burn his bones for me.

So she bundled me up and carried me through the endless woods. Her prayers poured out from her as copiously as did her sweat.

We skirted villages and towns for nearly a week, traveling mostly at night by the light of the stars and a waxing moon, until at last we reached an abbey. My mother found his tomb, and had work prying the stone from his grave. If the bishop were truly a good man, I do not know. His spirit had already fled the place.

But we found his rotting corpse, and my mother severed his hand, and then we scurried away into the night. The abbot must have set his hounds on us, for I remember my mother splashing through the creek, me clinging to her back, while the hounds bayed.

Two nights later, when the moon had waxed full, we found a hilltop far from any habitation, and she lay the bone fire.

We piled up tree limbs and wadded grass into a great circle, and all the time that we did so, mother prayed to her god in my behalf.

"God can heal you, Mooncalfe," she would mutter. "God loves you and can heal you. He can make you look like a common child, I am sure. But in order to gain his greatest blessings, you must say your prayers and walk through the fire of bones. Only then, as the smoke ascends into heaven, will the Father and his handmaid Mary hear your most heartfelt prayer."

It seemed a lot of trouble to me. I was happy and care-free as a child. My greatest concern was for my mother. Having seen all the work she had done, I consented at last.

When the fire burned its brightest, and columns of smoke lit the sky, my mother threw the bishop's severed hand atop the mix, and we waited until we could smell his charred flesh.

Then my mother and I said our prayers, and my mother bid me to leap through the fire.

I did so, begging the blessing of the Virgin and leap-ing through the flames seven times.

Even as a child, I never burned. Until that time, I had merely thought myself fortunate.

But though the fire was so hot that my mother dared not approach it, I leapt through unharmed, untouched by the heat.

On my last attempt, when I saw that the bone fire had still not made me look human, I merely leapt into the conflagration and stood.

I hoped that the flames would blister me and scar me, so that I might look more like a mortal.

My mother screamed in terror and kept trying to draw near, to pull me from the fire, but it burned her badly.

I cried aloud to the Virgin, begging her blessing, but though the flames licked the clothing from my flesh, so that my skirts and cloak all turned to stringy ashes, I took no hurt.

I waited for nearly an hour for the flames to die low before I wearied of the game. Then I helped my mother down to the stream, to bathe her own fire-blistered flesh and ease her torment.

She wept and prayed bitterly, and by dawn she was not fit for travel. She had great black welts on her face, and bubbles beneath the skin, and her skin had gone red—all because she sought to save me from the flames. But as for me, my skin was unblemished. If anything, it looked more translucent. My mother sobbed and confirmed my fears. "You look more *pure* than before."

So it was that I foraged for us both, and after several days we began to walk home in defeat.

After that, mother seemed to lose all hope of ever healing me. She confided a few days later, "I will raise you until you are thirteen but I can do no more after that."

She wanted a life for herself.

She took to making trips to the village more, and I knew that she fell in love, for often when she returned, she would mention a young miller who lived there, a man named Andelin, and she would sometimes fall silent and stare off into the distance and smile.

I am sure that she never mentioned her accursed daughter to him, and I suppose that he could not have helped but love my mother in kind.

One night, late in the summer, my mother returned from the village crying. I asked her why she wept, and she said that Andelin had begged for her hand in marriage, but she had spurned him.

She did not say why. She thought I was still too young to understand how I stood in the way of her love.

Later that night, Andelin himself rode into the woods and called for my mother, seeking our cottage. But it was far from the lonely track that ran through the wood, and my mother was careful not to leave a trail, and so he never found us.

Though I felt sorry for my mother, I was glad when Andelin gave up looking for us.

The thought terrified me that my mother might leave someday. She was my truest companion, my best friend.

But if I was raised alone as a child, the truth is that I seldom felt lonely. In a dark glen not a quarter mile from my home, was a barren place where a woodsman's cottage had once stood. A young boy, Daffyth, had died in the cottage, and his shade still hovered near the spot, for he longed for his mother who would never return.

I could speak with him on all but the sunniest of days, and he taught me many games and rhymes that he'd learned at his mother's knee. He was a desolate boy, lost and frightened. He needed my comfort more than I ever needed his.

For in addition to conversing with him and my mother, I could also speak to animals. I listened to the hungry confabulations of trout in the stream, or the useless prattle of squirrels, or the fearful musings of mice. The rooks that lived against the chimney of our cottage often berated me, accusing me of pilfering their food, but then they would chortle even louder when they managed to snatch a bright piece of blue string from my frock to add to their nests.

But it was not the small animals that gave me the most pleasure. As a child of four, I learned to love a shaggy old wolf bitch who was kind and companionable, and who would warn me when hunters or outlaws roamed the forest.

When, as a small girl, I told my mother what the birds or foxes were saying, she refused to believe me. I was lonely, she thought, and therefore given to vain imaginings. Like any other child, I tended to chatter incessantly, and it was only natural that I would take what company I could find.

Or maybe she feared to admit even to herself that she knew what I could do.

Certainly, she had to have had an intimation.

I know that she believed me when I turned five, for that was the year that I met the white hart. He was old and venerable and wiser than even the wolf or owls. He was the one who first taught me to walk invisibly, and showed me the luminous pathways in the air that led toward the Bright Lady.

"You are one of them," he said. "In time, you must go to her." But I did not feel the goddess's call at that early age.

It was that very year that my mother became ill one dreary midwinter's day—deathly ill, though I did not understand death. Flecks of blood sprayed from her mouth when she coughed, and though her flesh burned with inner fire, she shivered violently, even though I piled all of our coats and blankets on her and left her beside the roaring fire.

"Listen to me," my mother cried one night after a bout of coughing had left her blankets all red around her throat. "I am going to die," she said. "I'm going to die, my sweet Mooncalfe, and I'm afraid you'll die because of it."

I had seen death of course. I'd seen the cold bodies of squirrels, but I'd also seen their shades hopping about merrily in the trees afterward, completely unconcerned. I did not share my mother's fear.

"All right," I said, accepting death.

"No!" my mother shouted, fighting for breath. Tears coursed from her eyes. "It's not *all right*." Her voice sounded marvelously hoarse and full of pain. "You must promise me you'll stay alive. Food. We have plenty of food. But you must keep the fire lit, stay warm. In the spring, you must go north to the nunnery at the edge of the wood."

"All right," I answered with equanimity, prepared to live or die as she willed.

She grew weak quickly.

In those days, I knew little of herb lore or magic. If I'd known then what I do now, perhaps I would have walked the path to the Endless Summer and gathered lungwort and elderflower to combat her cough, and willow and catmint to help ease her pain and gently sweat out the fever.

But as a child I only prayed with her. She prayed to live; I prayed for a quick cessation of her agony.

Her god granted my prayer—the only one that he ever granted me—and she died within hours.

But death did not end my mother's torment. Her shade was restless and longed to watch over me. She thought me abused because of her sin.

So she remained with me in that house, wailing her grief. Each night was a new beginning to her, for like most shades, she would forget all that had happened the night before. I took her to see Daffyth on some occasions, hoping that they might comfort one another, but she gained nothing from it.

She cursed herself for her weakness in allowing herself to be seduced by Sir Jordans, and she often breathed out threats of vengeance.

She loved me and wept over me, and I could not comfort her. Nor did I ever seek out the nunnery, for my mother seemed as alive to me as ever.

I lived and grew. The she-wolf brought me hares and piglets and young deer to eat, until she herself grew old and died. I gathered mushrooms from the forest floor, and the white hart showed me where an old orchard still stood, so that I filled up stores of plums and apples to help last me through each winter.

I foraged and fed myself. As I did, I began to roam the woods and explore. I would leave the old cottage for days at a time, letting my mother stay alone in her torment. On such occasions, she wandered too, searching for her little lost girl.

I found her once, there at the edge of the village, staring at Andelin's house. The miller had grown older, and had married some girl who was not my mother's equal. Their child cried within, and my mother dared not disturb them.

Yet, like me, she stood there at the edge of the forest, craving another person's touch.

I often kept myself invisible on my journeys, and at times I confess that I enjoyed sneaking up on the poachers and outlaws that hid in the wood, merely to watch them, to see what common people looked like, how they acted when they thought themselves alone.

But in my fourteenth summer, I once made the mistake of stepping on a twig as I watched a handsome young man stalking the white hart through tall ferns. The boy spun and released his bow so fast that I did not have time to dodge his shot.

The cold iron tip of his arrow only nicked my arm. Though the wound was slight, still the iron dispelled my charms, and I suddenly found myself standing before him naked (for I had no need of clothes). My heart pounded in terror and desire.

I suddenly imagined what the boy would do, having seen me. I imagined his lips against mine, and his hands pressing firmly into my buttocks, and that he would ravish me. After all, night after night my mother had warned me what men would do if they saw me.

So I anticipated his advances. In fact, in that moment I imagined that I might actually be in love, and so determined that I would endure his passion if not enjoy it.

But to my dismay, when he saw me suddenly standing there naked, he merely fainted. Though I tried to revive him for nearly an hour, each time I did so, he gazed at me in awe and then passed out again.

When night came, I wrapped myself in a cloak of invisibility and let him regain his wits. Then I followed him to his home at the edge of a village. He kept listening for me, and he begged me not to follow, thinking me a succubus or some other demon.

He made the sign of the cross against me, and I begged him to tarry. But he shot arrows at me and seemed so frightened that I dared not follow him farther, for his sake as well as mine.

Soon thereafter I met Wiglan, the wise woman of the barrow. She was a lumpy old thing, almost like a tree trunk with arms. She had been dead for four hundred years, and still her spirit had not flickered out and faded, as so many do, but instead had ripened into something warped and strange and eerie. Moreover, she did not grow forgetful during the days as my mother's shade did, and so she offered me a more even level of companionship.

One night under the bright eternal stars, I told Wiglan of my problem, of how my mother longed for me to look mortal, and how I now longed for it too. I could no longer take comfort in the company of cold shades or in conversations with animals. I craved the touch of real flesh against mine, the kiss of warm lips, the touch of hands, and the thrust of hips.

"Perhaps," Wiglan said, "you should seek out the healing pools up north. If the goddess can heal you at all, there is where you will find her blessing."

"What pools?" I asked, heart pounding with a hope that I had never felt so keenly before.

"There are ancient pools in Wales," she said, "called the Maiden's Fount. While I yet lived, the Romans built a city there, called Caerleon. I heard that they enclosed the fount and built a temple to their goddess Minerva. The fount has great powers, and the Romans honored the goddess in their way, but even then it was a sin, for in honoring the goddess, they sought to hedge her in."

"That was hundreds of years ago," I said. "Are you sure that the fount still springs forth?"

"It is a sacred place to the Lady and all of her kin," Wiglan said. "It will still be there. Go by the light of the horned moon and ask of her what you will. Make an offering of water lilies and lavender. Perhaps your petition will be granted."

Bursting with hope, I made off at once. I set my course by the River or Stars, and journeyed for many days over fields and hills, through dank forest and over the fetid bogs. At night I would sometimes seek directions from the dead, who were plentiful in those days of unrest, until at last after many weeks I reached the derelict temple.

The Saxons had been to Caerleon and burned the city a few years before. A castle stood not far from the ancient temple, but the villages around Caerleon had been burned and looted, its citizens murdered. Little remained of it, and for the moment the castle was staffed by a handful of soldiers who huddled on its walls in fear.

The temple on the hills above the fortress was in worse condition than was the castle. Some of the temple's pillars had been knocked down, and the moon disk above its façade lay broken and in ruins. Perhaps the Saxons had sensed the Lady's power here and sought to put an end to it, or at least sully it.

The pools were overgrown and reedy, while owls hooted and flew on silent wings among the few standing pillars.

There I took my offerings and went to bathe under the crescent moon.

I knelt in the damp mud above the warm pool, cast out a handful of lavender into the brackish water, and stood with a white water lily cupped in my left palm. I whispered my prayers to the goddess, thanking her for the gifts that the earth gave me, for her breasts that were hills, for the fruit of the fields and of the forest. I pleaded with her and named my desire before making my final offering of the lily.

As I prayed, a man's voice spoke up behind me. "She's not that strong anymore. The new god is gaining power over this land, and the Great Mother hides. You seek a powerful magic, one that will change the very essence of what you are—and that is beyond her power. Perhaps you should seek a smaller blessing, ask her to do something easy, like change the future?

"Still, pray to her as you will. It hurts nothing, and I'm glad that some still talk to her."

I turned and looked into the ice-pale eyes of a Welshman, recognized at once my features in his face. *He was my father.* I did not feel surprised to meet him here. After all, my mother had taught me well that demons always seek out and torment their own children.

He stared right at me, his eyes caressing my naked flesh, even though I had been walking invisible.

"Sir Jordans?" I asked. "Or do you have a truer name?"

The fellow smiled wistfully, drew back his hood so that I could see his silvered hair in the moonlight. "I called myself that—but only once. How is your mother? Well, I hope."

"Dead," I answered, then waited in the cold silence for him to show some reaction.

When he saw that he must speak, he finally said, "Well, that happens."

I demanded, "By the Bright Lady, what is your name?" I do not know if the goddess forced him to reveal it because we were at the pool, or if he would have told me anyway, but he answered.

"Merlin. Some call me Merlin the Prophet, or Merlin the Seer. Others name me a magician."

"Not Merlin the Procurer? Not Merlin the Seducer? Not Merlin the Merciless?"

"What I did, I did only once," Merlin said, as if that should buy a measure of forgiveness. "The omens were good that night, for one who wished to produce offspring strong in the old powers. It was the first horned moon of the new summer, after all."

"Is that the only reason you took my mother, because the moon was right?"

"I was not at Tintagel on my own errand," Merlin defended himself. "Uther Pendragon wanted to bed the Duchess Igraine, and he would have killed her husband for the chance. Call me a procurer if you will, but I tried only to save the duke's life—and I foresaw in the process that Pendragon's loins would produce a son who could be a truer and greater king than Uther would ever be."

"Igraine's son? You did not kill the boy?"

"No, Arthur lives with me now, and follows me in my travels. In a year or two, he will learn his destiny," Merlin said. "He will unite all of England and drive back the Saxons, and he will rule this stubborn realm with a gentle hand. . . ." He hunched down in the tall grass beside the pool, stared thoughtfully into water that reflected moon and stars.

"So you helped seduce the Lady Igraine for a noble cause. But why did you bed my mother?"

"For you!" Merlin said in surprise, as if it were obvious. "I saw that night that your mother had fey blood, and all of the omens were right. I saw that you would be wise and beautiful, and the thought came to me that Arthur would need a fair maiden by his side. The old blood is strong in you, both from me and your mother. If you marry Arthur Pendragon, perhaps together we can build a realm where the old gods are worshipped beside the new."

"Didn't you think before you mounted her?" I asked. "Didn't you think about how it would destroy her?"

Merlin said, "I looked down the path of her future. She would have married a stableboy and borne him five fine sons and a brace of daughters. She would have been happier, perhaps—but she would not have had *you!*"

"My mother died in torment because of you!" I shouted. "She died alone in the woods, because she feared letting anyone see me alive. She died friendless, because I was too young and silly to know how to save her. Her spirit is in torment still!"

"Yes, yes," Merlin cajoled as if I did not quite see some greater point, "I'm sure it all seems a tragedy. But you are here, are you not? You—"

I saw then that he would not listen, that my mother's suffering, her loneliness and shame, all meant nothing to him. She was but a pawn in his hand, a piece to be sacrificed for the sake of some greater game.

I knew then that I hated him, and that I could never allow Merlin to use his powers against a woman this way again. And suddenly I glanced up at a shooting star, and I knew that I had the power, that the old blood was strong enough in me, that I could stop him.

"Father," I interrupted him, holding the lily high in my left hand. Merlin shut his mouth. "In the name of the

Bright Lady I curse you: though you shall love a woman fiercely, the greater your desire for her grows, the more lame shall be your groin. Never shall you sire a child again. Never shall you use a woman as your pawn, or your seed as a tool."

I stepped through the rushes to the side of the warm pool at Minerva's failing temple, felt the living power of the goddess there as my toe touched the water.

"No!" Merlin shouted and raised his hand with little finger and thumb splayed in a horn as he tried to ward off my spell.

But either he was too late, or the spell was too strong for him. In any case, I tossed the white lily into the still waters.

As the wavelets rolled away from the lily, bounding against the edges of the pool, Merlin screamed in agony and put his hands over his face.

I believe that he was peering into his own bleak future as he cried in horror, *"No! No! No!"*

I knelt and dipped my hand in the pool seven times, cupping the water and letting it run down my breasts and between my legs.

Then I stood and merely walked away.

Sometimes near dawn, I waken and think that I can still hear Merlin's cries ringing in my ears. I listen then, and smile a fey smile.

In time I made it back to my cottage in the woods, and I told the shade of my mother about all that had transpired. She seemed more at peace that night than ever before, and so before daybreak, I introduced her to the child Daffyth once again.

I told Daffyth that she was his mother, and convinced my mother's shade that Daffyth was a forgotten son, born from her love for a man named Andelin.

In the still night I coaxed them to the edge of the woods, and let them go.

When last I saw them, they were walking hand-in-hand on the road to Tintagel.

As for me, I learned in time to praise the goddess for her goodness and for what I am and always hope to be—a mooncalfe, and no sorcerer's pawn.

Avalonia

Kristen Britain

Mist curled and wove about the ruins of the old abbey like trailing, winding strips of gauze. The Tor was long lost to sight in the fog, though once, a window had opened, revealing a brief, titillating view of the fourteenth-century tower atop it.

Vapor coated Anne Wilder's glasses, obscuring her vision further. She tore them off her face in vexation and rubbed the lenses clear with the tail of her scarf. What had possessed her to visit Glastonbury on such a foul day? Even the tourists, who usually came in busloads seeking the spell of Arthurian legend, had fled Glastonbury for the shopping districts of London.

She had come on the word of a blind musician.

Last night she had taken supper in a pub down the street from her bed and breakfast. During a break in the band's Celtic repertoire, one of the musicians made his way to the bar, uncannily avoiding the clutter of tables, chairs, and patrons as though he traveled a well-worn path. He sat on a stool beside her. The barkeep passed him a pint of dark, bitter ale, and he reached for it instinctively, whereupon he turned to Anne.

"You are new here, aren't you," he said. It was a statement of fact.

How did he even know she sat beside him? "Yes. How can you—"

"And American by your accent. What brings you to England?"

Anne wondered at his interest. She was but one of millions of tourists who inundated Britain yearly. He seemed friendly enough, however, and if he wanted a bit of conversation, she welcomed it after her solitary travels.

"A walking tour of Scotland," she said. "And some birdwatching along the coast, and . . ." A great weariness had prompted her escape, a weight on her shoulders. Too many battles she had fought, and lost. She shrugged, then remembered he could not see. "I came, I guess, for whatever reason anyone travels."

"Hmmm." He took a swig of his ale, then turned to survey her with eyes that could not see. They were a startling blue beneath frosty eyebrows. "You seek something deeper."

"Excuse me?"

He leaned close to her and said, "I hear it in your voice and words, m'dear. A longing to remember that not all mysteries can be answered with science."

Anne shifted uncomfortably on her stool, her own ale since forgotten at her elbow. Mysteries? His words didn't make sense to her, though he had spoken with the conviction of a prophet. And science? Did he somehow know of her work?

Maybe he was a nut. She glanced around for an escape route and tried to think up a polite excuse.

To her horror, the musician clamped his hand on her wrist, as if to prevent her from leaving. His knuckles were gnarled with age, like burnished tree roots. "Go to Glastonbury," he said.

"Why?"

"I've the second sight, you see." He thumped his temple with a stout index finger. "You will find memory in Glastonbury, and a power in the land that still dwells there. I know this."

Anne almost laughed in his face. What kind of New Age nonsense was this? A travel brochure had proclaimed Glastonbury as a major Arthurian site, as though King Arthur had been historical fact rather than overdone fiction. Yet she did not laugh, for the musician's expression was painfully earnest.

He sniffed the air as if it could tell him something. "In Glastonbury, you will find memory. Belief. And perhaps a choice." He then gulped down a swig or two of his ale and left her to rejoin his band.

Anne sniffed the air, too, but smelled nothing more remarkable than cigarette smoke, cooked food, and her own ale. The musician took up his fiddle, and the band worked its way into a slow, mournful ballad.

Anne sniffed the air now. It was laden with damp; not just the damp of air, but of reeds and mud and . . . well, a wetland. Legend held that the old abbey sat upon what was once the Isle of Avalon, but there was no lake to surround it now.

Natural succession, Anne thought. A shallow lake or pond soon turns to meadowland. Terra firma, the solid ground beneath her feet. This she understood.

Yet, when she took her next step, her foot lifted with a sucking sound. Her shoes were soaked.

So here she was in Glastonbury on a foul, damp, and

foggy day because a blind musician with the second sight told her she would find memory and belief. And perhaps a choice. She snorted in contempt. There were gift shops, museums, and the ruins. Ruins and museums held little allure for her. History confounded her, especially in a land such as this where it was layered like an onion—Roman walls, medieval castles, standing stones. And then there were the peoples—Saxons, Picts, Romans, Celts, and Britons. . . . Legends simply confused the issue. It was too much.

She thought she should return to her lodgings to fight off the chill with hot tea and biscuits, and maybe plan a hike in the Lake Country to watch more birds and take in the landscape. She turned back toward the abbey, but the fog folded in around her, a dense opaque cloak. She tried wiping off her glasses again, to no avail.

Anne combed her fingers through lank, sloppy curls. Though there was no discernible landmark and she was unsure of her direction, she did not panic. She had felt more lost, more overwhelmed, in the few great cathedrals she had visited. She would pick a direction and walk. Eventually she would come to some landmark, someone's house, a footpath, or maybe the abbey.

Ahead, a great swirl of mist was accompanied by wingbeats. She pressed forward eagerly, and witnessed a swan flapping its great pale wings before it vanished utterly into the mist.

A swan where there is no lake . . .

She halted to take her bearings, but there was no way to do so. Even on the coast of northern New England where she had lived for many years now, she had rarely seen so dense a fog. Still, her apparent isolation did not arouse panic, though she began to feel the first few pangs of concern.

The mist is an enchantment, maybe, but such whimsical notions were gone with her childhood. Her mind lay in the realm of science and fact and provable results. Not fantasy. Not history. Not legend.

Yet, she couldn't help but sense the antiquity of the place, and its charm. It almost seemed to flow from the ground, through her feet, and upward through her body. Odd she had not felt this way when standing in the awesome splendor of cathedrals with their multifaceted windows and detailed artistry. She had simply felt very small and alien, and she had not lingered. Instead, she sought out the countryside, avoiding historic structures of all kinds.

Maybe it was because she felt a kinship with the land. After all, wasn't her home in New England and parts of Britain composed of some of the same rock? A geologic phenomenon called a terrane, a bit of continental crust, transformed by Pangaea, when all lands became one. The terrane had been called *Avalonia* . . . The hills she walked back home bore a strain of the same ancient, ancient lineage of the land she now walked.

The antiquity of Glastonbury was in the very air she breathed, and in the sense of place. Legend lived in the mists . . . The musician had said there were mysteries that science could not answer.

She let the mists gently waft by her, settle on her shoulders, caress her cheeks. She denied his words. Better to know geology and the names of birds. Better to know the behavior of mammals and the scientific method. These things existed in her world and were tangible. The only mysteries she sought were those which could be unraveled by science.

Or so she thought. Her very certainty brought a sense of emptiness and sorrow and loss. It left no room for dreams, or the kind of mysteries the musician had spoken of.

She cleaned vapor from her glasses once again, and closed her eyes, feeling that resonance in the land flowing into her. She was a wildlife biologist because she loved the land and all the interconnections of species that lived on it. She armed herself with science, research, and facts in a battle to preserve the natural world.

A seemingly losing battle. Thus her weariness and the weight on her shoulders.

As she stood there, she imagined she heard a horse, and then more than one, gallop through the mist. The earth trembled beneath her feet with their passing. She imagined the shouts and cries of men, and a clash like the striking of metal upon metal; like sword striking sword. She scented iron and blood in the damp air.

She opened her eyes, but the imagining did not stop. The mist billowed and swirled, sculpting men and horses about her, gray and timeless, but with a certain substance. She turned around and around trying to make rational sense of what she saw, but her scientific mind could find no good conclusions about the gleam of light radiating from armor and weapons from another age. Warriors fought and fell all around her, their cries like those of a fading echo.

One warrior rode amidst the others, a crown encircling his helm. He was more radiant than the others, his tabard bloodied. He carried an exquisite sword, flaming in his hand. This he pointed at Anne, and over the distance that separated them, he said in a quiet, calm voice that belied the strivings and carnage around them, "Your disbelief will lose the battle."

And with an astonished blink from Anne, the warrior—the *king*—and the battle around her rolled away as mist.

Ghosts? But Anne did not believe in ghosts. She let go a shuddering sigh, desiring to be back beside the fireplace in her bed and breakfast, snug and dry, with nothing more extraordinary around her than Victorian furnishings and the drone of a television in the common room.

The scent of wetland carried more strongly to her now, overladen with apple blossoms though it was not spring. She heard a gentle lapping, as though of a lake upon the shore. She turned about again, and there, incredibly, the mist parted revealing the edge of a lake.

"I must have wandered farther than I thought," she murmured, not remembering a lake pictured on any of the glossy brochures about Glastonbury she had picked up.

"Far, indeed." A woman stepped barefoot among reeds and rushes of the shore. She was an elderly woman with ivory hair loosely braided down her back and a green laurel upon her brow like a crown. She wore a shawl and a simple dress of blue-green wool. Her eyes were as piercing as those of a kestrel that misses nothing, but still gentle. She approached Anne, clutching her shawl.

Another vision?

When the woman stood but a pace from Anne, she extended her hand, palm up, the lines that creased it clearly defined.

"Touch my hand, child, and you will know I am no simple vision."

Anne did, resting the tips of her fingers lightly on the woman's palm. She felt the warmth of earthly flesh, but there was more. It was the same sensation of the earth beneath her feet singing inwards through her veins and heart, and from the woman she scented loam, like one who works with the soil and brings forth green, growing things, as a gardener.

Anne withdrew her hand almost reluctantly, her heart

pounding. Here she found resonance, here panic swelled within her: mystery.

"Who are you?" Anne asked. "And—and where am I?"

"Don't you know?" The question was sad, not coy. "Yes, I see you do not know. You have been fighting for so long that you have lost sight of why." The woman transfixed Anne with her quick, piercing eyes. "You have come where so few can cross over, for the way has been nearly obliterated. Your coming is a sign of hope."

Anne stared blankly at her, and the woman chuckled.

"You hail from far away," the woman said. "There is a freshness of spirit about you. A child who thrives in a place of wild, tall pines and seaspray."

How did she know? "New England. I live in New England."

The woman raised both brows. "Truly." But there was no surprise in her voice.

Because silence fell between them and Anne felt a need to fill it, she babbled, "I am a biologist at a wildlife refuge there."

The woman sighed, and it was like a breath of a breeze that rustled tree limbs. "Such is the day that nature's creations must be set aside in refuges."

"If we didn't," Anne said a little defensively, "it would be all gone."

"As I said, such is the day."

They strolled the shoreline of the lake in silence for a time, the woman's skirts trailing along the ground. It seemed to Anne that tiny white flowers blossomed in the woman's wake.

"Tell me, child, how is it in this refuge? How do you care for what you protect there?"

Now Anne walked on solid ground. She recited her research into seabird populations. She spoke of monitoring the reproductive rates and successes and mortalities of terns, puffins, and razorbills. She spoke of data and papers and publications, and of a not-so-far-off doctorate.

When she finished, slightly breathless, the woman's expression had changed little. She halted and turned to Anne. She took both of Anne's hands into her own, and again there was that resonance, the grounding.

"Why do you pursue this, child?"

Anne drew her eyebrows together in consternation. She had just explained it all. "So we can understand the implications of—"

"No, child." The woman had not raised her voice. "Look deeper. You have neglected a part of your spirit. Gaze into the lake and look deeper."

The woman squeezed her hands in reassurance and led her to the very lake edge. She peered into the shallows, through the reeds. The water was glassy and she could see to the muddy bottom. A frog plopped into the water nearby, sending ripples in ever widening rings. A bluish light cast off the water's surface, and Anne began to see herself.

She is nine years old on a visit to Isle Royale National Park in Michigan. She is camping with her family. A ululating cry pierces the night, followed by others in an unearthly chorus. It is like a summons to her, and even now she feels its power.

"What is it, Daddy?" she asks.

His head is cocked, listening, a strange expression on his face. Everyone is quiet, even her little brother, Matt.

"Wolves," her father says. "They are speaking to one another."

She shivers.

Other images and sensations flowed through Anne's

mind: miniature alpine flowers blossoming on the mountain heights; gigantic Sequoia trees looming toward the heavens, more awesome to her than any cathedral; the sweet scent of pine resin on a hot summer day; the wingbeats and honking of wild geese rising into the bronze, autumn sky . . .

These memories and more surged through Anne, and when she opened her eyes, she found herself on her knees, the wet ground seeping through her pants, and a torrent of tears rolling down her cheeks.

"Do you remember, child?"

"Yes," Anne whispered. She had found memory. "Who are you?"

The woman smiled gently. "You have penetrated the mists between worlds, to Avalon. Once I was known in both worlds. The old beliefs are but gone, except on Avalon. Still, I think in your heart, you know me."

Anne scrambled to her feet, pulling off her glasses so she could dab at her eyes with the end of her scarf. "Avalon—just legend. And you . . ." She shook her head. "No, I can't believe what I think you're asking me to believe."

"You have removed yourself from belief," the woman said.

"I have no faith of the kind you suggest," Anne said. "I move in the world of statistics and results, not in a world of myth and legend. I believe what I can see."

"What do you see when you look at me?"

Before Anne could stop herself, she said, "I see the rain and rivers and the lakes. I hear in your voice the song of the ocean and the breeze. I see all living things and their strengths."

The woman nodded and wiped away a tear that glided down Anne's cheek. "It is so. And there is another you must see. Another moment of faith, if you will."

Unbidden, the warrior king stepped from the mist, his bright sword now sheathed at his side, his helm tucked beneath his arm. "My lady," he said. He bent to his knee before the woman.

"Rise, my child."

And he did.

Anne shuddered. The woman was asking too much of her; asking her to make too great a leap of faith.

"He does not exist," she said. "He's a story. Legend."

"Indeed?" The king glared upon Anne, his bearing imperious. "Legend gives me life. Belief. A story so oft repeated, and it changes with the telling. I have been Artorius, Artos, and Arthur. I am the warrior who comes again and again."

"A legend does not live."

"Your denial will not only close the way to this world, but deny it of the inexplicable, the mysteries. A loss of hope."

"You have memory once again," the woman said, "but only belief can give rise to hope and dreams. Without hope or dreams, you have lost the battle before it has begun."

"I was given this blade to bring hope," the king said. He drew the sword and held it aloft. "I betrayed that hope, and I must always return to the field of battle to redeem myself."

"The way between the worlds is fast closing forever," the woman said. "So few in your world believe. Without belief, all mystery will cease. That which you love and fight to preserve will wither, and you will have lost more than a battle."

Anne could not speak. Their words swirled great turmoil within her. She was used to a certain surety in her world. There was that which was true, and that which

was false. Cut and dry. Black and white. Yet two legends
stood before her. And it was not a dream.

"A choice presents itself," the woman said.

"A choice?"

The woman twined her fingers together in front of her.
"You are a child of the land. You sense it strongly—it's a
sense of spirit. One does not need crumbling walls or
castles to mark their place in the world. Your place, your
roots are here."

"Here?"

"The spirit of Avalon runs in your veins, child."

There was a prickling on the back of Anne's neck.

"A remnant of the old blood is within you. It has
drawn you here. And you may remain here, child, if you
wish, for Avalon is a refuge of sorts. But first you must
believe."

Anne looked from the woman to the king. Both were
grave. Both were as still as trees on a day without a
breeze.

Avalon runs in your veins, child. Anne had come here,
unsure of her purpose. Yet, she had found memory;
memory of why her work was so important to her, why
she fought so hard a battle. Never had she anticipated
this.

I cannot explain this. Nor could she explain the magic
of a wolf's cry in the night, or the sensation she felt
when she watched the aurora borealis. *Perhaps I am not
all fact and logic after all.*

"I believe," was all she said.

"And will you stay? You will not be able to return to
your world."

Anne wondered what lay beyond the mist. Should she
stay, would it be like traveling in time? What sort of
magics were at work there? What was Avalon like? Curiosity had made her a scientist, and she looked beyond

the woman and the king as though some vision might reveal Avalon to her. But she could only go there if she chose to.

"If I go, what will happen to this world?"

"It will continue on. There is great sorrow ahead—a grayness. Without a champion, your world will wither."

Anne nodded. The curiosity that had made her a scientist also reminded her that she left her work undone. She couldn't abandon it, but she could return to it with new insight. With memory of why she began it all in the first place. What better tribute to the lady was there than completing work that would help preserve at least a part of the world that moved out of sync with Avalon?

Anne passed her hand through her curls. "I must return to my work. I am one to help make refuges, not one to seek refuge."

The woman smiled. "I know, my child. And you will go with my blessing." She kissed Anne tenderly on the cheek. "Perhaps your work will open another path to Avalon, for though the way is closed, Avalon will always exist. And you will find places that resonate with the old power, even in a faraway place of wild, tall pines and seaspray."

The woman turned and walked away, the mists winding and folding about her, until she vanished.

The king made a short bow. "I, too, must go. My tale leaves off where yours begins. I am weary beyond measure."

And Anne saw it in his face. Too many battles, too many betrayals. This was not the Arthur of stories about chivalry, honor, and courtly love. This was not the Arthur of a dozen shallow Hollywood movies.

It goes deeper.

"I leave this in your keeping." He handed her the great sword, hilt first.

She expected it to weigh more, to be cold to the touch, but it was neither of these things. It possessed only lightness.

"When you are no longer able to carry it," the king said, "when you, too, are over wearied, bring it to this place and cast it into the lake."

The king, too, turned and faded into the mist.

For many moments, Anne stood where she was, suddenly feeling bereft and lonely, and realizing the opportunity she had forsaken. But as the dense fog thinned and she was able to discern the outline of the Lady Chapel up the slope, she felt her spirit renewed, a new sense of purpose now that her memory had been restored. A new sense of hope now that belief bloomed in her heart.

The swan glided from the mist and flew overhead in a circle before landing in front of her. The swan curved its long, elegant neck and folded its wings to its sides.

Not all legends had stayed within Avalon.

The swan then thrust its head upwards and it grew in a single fluid rush, transforming into the figure of a man— the blind musician. He extended his hand to her.

She took it into her own, marveling at how easy it was to believe.

"I will guide you," the musician said.

Anne smiled, knowing that she would not be alone on this side of Avalon after all. And perhaps the way to Avalon would reopen one day, just as the lady had said, and she would follow the path that led into the mists. But for now, sword in hand, she would return to her own work, to the land with the ancient soul whose lineage was also of the land she now walked upon: Avalonia.

Finding the Grail

Judith Tarr

"And why," asked Melisende, "may not a woman find the Grail?"

"Because," Queen Guinevere replied with that air of sweet reason with which she answered every question she was ever asked, "quests are given to men. To knights. Even kings, if the kings are suitably inspired. Whereas we," she said, pausing to admire the completion of yet another delicate flower in her tapestry, "remain at home, tend the castle, wait and pray for our lords' safe return."

Several of the queen's ladies crossed themselves. "We pray," they said to one another in voices like the twittering of birds—that being the fashion in Camelot this season; last season it had been laughter like little golden bells. "We pray that they may come back to us; that they be whole, or as whole as need be. And that when they go out again, as men must do, they go not too quickly, but not too slowly, either."

Melisende rolled her eyes. Having already stained the
fine linen with blood once today, she was relegated to
choosing the colors for the next portion of the tapestry.
Her finger still stung where the needle had pricked it,
but she had never minded pain. She minded much more
that she must sit here among these ornamental idiots, lit
by a shaft of sun, separating crimson from scarlet from
henna, and laying the twists of thread in tidy rows near
the queen's hand.

Try though she would, she could not help but hear the
sounds that drifted up to the queen's bower from the
courtyard below. The quest for the Grail would not begin
until the morning, but there was a great clamor and clatter in the palace as the knights made ready to go. Some
would go with retinues, squires and servants, trains of
baggage, and everything that they reckoned proper to a
knightly campaign. Others chose the simpler way, a single squire and a small train of mules, and no more than a
remount or two, and a groom for the heavy destrier that,
with his armor, made each knight a knight.

The women chattered heedlessly above the clamor.
They would weep and wail soon enough, but for the moment their minds, such as they were, were engaged in
the latest round of gossip, and a terrible scandal: Sir Di-
nadan's wife seen in, of all horrors, last year's gown at
this year's feast of Pentecost.

Melisende laid the last twist of crimson beside scarlet
beside henna, close by the queen's white hand, and quietly, under cover of the scandal, slipped away.

There was little enough quiet to be had in Camelot on the
eve of the Grail-quest, but such as there was, Melisende
found it. It was not, as might have been more usual, in
one of the chapels—those were full of knights and
squires praying to succeed on the quest—but in the stable

under the great hall. The king's horses were kept there, and the queen's palfreys, and a few odd beasts: a pony or two for the pages, the chaplain's mule, and an elderly but once noble creature who had, it was said, served honorably under the Lord Merlin.

Melisende's mare lived next to the old gelding. Blanca was much too opinionated to suffer any lesser companion. The two of them kept to their distant corner of the stable, shared bits of hay and cut fodder, and conversed companionably over handfuls of white barley. The stable-lads tended to avoid them, muttering that the mare was as witchy as the gelding—and everyone knew that he was half a devil like his master.

Melisende saw nothing devilish in that elderly and gentle beast. His eyes were strange, to be sure, as pale as glass, and his coat was the color of cream; but they were soft eyes for all their oddness, and his manners were impeccable in taking the bits of apple and honeycake that she had brought as tribute. Blanca was far more insistent, and far less polite about it.

Between the mare and the gelding, Melisende rested for a while. She stroked tangles out of Blanca's thick waving mane, and brushed the gelding with a twist of straw. He nibbled the long plait of her hair. "I would never wish," she said to him, "that I had been born a man, except for this: that men do everything worth doing in the world."

The gelding rumbled gently to himself, seeking in his manger for stray bits of barley.

"But they do!" Melisende insisted, as if he had taken issue with her. "What can a woman do but sit at home and wait and pray, embroider tapestries and weave war-cloaks and twitter like a bird in a cage? Why *can't* a woman find the Grail?"

There was no answer to that, which a horse might

give. Melisende set her teeth and knit her brows and attacked the cream-pale coat as if its cleanliness were the most important thing in the world.

As she set herself to make the Lord Merlin's old gelding immaculate, and after him her own moon-silver Blanca, voices drifted toward her from the outer door. Everyone, she had thought, was busy elsewhere, but it seemed that two men had found occasion to visit the king's horses.

One voice she recognized easily enough. There was no mistaking that deep lovely burr. Sir Gawain was a man for the ladies, everybody knew it, but Melisende had never liked him less for that.

The other needed a moment, and its owner's motion across the light. But of course: it was the new stable-lad, the one who looked after the king's horses, whose name was something or other, but whom everyone called Beaumains for his fine white hands and his pretty manners. He was some knight's by-blow, people said, with ambitions far above his station; but Melisende had never noticed that he put himself forward. He was a tall, slender, shy person with milk-white skin and a face as pretty as a girl's, for all that he tried to hide it behind a mask of dirt and a dusty black mane.

It was not so well hidden now; in fact it was glaring up at tall broad Gawain, who glared formidably down. "You will not," Gawain said.

"I will," said Beaumains as haughtily as any prince—and to the prince of Orkney, no less.

Gawain glowered at it, but he did not strike the boy for his presumption, nor reprimand him for it, either. "This is a quest for knights," he said, echoing the queen, if he had only known it. "Not for—"

"I will go," Beaumains said, "and you will not stop me. There is no way that you can."

"No way?" Gawain's head sank between his wide shoulders; his voice lowered to a growl. Something in the movement, and in the way Beaumains's own head turned, lifting its chin, made Melisende's eyes sharpen. Was it—could it be—?

No. Not likely. Gawain was hardly old enough for a son as old as Beaumains. Brother, then?

Yes, that could be. Gawain was older, broader, heavier, and the black beard hid somewhat of his face; but the breadth of the brow, the blue flash of the eyes under the thick dark hair—those were very like. Very like indeed.

They quarreled like brothers, that was certain, face to face and no quarter given. "Maybe *I* cannot stop you," Gawain said deep in this throat. "Mother, on the other hand—"

"No," said Beaumains. Simply, and obstinately, that.

"Are you daring me to try?"

Beaumains's chin came up even further. It was vastly provoking; Melisende marveled that Gawain, great knight and prince that he was, did not simply slap the boy silly and have done with it. But Gawain never lifted a hand, even when Beaumains said, "You don't have time to send to Mother. In the morning, at dawn, you ride out with all the rest, hunting a thing that you know you'll never find."

Gawain started as if struck. His face above the beard had gone as white as Beaumains's own. "I have given my oath," he said.

"So you have," said Beaumains. "So have all the knights, every one. Fools and dreamers, the lot of them."

"And you, who tend the king's horses—are you any less a fool?"

"Maybe not," Beaumains said. "But I will go. I would like to see it if I can."

"Only a pure knight may see it," Gawain said. "That is the prophecy."

"Of all men," said Beaumains, "a pure knight only. Yes." He smiled, a strange, tight smile, like the curve of a blade in his pale face. "I will go, eldest brother. I will find the Grail. That I swear to you, before God and His Mother and the king's fine horses."

Gawain hissed between his teeth and lifted his hand— but only to cross himself; not to strike that odd and insolent boy. "On your head be it," he said, "and if your life is forfeit, then may God's Mother defend you."

Beaumains bowed his head, that was far too haughty for a stableboy's, and murmured something that sounded like a prayer. But when he looked up, he was as arrogant as ever. "You'll not find the Grail," he said, "but if God and His Mother hear my prayer, they'll bring you home again, little sadder and somewhat wiser than you were before."

It was a blessing, in its way. Gawain bent his head to it—as startling as everything else he had done—and turned on his heel with a jingling of knightly spurs, and stalked out into the stableyard.

He left a great quiet behind him, and a brother who stood for a long while stiff and still, with his white hands clenched at his sides. Then, all at once, Beaumains gave way, not quite falling, but shrinking and dwindling into the stableboy whom Melisende had thought she knew: gangling, awkward, with tangled black hair half-hiding his face. The eyes that had shown themselves so vividly blue were veiled under lowered lids. He drew a breath that shook a little, and turned slowly, as if he did not know quite what to do with himself.

Melisende did not think, until too late, of sinking down behind Merlin's old gelding and letting the boy think himself alone. Even as she thought of it, Blanca snorted and stamped, demanding her royal share of Melisende's attention.

Beaumains spun about, staring full into Melisende's face. Oh, those eyes were blue—blue as flax-flowers, blue as the sky in summer. She had never seen eyes so blue.

They startled her out of all good sense. They made her say, "If you can find the Grail, then so can I."

Beaumains did not say the thing she expected, which was that only a man could go questing after magic and mystery. Nor did he laugh, which astonished her. He regarded her gravely, as if her words were actually worth considering—and that, in a prince disguised as a stable-boy, was a wonderful thing. "The queen will let you go?" he asked her.

"I don't care if she does or not," Melisende said more than a little crossly. "I *want* to go."

"Then go," Beaumains said. Just that, as if it were a perfectly reasonable thing to say.

Melisende gaped at him. "You aren't supposed to encourage me!"

"Why not?" Beaumains made his way slowly down the aisle. The horses whickered at him—even Blanca, the hussy, who arched her lovely neck and begged, and all but purred as he rubbed it. Beaumains's fingers were very clever and very skilled. He focused himself on them, as if to shut out Melisende and Gawain and every other unpleasant thing.

"I want," said Melisende, "to find the Grail."

"Why?"

He had startled her again: he was listening after all, and aware of her, even with his eyes fixed on Blanca.

"Because," she said after a moment, "I want to. Do I need more reason than that?"

Beaumains did not answer.

Maybe he did not require more answer than that. But
Melisende went on, because after all she needed to. "Do
you remember on the feast of Pentecost, when the king
wouldn't sit to dinner until he saw a marvel, and when
everyone was ready to go to war for hunger, the vision
came on us all? Even we saw it—even we women: the
cup full of light, floating in the air. That was magic, I
know it was; I could see Merlin in the shadows, shaping
it. And maybe others saw him, too, and knew; and
maybe not. But it doesn't matter. He made a marvel for
us all, and it possessed us. It called us to it. It made us
want—it made us yearn for the Grail."

"Yes," said Beaumains, "and Merlin is half a devil.
Maybe he did it to break the Round Table, and to empty
Camelot, and lay it open to its enemies."

"Maybe," Melisende said. "And maybe it was time—
maybe the knights were bored, with all their battles won,
and no enemies left to fight, and nothing to do but lie
about and play at dice and indulge in petty squabbles.
Maybe they needed a great quest. Maybe they needed a
purpose, a reason to be what they are."

"That doesn't explain why you want to do it," said
Beaumains.

"Or you." Melisende shook her head. "There isn't a
good reason, is there? Except I think it's real. I think
there is a Grail, and it calls us—yes, even me. Even a
woman, and an excessively young one at that, who has
much more skill with the bow than with the needle, who
has never had any talent for the arts of courts, and who
would rather sit on a horse than in a lady's bower.
Maybe that's why? Maybe the magic takes me for a kind
of crooked boy?"

Beaumains laughed suddenly, startling her speechless.
"Maybe," he said. "There are so many maybes in this
world. Shall we go questing together, then? Two may be

stronger than one, after all. And I can shoot, and use a sword, too, and a lance."

"I can use a spear," said Melisende. "I killed a boar once."

Was that admiration? Or disbelief? Maybe both. "Then you'll be a strong companion."

"But hardly a proper one," Melisende said—not willingly at all, but her upbringing was too strong to keep her silent. "A lady of rank and a stableboy—even if he is really a prince—"

"I solemnly swear to you," said Beaumains, "that my conduct toward you will never be less than perfectly proper. This on my mother's soul, by the very Mother of God."

"It's still not—" Melisende bit her tongue. No, it would never be proper, unless it were a proper scandal: Count Bleys's youngest daughter running off on quest with a scapegrace prince from Orkney. And yet that prince had sworn a vow. Meeting those blue, blue eyes, Melisende knew that he would keep it. He was as honorable as his brother Gawain was ever known to be, that was clear to see; but he had none of Gawain's weakness for the ladies.

Maybe he was simply too young. He had no beard at all yet. His cheeks were as smooth as Melisende's own, and notably fairer.

With beating heart and breath catching in her throat, she held out her hand. "Very well, then. We'll hunt the Grail together. And if we find it—well, we'll be a scandal together, or a marvel for the next feast of Pentecost. Or both."

Beaumains's fine white hand clasped her broader, plumper, browner one. They bound the pact so, with the horses to witness. Then they went their separate ways,

Melisende to prepare as she could—but never to repent of it—and Beaumains, she did not doubt, to do the same.

"Until the dawn," she said.

Beaumains nodded. Then he was gone, vanished in the shadows of the stable.

Melisende was ready long before dawn. The air was chill, the stars hidden in haze, though no rain fell. She crept out of the room she shared with the rest of the queen's ladies, dressed in clothes that she had brought with her from home but thought never to wear again: old riding clothes that had belonged to her brothers, worn leather and age-softened linen, and a mantle that she had woven herself of wool from her father's sheep. She carried her bow and the quiver of arrows and a knife, but no spear; for all her bravado, she had known of no way to conceal such a weapon, nor was she bold enough to steal one from the king's armory.

The horses were waiting, saddled and bridled, and Beaumains standing between them: Blanca, of course, but the other widened Melisende's eyes. Merlin's gelding snorted gently in the quiet. A mule stood behind him, carrying more baggage than Melisende might have imagined they would need. Beaumains was, after all, a prince, though he played at being a stableboy.

As Melisende approached, Beaumains mounted the gelding with the air of one who has every right, and took the mule's lead in his hand. He barely left her time to claim her own and mount before he sent the gelding forward. The gelding, whose name Melisende had never known, if indeed it had one, submitted with good will to this new master, nor seemed in any way disturbed to be put back to work again.

The guards on the nearest gate were asleep or absent, the gate unbarred. Beaumains rode through it as if it were no more than he had expected. Melisende followed as close as she could, biting her tongue against the crowding questions. He was what he was. Nothing that he did should surprise her—except, maybe, that he accepted her as his companion.

The light grew slowly, a grey morning, but the sun rose above the haze. Melisende could feel it in her skin. By noon the clouds would all be gone, and the day as fair as a day could be in this isle of Britain.

By full morning, Camelot was well behind them. Melisende had found her wits and, somewhat more slowly, her tongue. "You're riding Merlin's horse," she said mildly.

Beaumains, who was riding somewhat ahead, did not pause or look back, but the set of his shoulders told her that he had heard.

"If you've stolen him," Melisende said, "Merlin might object."

"Merlin told me to take him," Beaumains said.

"He did not."

"Are you calling me a liar?"

"No," Melisende said after a moment. "But—"

The gelding halted. Blanca came up beside him. Beaumains did not seem angry, but his face was stiff. "My brother would have given me one of his palfreys," Beaumains said, "but the Lord Merlin offered this one instead. The old gentleman is bored, he said, and sad with confinement. A quest will bring him back his youth again."

"How kind of the Lord Merlin," Melisende said.

Beaumains shrugged, as if her doubt mattered little to him after all, and let the horse walk on. Melisende, who had seen the Lord Merlin only at a distance and only in sorcerous robes, tried to imagine a world in which wizards were kindly old uncles, and their horses free to be

borrowed for quests and ridings about. It was not a
world she had ever lived in, away in her father's country.
It had seemed great and terrible enough that, rough child
that she was, she was sent to Camelot to be the queen's
waiting-woman.

And now she had run away with a stableboy who happened to be Sir Gawain's brother, questing for the Grail
as only knights were supposed to do. Her father would
be terribly angry. Her mother would throw up her hands
in despair. And the queen . . .

The queen would not care, except for the insult to herself.

Melisende could have turned back then. There was
time. She could pretend that she had gone for a morning
ride before the courts filled with knights setting out on
the quest, and forgotten the time and come back late.
Her punishment would not be too heavy, with so much
else to distract the queen and her ladies. No one would
even remember the infraction after the sentence was
meted out.

But Melisende did not turn Blanca's head, or even
glance over her shoulder at the distant towers of
Camelot. Her face fixed resolutely forward. She was
going to find the Grail. Or, at the very least, she meant to
try.

Beaumains rode westward. Melisende, for lack of greater
inspiration, let him choose the direction, though she
asked, in one of their first camps, "Why west? Most of
the knights are going east, over the sea. The Grail is in
Spain, some say, or in Rome. Or in Byzantium, or the
kingdom of Prester John. West is little enough country,
and then the sea again."

"The Holy Spear is said to be in Spain," Beaumains
said, "and there are relics enough in Rome and Byzan-

tium, and maybe one is the cup of the Last Supper. But," he said, "I think the Grail is close by. And the Lord Merlin knows where it is."

"If he knows that," Melisende said, "wouldn't he have brought it to Camelot? Wouldn't that have been simpler than sending all the knights away?"

"Maybe," said Beaumains. *And maybe not,* he did not say, but Melisende heard it clearly enough.

"I'm surprised he didn't tell you what he knew," Melisende said rather nastily, "since you're so much in his confidence."

"No one is in the Lord Merlin's confidence. Even the king." Beaumains prodded the fire, which was dying too quickly, and fed it with a dry branch. Green ones whispered above them, a wood of oak and ash which offered them shelter against the threat of rain.

Beaumains's face in the leaping light was strange and rather wild. He looked like a creature of the wood, half a devil himself perhaps—and who was to say that he was not? His mother Morgause worked great magics in her cold bower in Orkney, it was said—though her sons who had come to court, except for this one, seemed mortal enough, with human gifts and failings.

Maybe this was her devil-child, and the Lord Merlin had recognized the kinship. And maybe that was preposterous, and he was only what he seemed: a tall thin boy not quite a man, beardless still and light voiced, but strong. He had offered Melisende no impertinence, kept to himself and made no effort to spy on her when she dressed or bathed. He was as faultless a companion as a lady could wish for, with his inborn princely grace and his quiet manners.

She found him more annoying the longer she traveled with him. No man was as pure a spirit as that. He did everything well: rode, hunted, made camp. He always knew how to conduct himself, as much in the lowliest village as in the occasional town. People took him for a knight, though he wore no spurs, and Melisende for his grubby brown-faced squire, though surely anyone with eyes could see the shape of the woman's body under the well-worn riding gear. Except that no one looked, or admitted to looking. They were all enraptured by the young man on his fantastical quest.

Melisende began to lose count of the days, would have lost them altogether except that sometimes, in this village or that abbey, they were celebrating a feast-day. So she knew when St. John's Day came and went, and Peter and Paul, and St. Benedict, and Mary Magdalene. They wandered an endless while, through more of the west of Britain than Melisende had known existed, to places so old that the magic was still rank in them, and places so new that the carpenter still hammered in the roofbeams or the masons labored in the apse. No vision of the Grail ever came to them, nor did any of the cups in any of the abbeys or churches or chapels present itself as the one they looked for. Even when there was magic, it was magic of a different sort, dreams and illusions mostly, or a chill down the spine as they rode past an ancient ruin.

If this was questing, it was a quieter thing than knights ever admitted. They would have been reckoned terribly unheroic in Camelot, for hiding in hedges when companies of knights clattered past, or avoiding roads that were known to be infested with brigands. Monsters they saw none, except the odd herd bull, and once a pack of dogs that pursued them till Blanca's well-aimed heel caught the leader and shattered its skull.

As the feast of the Blessed Virgin approached, they entered into the Summer Country, the borders of old Lyonesse, such of it as had not sunk beneath the sea. Parts of it were sinking even yet, long lakes, bogs and fens, and dank woodlands full of mists and midges. The roads were old Roman roads, which were the best in the world, but the tracks that ran to and from them were older by far, and stranger.

Then Beaumains, who till now had wandered in desultory fashion, seemed to have found a purpose. They had fallen into a habit of silence, long days' riding and short nights' sleep, no chatter, no singing, no sound but the horses' hooves on Roman paving or trodden earth or, faintly, green turf. It was like a ride in a dream.

Now the dream grew sharper, and yet also more dreamlike. Beaumains took the lead as he always had, but with greater speed, as if he had settled at last upon a destination, and would come there as soon as he possibly could. It was not the old city, Isca of the Dumnonii, nor the Baths of Sul, the ancient goddess given a Roman face; he rode through or past them. Nor was it any of the monasteries that seemed to fill this country as full of holiness as of magic.

At least, not any of them but one. They came to it on a morning of mingled mist and sun, the day before the feast of the Queen of Heaven. It was an island in a lake of glass, and a tor rising up out of it like a tower in a castle. The isle was full of the scent of flowers, impossible in this season, and yet unmistakable: apple blossoms, strong and heavenly sweet.

"Avalon," Melisende said as they stood on the shore of the lake. "You've brought us to Avalon."

Beaumains nodded. She was a little surprised. He had seemed buried so deep in himself as to be oblivious. But his eyes when he glanced at her were clear.

"You don't think it's here," she said.

"Why not?" he asked, reasonably enough when all was considered.

She peered over the water that was as grey as glass, into a mist that would not clear or shift, though she sharpened her eyes to the point of pain. "This is an isle of women. Even I know that. If the quest is for knights, and only knights, then surely the last place the Grail would be is a place where no men go."

"One would think so, wouldn't one?" Beaumains said mildly, and without irony that Melisende could discern.

"You're mad," she said.

"And a fool, too." He began to walk along the edge of the lake, treading lightly amid the sedge.

The horses followed as if they knew nothing of fear. Melisende trailed behind. There were tales of this place, whispers and murmured hints. It was a house of holy women, they said, of nuns sworn in devotion to the Queen of Heaven. What rite they kept, or what worship they gave to the Lord Christ or to his Father, was a matter of some debate. They were good Christian ladies, some insisted, sworn to a holy rule, and faultless in their piety. Others observed, if circumspectly, that there had been holy women in this place since long before the Lord Christ was born—and it was great in magic. Very great indeed.

King Arthur's sisters had dwelt there, Morgan called le Fey, and Morgause who grew to be queen in Orkney. Which surely Beaumains knew; and what else he knew, Melisende began to wonder.

As she pondered all of that, Beaumains paused. She nearly collided with him. He had come to what was clearly a ferry. It was little enough to deserve the name: a little shore of sand and stones, and a coracle upended on it like an emptied bowl. The coracle was shabby and small, but it seemed seaworthy. There were paddles under it, as battered as the boat, and as evidently service-able.

There was no ferryman—or woman, it would be here. The passage was theirs to take or to refuse.

Beaumains slid the boat into the water and held it there, waiting for Melisende to take up a paddle and clamber in. She almost refused—almost turned away.

But she had not come so far, abandoning everything—honor, duty, service—to turn back from what might be no more than a night's lodging. And if it was more . . .

She stepped gingerly into the boat. It was no more than a shell of wicker and hides, round and light and given to spinning crazily at slight shifts of weight. Beau-mains had some skill in paddling such a beast. Meli-sende had less, but she could match her strokes to his.

As they made their wobbling way out into the water, the horses, abandoned on the shore, snorted and shook their heads and plunged in behind. The gelding led. Blanca followed. Melisende opened her mouth to up-braid them, but shut it again. Of course they must come. They were too fine to leave behind; too obviously worth stealing.

The leather of saddles and bridles would dry, she sup-posed. After a while. With oil and rubbing and much help, it might even survive intact.

The mist curled about them, thin at first, then more thickly. When Melisende glanced back, her breath hissed between her teeth. There was nothing behind but grey emptiness. They could not see where they had come from or where they were going. There was nothing in the world but the boat and the two horses, and mist. It took the splashing of paddles and the horses' snorts and whuf-fles as they swam, softened and deadened the sounds, and buried them in silence.

Beaumains knelt in front of her, his back straight, as if

he had no fear in the world. Maybe he did not. He was a witch's child. Such things well might be as common to him as daylight.

They paddled for an hour, or likely more; perhaps for half the day, or half a lifetime. The lake could not be so wide. They must be paddling in circles.

At first she thought she had imagined it. Whispers. Murmurs like voices, or like the rushing of water. The lake, which had been as still as glass, began to ruffle, though there was no wind. Ruffles became ripples. Ripples became waves. Waves lifted the boat and let it fall, each rising higher than the last.

Melisende stopped paddling. The waves were carrying them forward. Beaumains had paused in his strokes, holding still, moving only to keep the light whippy craft from spinning. He seemed as calm as ever.

She shipped her own paddle, clung to the sides, and prayed. She could not see the horses. For all she knew, they had drowned.

Then, as her eyes darted, she saw a maned head rise beside the boat, riding the wave with it. Blanca swam without distress, and the gelding beyond her.

They comforted Melisende a little in that nightmare of surging water. And still no wind, no storm, only the mist and that terrible stillness.

Then, as if her thought had conjured it, the wind came. It smote them like a fist of air and water, lifted them up and cast them down, and drove them headlong into the void.

Melisende was beyond prayer. She was blind with water, breathless in the gale, shivering convulsively. Nothing in the world mattered but that she cling to the boat, which had a coracle's gift for staying afloat, if spinning, through any maelstrom. She had to trust to it. She had to hold still, though all her spirit shrieked at her to do something, anything, however useless, and however great the danger.

She held still. And the wind died. Slowly, so slowly she was unaware of it, until it struck her that she could see. They rode the waves, but those too had abated a little. Then a little more. Then, with a sound like a sigh, they cast the boat up on the shore, grey itself as the mist, yet solid enough to strike the breath from her as she tumbled along it.

Then at last, truly, there was stillness. Melisende lay on her back on wet sand. She was not dead, though she might almost have wished to be. Her body felt like one great bruise.

Slowly, groaning, she sat up. The coracle lay upended not far from her. Beyond it a sodden bundle stirred and muttered and unfolded itself into the long lean form of Beaumains. And there, treading through fraying tendrils of mist, walked the mare and the gelding. They were still bridled, still saddled—and miraculously, impossibly dry, as if all that wild voyage had been a gallop across a mortal meadow.

They were not in any earthly country. The mist lay thick over the water, but thinned and scattered over land: a green isle, heavy with the scent of apples and of apple blossoms. It was the same impossible fragrance that had wafted toward her across the lake from the isle of Avalon.

There beyond the shore was an orchard, and in it trees heavy with both blossom and fruit. And yet they were solid enough to the touch, the earth green and rich underfoot, and the mist melting from a sky in which the sun rode high.

Beyond the orchard she saw the rise of the tor, and at its feet the low dark shape of the nunnery. It was a remarkably prosaic thing for so magical a place, plain

hewn stone and wooden doors, thatch on the roofs of the
outbuildings and slates on that of the central house, and
a squat tower that must mark the chapel.

Melisende stood on the orchard's edge and stared.
Blanca moved up beside her, grazing with single-minded
determination, in a chinking of bit and champing of jaws
that sounded loud in the silence. No bird sang here, nor
did the wind blow. The lake was as flat as glass.

She caught the reins before they slipped under
Blanca's heedless foot. Blanca led her onward. The gelding followed, and Beaumains last, stumbling a little as if
with exhaustion.

The touch of earth underfoot revived them, and the
sweet air wafting about them. Melisende did not dare to
pluck an apple from a tree, though some were ripe. Her
heart warned her to touch nothing. Foolish perhaps, but
who knew what magic was here? She might pluck the
apple of Eden and know it only when it was too late.

The nunnery seemed more ordinary rather than less,
the closer they came to it. The sun dried and warmed
them, plain sun of summer in Britain. The orchard here
was as it should be, green apples and ripe, no blossoms;
no memory of spring in high summer.

Beaumains moved past her. She did not try to stop
him. He was the prince, after all, and would be a knight.
It was his quest, she supposed. Women did not go questing. Had not the queen said so?

Such bitterness. She did not know where it had
come from. She thrust it down and pressed forward,
close on Beaumains's heels. A woman could go questing. Melisende had. And whatever she had found, she
thought it might be worth finding.

The nunnery's gate was shut, and silence within,
though it must be near time for the singing of the Angelus. Beaumains approached the bell that hung beside

the gate. It was an iron bell, ordinary and rather ugly, but the sound that rang from it was as sweet as all heaven.

It died in a shiver of echoes. Beaumains waited. Melisende, for lack of greater inspiration, followed his example.

A smaller door opened within the larger gate. A figure stood in it. Like the nunnery, it was a very earthly shape: small, rotund, and swathed in black. The voice that came from the veil was a woman's voice with an accent of the West Country, broad and not at all queenly. "Welcome, strangers, to the house of Our Lady of the Lake."

Beaumains inclined his head. He did not cross himself, Melisende noticed. "I come seeking lodging," he said, "for love of the Queen of Heaven."

"You may seek," the portress said, as amiably as before, "but only the Lady can give you leave to find."

"And may I ask her for it?" asked Beaumains with remarkable lack of temper.

"This is a house of women," the portress said.

Beaumains laughed. It was a strange sound, bright and cold. "And you trust your eyes, good sister?"

The portress peered through her veils. So did Melisende, through veils of incomprehension and expectation and—above all—astonishment. But he could not—but he could—but she—

And why might this not be a tall lean young woman with a shape too scant for curves? Those white hands, that fair face—no wonder they were so good to look on, if it was a woman she looked at, and not a boy.

Beaumains, who was not a prince at all, but a princess, spread those white hands and bowed to the portress, and said, "Surely a woman may walk in a house of holy women. Even a woman who rides as a man."

"Surely she may," the portress said without visible

discomposure. She drew back, beckoning them in—even the gelding, Melisende noticed; but was not a eunuch welcome in the courts of queens?

They were received as guests in the house of Our Lady of the Lake, shown to lodgings such as any abbey would offer, plain and unadorned but comfortable enough. The table there was spread with simple fare, brown bread and yellow cheese, wooden cups of ale, and a basket of apples; and in the stable, for the horses, sweet hay and a handful of barley for each. There was no one to look after the horses, or to serve the daymeal. All the sisters would be in chapel, where the singing had begun, high and piercingly sweet, chanting the office.

Beaumains made no move toward the chapel. After he—she—had tended the gelding and Melisende her mare, they went in to eat and drink in silence that Melisende could find no simple way to break. Words she had plenty, and more than plenty. There were too many. They drowned one another out before she could speak a one of them.

Silence was not so ill a choice. She watched Beaumains covertly, seeing what was obvious now she knew: the delicacy of the features, the lightness of the carriage, and yes, those fair hands.

When at length Melisende spoke, it was to say, "No wonder you were willing to take me with you."

Beaumains finished eating an apple and set the core on his—her—plate, carefully, as if it were made of glass. "You really didn't know?"

"I really am an idiot."

Beaumains laughed. "Yes, you are. But a determined idiot. And a trusting one. If I had been the man I seemed, don't you think I might have tried to take advantage of you?"

"Not you," Melisende said, and she meant it. "I think that I would call you pure in heart."

"Or pure in folly." Beaumains tilted her head, blue eyes narrowed a little, as if she weighed Melisende and found her—not wanting. No. After all. Not insufficient. "My name is Elaine," she said.

"Were you going to uncover yourself in Camelot?" Melisende asked her.

She shrugged. "Maybe. Someday."

"Or your brothers would do it for you."

"Not my brothers," said Beaumains, whose name was Elaine. "They know better."

"But if the Grail is here, they must know—"

"The Grail is here," she said. "Don't you feel it? I wasn't certain, not till I came here—else I'd have come straight and not wandered all over the west of Britain. But now there can be no doubt of it. And why not? Why should not the Grail be a women's mystery? My brothers know what men know. And only that."

"Men have been sent in search of the Grail."

"So they have," Beaumains said. "Some of them will find manly things, I'm sure: sacred spears, enchanted swords. One or two might even find a cup, though what cup it is, who knows? The true cup, my heart tells me, is here. In this place. Where only women walk."

"And will we see it?" Melisende demanded, doubtful still, and not easily able to hide it.

Beaumains spread her hands. "If we are pure of heart," she said, "and if the Lady grants. And if not . . ." She shrugged. "Then not. We can but try."

That was no more than Melisende had ever ventured to think. And yet it was a stronger thing here, in sight of what she had come for. If it was here. If Beaumains's heart was telling the truth.

And why should it not? However Melisende might

like to imagine that she mattered, if she faced the truth,
she was a very small drop in a very large sea that was
the world. Beaumains had come for her own sake, and
been generous enough, or lazy enough, to let Melisende
follow. She would see no use in a lie.

The Grail was here. Melisende's heart began to beat
hard, as hard as Beaumains's must have done. It was
here. After all, and however belatedly, she knew. She
knew, too.

"Rest if you can," Beaumains said, breaking the
thread of Melisende's maundering. "Sleep if you will.
The sisters keep monks' hours here. They rise soon after
midnight. Then, if it's to be shown, what better day for it
than Our Lady's own day?"

Melisende nodded. She understood. Or near enough.
Whether she could sleep, she did not know; but she
could make herself rest.

The day faded. The sisters marked it in the chants of the
hours and the sweet ringing of bells. At sunset a small
shy novice brought another meal, bread again, and
cheese, a bowl of something savory with roots and herbs
and a whisper, perhaps, of meat, but no more. Peasant
fare, as the rest had been, but plentiful. Melisende could
hardly disdain it, and Beaumains fell to with as good a
will as if she had never been a princess born.

Melisende could have sworn that she would never
sleep—not so close to the end of the quest. She woke
with a start and a stiff neck, to find that she had fallen
asleep where she sat, over a half-eaten loaf and a remnant of cheese.

Beaumains was nowhere to be seen. She scrambled
herself together and went looking where she hoped—she
knew—Beaumains must be.

It was deep night. Stars crowded overhead as she

groped her way through the cloister court. The tor loomed dark against them, standing like a pillar to uphold the sky.

A lone light glimmered, a torch set in the wall beside the entrance to the chapel. Melisende guided her steps toward it.

Within was silence. It was a chapel such as she had seen before in poorer abbeys, bare stone unadorned, with little beauty of carving or painting. The altar was plain, its cloth of linen that must have been woven here in the nunnery. No cross stood on it, only what must be a chalice, veiled in linen as plainly homespun as the altarcloth.

Only one figure knelt before the altar, one Melisende knew well: straight shoulders, narrow for a man's but wide for a woman's, and thick black hair cut short, and an indefinable air that marked one royal born. Melisende, noble enough but gifted with neither beauty nor elegance, smiled faintly, but shrugged, too. She was what she was. It was enough.

She stepped through the door into the chapel.

Fire. It burned like fire. It was like the water rising in the lake, like the wind that had come out of nowhere earthly to bar their way to the isle of Avalon. This too was unnatural, beyond nature.

This too was a test. She had been too much a fool to know what the others were. This she knew. It raised a wall against her. It promised to flay flesh from bones, and char the bones.

The chapel was empty, and yet it was full of voices. High voices, supernally sweet.

Blessed are the meek: for they shall inherit the earth.
Blessed are the merciful: for they shall obtain mercy.
Blessed are the pure in heart: for they shall see God.
With each verse the fire burned more fiercely.

Melisende knew she was none of those things: not meek,
not kind, nor ever pure in heart. She was as mortal as
any, and as deeply stained with sin. Sin of which she re-
pented as good Christian should, but there was no priest
to shrive her. There was no one but Beaumains, of
whose purity she must be certain, for the princess from
Orkney had passed this door unharmed and come even
as far as the altar.

Melisende was not worthy.

Lady, the voices sang, *we are not worthy; speak but
the word and we shall be healed.*

Lady?

Beaumains was not, after all, alone in the chapel. A
figure stood behind the altar where Melisende was used
to a priest: a figure robed in white. But a priest could not
be a woman, and this unquestionably was. She might be
kin to Beaumains, slender as she was and tall, with eyes
as blue as speedwell, and hair that though greying had
once, without doubt, been black. Her hands were as long
as Beaumains's, and fair, and yet even from so far,
Melisende could see that they were roughened and reddened as if with a lifetime of labor.

She was mortal, then, and earthly, though the light
that bathed her came from no simple lamp or candle. She
bowed as a priest would bow in the Mass, and set hand
to the veil that hid the chalice.

Melisende had forgotten to breathe. This was the thing
she had come for. She knew it through the fire in her
heart, that seemed no longer to burn, but to warm her
like a hearthfire on a winter's night. She walked through
it without thought, into the whispering space of the
chapel.

The woman at the altar had paused, or else Melisende
had taken no time at all to come up behind Beaumains

and to kneel as she knelt, rapt before the altar and the light.

The veil lifted. Melisende narrowed her eyes against what surely would be a gleam of gold and a blaze of heavenly splendor.

There was no gold. There was no splendor. There was not even a cup. Only a bowl of wood, dark with age, neither beautifully nor intricately carved. Such a bowl would have served to bear a peasant's porridge or a beggar's alms. It was a poor thing, a common thing, a thing without either wealth or glory.

She almost laughed. But if she did—who knew what would become of her? A woman had laughed, it was said, at the Lord Christ as he stumbled toward his death, and suffered a terrible curse.

Melisende would not laugh. Nor would she weep. To quest so long, to hope so much—and to find so ignoble a thing.

The woman—priestess? abbess?—lifted the cup toward the light of heaven. Even that could not make it seem more than it was.

It was a cup for a poor man, a carpenter, a commoner who had died a criminal's death. Not for a king, nor yet a prince. In this world, he had never been that.

Awe fell on her. She bent beneath the weight of it. A simple cup. A cup of olivewood, none too finely carved.

"It came," said a low sweet voice, "from the Holy Land, years after he was dead. An old man brought it, a man who had been his friend, who had given him his own tomb to lie in—though he lay there but three days before he rose and left it. The cup was entrusted to this good man, this Joseph, that he might keep it safe. But when he grew old, he received another calling. Go, it bade him, to the ends of the earth. And when you come there, take my cup. Give it to those who wait, whose trust it shall be. They shall keep it safe. Do it, and remember me."

"Here?" Melisende might not have dared to speak, except that she dared do no other. "To this place? But—if only women—"

The priestess smiled. Yes, she was kin to Beaumains; they were most wonderfully like. "Where better to keep such a thing safe? Men would look for gold and jewels, for a king's cup. Women would know. That he was a poor man. That he owned nothing of value but his life. And that, when he took this cup in his hands, his life was near its end."

"I can see," Melisende said slowly, "why this is such a secret. But if the knights are sent to seek it—then surely—"

"No man may enter here," the priestess said. "And no woman but one pure of heart."

"But I'm not—"

"She judges that," the priestess said, with a glance and a turn of the hand that took in all about them, both above and below: earth and heaven both. "God is not only Father, child. She is Mother, too. This cup belonged to her son. Would she do aught to dishonor it?"

Melisende could hardly argue with that. But she could say, "You're not going to let us go back—not with the cup. And not with your secret."

"The Grail is no human possession," the priestess said. "It was never meant to be paraded before princes."

"And if we did," Melisende said more than a little wryly, "they'd only laugh."

The priestess smiled. She came down from the altar with the cup in her hands, and held it out.

Melisende's breath caught. "You can't—"

"Take it," the priestess said.

Melisende must, or the woman would let it fall. It was

a simple thing, smooth wood, old, with a crack beginning, and little enough heft. And yet in it was all the world. Melisende's hands had never known anything so holy.

She could keep it. She could walk away. Who could stop her?

She gave it back. She set it in those long fair hands, bowing over it. Her heart was full beyond measure.

It did not matter what she went back to—what punishment was meted out to her for running away, for abandoning her place, for pretending that she could seek the Grail as if she had been a man and a knight. It did not matter even that she could not tell anyone in Camelot that she had done it—she had found it. She had seen, had touched, the Grail.

She had done it. That was enough.

"A man would never understand," she said.

The priestess smiled. Beaumains laughed. "No," said the princess who had feigned and still no doubt would feign to be a stableboy, "a man would not. Men go questing for things both rare and magical, and sometimes even holy. But women," she said with satisfaction— "women find them."

Me and Galahad

Mike Resnick and Adrienne Gormley

I'd just finished milking Wilma and was following my sister back to the house when this truly glittery young dude rode into town. Lordy, he was something, with his yeller hair hanging in his eyes, his tack all polished fit to blind a hog, and rhinestones and sequins all over his shirt and chaps. So I said to Viv, I said, "Ain't he purty?"

Viv, she never held much truck for none of them fancy-dancy cowboys what rode for the King's spread, so she just turned up her nose and hied off for home. But me, I stayed to watch as he lit down and walked up to the Padre, who'd just come out of the church.

Then Viv yelled, "Kate! Get your lazy fanny in here—*now!*" So I picked up my milk pail and marched off, and as I walked into the kitchen, Viv was busy being Viv and yammering, "You should've seen her, Ma, standing there slobbering like a bitch in heat."

"Aw, I was just looking," I said. "Ain't no harm in that, is there? Anyway, he warn't interested in nothing but Brother Dave, which leaves out any trips to the hay loft, for dang sure." And I guv Viv such a look, letting her know that I knew what she did up there. So she went for me with her claws, and I grabbed her by the hair and yanked hard as a gentle reproof, and Ma had to get between us to break it up.

Next morning, I was hanging out the washing to dry when Brother Dave strolled past.

"Morning, Kate," he said, stopping to chat a bit.

"Morning, Padre," I replied as I smoothed the wrinkles out of Pa's best shirt. "I ain't seen your visitor around these parts today."

"Oh, he's gone, after spending the night praying in our little church," he said. "He told me old Artie's got the whole passel of 'em riding trail, looking for some fancy antique cup what the Spanish lost back when they was driven out of the territory. Seems it's worth a lot of *dinero*, and King Artie's always looking for something to help him keep his hold on that Flying Snake Ranch of his."

I stood up from where I was bent over the basket and shook out my skirt. "He looks a mite younger than the rest of them that's rid through here," I said, hoping Brother Dave would take the hint.

"Oh, he is, and he's even the son of one of them, would you believe?" he replied, taking the bait. "That Lance is the young bastard's old man. Looks just like him, he does."

Well, knowing what I did about what Brother Dave thought of That Lance, I could understand him calling the feller a bastard, since Lance hadn't never got hitched—and according to the minstrel shows that come through, he was messing with Miz Gwen when Artie was out protecting the herd from the Saxon Boys. And considering how Miz Gwen was more than a mite jealous of any other gal what caught her fancy man's eye, she must have been royally pissed when this young feller came riding onto the spread, all bright-eyed and bushy-tailed, let me tell you.

It must of been a week later that the glittery young feller came back our way. When I spotted him dragging his feet down Main Street, I hopped into the house, set down the batch of eggs I'd been carrying, and grabbed the fanciest thing I saw, which was Ma's silver wineglass that she'd been given years ago by old Lady Cynthia, because Ma had done good work caring for her kids when she was young. Well, he was going so slow, leading his horse, that I made it to the crick afore he did, and I had the glass full by the time he got there. His horse was limping, which was just a nasty thing to do a good horse, if you asked me. And he had a new John B., which he must of got from somebody he whipped. Whoever it was, the guy had fought back, because the sparkly shirt had a rip or two and a few of the sparkles was missing. He'd lost some conchas from the chaps, as well.

So I put on my best not-quite-pure look, and said to him, as polite as I could, "If you're thirsty, here's something to drink."

Well, he took Ma's wineglass from me, right enough, and I was scared he'd drop it, but he turned and let that gimpy nag drink out of it instead. Which really riled me, because that was Ma's most prized possession! And now I'd have to give it a good washing and polishing before it was fit for people again.

And did he notice me? He never said word one to me, let alone look. Not on your life. He just handed the glass back to me and dragged off, back to the church and Brother Dave.

*   *   *

It was some time before the young feller came riding into town again. I thought he'd done rode off into the sunset, for sure, and that maybe Miz Gwen had old Artie fire him. So I figgered maybe this time I'd catch his eye another way, and keeping Ma's saw in mind that the way to a man's heart is through his stomach, I'd put together a meal for him. After all, if he was out hunting for that fancy cup that King Artie was so hot after, he sure needed his energy.

Anyway, I got some cheese, a bowl of stew, a hunk of Ma's bread, and some of Wilma's finest milk in Ma's good glass, and carted it all off to the parsonage, where I'd seen Brother Dave take him. And this time, even with the Padre there, I figgered I'd do something a bit brassier to catch his eye. So I let my hair hang loose and opened the top button on my shirt so a hint of what lay within made itself known, and rapped on the door.

I heard Brother Dave say, "Enter, please," just like he was talking to some of them high-toned folks what visited the bankers from time to time, so I hitched myself straighter and went in. The young feller was sitting there at the table, while Brother Dave was fixing up his shoulder. I figured it must have been some fandango for this boy to have got hisself nicked.

Brother Dave looked at me and said, "Thank you, Kate, for thinking of my guest." He really was talking in that highfalutin way he did to folks like Artie and his family. Probably because of the young cowboy. He must not have wanted the guy to know he talked like normal folks when the hoity-toity types weren't around.

Well, I set the grub down, but the cowboy, he said nary a word, and didn't cast one eye in my direction. And I'd copied Viv's moves that she'd used on old Mr. Ector's son, too. What a waste.

He kept speaking to the Padre like I wasn't there, and he said, "So even for someone who's been through the Academy as I have been," he said, "it was rather a tiff, what with there being twenty of them, all set on having at Percy, who is as true-blue a man as ever there was, and taking his life. I truly appreciate the sanctuary you have offered me here while I wait for the final call for my destiny."

Destiny? What in tarnation did he mean by that? It didn't matter; he just sat there like a bump on a log, and kept on talking. "In appreciation of the sanctuary you've offered, Brother David," he said, "I'll have only a part of the bread and a cup of water, and you can have the rest of this fodder. My righteousness will be my sustenance." And he swung his hand around and dang near upset the glass of milk.

Now I was getting really stymied, but I tried not to let it show. Instead, I said to Brother Dave, "Any idea when I can come by and pick up the dirty dishes, Padre?"

"Don't worry, Kate," he said back to me, "I'll return them myself. We don't want your mother to fuss, now, do we?" Then he escorted me to the door and patted my shoulder. I ambled on home, wondering what I had to do to get that young man to notice me. Maybe jump on him buck naked? (Or would that scare the living daylights out of him?)

It took me a bit, but I finally got up the gumption to talk to Brother Dave about what motivated this guy. So I said, "Padre, how come he don't notice when I do something nice for him?"

Well, Brother Dave scratched his bald spot and looked up like he were asking the Lord to give him the answer. Then he said, "It's like this, Kate. He don't see you because you're regular folks. To him and his kind, regular folks like you and your family ain't here for nothing but to give service, like the kind that Viv performed for the Ector boy." I swallowed hard, and he grinned. "I'm not blind," he continued. "I can't be blind and watch over my flock."

"But I can't even catch his eye that way!" I blurted out, and then covered my mouth, realizing what I'd just said.

Well, Brother Dave just shook his head and said, "This one's different somehow, Kate, because he has this strange belief that the cup Artie's got them looking for is the one the Lord drunk out of at the Last Supper." He paused for a bit and shook his head. "What he means by his destiny, Kate, is he believes he's the one that's supposed to find it."

"So what's wrong with a plain 'Thank you,' or a 'God bless'?" I asked Brother Dave, but he didn't answer.

I thought again we'd seen the last of the young feller, and was about to put paid to my plans to get him to spot me. I was even thinking of resigning myself to giving in to Owen Baker, when he done showed up again. I found out later that he liked to make his way back to see the Padre whenever he got a scratch or three from saving any of the other fellers what worked for the king. So I decided to give him one last chance.

That night I couldn't get away until the supper dishes was done, but finally I saw my chance and snuck out, and by then he was on his knees in the church, praying up a storm. So I slid in the back, and to be respectful I covered my head with Ma's shawl, and knelt down, figgering to spend as long as I could until he was done. I was too scared to fake praying, knowing that the Lord would take that wrong, so I honestly prayed, prayed he'd finally spot me and want to take along a memento from me to remind him of me when he was taking on the bad guys. It must have been purty near midnight when my knees finally cried uncle, so I hauled myself to my feet and dragged myself out of the church.

And boy, was I surprised when I found out I wasn't leaving the church alone. The young cowboy hisself was walking beside me. And danged if he didn't look me right in the eye and speak to me.

"You kept vigil with me," he said. "For that I thank you."

My face got warm, but I kept my manner calm and said, "Thank you." Well, he turned away, but I stopped him with my hand on his arm, and said, "The Padre done told me of what you're about. You want I should pray for your success?"

"I thank you again," he said to me, and then to Brother Dave, "How odd to find someone who truly believes among the hoi polloi."

How odd? How odd? I wasn't just confounded, now; I was getting annoyed. What made him think that he had a lock on holiness, anyway? Well, I forced my anger down a bit, and decided to risk it all for what I'd planned, so I took Ma's shawl off my head.

"Could I ask a favor?" I asked, again trying to talk like they did up at the Hotel Biltmore. "As a reminder of everything, would you carry this with you? It were Ma's—"

Well, he grabbed it from me, threw it in the dirt, and stomped on it something fierce. "What?" he hollered. "How dare you tempt me with such worldly symbols!"

I blew up. A stick of dynamite couldn't compete. "Listen, your High and Mightiness," I snarled, "what makes you think that you're so bleeding pure? What makes you think you're better than the rest of us? Didn't Our Lord hisself spend time with the poor and the sinners? Least-

ways that's what I learned in Bible class." I snatched
Ma's shawl up from the dirt and shook the tatters in his
face. "This here was a courting gift, from my pa to my
ma, and their getting hitched was carried out in church.
Brother Dave even married them, and last I heard, marriage in the church is blessed by the Lord, and if that
ain't holy, what is?"

He just stood there, his purty pale blue eyes bugging
out at me. "So why don't you get your self-righteous self
back on that nag of yours, and get yourself out of here?
If you ain't the most selfish bastard I ever seen in all my
born days, I don't know who is!"

I guess he felt the need to get away, because he
knocked the Padre down in his hurry, and the last I saw
of him, he was riding out as fast as that big old cayuse of
his could carry him. Me, I helped Brother Dave to his
feet, and let him lean on me on his way back to the parsonage. We were partway there when Viv joined us. "I
saw. I told Ma," she said. "She sent some wine."

We helped Brother Dave to sit down, and Viv lifted
his foot up to wrap the ankle that was all swelled up. I
noticed Ma'd sent her old wineglass along with the bottle, and I figured the Padre would need the painkiller, so
I poured him a healthy amount. And why not? Brother
Dave was worth a lot more courtesy than some stuck-up,
priggish eastern dandy and his sorry horse.

So I handed over the glass, and the Padre drank down
the whole thing, then sat there, staring at Lady Cynthia's
wineglass. After he was done, he handed it back to me.

"You sure had him pegged, Padre," I said.

"I sure did, Kate," he replied, straightening as the
color came back to his face. "He's about the coldest fish
I ever did see. He's keeping himself physically pure, but
that's about it . . . He ain't righteous in the heart, like
you." Brother Dave stood up then and stretched, and

wiggled the injured ankle. He grinned. "I feel twenty years old," he said. "How are you gals doing? Kate?"

I smiled. I was still feeling good about myself, from what the Padre'd said, about being righteous in the heart. I could sense Viv felt that way, too, from the way she smiled.

"Think he'll get what he's aiming for?" she asked.

"Well, now, what he's aiming for and what he's asking for are two different things," the Padre said. "And I think it's what he's asking for that he'll end up getting."

Viv was already out the door and waiting on the step, so I picked up Ma's glass and the rest of the wine.

"Oh, Kate," the Padre said, "wait a minute." I stopped and looked back at him, while Viv went on. I shook my head. Danged if he wasn't looking angelic as well as healthier. "Don't you let anybody get away with that wineglass of your mother's. After all, Lady Cynthia must have had her reasons for choosing your ma to keep it." Then he shut the door and went back inside the parsonage.

I stood there in the street, thinking hard, and after I'd thought a bit, I chuckled. And then I figured that if I was going to be the one to take care of it after Ma was gone, maybe hitching up with Owen Baker wasn't so bad an idea after all.

A Lesser Working

Jennifer Roberson

"Sir," I said, "won't you come into the inn?" It wasn't much, perhaps not properly an inn as others might name it, being little more than a smoke-darkened square of rough-hewn wood mortared with clay, but it boasted a sound roof and a common room men might nonetheless be grateful for in a storm such as this. "No need to stay out here, sir, when you might come inside."

"Might I?" he murmured tonelessly, as if he didn't care.

"Sir," I began again; what profit in staying beneath the weathered and leaking limbs of the lean-to currently sheltering four horses as wet as this man? "There is ale, a little mead . . . and Mam has made a stew of two hares and tubers and sage and wild onions."

"A feast." His tone was far more dry than the black hair clinging to his head.

It stung, that tone. "Better than naught," I retorted, "unless you wish to share the horses' fodder."

He looked at me then, noticed me then for what I was, not merely a voice he preferred not to hear. In the freckled illumination of the small pierced-tin lantern I carried, his face was every bit as white as his hair was dark. Thin, pale skin stretched tightly over sharply defined bones. The eyes too were dark, though perhaps the rims, in daylight, would be blue, or brown, or even winter-gray. Here, in the night, in the storm, he was all of darkness, cloaked in oiled wool that dripped onto straw and packed earth.

One of the horses chose that moment to sneeze violently, banging its nose on the wooden feed bin chewed nearly to pieces by countless teeth. The horse was startled by unexpected pain and jerked back abruptly, bumping into me so hard that I was knocked off-balance. Staggering, I dropped the lantern altogether; as I saw oil and flame spill out I immediately went to my knees to make sure no fire was started. But the roof leaked, and the straw was too damp to kindle. Oil hissed, and the flamelets went out.

A hand on my arm pulled me to my feet. With the lantern doused there was no light, for rain-laden clouds obscured the moon and stars. I could find my way back to the inn because I had countless times before, but surely the stranger could not.

He released me then and turned to the horse, even in the dark urging it toward the feed bin again. A few quiet words soothed it; though I didn't know the language, the horse apparently did. It quieted at once.

"Put your hand on my shoulder," I urged. "I will lead you to the inn. No sense staying out here in the storm *and* the dark."

"In Tintagel," he said obscurely, "there is no rain."

I blinked. Likely not; the duke's castle was undoubtedly sounder than the stable lean-to.

"Though a storm will come of it," he added.

Was he mad? He kept to the company of horses when the men he had rode in with had already dried their cloaks by the fire. Fa had sent me out after the straggler to light his way in; that he might prefer the storm had not occurred to anyone.

"A storm *has* come of it," I said tartly, and winced inwardly; Mam, had she heard that, would no doubt cuff me for it.

"Ah, but this one was not of my making," he said mildly, seemingly unoffended. "Nor the one in Tintagel; that is merely a man's lust. But the storm to come . . . well, that one *shall* be mine."

Perhaps he was made to stay with the horses because he was mad. If so, then I needn't remain. But I tried one last time. "Sir, it is too dark to see. Will you come inside? I know the way even without light."

"Light," he said, "is what I have made this night. A lamp, a lantern, a torch. A bonfire for Britain in the shape of the seed, the infant, the child who will become the man."

He *was* mad. Sighing, I made to move past him, to go out into the rain, hoping to think of an explanation suitable for Fa and Mam, but a hand came down on my shoulder. It prisoned me there, though the touch was not firm. I simply knew I must stay.

"Boy," he said, "what do you know of politics?"

"It's a spell," I answered promptly.

The grip tightened as if I had startled him. "A spell?"

"It makes men behave in ways they perhaps should not."

I had more than startled him. I had amused. He laughed briefly, but without ridicule, and took his hand from my shoulder. "What do you know of such—spells?"

"What my uncle told me. He was a soldier, sir. He came home from war, you see, and explained it to us. How men conjure politics to order the world the way they would have it be ordered, even if others would have it be otherwise."

"Well," he said after a long moment replete with consideration, "your uncle was a wise man."

"It killed him," I said matter-of-factly; it had been three years, and the grief was aged now. "The wound festered, and he died. Of politics, he said."

"It is true," the stranger said meditatively, "that politics kill men. Likely Gorlois will die of that same spell, after what I have done this night."

The duke? But what could this man have done to him? "Duke Gorlois is away from Tintagel," I said. "He and his men rode away days ago."

"Ah," he said, with an odd tone in his voice, "but he is back. Even as we speak he is home in Tintagel, sharing his lady wife's bed."

"But—he has not come this way," I blurted. "He always comes this way."

"Tonight," he said, "the duke found another way."

I did not see how. There was only one road from Tintagel, and it ran by the inn. "A new road?" I asked; Fa would need to know. "Is there an inn on it?"

The laughter was soft, but inoffensive. "There is not," he answered. "You need not fear for your custom."

Lightning abruptly split the sky. I squinted against the blinding flare that set spots before my eyes, and steeled myself for the thunder. It came in haste and hunger, crashing down over the lean-to as if to shatter it. Even knowing it was imminent, I jumped. So did the horses. Only the stranger was immune.

"I wonder," he mused, "if that heralded the seed."

"The seed?" I was busy with the nearest horse, hold-

ing the halter as I rubbed its jaw, attempting to ease it in
the aftermath of thunder.

"A man's seed," he explained almost dreamily, though
he spoke to himself, not to me. "And the woman believ-
ing it of her husband's loins."

Even Fa would not expect me to stay outside in a
storm with a madman. I opened my mouth to take my
leave, but the stranger was speaking again. And he
seemed to know what I was thinking.

"Forgive me, boy." His tone was crisper now, though
still clearly weary. "It takes me this way after a Great
Working of—politics. I am not always fit company for
others, after."

I ventured a question. "Is that why you're staying out
here in the dark with the horses?"

He answered with a question. "Do you fear the dark?"

"No," I answered truthfully. "But it is difficult to tend
my chores when I can't see—*ah!*"

He had caught my hand in his own. "Forgive me," he
repeated. "I did not mean to startle you."

He touched the palm of my upturned hand with two
cool fingertips. "Sir, what—?"

And then light flared, a spark of brilliant blue that
bloomed in my hand like a fire freshly kindled. He
cupped my hand in both of his and held it, keeping me
from leaping back. "It will not burn, boy. That I promise.
No harm shall come of it."

I stared at the light pulsing in my palm. It was neither
flame nor lightning, but something in between. It was
the shape and size of a raindrop.

"Now you can see," he said, "to tend your chores."

He let go of me then. His hands dropped away from
my own. I stared at my hand, at the light in my palm
burning steadily, neither hot nor cold. I tipped my hand,

wondering if the "raindrop" would spill out and splatter against the straw, but it did not.

I looked up at him then, seeing him more clearly than I had with the light of my pierced-tin lantern. His eyes were black, but even as I watched them the blackness shrank down. The color left behind was clear as winter water.

"Are you ill?" I blurted, for this light showed me the truth: the eyes were gray, but the skin beneath them etched deeply with shadowed hollows, and the lips were white.

"Not ill," he answered. "Rather, diminished. It was a Great Working, what was done tonight."

"This storm?"

His pale mouth twitched in something like a smile. "Not this one."

"But—you can?"

"Make storms?" He shrugged, little more than the slight hitching of a single shoulder. "Storms are Lesser Workings, and inconsequential in the ordering of a realm. I leave them to themselves."

"Then what did you do? What politics did you conjure?"

He said, with no humor in it, "Your future."

I stared at him, wishing to name him mad to his face. But the truth burned in my hand. Not mad. *Enchanter.*

What boy, what man, would not wish to know the answer? And so I ventured the question. "What of my future, sir?"

"Your uncle went to war, you say."

"He did."

"So will you go."

I twitched with startlement. "I? But Fa has said I may not; that I must stay and tend the inn when he is old."

"And so you shall. But there is time for all: to go to

war, to come home from it—safely—and to tend the inn."

My hand shook a little. The blue light danced. "Sir— do you See this?" Meaning: *In a vision?*

"I See a boy your age, discovering the truth of his begetting. I See him grown to manhood, discovering the truth of power. And I See him serving Britain *with* that power."

I licked dry lips. "Is he an enchanter, too?"

He smiled. "Not that kind of power, boy. Magic of a sort, but no more than that which lives in *your* heart."

"Mine?"

"The power to lead," he said. "The power to inspire."

"In—*me*?"

"You will not be king," he told me. "That is for another. But kings have need of good men, strong men, men such as you will be."

"The Pendragon?" I asked; he was king now.

The smile fled his face. "No, boy. Not Uther. Another."

"Who?"

His eyes had gone distant, as if he saw elsewhere. "The Lady Ygraine's son."

"The Lady Ygraine *has* no son," I blurted; everyone knew it was the duke's great regret.

"In nine months' time," he murmured.

"Then—will Duke Gorlois be named king? In the Pendragon's place?" How else would Lady Ygraine's son become a king?

The distance was gone from his eyes. Once again he put a hand on my shoulder. "Weariness besets my tongue; I have said too much. Shall we go to the inn? I am famished. Hare stew with tubers and sage and wild onions should suit me well."

I hesitated. "But—who shall be king? Who is this king I shall serve?"

His smile this time held no weariness, but lighted the lean-to as if it were the world. "You shall know him," he promised, "when you see him."

"I will, sir?"

"Down this very road he shall ride, and come to this very inn, and you shall see him and know him for what he is: king that was, and king that shall be." His hand guided me out into the storm. "Go, boy. Lead on."

But I hesitated. "Who are *you*, sir?"

"I? I am merely a Welshman, a man born to a mam and a fa even as you were. My gift is to see a little farther, perhaps, but no more than that."

I glanced at the glowing raindrop in my hand, then gazed at him steadily. "I do not believe you, sir."

"No?" He sighed, and his hand tightened. "Well, then, perhaps a bit more than that. But not this night. I am done with all Workings this night, even the Lesser ones . . . except perhaps for this small light meant to show us the way."

"Done with politics, sir?"

He laughed, and the weariness fled. "Ah, but I shall never escape *that* Great Working. I am a meddler, you see. Men—ask me things. And ask things *of* me."

I ventured it very quietly. "What things, sir?"

He gazed over my head into the darkness beyond. "A new face," he murmured. "A new form. The wherewithal to pass beyond the guards, and to enter the lady's bed."

"Sir—"

"Come," he said firmly, and pushed me out into the rain. "Show me the way, boy, before your fa comes out to find us."

Fa would, and punish me for lagging. I preceded the enchanter as he wished, the light in my palm undiminished by the storm. It was but fourteen steps to the inn, and as I reached for the doorlatch the light flickered and died. The Lesser Working was done.

I felt so bereft I stopped short. Patiently he put his hand on mine, closing his fingers and my own upon the latch. He lifted, and so I lifted as well; the door swung open into the quite ordinary yellow light of the fire on the hearth and the lamps in the common room, where three men waited as well as Mam and Fa.

"Good lady," said the enchanter, "might I trouble you for stew?"

Grievous Wounds

Laura Resnick

"Comfort thyself," said the king, "for in me is no further help; for I will to the Isle of Avalon, to heal me of my grievous wound."

—Thomas Bulfinch
The Age of Chivalry

The agony of the wound unmanned him, but he must not cry out. A king should not die wailing like a child. He ground his teeth against the pain and tensed his throat to block the sounds of anguish, which threatened to tear through him with every jolt of the litter upon which he lay dying.

They were carrying him somewhere. Away from the battlefield. Away from the ruins of all their dreams. Away from the bitter destiny of all he had wrought with his life. His bastard-born, incestuous, cuckolded life.

"Ca- Car- Carr—" *Carry me away.*

"Sire . . ."

He heard doubt and weakness in the voice.

"Lucan?" he asked vaguely. Carrying his litter? No, surely not. Lucan had been wounded. He was sure he remembered that. Were his troops so decimated that a wounded man must carry the king's litter?

"Yes." The word came out as a hiss of pain. "Sire, I . . . I am not . . ." Then, on a note of desperate pain and panic. "Bedivere!"

Lucan fell to his knees. The litter hit the ground, and Arthur's self-control vanished as pain swallowed him whole, gulping him into its fiery belly. His screams echoed all around him, but they were not loud enough. Not loud enough to block out the agony engulfing him, not loud enough to drown sorrow, defeat, and torment. Not loud enough . . .

The clatter of hooves on stone confused him. He had landed in mud when they dropped him. Yet the hooves sounded close—perilously close—to his head. He rolled his head slightly. Felt paving stones beneath his skull. Surely not? Wouldn't his skull be split if it had hit stone instead of earth? He moved restless hands and felt hard stone beneath them—where only a moment ago there had been cold mud.

"Please, sir, are you well?"

He felt light bathing his face.

But . . . it's night now.

He was dying in the dark and the mud. How could he be lying on stone pavement in the sunlight?

And the pain . . . where was the pain?

His eyes snapped open—then immediately shut again, watering in the brilliant glare of the sunlight. He raised a hand to shield them . . . then froze as he realized he had just moved with no ill effect whatsoever.

It doesn't hurt.

It should hurt. It was a mortal wound. The battlefield at Camlan now held more of his blood and guts than he did.

"Please, sir, are you *un*well?"

It was a boy's voice, wavering awkwardly in the uncertain range between childhood and manhood. Bewildered, Arthur opened his eyes, squinting against the sunlight. He nearly flinched when he found himself staring directly into a young face puckered with worry.

"Please, sir, are you—"

"Yes, I heard you." His voice felt strangely distant from his body. He swallowed and admitted, "I'm not sure."

He turned his head away from the boy to get a view of his surroundings. He seemed to be lying in a town square. Common folk bustled all around them. Knights on horseback rode past, which accounted for the clattering that had first roused him. The smell of nearby livestock was pungent in his nostrils. The rhythmic cry of a passing peddler competed with all manner of sounds, complaints, and pleas coming from man and beast alike. Looking around more alertly now, Arthur saw that some people were staring at him with suspicion or dismay, but most chose to ignore him and go about their business.

It occurred to him that a king—even a very confused one—should not be lying like a drunkard in a town square for all the world to see. "Help me up, boy."

"Yes, sir."

The lad was strong, hauling Arthur to his feet with virtually no cooperation from the king's trembling limbs. Arthur leaned heavily on the boy's shoulder and gasped for air as the world reeled around him. Sounds scraped along his skin, colors felt hot in his mouth, and scents enveloped him like a scratchy blanket. What in God's name was happening to him? He breathed deeply, still amazed that it didn't hurt. Only minutes ago, each breath had been an unbearable agony taking him one step closer to death.

Bit by bit, the world stopped swirling, his legs stopped shaking, and he was able to stand like a man instead of cling like a weaning child.

"Thank you," he said to the boy helping him. "I'm better now."

"Would you like me to take you . . ." The boy paused and shrugged uncertainly. "Back to your people?"

"My people?"

"Or wherever you belong?"

"I belong . . ." Arthur looked around as his senses calmed. Something stirred in his memory as he studied his surroundings. "I know this place."

"If you're better now, sir . . ."

"Those stables . . . This marketplace . . ." Arthur nodded slowly. "Yes, I've been here before." But when? And where was this? "And how did I get here?"

"I'm afraid they're waiting for me," the boy said apologetically. "Kay will be vexed if I make him wait much longer."

"Kay!" Arthur's head snapped around. "Then he . . . He isn't dead, after all?" No, that was impossible. Kay was dead on the blood-drenched field of Camlan.

"Dead? No, indeed, sir." The boy gave him a puzzled look. "Do you know my brother?"

"*Your* brother?"

"My foster brother," the boy amended.

No, not Kay, then. Just this lad's . . . A strange sensation crept into his bones. "I had a foster brother named Kay."

"I see, sir. And is he . . ."

"Yes. Dead."

The place. So familiar. The boy's face. So familiar, too, he now realized; only seen from an unfamiliar perspective. *My God . . .* "Ar . . . *Arthur?*"

"Yes, sir!" The boy smiled. "Forgive me, sir. Have we met before?"

Polite, yes. His stepfather had drilled courtesy into them. Tall. Stronger than other boys his age. He would grow into those hands and feet in time to fight the Saxons . . . Arthur sat down rather abruptly on the hard pavement.

"Sir!" The boy knelt beside him. "You are *very* unwell!"

Well, yes, I'm dying . . . He started to laugh.

"We must find someone to tend you," the boy said worriedly.

The sword, Arthur realized.

"Can you walk?" the boy asked.

This was where it all began. This was where he had pulled the sword out of the stone. The sword that marked him, blessed him . . . *cursed me* . . . as king.

"The sword," he whispered to the boy—*Arthur*—his head reeling.

"Never mind the sword Kay sent me to find. He can wait," the boy said firmly. "You need help."

Everything could be different. Now was his chance to change all that he had wrought. "The sword in the stone . . ."

"I will find a healer. Can I leave you here alone for a few moments?"

"Don't . . . Don't . . ."

"I'm sorry, sir. There's no other way. You can't move, and I don't know how to help you."

"No, you don't understand." He reached for the boy's arm. Young Arthur eluded him with the speed and agility that would keep him—had kept him—alive in many battles.

"I do, sir, but I'll be back before you know it. Lie still. Don't fret."

No!

But young Arthur was gone without hearing the words which could have saved him.

Don't touch the sword in the stone.

Go home, boy, go home and live a normal life. Don't become the man whom thousands will follow to their deaths. Don't drench this land with the blood of your friends as well as your enemies.

Arthur tried to rise again, but his legs would not support him. His vision swam, darkening at the edges. The sunlight dimmed as shapes became shadows, voices turned into echoes, and the scents of his youth drifted away on the summer breeze . . .

Pain cut through him with brutal force. Echoing sounds shimmered through shifting light and darkness. Nausea overwhelmed him, but when merely breathing hurt so much, the thought of vomiting was unbearable.

"He's awake!"

Bedivere's voice. Exhausted and grim, but still buoyed by the courage and common sense that had made him Arthur's most trusted companion for so many years. His dearest and most valued friend . . . until Lancelot.

Lancelot, who'd come to Camelot like a breath of fresh air, who'd had the imagination and vision that Bedivere lacked, while lacking none of his courage. The knight who could see what Arthur saw, the man who could understand better than any other what Arthur envisioned, what he hoped to create and shape from the shambles he had inherited after the Saxon wars. Lancelot, his dearest friend, his most capable enemy . . .

"Yes, I'm awake," Arthur mumbled.

Awake now. But how real the dream had seemed! And how his bewildered dream-self had longed to alter his destiny.

Ah, yes, if only things could be—if only they had been—different. If only he hadn't sired a bitter son on his own half-sister, become king of a chaotic and war-torn land, loved and made a queen of the woman who would fall helplessly in love with his own best friend. If only, if only, if only . . .

Well, it was all over now. And what man did not have regrets, after all? What king did not drown in them?

"Sire," Bedivere said, bending over him. "We must lift you onto the barge."

"And it will hurt," Arthur guessed.

A weary smile flickered at the edge of Bedivere's grim-set mouth. "Only when you laugh."

"Oh, in that case . . ."

He felt Bedivere briefly clasp his hand in the dark. "Avalon is not far now, sire."

"Only across the water. Ah, if only I could walk on it . . ." He closed his eyes, sorrow overriding the pain. "No, we'd still have lost."

Bedivere said nothing. No empty boasts about the next battle. There would never be another battle for them. They were done. Utterly destroyed at Camlan. The dream was over.

"Lucan?" Arthur asked.

"Dead," Bedivere replied briefly. "While you were unconscious."

"So many dead. So many." It hurt to speak, yet he felt he must say their names aloud, if only to hear the words one more time. Some would get no other epitaph now. "Gawain. Kay. Lucan." All had died since dawn . . . "Gareth. Gaheris." They had died trying to prevent

Lancelot's rescue of Guinevere after she'd been sentenced to burn.

After I sentenced her. Guinevere, Guinevere . . .

Don't think about it. Not now. May death come for me before I remember it again.

"Galahad," he continued aloud. Lancelot's son had died searching for the Grail. "Percival." Well, *someone* had to find it.

"That was a long time ago." Bedivere's voice was terse. "Best not to dwell on it now."

"Elaine." The lily maid of Astolat, dead for love of Lancelot, for a king's poor judgment, for a queen's passion. "Torre." The brother who had fought for the dead Elaine's shattered honor and wasted heart. "Ambrosius." So long ago. "Uther." Kings died harder, it seemed.

"Sire?" Bedivere's voice was concerned.

He felt a hand on his brow. *He thinks I'm delirious.*

"I'm still here," Arthur said. *But not for much longer.*

"Try to hang on until we reach Avalon."

Why?

Bedivere added, "We're going to lift you onto the barge now."

"Sagramore, Lionel, Bohort, Hector, Blamor, Lawayn . . ." All dead now.

Bedivere spoke to someone else. "Don't jostle him! The wound is . . ." More softly now: "Don't jostle him."

"Tristam . . . Or perhaps not." Who knew for sure? If anyone could live forever, it would be Tristam.

"Steady now," said Bedivere.

Arthur's throat tightened as he added the name that hurt more than any other. "Mordred."

Dead by my hand.

"If only we'd killed him sooner," Bedivere said.

It was certainly, Arthur reflected as his litter wobbled precariously between land and barge, the course of ac-

tion Bedivere had always favored and urged. And maybe
Bedivere blamed Arthur for the disaster that Mordred,
allowed to live and even granted royal power, had finally
wrought.

"The sword in the stone . . ." he murmured on a sigh,
thinking about his dream.

"What about it?"

"The moment a boy becomes a man," Arthur said.
"The moment his destiny is revealed."

"The sword in the stone," Bedivere repeated.

"My destiny was granted. Mordred's was denied." He
gritted his teeth as pain curled its burning fingers into his
flesh. "So he sought it as best he knew how."

"Don't make excuses for him," Bedivere snapped at
his king. "Not now."

"Isn't it enough that I killed him? Isn't it enough that
his blood stains my hands?" Arthur gazed up at the night
sky, trying to see the stars through the clouds. "May I
not at least remember my son with love?"

"How could you love that—"

"You aren't a father. You can't understand."

Lancelot had understood. Somewhere out there in the
bleak night, he understood even now.

Born in bastardy and incest, Mordred was Arthur's
son. His child. *His.* "A child is . . . God's gift."

"Forgive me, Arthur, but Mordred did not come from
any Christian God."

"I should have had your tongue cut out years ago,"
Arthur said mildly.

"The night is young."

"God's gift, I tell you." Speech became more difficult
as each breath became more agonizing. "Perfect at birth.
Innocent." He closed his eyes again. "Then life shapes
us to its will."

He heard shouting. Something about a log in their

path. Bedivere left his side. A high-pitched cry screeched along his skin. The barge tilted slightly as its captain tried to avoid the obstacle. Arthur choked on the sound that tried to escape past his lips as he felt his guts shift with the barge.

Bedivere's voice: "No!"

Then the jolt and the shock and the pain and the sound of his own screams . . .

The cushion beneath his cheek was velvet. He smelled beeswax candles and fresh rushes. He heard waves in the distance. A soft breeze touched his face briefly, carrying the scent of the sea to him.

No scent of blood or sweat. No pain.

His eyes snapped open. He was reclining in a large, well-appointed tower room, the sturdy walls curving around fine furnishings. He sat up slowly, his head spinning, his senses reeling at the intensity of colors, sounds, and smells.

I've been here before.

"Yes, you've been here before," said a dry voice.

He stiffened, knowing that voice instantly despite the passage of time. "Merlin," he said even as he turned around to face him.

The old sorcerer sat in a corner, his wild white hair and beard flowing down to his rumpled array of simple homespun clothing. His remarkable blue eyes still held all the life and intensity Arthur remembered. One side of his mouth curled slightly—his version of a smile. "Hello."

A wealth of emotions flooded Arthur as he gazed upon the magician who had been father figure, friend, advisor, and conscience to him throughout his youth and early manhood. Merlin and his teachings had shaped Arthur more than any other person or experience in his life. Of all the people he missed desperately in these final hours, no one's absence hurt more than Merlin's.

"Is this a dream?" he asked.

"No. This is a lesson."

Arthur smiled sadly. "I'm too old for lessons, Mer—"

"You are never too old for a lesson!" Merlin snapped.

It was so familiar, Arthur laughed. "It must be a dream, though. You're enchanted and . . . gone from us. You even warned me it would happen."

"Yes," Merlin agreed. "In your time, as you lie dying after Camlan, I have been gone for many years. But here in my time, all of that is still many years away. You haven't even been born yet."

"Born? But I—" He stopped and looked around him again, realizing. He got up, went to the window, and looked down at the sea-weathered cliffs and the ocean below. Just to be sure, even though he already knew. "This is Tintagel!"

"Precisely."

He whirled to face Merlin. "Why have you brought me here?"

"Because you made such a muddle of your meeting with young Arthur."

"What?"

"You saw none of his enthusiasm and spirit, none of his ambition to help others and change his world. You just stayed mired in your own regrets." Merlin shook his head. "Young Arthur is—er, will be—young and impressionable. Not to mention polite. He might have listened to you. He might not have taken the sword from the stone. And then where would Britain be?"

Arthur sat down again, feeling the weight of his age. "What was the point of sending me there then, Merlin?"

"I don't wish you to die engulfed in remorse and sorrow and self-pity."

Arthur glared. "I do not indulge in—"

"Self-pity," Merlin repeated. "So you're dying in pain and seeing all your work reshape itself into something else—or maybe even fall apart completely."

"Yes!"

"You're a *king*, Arthur. What did you expect? Do you have any idea how many kings have died this way, how many more will? Did you think *your* great destiny would be the first that required no sacrifices?"

Arthur drew in a sharp breath as he realized the truth. "And you *knew*, didn't you? You've known all along!"

"Naturally."

"Then why? Why make me do it? Why—"

"I didn't *make* you do anything, you young rascal!" Merlin snapped.

Arthur reflected wryly that the phrase hadn't even applied to him the last time Merlin had used it, more than twenty years ago.

Merlin continued, "I merely taught and encouraged you to live up to your full potential, to seek and fulfill your destiny, to create instead of destroy, and—having created something—to tend it well and wisely."

Always a fair man—a quality taught and ingrained by Merlin, in fact—Arthur supposed this was true. Merlin had taught and guided him, but he and his life's work were of his own making, his own choice. He rubbed a hand over the place where, in his own time, his life force was flowing out of his body in a river of blood. "But why didn't you warn me?" he asked plaintively.

"Why should I?" Merlin asked.

"So that I . . ." He couldn't finish.

"So that you would have stayed home and lived a normal life?"

"Yes!" He smarted under the contempt in Merlin's voice, but he would not deny it.

"Oh, Arthur." Merlin's mouth curled again, but this time in sadness. "Perhaps you've forgotten what a normal life was like when you were born. Don't you remember how you wanted to change 'normal life' for people when you were young? Don't you understand how great was your triumph, that you *did*?"

"And now—"

"She's coming." Merlin rose suddenly. "Perhaps talking with her will remind you."

"But I—"

"Goodbye, Arthur. We will meet again . . . Well, no, I will meet you again, but you will never see me again. Not unless all that priestly rot about heaven and the hereafter happens to be true, that is."

"Merlin, wait!"

"Die well, Arthur. It's all you have left." He paused and added more gently, "It's what I'm trying to give you. The first and last thing I can do for you. My once and future gift."

"Wait, I want—"

But Merlin didn't wait, he simply vanished, leaving Arthur alone. So alone. But only briefly.

He recognized her the moment she came into the chamber. She was much younger than when he had met—er, would meet—her. "Igraine," he murmured. The wife of Gorlois. Uther had loved her madly and had convinced Merlin to help him magically slip into Tintagel Castle in Gorlois's absence to make love to the duke's beautiful wife. Merlin's price for the task had been the child who would be born of that night's adulterous union. Igraine, destined to bear the bastard, was the only one ignorant of the agreement on that fateful night so long ago.

How typical of Uther.

It was only now that Arthur realized it had evidently been pretty typical of Merlin, too.

However, having given up the child at their insistence, and with the empty promise of many more babies to come, the (by then) widowed Igraine married Uther. They would never have another child, though, and fifteen years later—fifteen years from now—Uther would order Merlin to bring Arthur here to meet his real parents for the first time. It was the only time Arthur ever saw his own mother.

Uther had died within a year, and Igraine did not survive him for long. But Arthur had never forgotten what she looked like. Or Tintagel, the dark and windy castle where he had been born.

Now Arthur saw that Igraine was hugely pregnant. He realized that Gorlois must have been dead for some months, for she was obviously going to give birth any day now. The fiction of this child's birth and sudden disappearance would be that it was Gorlois's stillborn son. Attempting to rule a fragmented association of petty kings and chiefs in a chaotic and war-torn land, Uther had told his future wife that he couldn't afford an heir whose parentage might be questioned, and since Igraine had been Gorlois's wife when she conceived this child . . .

Well, kings must often be ruthless, even with their wives, Arthur acknowledged with renewed sorrow. To protect the realm he was trying (and would fail) to build, Uther had made his wife give up her only child. Arthur, who had sentenced his own wife to burn at the stake in a vain attempt to save his disintegrating realm, was hardly in a position to criticize.

Igraine regarded him across the chamber, her blue eyes wary and assessing. "He says I must speak with you."

"Who says?"

"Merlin." Her smile was bitter, no smile at all really. "As if I have not already agreed to do more than enough."

"You mean giving up the child?"

"He told you?" she asked in surprise. "I thought it was supposed to be a secret."

Arthur hesitated. "Did he tell you who I am?"

She shook her head. "He said only that you could tell me things about the future. About my baby's future."

"Oh. Well. Yes. He's right about that."

She took a seat, graceful despite her bulk, and gestured for him to sit, too. She seemed to gather her courage before finally saying, "You know . . . Do you already know that this child is a king's son?"

"Yes."

"He deserves better than to live as some foster child in obscurity," she said bitterly. "His destiny should be greater than that."

"Actually, it will be," Arthur assured her.

"Uther's son should be a great warrior, not some—"

"To tell the truth," Arthur interrupted, "he *will* be a great warrior."

Her face lit up with surprise and pleasure. "Are you sure?"

He supposed it was no time for modesty. "I'm sure. A very great warrior."

"We need great warriors," she said fiercely.

"Yes, you do," Arthur said slowly, "don't you?"

"Vortigern left us a land divided by warfare, chaos, and poverty." Her tone was as bitter as her earlier smile had been. "Fields lie fallow. Roads disintegrate. Roaming bands of outlaws burn, pillage, rape, and murder, and no one is strong enough to stop them."

"I remember . . ."

"People starve. Begging orphans fill every town and village."

How could he have forgotten?

"And we all fight amongst ourselves, giving our enemies every opportunity to conquer our native land and destroy us all."

But he *had* forgotten. As he lay dying in despair, he had forgotten how he had changed all of that. He had forgotten the hopeless desperation and mindless violence of the era in which he had been born and grown to young manhood. He had forgotten how badly his vision and his strength had been needed by this tormented land.

"What's to become of us all?" Igraine muttered. "What's to become of my child?"

"Things will be different," Arthur said. Igraine would not live to see the future he would shape, but he wanted her to know. He wanted to comfort her with the truth. "*He* will change it."

She looked down at her swollen belly. "You're positive it will be a boy?"

"I guarantee it."

"A great warrior?"

"There is no doubt."

"How will he change things?" she challenged.

"He'll stop the Saxons. He'll unite the Britons. After years of warfare to accomplish this, he will rule in an age of peace and prosperity. Until . . ." No, why tell her about that? Tonight, his defeat and death were still unthinkably far away, and not very important compared to what he would achieve in the meantime. "People born in his reign . . ." He made a gesture which encompassed the despair and chaos Igraine had described. "They won't even know about all this unless older people tell them stories about these dark times."

She regarded him intently. "He will do all this?"

He nodded.

"If I give him to Merlin, as promised, he will do all this?"

"Yes."

She put a protective hand over her belly. "And what if I don't give him to Merlin?"

He realized for the first time, with the only feeling of affection he'd ever felt for his mother, that giving him away had been very hard for her. "Then I don't know what will happen."

"I see." She looked down at her belly again. "But if I give him away . . ."

"Then I promise you, all that I have described will come to pass." He felt pain slide back into his own belly, throbbing slowly.

"Then . . ." She sighed and slowly lifted her hand away from her body, away from the child within her. "I will keep my promise. When he is born, I will give him to Merlin. And never see him again." There was no mistaking her resolve.

Pain, seeping through his senses, making his breath hurt, making his limbs weak. "Oh, but you will see him again. Once."

"I will?"

The hope in her voice made his eyes water. Or maybe it was just the pain. Eating away at his strength, burning through his flesh . . . He doubled over, fighting it.

"What's wrong?"

Her voice seemed to come from a great distance as his body called him back to his own place and time, the final hours of his own destiny . . .

"What's wrong?" A stranger's voice.

"What do you think is wrong, you idiot?" Bedivere's

voice. "Half his innards are back at Camlan. Try not to hit anything else with this damn barge, will you?"

"I'm sorry. It's dark, and—"

"If I want excuses, I'll ask for them."

"Easy, Bedivere," Arthur chided weakly. "Who will look after me if you force that man to throw you into the lake?"

"Ah, you're back with us." The words were terse, but Bedivere's voice broke.

"Briefly."

"Sire, they will heal you at Avalon. They will—"

"I'll be dead by dawn."

"Arthur."

"But . . ." He recalled the visit. Merlin. Igraine. The dark world he'd been born into and had re-made into a shining land of prosperity. "But we did good work, didn't we, Bedivere?"

"Of course. Did you ever think otherwise?"

"Well, I'll confess to a moment or two of doubt today," he said dryly. "But . . ." He had had the vision, the strength, and the will to create instead of destroy, to build a new world and nurture its development. How could he have turned his back on such a destiny, after all? "Yes, what else could I have done?"

Pull the sword from the stone, boy. Seek your destiny.

"He had to be killed, Arthur," Bedivere said, misunderstanding. "It was battle. It was war."

Poor Mordred. "That wasn't . . . what I was . . . thinking about." It was becoming difficult to find enough air to speak. He was growing weaker, dizzier, fainter. But at least the pain had numbed slightly and wasn't as soul-destroying as it had been before. Death was coming closer with every moment.

He had conceived Mordred in blind passion and total ignorance, and later dealt with his shame and regrets as most men dealt with such things—foolishly. *Hide away the bastard got on your own half-sister.* Yes, he had hidden away his shame and regrets—in the person of his only son—until so many mistakes made as a man finally overwhelmed so many great deeds performed as a king.

"So many regrets . . ."

"Well, then . . ." Bedivere hesitated before saying, "She had to be sentenced, Arthur. Adultery in a wife is high treason in a queen. She knew the risk."

"Yes . . ." So many regrets, indeed.

And what sorrow and loneliness had driven Guinevere to such a risk? They had loved each other once. He remembered it well, though it was long ago. They had been so young. But that simple, youthful, conjugal love had not been strong enough to survive the demands of kingship, the humiliation of a barren queen, and the unspoken but unmistakable devotion of another man. By the time her preoccupied and frequently absent husband realized she had already turned away from him for the love of another man . . .

By then, I only cared that she should be discreet and not get caught. Poor Guinevere. It must have been the ultimate humiliation, that her own husband didn't really mind when she fell in love with another man.

Well, if she was going to betray her husband, Arthur supposed it might as well be with the best man in Britain, the best man any of them would ever know.

"And it was love, after all . . ."

Love, which Lancelot had kept locked in his heart, barren and unnourished, for years. Love, which shone in Guinevere's radiant face for a short while, before jealousy, sorrow, and frustration had started intruding upon what they shared. Love, which survived secrecy, unhappiness, recriminations, suspicion, the heavy burden of guilt, and—in the end—even public disgrace.

If Arthur's life had lacked one great thing, it was a love such as that shared by his wife and his best friend.

"Love . . ." he repeated.

Bedivere said nothing, as Arthur expected. The infidelity had lasted for years without exposure precisely because no one wanted to talk about it. Not until Mordred and Agrivaine (thank God that viper was dead now, too) started casting their long shadows over Camelot.

So many regrets. And no time left to save what he had spent his life building; someone else must do that, if it was to be done. That he had built it must be enough. Now he had only time left for one task: to die well. Even in this, a king should impart courage to those around him.

There was only one more thing he would like to do, one last person he would like to see before he died. One last grievous wound to be healed . . .

He recognized Joyeuse Garde, Lancelot's home, because he had laid siege to it not long ago. He knew he was in the past again because the high stone walls and surrounding land showed none of the damage he had reluctantly done to it when forced to pursue Lancelot here after the knight's rescue of Guinevere.

And while I was here, my son was stealing my throne.

And now it was here that he hoped to find the heart to die well, as Merlin had advised.

"Who goes there?"

Recognizing the voice, Arthur turned to face him.

"Lancelot," he murmured. So young, so fresh, so eager for life. Filled with dreams, vision, and noble ambitions.

The young man—armed with quiver and bow, evidently returning from a morning of hunting—approached him.

"Yes." Lancelot studied him, seeing—Arthur knew—a much older man. "You are a friend of my father's?"

"Yes. But I didn't come to see him."

Lancelot tilted his head, alive with curiosity. "Me, then?"

"Yes. I . . . I understand you want to join Arthur."

"Yes!" Enthusiasm flowed forth. "My father wants me to stay here with him, but I—I want to join the young king in freeing and uniting the people, in creating a just and noble world!"

"And if I tell you there will be hardships, losses, sorrow?"

"Then I say: I am needed!" His eagerness was like a tameless horse.

Arthur felt pain seeping into his body again, even here in Merlin's magic realm. Death was very near. *Wait, wait, give me time, just a few more moments . . .* He sank slowly to a stone bench and gestured for Lancelot to join him. The young man's energy was exhausting.

"Are you ill?" Lancelot asked.

"Just . . . a wound. It is not healed." True enough.

"You must come into the castle!"

"No." He shook his head. "I must go in a moment."

"But—"

"I came on Arthur's behalf."

That got Lancelot's full attention. "The king sent you? To *me*?"

"Not exactly, but he needs good men, and he . . . he trusts me to recognize them."

"Then . . . you think I should go to Camelot?"

He sighed. "Tell me, Lance. What do you hope to find at Camelot?"

"Great work," the young man replied promptly. "The chance to fight injustice and defend the weak. To answer the call to noble deeds and to achieve difficult victories."

"Oh, you will find all of that," Arthur admitted, "and more."

"Will I meet the king?" he asked hopefully.

"Yes." Why not tell him? "In fact, you will become his cherished friend."

"No! Truly?" He frowned. "But how could you know this?"

"That doesn't matter right now. But I need to know one thing. What price are you willing to pay?"

"Pay?"

"I mean . . ." Arthur gritted his teeth as the throbbing in his belly grew worse. "What sacrifices is this destiny worth to you?"

"Every sacrifice!"

"Even if I told you . . . you will love in sorrow and one day leave Camelot in disgrace?"

Lancelot stared, dismay clouding his sharp young features. After a moment, he asked, "Will the king condemn me? Will Arthur revile me?"

"No. Whatever happens, Arthur will love you until he dies."

"And . . . there *will* be great work?"

"Yes."

"I will fight injustice and defend the weak?"

"Yes."

"There will be noble deeds?"

He thought of the Grail. "Yes."

Lancelot took a breath. "Then surely what happens to me—this sorrow and disgrace—surely this is unimportant. I will follow my destiny at the king's side."

"Are you sure?" Arthur asked. The young could be so arrogant, so self-assured, so naive. "Are you *sure*?"

"Yes."

"Your suffering will be great. Your sorrow unbounded."

"I am sure," Lancelot said.

And Arthur saw that he truly was.

"There is one other thing," Arthur added. "What we build . . . I mean, that which you help Arthur build—it may not last."

"All things come to an end," Lancelot said. "Even Rome eventually fell."

"True," Arthur admitted, his head now spinning from pain and weakness.

"But if we do the things you say we will do, then surely what we build will be remembered."

"Remembered? Does that matter?"

"Of course!" Lancelot smiled at him. "And the memories will inspire those who come after us to build again. Do you not think so?"

"I . . . I hadn't thought about it," Arthur realized with surprise. He'd been too busy trying to hold his world together. "I hadn't considered that."

"Then you should," Lancelot said simply.

"Yes," Arthur agreed slowly. "Yes. I should."

"I think your coming here is the sign," Lancelot said.

"Sign?"

"That it's time for me to leave, to go to Arthur's side."

"Yes," he agreed after a pause. "Yes, I believe the time is right."

"Will you accompany me?"

"No," Arthur said, regret flooding him. Those days—those years—had been golden, but a man could live his life only once. "You go now. I must return to my place. My own . . . task awaits me now."

"As you wish." Lancelot rose to leave Arthur. After a few steps, he turned hesitantly and said, "Thank you for coming. Thank you for giving me a choice. But you see . . ." He shrugged. "There could be no other."

"Yes." Arthur gazed at Lancelot, gilded in the morning light of youth and hope. "Yes, I see that now."

There could be no other choice for any of them.

And the memories will inspire those who come after us to build again . . .

"Avalon?" Arthur asked weakly.

"Just ahead, sire," Bedivere promised.

Bedivere, one of the few survivors. One of the few left to go on after this dark night, to live through the chill dawn and carry the torch of their dreams.

"All that we did . . ." Arthur began.

"Don't tire yourself," Bedivere advised.

"Listen to me." It was a king's command, weighty despite his physical weakness.

"Yes. Yes, of course." Bedivere bent close to hear his breathless whisper.

"Our work . . . has been worth . . . every sacrifice."

"Yes, sire. I know it has."

He heard the repressed tears in Bedivere's harsh voice.

"Ah, don't weep . . . my friend." He struggled for air. "It's a good death." He grasped at consciousness. "Only . . . one more . . . task."

"What is that?"

"Don't bury the dream . . . with me."

"What do you—"

"Excalibur," he rasped. "Into the water . . . Give it to . . . the Lady of the Lake . . ."

"But sire!"

"Into her keeping . . . for whoever will come, someday, to take it up again . . ."

"Arthur, please . . ."

"Someone will . . ." With the last of his strength, he gripped Bedivere's hand. "I promise . . . this is only a . . . pause . . . The end, no . . . I promise . . ."

A king should impart courage to others even in his death.

"So take . . . the sword . . . and fling it . . ."

"Yes, Arthur. Now?"

"Now," he confirmed.

He felt the weight of Excalibur lifted carefully away from his side. He floated in the quivering realm between life and death, between wakefulness and the final sleep. After what seemed a long time, he heard a faint splash. He was too weak to open his eyes when he felt Bedivere return to his side.

"Her hand," Bedivere said in amazement. "It came out of the lake to catch the sword and drag it under."

"The final task . . ." He was too weak to smile. "A good death . . . A good life . . . All wounds healed . . . but *this* one . . ."

"This is the one that counts," Bedivere said in despair.

"No, my friend, no . . ." In his last moment of life, he managed to find the strength to smile briefly, after all. "It is only the one which sends me to my rest."

Black Dogs

Lorelei Shannon

Though the hearth-fires of Ehangwen blaze high on this night, they have no power to warm me. The air is rich with the dizzying odors of roasting venison, spiced wine, fresh bread. I hear the strains of lively music and the strange, coughing sound of human laughter. Silk flashes as the dancers whirl past me. I gaze at their long, frail-looking limbs and wonder that they can gambol so.

There is a wildness to this revel, a desperation that makes my hackles rise. There is unrest in the kingdom. All here know that. But they know not what I know; that my lord the King will be dead within the fortnight.

I know this as surely as my own name, or the forests surrounding the castle, or the scent of my master's body.

It is not truly the treachery of my lord's own whelp that will end his life, although he shall be fate's instrument. It is the event that occurred in the deep forest outside Dinas Bran nearly one year ago that has brought doom to the King. This event only he and I were witness to, so it will never be written in books of history. There is nothing that I or any other earthly creature can do to prevent what it will cause. I cannot even cry; the human release of tears is denied to my kind. I can but lie here at his feet and remember, and wish to all the powers of nature that it had never happened.

What a day it was! A fine, blue morning, clear and shining. We hunted that day, just my master, his beloved mare Llamrei, and I. That happened so seldom; we were usually surrounded by knights and courtiers, noble men and sycophants. But the King had tired of ignoring his lady the Queen's continued betrayal; he had tired of the politics and lies and complex ways that humans seem compelled to affect. Like a young knight errant, he had taken us, his loyal companions, and traveled to the kingdom of Powys to seek adventure. I was overjoyed to be with him.

We charged through the woods like the Wild Hunt, mad with the thrill of the chase. Oh, the smells! Rich earth, green trees, squirrels, birds, horse, man, the boar we pursued, musky and sweet.

He was no magical thing, no wicked king transformed like the strange beast Twrch Trwyth, but a mighty creature nonetheless. Ysgithyrwyn by name, this beast was brave and clever and fierce. My admiration for him was as strong as my desire to have his blood in my mouth.

"Come, Cabal!" cried my lord, grinning like a wolf. Llamrei snorted and pawed at the leafy ground. "The boar is just ahead!"

With a burst of speed, I pulled away from my master and shot through the bushes, roaring a challenge to the boar. I could see the great flanks of the beast not far ahead, crashing through the underbrush on the far side of a clearing. I brought my haunches beneath me, preparing to leap.

It happened so fast.

A flash of teeth as long and sharp as daggers. A savage roar, icy breath on my face, a scent of Faerie strangeness, which turned my insides to stone. A great black dog reared up before me, seemingly from nowhere. I screamed a war cry and lunged for his throat.

My jaws closed on nothing. The beast was gone. I am not ashamed to say that I ducked my head in fear and whined like a weanling.

Behind me, I heard a whinnying shriek, a crash, and curses. Moments later my master came running through the trees.

"Llamrei threw me, can you believe it, boy?" He stopped, looked over his shoulder. "I can't imagine what's come over her! Good God, look at her run."

My lord smiled, patting my head. "She'll be back, that one. She'll return when the wildness leaves her—what on Earth . . . ?"

I rammed my head against his hip. I wanted, of a sudden, to leave this place.

"And what of you, my lad? Where is that boar? He didn't slip away from you, did he?"

I whined, pawed at his boot. My lord laughed, thinking that I was ashamed to have let the beast get by me. In truth, I was consumed by a creeping yet urgent terror. I stood up, placing my paws upon my lord's shoulders, seeking to push him out of the clearing.

He playfully gripped my ears, scratched my cheeks. "It's all right, Cabal. The day is young. We may catch him yet."

I could feel wyrd magic sizzling around us like fat drippings in a roaring fire. The creature, the Black Dog, was coming back. And I knew, I *knew*, that my master must not see it. I groaned and threw my weight against him.

But my lord is a mighty man. He did not give ground, did not fall. He laughed and wrapped his arms around me, as if to grapple, as we sometimes do.

And then he froze. His eyes grew wide, his mouth opened, he gasped. With sinking despair, I knew that the creature had appeared behind me.

I dropped down to the ground and whirled, baring my teeth and snarling.

The Dog made not a move, but stood there, staring at my lord with unnatural eyes of luminous green.

It was a massive thing, bigger even than I am. Like me, it was as black as midnight, but where my coat is smooth and shining, this creature's was rough and shaggy. Its eyes burned with witchfire; the whole beast seemed to shimmer with the stuff. Wave after wave of cold, searing rage came boiling out from the very heart of the thing.

"Where did you come from, big fellow?" my lord whispered, head cocked like a hunting falcon. I realized that he could not see the wyrdness of the creature at all. To his blunted human vision, it was simply a massive dog. I felt that made him all the more vulnerable to whatever witchy mischief it might be up to.

I took a step toward the Black Dog, growling more loudly, showing all my teeth. I would chase it all the way to the Christians' Hell before I would let it harm my king.

"Easy, my lad." My master set his hand gently upon my back. "This great fellow means us no harm. See, he's but standing there like a startled hart. Most likely, he's lost."

It was true that the beast was not moving. It was as still as one of the wizard's stones on the Salisbury Plain, staring, staring. But its rage was so strong I could taste it. I turned to look at my master, yipped with frustration. How do humans get through their lives with so little perception?

His eyebrows raised, just slightly. I whirled around, and saw that the Black Dog had gone.

"My, but that big creature moved fast, Cabal! It seemed to melt into the woods like smoke."

Seemed to? It did, I was sure of it. But I had no way to tell this to my lord.

"That must've been what frightened Llamrei. Imagine that, being frightened away by a damned dog after all we've been through together! Perhaps she's getting old." My master shook his head.

But I could not blame Llamrei. Horses are sensitive to the world of Faerie. The Black Dog was simply too much for her delicate senses to bear, like the blast of a thousand war trumpets, or the rays of the sun on the eyes of a nightbird. But I wished she had taken my master with her, and left me to deal with the creature myself.

We spent the day walking together, running, stalking. We never spotted the boar again, but my master shot a fine fat hare with a single arrow, roasted it, and we ate it like a couple of woodsmen, with lots of lip smacking and very few manners. It was delightful, but still, I could not be rid of my anxiety over the Black Dog.

At last we headed back toward town. My master chatted with me, pointing out squirrels, petting my head. The sun was sinking low over the trees.

"I believe we'll stop for the night," said my lord, face turned up to the sky. "I've begun to worry about Llamrei. Perhaps she will see our fire and come to us. Shall we make camp?"

Dear Mother Earth, that was the last thing I wanted! I ran ahead, barking and prancing.

"Very well," he laughed. "We'll go a bit farther."

We were silent as walked through the trees, side by side. Occasionally my master would rest his hand on my head or pat my back. My love for him was as strong and fierce as a thunderstorm.

"What's that, my lad?" My master peered through the branches at a simple building of timber, sod, and thatching. The shape of a cross was carved into the massive wooden door.

"A church! Shall we pay a visit?"

I whined, pranced away. It wasn't merely that my kind do not worship the god of Judea. I could sense the strange presence of the Black Dog nearby.

"No time to play, Cabal, we're losing the light. Come." And with that, he strode toward the church.

"Good God . . ."

My heart began to pound. As I drew near I saw that there were claw marks on the door, deep and head-high to my master. Obviously the work of a great dog or wolf. But what froze my guts was the fact that the claw marks were scorched, blackened, as if the very beast who made them had been ablaze.

"What deviltry is this?" My lord had one hand on the pommel of Excalibur as he slowly opened the heavy door. I was there immediately, pushing my way in front of him. I was prepared to defend him with my last breath.

The church was silent, empty, and very dark. The heavy beams spaced along the walls and ceiling gave the impression of ribs, as if we were in the belly of some monstrous animal. The stench of candles and incense was first overpowering, then painful. It filled my nose, coated my tongue. I pawed my muzzle and sneezed, and it sounded very loud to me.

Gradually, I began to smell other things, beneath the

tar-thick scent of ritual. The wyrd scent of the Black Dog, and another, muted odor: the lush and compelling smell of death.

I groaned, licked my master's hand, wanting him to leave immediately. Instead he absently patted me and went to inspect the small altar.

I went with him. The candles were cold and unlighted, but they smelled pleasantly of tallow. There was a great cross of hammered copper on the wall behind them.

My lord peered around the thick wooden wall that separated the altar from the sacristy.

"Hello?" he called. I woofed softly, although I knew the church was empty of mortal beings. I could see in the darkening shadows; he could not.

After a moment, my master turned away and made to leave, and I eagerly followed. I paused to sniff one of the rough-hewn, simple timbers. My lord brushed his fingers over it, and they came away covered with soot.

We reached the town of Dinas Bran in the purple twilight. There in the middle of the street stood Llamrei, looking rather embarrassed. My master gladly embraced her graceful neck, and she nickered to him in her strange, liquid language. My kind has always understood the languages of Man, since our tribes were bonded by the Lady herself at the dawn of time, but the speech of horses is a mystery to us.

My lord found a safe, warm stable for Llamrei at an inn called the Fat Corbie, and secured a room for himself while I waited patiently outside. Then we ventured into the adjoining tavern for some supper.

My master pushed the door open wide, then surveyed the room, hands on hips, before entering. I stood proudly at his side and inhaled the delicious smell of roasting mutton.

"Sweet Jesus! 'Tis old Padfoot himself!"

The hoarse cry was followed by other human shrieks and bellows of alarm. A heavy man with a beard like a gorse bush pointed at me. A young girl cowered by the fire. A tall, thin fellow in the robes of a priest shot to his feet and stared at me with accusation and horror.

My master looked back at them, and raised an eyebrow. The young girl shrilled incessantly, like a wounded blackbird. My King looked down at me, as if to see if I had sprouted horns or grown a third eyeball.

"You mean this fellow?" He patted my head. "This one's name is Cabal, not Padfoot. You've nothing to fear from him. He's got better manners than most noblemen."

And with that, he stepped into the tavern. He sat at a heavy wooden table as if he owned it, and motioned to me to lie at his feet, which gladly I did.

There was silence for a moment. Then the bearded man burst out laughing.

"By all that is holy, we thought your hound was the black devil who's been plaguing our village. Sit, stranger, and welcome. I am Gwrhr. This is my daughter, Morwen, and our good priest, Father Dywel."

"I am John, of Glastonbury." My lord gave a wink, which only I could see. "Some ale, Gwrhr, if you please. And some of that mutton for myself and my companion."

The young girl, a thin, blonde creature with the dark eyes of a doe, immediately attended to it.

"What is your errand in Dinas Bran, Sir John?" The voice of the priest was deep and strangely flat.

"No errand, Father. I merely seek adventure, and honor for my king."

The holy man rubbed his bony chin. "Your time would be put to better use in the service of our Lord and Savior."

Anger flashed in my master's eyes. "I serve him always, Father, as all good Christians do."

Young Morwen approached with ale and great plates of meat. She was but a child, I saw, no more than twelve.

She placed my lord's supper on the table, then hesitated, still holding my plate.

"Just set it on the floor before him, lass. He'd sooner die than bite you." My master's smile was kindly. He cocked his head. "Do you like dogs?"

"I do, sir," said the girl, with a tiny smile. She gave me my platter. I paused to lick her cheek before gobbling the delicious feast.

Morwen stroked my back with her fingertips, as if she thought I would break. "I had a dog once."

"Leave Sir John be," said Gwrhr, stirring the fire.

"She's no bother. I'm glad of the conversation," my lord said, wiping his mouth politely on his sleeve. "Tell me about your dog, Morwen."

The girl's eyes shone, perhaps with tears. "Oh, he was something, my Soot. A fine big pup, brave and loyal and gentle as a lamb. He wore a little brass bell around his neck on a cord, which I bought for him at the summer fair. So I'd always be able to find him." Her lip began to tremble, and she caught it between her teeth.

"What happened to him, lass?"

"He vanished, sir. Just vanished, into thin air, more than two years ago now. I think that thing, that terrible Black Dog, must've killed him." Big, silent tears slipped down her pale cheeks.

"Perhaps he still lives," said my lord gently, touching the girl's blonde hair.

"He is dead," she whispered. "I can feel it in my heart."

"Then," said my master, scratching the base of my

ears, "you shall see him in Heaven. He will be waiting for you."

Morwen smiled. "Truly?"

"Of course not." The priest strode over to my master's table, face pinched and angry. The girl sobbed once, and ran to her father.

The King scowled. "Why would you say such a cruel thing to her?"

"Why would you tell her such lies?" The priest crossed his arms, as if he were scolding a naughty child.

"No lies, Father. Who on this Earth is more virtuous, more loving, more deserving of Heaven than a dog?"

"Animals have no souls. Everyone knows that but idiots and heathens."

My master stayed seated, gazing up at the priest with a clear eye. "Then idiot I must be, for I shall never believe that. Animals are God's creatures just as we are."

"Animals were created by God, but they are merely here for our use. For our consumption. Does wheat have a soul? Does a pear tree?" Father Dywel spoke slowly, as if addressing a halfwit.

My lord's eyes twinkled. "Perhaps."

"Heathen!" roared the priest. "If you honestly believe that, Sir John, you are no Christian man."

"Indeed I am, Father. I love the Lamb more than I love my own life. I am a pious man. But when I look into the eyes of a dog, I see such purity, and such goodness . . . I know I see something of the divine. The soul of a dog is as visible in his eyes as are the tears in young Morwen's. I will continue to believe that, unless you can prove to me that the Almighty has whispered otherwise in your holy ear." My master smiled, but his tone was steel. Gwrhr and Morwen watched him with eyes wide.

Slowly, the priest's face went from whey to ash to crimson.

"Blasphemy," he hissed. "No wonder our town has been cursed with a demon." He started for the door, then paused to cast a venomous look over his shoulder. "A demon, John of Glastonbury, in the shape of a dog." And with that, he was gone.

My lord had already turned his attention back to his dinner.

"Please, sir, forgive the Father. His church has been plagued since the day it opened its door to us. Poor Soot's disappearance was but the first of many diabolic events." Gwrhr refilled my master's cup himself. "Now all but the most pious fear to set foot in his church. Some have even reverted to the Old Ways."

My lord nodded slowly. "Tell me of this demonic hound, this Padfoot."

As the words left his mouth, I was filled with a most terrible dread. I began to shake. I whined and nudged at my master's leg with my nose. He absently patted my head as Gwrhr replied to him.

"He is a creature of Hell. He destroys crops and sours milk with a glance. He sets fires. He kills sheep and goats."

The King swirled the liquid in his cup. I could tell that he was skeptical. We had investigated "witches" and other beings thought to cause such mischief before, and always had we found the cause of sour milk to be warm weather. But this . . . this was different. I felt it in my bones. Why could my master not?

"Tell me about the claw marks in the door of the church, good Gwrhr. About the soot on the timbers."

My dread increased. I did not know why, but I wished my master to stop speaking of the terrible hound. I growled long and low.

"Quiet, lad," my lord whispered. Gwrhr glanced at me with trepidation and went on.

"It was a year ago, sir, during Michaelmas. The church was filled with the faithful, peacefully at worship, when that devil came calling. The Black Dog scratched at the door, howling fearfully, burning like brimstone. Then the church door just flung open, and Padfoot ran blazing into the church, biting, clawing, murder in his eyes. He leapt onto the altar, reared up on his back legs, so that he resembled some form of hideous man-beast. The church grew hotter and hotter 'til the very air seemed to shimmer. The worshippers thought they would be incinerated. But before the church could burst into flames, the Black Dog vanished."

"Mmm," said my master. "Did you witness this yourself?"

"No, Sir John. I was here with Morwen, who was ill on that day."

"Mmm. Was anyone badly hurt?"

"A few were scorched, a few bitten. But they're not likely to complain about it. No one dares, for fear of the curse."

"Curse?" My master was as courteous as always, but I could tell he did not believe Gwrhr at all. I, however, did. I whined and licked at my lord's hands.

"Hush, now!" he said, irritated. "I'll take you out in a moment. Gwrhr?"

"Indeed, sir. If you see Padfoot with your own eyes, you mustn't speak of it for one year and one day. If you do, you'll die, good Sir John. You'll die a year from the day you spoke his name."

I was seized with an overwhelming terror for my master. I knew in my gut that Gwrhr's words were true. I began to bark loudly and rapidly, to beg my King not to speak. Gwrhr took a step back, and Morwen cowered in a corner.

"Cabal! No!" cried my master. Although it rent my

soul to disobey him, I continued to bark, pleading with him to be silent.

My lord rose angrily and strode to the tavern door, throwing it wide. "All right! Out with you!"

I crept out from under the table and stood in the center of the room, barking like a mad thing. I desperately hoped that my master would take me outside, and we would leave this place.

"Cabal! *Out!*"

I wouldn't budge. Dear Mother Earth, why couldn't he understand me?

My master seized me about the middle and half carried, half dragged me to the door like a pup who's soiled the rug.

"Bad!" he cried. My disgrace burned inside me like liquid fire. He flung me out bodily, and slammed the door.

I continued to make noise; clawing at the door, barking, whining, until I realized that it did no good at all. I could hear the men talking still. I cocked my ears to listen.

". . . And how, exactly, do you know that the curse exists?"

"Everyone else was too frightened to breathe a word of it, sir, save Llewelyn the blacksmith. He came in here that very night, saying he needed strong ale, and told me the whole story. He always was a bold one. Well, Sir John, no sooner had the last word left Llewelyn's mouth, when he was struck dumb. He couldn't so much as squeak. And a year to the day later, he dropped dead, just fell lifeless to the Earth two feet from the church door. We learned our lesson, we did. There's no one in this town will admit to seeing the beast, although he seems to be everywhere at once."

There was a brief pause.

"But you speak of him, Gwrhr."

"Only of that incident, sir, which I did not witness. As it happened more than a year ago, y'see."

A longer pause. I whined, scratching at the door.

"Nonsense,"

No, I barked, *no!*

"Nonsense. Why, I saw the hound this very day. A big beast, indeed, with a strange green cast about its eyes, but no demon. Just a big black dog, like my own Cabal."

I threw back my head and howled.

When my lord at last emerged from the tavern, I danced anxiously around him, wondering if he had been struck dumb like the unfortunate blacksmith.

"Hey, my boy. What's got into you this night? I've never known you to be a naughty fellow. Was it something you smelled?"

Your death, I thought.

It was true. Although my master still had his voice, he had the stink of the curse all over him. A rancid magic, sparking with anger and pain. It was with a broken heart that I followed him to the stable, where he left me for the night. Llamrei felt my anguish, and rubbed her velvet muzzle against mine.

My master came to get me before dawn. He was as excited as a child. "We are going to the church this day, Cabal, to summon Dinas Bran's 'demon.' Won't they be surprised to discover he's just a great mongrel?"

I licked his hand, loving him desperately.

The morning light was a soft, buttery yellow. A crowd gathered around us at the front of the church, muttering, speculating about the brave knight who meant to rid them of the Black Dog. Some thought him foolish, others thought him mad. Wagers were placed on his survival. My master was in high spirits, laughing and joking in the easy way of a true leader. I stood nearby, head and tail drooping, listless with pain and fear.

"Black Dog!" My master's voice was like rolling thunder. "Black Dog, I summon you! Come and face me on this holy ground, you child of Satan! Come! Come, boy, and I'll give you a fine soup bone!" He winked at me.

Many in the crowd gasped at my lord's audacity. One or two laughed. The church door swung wide. Father Dywel stepped out, bony face an angry, boiled scarlet.

"Leave this place, you heretic! How dare you summon a demon to the House of the Lord?"

"How?" My master laughed. "Like this, Father. Come, boy! Come, Black Dog! Come to me now!"

Everyone was silent, waiting. A tiny lad began to cry. Morwen, eyes wide and fearful, took her father's hand.

"See? Nothing. I tell you, it's but a dog—"

There was a terrible crack, as if lightning had struck right next to us. In an acrid flash of smoke and flame the Black Dog was there, blazing like the fires of Hell. It reared up on its back legs, roared a challenge in my master's face, and lunged for Father Dywel, great jaws gaping.

The giant paws struck Dywel's chest, knocking him to the ground. The priest began to shriek. But the Hound did not pause; he leapt over the man on the ground and dove into the church.

"Mother of God!" cried my master, more excited than afraid. He charged in after the beast.

It leapt up onto the altar, scattering candles, setting one sod wall ablaze. I lunged ahead of my master and screamed a battle cry. The Black Dog whirled. It did not hesitate; it flung itself at me.

We fought. This was no gauzy spirit, no phantom of

smoke. My jaws closed on the Black Dog's furry shoulder and met with hard-muscled flesh. The creature's teeth were like knives as it snapped at my face. Heat came from the Hound in blasting waves. Smoke from the blazing wall choked me and burned my eyes.

We slashed, bit, tore with paws, each vying for a grip on the other's throat. I threw my weight against the Dog, attempting to flip it onto its back. It was like running into an oak tree. With a growling roar, it feinted at my foreleg. When I drew back, it struck like a snake and seized my neck in its deadly jaws.

"Cabal! Move! Get back!" My lord sought to save me; he held his sword aloft and ready to strike, but we were entwined, my foe and I. He could not strike at the beast without hitting me as well.

I knew in that moment that I was dead. All the Black Dog had left to do was close its jaws and tear my throat out.

But it did not. I realized, with no small surprise, that it was simply maintaining its grip on my neck, and pushing me backward a step at a time. Why did it not end this? I had failed my lord the King; I had nothing left to live for.

The Dog shoved me again, and I bumped into something: the wall between the altar and sacristy. My lord circled around, eyes wild with frustration and anger.

"Move, you devil!" he roared. "Let him go, and face me!"

The teeth of the Black Dog pressed harder against my neck. I felt its teeth break my skin. I gagged, unable to breathe. I shut my eyes and hoped death would be quick.

Then it was gone. The pressure, the pain. I took in a great whooping gasp of air. The Black Dog's paws hit me square in the chest, bowling me over like a clumsy pup.

The beast reared up, snarling at my master. Its eyes,

like molten emeralds, were fixed on him. Witchfire danced around it madly. The blaze from the wall near the altar, which had spread to the ceiling, filled the church with bitter smoke.

My master howled and brought Excalibur down in a mighty arc. The sword passed through the creature as if it were made of water and smashed into the wooden wall behind it.

The Black Dog vanished. There was a great whooshing sound, as if all of the air had been sucked from the church. The fire, which had consumed the altar, went out instantly as the wooden wall came crashing down.

My master jumped back and covered his head. I looked up, cowering, expecting the ceiling to fall. It didn't.

The smoke was clearing. My lord took a step toward the fallen wall, and then another.

"Sweet God," he whispered. I moved quickly to his side to see.

The wall had been hollow; more a tall, narrow box than a wall, really. Something lay curled inside it; something I did not wish to see.

It was the skeleton of a dog. A pup, in truth; a strapping big fellow but only half grown. It lay on its side, curled up miserably, muzzle tucked against its bony chest. I could see curls of rough, shaggy black lying beneath it like a carpet. Deep claw marks, some stained with old, brown blood, scored the inside of the shattered boards. Something caught the light at the base of the pup's throat, or where its throat once had been.

My master bent down and took it; a small metal object on a rotten cord. Silently, he turned and left the church. I followed.

He approached a wide-eyed Morwen, and placed the

object in her hands. She stared at it, unmoving for a moment or two. Then she began to sob.

"Why?" roared my master into the face of Father Dywel. "Why?"

The priest's face was pale. "It—it is tradition," he said, not meeting my lord's eyes. "It is protection for the church—"

"Protection? How the bloody Hell is a dead dog meant to protect your church, man?" Seldom had I seen my lord so angry. If I did not know that he would never kill a priest, I would have thought Dywel a dead man.

"It—the dog's spirit is meant to—"

"His spirit? But dogs have no souls, have they?"

"It is part of the Old Ways, and we must strive to integrate—"

My master shoved his face but inches from Dywel's. I was surprised that the priest did not roll over and show his throat. "I am well acquainted with the Old Ways, priest. Sometimes there was sacrifice. Never torture."

"It was but a dog! A rude beast—"

"Hypocrite."

My King's voice was ice.

The priest drew himself up to his full height. "Do not speak to me so. I am a man of God."

"Not my God." My lord turned his back on Father Dywel. "Come, Cabal. Let us leave this place. I find its odor foul."

Prancing, happy, I danced around him. It was over! The Black Dog, no demon at all, was at peace. Surely my master was free of his curse! I leapt up to lick his face.

Imagine my sickening shock. He still was soaked in deathmagic.

With a tormented howl, I whirled and ran into the forest.

"Cabal!" he cried after me. "Cabal, come back, lad!"

* * *

I ran and ran. I saw nothing. I heard nothing. I felt nothing but my own anguish. When I could run no more, I collapsed beneath a great oak tree. There I lay, curled up on my side like young Soot, howling. I intended to lie there until I died.

I heard something; a light step, the crack of a twig. I raised my head, not caring if it were a child or a dragon.

It was a stag. A great, lordly creature with antlers like the branches of a tree in winter. He stared at me with an uncanny, golden eye.

My breath caught in my chest. I felt wild magic wash over me. I rolled over to show the Horned God my belly and throat.

"Your heart is broken," said the stag, in a voice rich and strange.

I stood, head bowed. "Yes, my lord. My master, the King, is cursed to die."

The stag was silent, but there was compassion in his eyes. I was taken with a mad notion.

"Horned Lord, please help him! Your magic is strong. Can you not take the curse from my master? He is a good man, honest and worthy and true. I beg you!"

The stag slowly shook his noble head. "I cannot. For it was I who breathed life into the curse, good Cabal, and nothing can take it from him."

"You? Why?" My world was crumbling. I willed my heart to stop.

"During the many long, agonizing days it took Soot to die, he summoned me with his piteous cries. First he begged for freedom, which I could not give him. I have no power in the house of Yahweh. Then he cried for death. I could not grant that to him either. In his anguish, he went mad. With his dying breath Soot called for terrible vengeance; he uttered a curse, random and ruthless.

He beseeched me to give him the power to enact it. I could not deny him. How could I?"

How indeed. Soot had been grievously wronged. "Is he truly at peace now, Forest Lord?"

The stag turned his head to look at a shadowed hollow. There for a moment appeared Soot; the real Soot, not the terrible form his angry shade had taken. A frolicsome pup gamboling in the woods, his mistress's little bell around his throat. *Poor lad,* I thought. *You deserved better.*

The ghost dog barked once and was gone. With what little was left of my heart, I was glad for him.

"My master set him free," I said, pleading, groveling at the stag's hooves, not caring for my dignity or my pride. "Please, Horned Lord. Please do not condemn him to death. Take my life for his. Please. *Please!*"

"I cannot. No power in this world can remove a curse spoken by the dying. Not even he who spoke it."

"What—"

"After the death of the blacksmith, Soot regained some of his senses. He bitterly regretted what he had done, but he was powerless to stop it, until the day he saw your master. Soot knew he was the one. I am truly sorry, dog, that it must end this way."

I crumpled.

The Horned King towered above me like a mighty tree. His golden eyes locked with mine. "You must stay with him. Be his friend, for all others will turn away from him. Spend what time you have left in his company."

"I do not think my heart can bear it," I whispered.

"It must. The duty and the destiny of your kind is to give without question."

He turned silently, and was gone.

* * *

I returned to my lord the King. He was mightily glad to see me, and threw his arms around me in a fierce hug. I breathed in his scent and kissed his bearded face.

And so our lives went on. We left Dinas Bran and tracked the boar Ysgithyrwyn through the deep woods. He fought bravely, but with my help, the King dispatched him quickly and cleanly. I did what was required of me, but I had lost my taste for killing.

I have spent the year at my lord's side, fighting, hunting, playing, keeping him quiet and faithful company. There have been fine, joyous days when I nearly forgot how it will end. There have been days when the weight of it was so great that I could barely rise from my bed. But it is almost finished now.

And so I lie at his feet, savoring every second of the time we have left together. And when it is over, I shall leave this place. I will journey into the woods to seek my death in the jaws of a lion or a pack of wolves, that I may be with my lord the King once more, this time for all eternity.

Marwysgafn
(Deathbed Song)

Eric Van Lustbader

Good morning, or is it evening? When you get to be my age it does not seem to matter. Really? Well, there are many, many things you have yet to understand. Just add this to the list.

So you have come after all. I confess that I did not believe that you would. Why? Well, for one thing, it is such a long way for you to come—all the way to the brink of the Underworld. For another, I had great doubts as to whether you could. I mean to say you are only human. No disrespect intended, you understand. In fact, as you know, no one could have more respect for humans than I. Then, again, I had all but forgotten our appointment. It was made so long ago, and I am so very, very old.

First of all, can you understand me? Good. Welsh was my first adoptive language—never mind about my native tongue; such as you can never hear it—but I have tried over the years to improve my English. So. I expect

you have a thousand questions. Patience, my child! I will
answer them all, in time. Time. Ah, in the end, I have
outlived all of them: Uther, Ygraine, Morgause, Morgaine, Arthur, and Elaine. But how they live on in my
memory! That is why you have come all this way, at
such personal peril, is it not, to find out the truth. I was
charged with protecting Arthur, the king, and yet I stood
by and watched him be destroyed by the people he loved
most dearly. You want to know why. Oh, do not bother
denying it, my dear, I can sense your questions gathering
like clouds upon the horizon. Well, I have no doubt that
the history I am about to relate will not disappoint you.
But because you have read all the legends and the lies
that grew up in the centuries since those people lived
and loved and schemed and sinned and died I know that
it will surprise you. Yes, indeed it will. Hell, my girl, the
truth always surprises, have you not yet learned this simple lesson? So now I say to you, brace yourself, for you
may not care for what you are about to hear.

Well, then, let me see, how to begin? Call me Myrddin; my mother would have, if I'd had one. Having had
neither a mother nor a father I am now of an age when I
can admit that it has often been difficult, if not outright
impossible, for me to understand the ways in which the
human psyche is swayed, torn, and distorted by its rela-
tionships with its parents. However, I can claim to understanding with a certain degree of experience the ways
in which a man can be swayed, torn and distorted by a
woman.

I emerged from the bole of a massive ancient oak tree
that had been lately struck by a bolt of lightning and was
thus hollowed in its core like the heated womb of Vul-
can's mate. I was fifteen years old then, as humans de-
termine age, and the sky was dark, indeed, over the
ravaged British Isles. Fortunately or not, depending on

one's point of view, I was born near enough Tintagel to have had a hand in subsequent events. Of course, the ensuing years have cast a different light upon these events than that which I then perceived. Shadows have emerged that I was then too young to have imagined, let alone have recognized. I imagine now that I could have been born in the Loire valley or, for that matter, in the steaming hinterlands of Borneo if that was where I had been needed. As Fate would have it, however, it was in the bloody heart of England that I first stepped forth upon the Earth.

Possibly Fate is too vague a word for the happenstance of my birth, for I was summoned to that particular age and specifically to the dank and forbidding castle of Tintagel by the Lady Ygraine. At that time, Ygraine was the wife of Gorlois, the current duke of Cornwall, who was waging a savage and bloody war with Aurelius and his brother Uther Pendragon.

I was guided to Tintagel by a great horned owl, whose passage above my head I could hear, though no human being could. We went across marshlands and fens rife with minuscule life, skirted lakes in which the blue-and-silver sky was reflected in serene dioramas, crossed battlefields mired in the blood and rent flesh of brave soldiers and foolhardy kings. Apart from the horned owl's passage, the only sound I heard was the harsh cries of the skittish carrion birds, come to feast on the stinking remains of mankind's great folly. Using a secret underground passage disclosed to me by the owl, I passed undiscovered into the castle keep and there, high in an octagonal turreted chamber pierced with slender windows to gather the sunlight at every hour of the day, I came face to face with Ygraine. She was surrounded by her three daughters: Morgause, Morgaine, and Elaine. Not to mention two hundred lit candles. I confess that I never saw Ygraine when she wasn't surrounded by candles. But more about that anon.

I must tell you that the lady and her daughters were of one visage, as if chipped from the same magnificent block of gemstone. They were dressed alike, as well, in thick, floor-length cloaks of purple finespun cloth interlaced with gold thread, the backs of their heads shrouded in cowls. For good or ill, these women and I had an immediate kinship, for I could tell that like me, they were not born of man.

I have said that the four women bore the same face. Ygraine's enormous hooded eyes were without color, undoubtedly they were the orbs of the great horned owl that had been waiting in the limbs of the oak for me to be born. In her daughters, however, there was a difference. Morgause's eyes were jet black, Morgaine's were an intense jade green, and Elaine's were a calm sea blue.

"I had thought to call you Ambrosius," the Lady Ygraine said almost at once, "but now that I see you in the flesh, as it were, I believe Myrddin suits you more." She had a strong voice, which rang in the room like a church bell. For all her voice's beauty, however, her syntax was as clipped and terse as a battlefield general's. This was a woman used to getting what she desired. She cocked her head thoughtfully while her penetrating gaze parsed me as if I were composed of mere words. An apt simile, as it happens, since she had conjured me with an incantation. "Yes, I do believe Myrddin suits you quite well. And why not? At the time of your birthing I had the brawling Celts in mind rather than the decadent Romans."

"How may I serve you, Lady?" The words flew out of my mouth seemingly without assistance from my brain. One moment I was listening to her, the next they were simply *there*. Here was the first clue to my own Fate.

"Come, sit down." She lifted a slender arm, ushering me to a carved wooden chair. Her smile was genuine enough, but there was a chill about it that made one want to hunch one's shoulders. "Have some mead." She slid into my hand a chased silver chalice incised with the Duke's coat of arms: a single black dragon, its tail curled about its body like a serpent. "It is a favorite of the humans; possibly you will develop more of a taste for it than I have."

It was cold in the room, despite the sunlight and the tapestries of violent hunting scenes that hung upon the thick stone walls. I would have preferred something to warm my insides, but I drained the dark liquid as I imagined she wanted me to do. It was thick and sweet and fermented, like the dead on the battlefields I had passed on my way here. When I told Ygraine that her daughters laughed, the three as one, as if giving voice to the reaction in their mother's mind.

"Do you like it, then," she asked, "more than I do?"

"That remains to be seen, my lady."

"No, it will not." With a spidery forefinger she tapped the center of her forehead. "You sprang full-blown from my head. You feel what I feel, you know what I know. As if you were my right arm, you obey me in all things."

"I understand, my lady." As it happens I did not. But the more curious thing was that she did not, either. Because, in the end, she was wrong about me.

Ygraine had closed her eyes. Her pale, strong hands were clasped in her lap as if she were a holy woman in prayer. She had a wide brow and long, curling hair the color of a moonless night. Her nose was straight as a sword, with curiously flared nostrils that had the ability to make her at times seem dangerous. In all, she was striking without the burden of being beautiful. Hers was a countenance in perfect balance between animal cunning and remarkable intelligence. In my newly arrived naïve state, this observation could not fail to impress me. This, too, she wished, though I could not know it then. It was only many years later that I came to understand all the facets of her intelligence, including duplicity and deceit.

Her eyes flew open, her pupils dilating with the light. She took the chalice from me. "Now that we have celebrated your arrival in our own small way, it is time to get to work. For there is much to be done." At this, her daughters closed about her like a mantle thrown across her shoulders. "Myrddin, we embark here upon a great experiment. My daughters are the last of their line—besides you, I dare say, the last of their kind. *Our* kind. Gorlois has given me five daughters."

"I see here only three," I said.

"I mean there are five others." Ygraine smiled so that the points of her teeth showed between her pink lips. "Morgause, Morgaine, and Elaine are not of his seed, though naturally he believes that they are. They were conceived as you yourself were conceived, Myrddin, through focused thought and incantation. But this is not the way to perpetuate a race. Already in these three I see flaws that even I cannot address. If the incantations continue the flaws will begin to overwhelm the whole in the subsequent issue. So another means must be found to ensure that our kind will not die."

"My lady, if I may ask, just what is our kind?"

Ygraine lifted a hand and Morgaine came around to take it. She looked at her mother while Ygraine again closed her eyes. At once, Morgaine's shape began to shimmer and deliquesce. In her place appeared the great horned owl that had led me to Tintagel. The bird clasped Ygraine's wrist with its yellow talons.

"If I may say so, my lady, this is nothing more than a

conjurer's trick." So saying, I placed my hand on Elaine's shoulder. With the contact, I felt her entire body tremble and in the space of a single heartbeat something inexplicable and wholly unexpected raced through me. Her head turned and in her sea-blue eyes swam an emotion with which I was entirely unfamiliar. Then I had uttered words I had never spoken before, part of a language the origins of which I was ignorant, and Elaine's fair form shimmered and dissolved. A large and fierce-looking hawk gripped my wrist. I passed my hand through the image of the hawk and it shattered like a porcelain vase. Elaine was again standing beside me. I took my hand quickly off her shoulder before that disturbing sensation could run through me again.

"Is that what you think me, a base conjurer?" Ygraine bestowed another of her curious smiles upon me. She waved a hand and, with that, the walls of Tintagel fell away. We emerged as a flock of snowy egrets, supported by the currents in the air. And we flew, the five of us, over the Cornwall landscape, out of the sunlight and into a curious colorless mist that swirled, as I came to see, above a huge circular lake. As we descended farther into the mist I saw a land mass in its center rising up as if to greet us, and the mist blew away from us in all directions at once. When we landed, we were our normal forms again. The sun shone strongly from a cloudless sky and songbirds twittered sweetly. Insects droned in the somnolent heat. Above our heads a line of egrets flew in formation. They were sharply outlined against the bowl of the sky, but on all sides the horizon was shrouded in dense fog.

"Welcome to Afalan," Ygraine said. We stood in the center of an enormous apple grove that appeared to stretch out as far as the eye could see. I knew without her having to tell me that *afal* was the Welsh word for apple. "This is our land, all that is left of it. The scourge of humankind, bringing with it its pestilent baggage of war, deities, and devils, squats like a pustule on the rest."

Her glowing eyes swept through the neat and orderly rows of magnificent gnarly trees before she turned to me again, watching with ill-concealed contempt as I ran my hands over the tree trunks, gathered up handfuls of earth, tasted of its curious sweetness to assure myself that Afalan was real and not another of her clever glamours.

"It is so very lovely, is it not?" Elaine, drawing close, asked me.

"A more peaceful place I cannot imagine, my lady."

"Peaceful, yes, precisely." She allowed the rich black earth to sift through her fingers. "I find when I come here a glorious serenity that reaches into my very bones." Her eyes were bright and sharp and somehow intimate as she proffered a shy smile. "I am at peace here. I am home."

"And so it should be," Ygraine broke in. "We are the first people to inhabit the Earth, before humankind rained down upon us like locusts." Her colorless eyes seemed to take on a fiery hue as Elaine and I stood, moving a little apart from one another. "They are a plague, an abomination against nature, with their endless wars, their restless bestiality, their astonishing capacity for cruelty, and their jealous, vengeful male gods. They are our nemesis."

"If it is a war we are waging with them, then surely our power—"

Her voice was almost a wail of despair. "What good is the power against a host so huge as humankind?" Ygraine shuddered. "They breed like rabbits, and they birth *males* at an alarming rate. This is something we cannot easily do. It took me a long time to conjure you. You can walk among them as an equal, while we females can only wield our powers from the deepest shadows, lest they come to suspect us of witchery and behead us with one stroke of their broadswords."

She came so close to me I could smell her breath, which was spicy, as if scented with cloves. "And so I bethought myself to wed Gorlois, and by his seed create a new race—not us, not them—something new, different, able to carry on our traditions in the new world that humankind's coming has wrought." Her eyes closed once again and, as if scenting danger, her daughters closed about her. "Five times I mated with that hirsute, stinking beast, gritting my teeth while making the necessary incantations, and five times I failed." She thumped her chest. "My essence is nowhere to be found in his offspring. They are like him, a lump of stone, nothing more. Swiftly, swiftly, they will follow him to the grave, if there is any justice left in this world."

I felt a sudden dizziness. The space around us went black, and when again I opened my eyes we were back in the octagonal tower of Tintagel. By the acute angle of the sun I could tell that it was hastening toward twilight. Time had passed, but where it had gone I knew not.

Ygraine was re-lighting the candles that in our absence had guttered. As each was lighted, her three daughters repeated the incantations of holy blessing. "But now I have you, Myrddin," Ygraine said, when she had finished. "You will help me in my plan to plant *our* seed among humankind. To ensure that we will not perish from history." She blew out the flame on the tinder stick, and I could not but help follow the few lines of smoke, which curled from it like a cat emerging from sleep. "I now perceive the flaw in my calculations. Gorlois is the wrong man. Though he be the duke of all this land he is doomed to be defeated by the Pendragon. I have seen that the Pendragon will unite all of Britain and rule the land for many years. Already I perceive their lasting place in history. From *them* will I receive the seed that will save us."

She took me by the elbow as we paced around the room while the three girls watched and bided their time. "The problem is the two brothers, Aurelius and Uther. They are inseparable. And now, especially, when the war fever runs high within them, I have no chance of gaining their interest. Therefore, go you now among the Pendragon war camp. Make yourself indispensable to the kingly brothers, and when you have, spread over Uther a glamour—take the form of Gorlois and slay Uther. This will serve to inflame Aurelius, so that when I come to him as the wife of his mortal enemy, when I allow him to seduce me, he will be vengeful and rampant, ready to impregnate me. For I tell you this truly, there is nothing that inflames their males more than the bloodlust of taking revenge on their own kind."

And so I began my initiation into the world of the humans. What a stink they make! Their bodies manufacture an agglomeration of acrid and sulphurous odors the likes of which I could not have imagined. And they rush about like mayflies, often taking action without proper thought or deliberation. They react by instinct and call it justice. They are self-righteous in their rage. And yet . . . And yet they have the capacity to love that inspires an awe in me I cannot with any accuracy describe.

I entered the Pendragon war camp as a full-blown wizard. Claiming to have seen the future, I was taken before Uther himself. In this, Ygraine had been correct. Had I been female, making the same claim would have precipitated only the swift and sure removal of my head from my shoulders.

As it was, Uther at first regarded me with a dark and

suspicious gaze. "Where was it you said you came from, wizard?"

"As it happens I did not say," I told him solemnly. "But as you asked, I come from an isle known as Afalan."

"Avalon, you say," he growled, mangling the name in his Celtic language. "This is a land of which I have no personal knowledge." He stalked around my person as if he were a caged animal. "Nor have I heard it mentioned by my scouts, cartographers, or minstrels. Does it lie south across the water from here—in Bretonne, mayhap, or even beyond?"

"Oh, not so far away as that, my lord," I said. "It is in your own backyard."

"Now you mock me, if I take your tone." He drew his sword halfway out of its scabbard. "Have a care, wizard," he thundered. "I tolerate no disrespect."

"I hear your roar, my lord," I said, bowing slightly.

Uther froze. Had I offended him? "Yes, as you have marked me betimes I am rather the beast." He threw his head back and laughed, and clapping me heartily on the back, cried, "Wizard, if your magic be half as sharp as your sense of humor, it will do me well to draw closer to you." He kept his exceptionally strong arm about my shoulders. "Come, walk with me!"

We strode out of his tent, a pair of armed retainers several paces in our wake. At first blush, the camp appeared to be in a state of utter chaos—as I say of humans, a morass of men rushing about at an hysterical pitch, all seemingly without a coherent thought in their heads—but I soon learned that there was a method to this chaos. The archers and arbolasters ringed the encampment, making of themselves a living fortress. Within, the foot soldiers mingled with the cavalry, giving both brief respite from their arduous labors. In the camp's very center lived the generals and the carpenters, chemists, smithies, engineers, and strategists who, each in their own separate way, were busily preparing the host for its final assault on Tintagel. Once, a small contingent of lightly weaponed scouts on horseback reined in long enough to give Uther the latest report on the enemy's activities. They were given fresh horses and then they were gone.

Uther returned his attention to me. "My man tells me that you can predict the future, Merlin." Again his Celtic tongue mangled a name. "If this be truth, pray tell me what lies ahead for the house of Pendragon."

"Victory, my lord," I replied without hesitation. "Victory most sweet over Duke Gorlois. It is the Pendragon's Fate to unite these islands in a reign of unprecedented peace and prosperity."

"A bold prediction, wizard. But I warrant I could as easily get the same from the madman who lives in a cave five leagues to the west. Should I then ask him as well? In these parts, I daresay he has more of a reputation than does the young wizard Merlin."

"My lord, I confess I know nothing of repute." I put my hand on his shoulder and the two retainers sprang into action, drawing their swords and brandishing them at my person. "Too soon for you comes this time of trust." I looked deeply into his eyes. The eyes, as Ygraine would have me believe, of the nemesis. "Believe me, Uther, when I tell you this moment will come to you only once."

For a moment, Uther did nothing. The hungry swords were ready to disembowel me, and I perceived another truth of Ygraine's. Despite our power, we were nothing compared to the monolithic might of the humans, who were at once less and more than we were.

Then the future king nodded and said to his retainers, "Sheath your swords. This man is friend to me and mine." He glanced at them. "Now go. Make my wish known throughout the encampment."

When they had left, Uther said to me, "Now is the moment, Merlin. We are alone amidst a mighty warhost. Declare yourself. Show me my trust is well placed."

In answer, I passed a hand across his eyes and at once we were transported to the secret underground entrance just outside the towering stone battlements of Tintagel. Uther's eyes became as big as the full moon in a cloudless sky. But he uttered not a word as we went into the tunnel, emerging into the keep itself. He made to draw his sword as a contingent of Gorlois's knights marched into view, but I stayed him with my hand.

"Nay, my lord. Be calm. I have thrown a glamour about us. No one may mark our presence nor overhear our voices so long as we remain within Tintagel's walls."

Uther rubbed his eyes and looked at me with a kind of awe. "Merlin, from this day forward I am in your debt." He looked around eagerly. "Take me to Gorlois. I want to look again into the bastard eyes of my antagonist."

I led him across the main yard, filled with the bristling preparations for siege and fierce warfare, and indeed Uther could mark well that none took so much as the slightest notice of our passage. Gorlois was recently come from a council with his generals, taking his leisure, goblet of mead in hand, with his wife. They were in conversation when we arrived, but of course Ygraine sensed us, and she turned her head slightly in our direction. When she did, Uther gave a gasp and gripped my arm like a man on the verge of drowning.

"Merlin, is that the Lady Ygraine, of whom I have heard much?"

"Aye, my lord. This is the duke's wife."

"I want her," Uther said with a kind of glazed look in his eye.

By this time, Ygraine had turned back to her conversation. I could see that Uther was too smitten with her to have noticed that she had marked us.

"I must have her, Merlin."

"My lord, a word of advice. With wizards it is best to take care what you wish for."

He turned to me, and I saw in his face that nothing I might say would turn his mind from its chosen path. "Can you arrange it? Having brought me here to the heart of my enemy's keep, how difficult would it be to effect our quick joining?"

"She may be true to her husband, lord. Or again she may not find you fair of visage."

"But I am swept up with her. My god, man, just the sight of her consumes me," Uther said. "Quickly, use your glamour."

"It is not so easily done."

"And why not? Use it, wizard, otherwise of what earthly use are you to me?" A sly smile crept over his face. "Ah, Gorlois is with her now. I take your point. Then at a time of your choosing throw a glamour about me so that when you bring her to me she will think I am Gorlois. Then will she willingly join with me as if we were in their own marriage bed."

Uther made his intimate measure of the forces arrayed against him and then we took our leave of unlovely Tintagel. Back in his tent, he uncorked for Aurelius and me a bottle of an amber liquid that tasted like fire as it went down. I could scarcely complain, however, since within the walls of that dark and unseemly castle, my stomach never failed to shrivel and grow cold.

"Merlin, we hardly know one another," he said, loung-

ing on a canvas and wood stool, "but I mean that to
change starting now."

I had already spent an hour with him and his generals
as he relayed the information he had gathered from inside the enemy's stronghold. Wisely, he chose a ficti-
tious explanation for this sudden wealth of strategic
information, inventing a spy inside the duke's forces. No
one gainsaid him, save his own brother. Possibly this
was to be expected. While Uther was a calm and reasonable man, Aurelius was cursed with a vexatious nature
that sorely tried those who loved him best, not the least
of whom was Uther himself.

"Why have we heard nothing of this spy before now,
brother?" Aurelius queried. "And having him unknown
to us, how are we to trust his information? What if Gorlois has turned him? We could be walking into a trap
cleverly set by the duke."

"For one thing, though Gorlois is a formidable general, he is hardly that clever," Uther said in a calm, rational voice. "For another, I myself recruited this spy. His
information is unimpeachable. I saw with my own eyes
the underground passage that will gain us access to Tintagel."

But Aurelius was hardly listening. "And what are we
to make of this wizard, who miraculously appeared at
just the right time? A stranger in our midst who you have
already granted more status than he might deserve." He
glowered at me. "Have a care, brother! Mayhap the man
to whom you so willingly grant your friendship in these
perilous times is a spy or an assassin." Aurelius had a
scar on one cheek, which ran up into a milky eye, which
slouched like a wounded animal behind permanently
slitted lids. "I have marked him, brother, and men who
have my ear have marked him, and we are agreed on one
matter: We trust him not."

"Gainsay not Uther," one of the generals said, stepping forward. But before he could continue, Aurelius landed a prodigious blow to the side of the man's face, knocking him cleanly off his feet. The other generals stirred in agitation, and I have no doubt that a terrible row would have ensued, had not Uther put his arm around his brother and hugged him to him. In so doing he turned him right away from the downed man and the gathering crowd and steered him toward the tent flap.

"Merlin has already proved himself a loyal friend," he said into Aurelius's ear. "Calm yourself, brother. Let us away to my tent, where we will drink and tell stories of the golden days of old and drown in the past any bad blood that has arisen."

In this manner was Uther able to cajole good humor back into a man given to bouts of quixotic pique and fits of paranoia. So it was that I proceeded to drink with the brothers Pendragon while Aurelius told stories of the founding of Bath by Bladud and the settling of Leicester by the great tragic king known as Leir, all of whose work was undone when his kingdom passed into the hands of his two bickering daughters. But he waxed most eloquent when it came to delineating the Pendragon line, which he traced back to the knight-regent Vortimer, who successfully repelled the Saxon invaders after they had successfully usurped the crown with the connivance of the hated Vortigern. It was Vortimer, Aurelius stated, who had restored the rightful lineage of Britain's kings that had now devolved upon the Pendragons.

One could see by the look in Aurelius's good eye that this was the kind of talk he liked best and, as he became more loquacious, he lost his sullen and guarded air. He was a simple man—a soldier to his heart and soul. Knowing his passion made his erratic behavior somewhat understandable: He had a vision of a united Britain under the Pendragon standard and he was fearful of allowing anything or anyone to get in his way.

For his part, Uther spoke of the founding of the British Isles by the Trojans, Brutus, the great-grandson of Aeneas, and Corineus, who founded Cornwall. Uther seemed particularly taken with Aeneas, who, according to legend, survived the sack of Troy to travel with the Sibyl all the way into the Underworld and back. "Aeneas is linked in some way to the Holy Grail," Uther said. When I asked what that was, he laughed good-naturedly. "Where have you come from, wizard, the bole of a tree? No matter. The Grail is said to be the cup Christ the Savior drank from during His Last Supper on Earth. It is most holy. Where Aeneas discovered it is a matter of speculation. For myself, I believe it was a gift from Queen Dido of Carthage, who fell in love with Aeneas the moment he set foot in her African city." I could see from the gleam in his eye, the words that tumbled forth from him as eagerly as schoolchildren on an outing, that this was a topic close to his heart. "In any event, it is clear from the texts that Aeneas had the Grail in his possession when he returned to Rome. But soon after, it was stolen or lost, I know not which, appearing subsequently in the Middle Eastern kingdoms closer to the point of its origin." He sighed as he drank deeply of the liquor. "I tell you the truth, I would gladly go to war with the Devil himself to possess it. With it in hand, we would within months unite these war-ravaged islands."

The Romans had a saying: *In vino, veritas,* and I suppose it was true. The brothers, in their cups, revealed their true natures.

As I watched, Aurelius slid further and further into oblivion, until only his maimed milky eye remained open. When he was asleep, Uther rose, and walking unsteadily across the tent, placed his hand tenderly upon his brother's brow. "Now you know the truth about him, Merlin," he said softly. "You see before you a righteous man. Our priests insist that the Pendragons have been touched by God, that our mission is pure and holy. We want only what is best for this land. My brother longs for the endless bloodshed to be finished as, God knows, do I. If he is gruff and unforgiving, if he is even at times difficult, then so be it. For myself, I cannot love him any the less for his faults, for they are as much a part of him as are his gifts of unshakable courage and vision. Our priests tell us that God made man in His image. Then man sinned, tasting of the forbidden apple of knowledge, and was cast out of Eden into the world. We are a people of sin and redemption. It is the Devil himself who throws temptation into our path at every step we take and, God knows, our flaws make us vulnerable. But without any one of those flaws we would be lesser men, and that, I warrant, I could not abide."

His hand still curled in his brother's damp hair, he turned to me. "Now, wizard, do not obfuscate. In the matter of the Lady of Cornwall, will you give me what I want, what I must have?"

Not in the way you want it, I thought. Not given the Lady's extreme antipathy to the duke. And, in any case, this very woman who Uther desired so feverishly had ordered his murder. And I, the assassin, was standing beside him as serenely as a contented shepherd with his flock. Except I was not contented at all. In fact, now that I had spent time with Uther, Ygraine's directive seemed unconscionable. These humans—or at least this one— was not at all as she had portrayed them. Instead of despising Uther, I found myself feeling protective toward him, as if he were my wayward but beloved child. Casting my mind back to the moment he came under the spell of Ygraine's otherworldly nature, I now saw that he was as innocent as a babe in the manger. It was then I realized I could never kill him. Strangely enough, by some alchemical process of which even Ygraine was ignorant, I seemed bound to him as thoroughly as I was bound to her.

His eyes blazed. "Answer me, damn you!" But almost immediately that fire died and he slid to his knees before me, his forehead bent upon my lap. "Ah, no, I cannot ask this. God forgive me, it is wrong. I cannot think but that because she is the wife of another she mayhap is the Devil's work. And yet . . ." He raised his head and I saw tears glistening in his eyes. "And yet I find it matters not," he whispered hoarsely. "I do love her so, my Merlin."

"Because she is the most precious possession of your enemy?"

"I recognize the truth in that, wizard. But I swear to you if that were all the allure I felt I could in faith forego her." He shook his head as if in disbelief at his own words. "You are the master of mysteries. Can it truly be so? Can a man love a woman from the first look?" When he said this a curious vision bloomed in my mind. For an instant, I was back in the octagonal tower with Ygraine and her daughters. My hand was on Elaine's shoulder and there was fire running through me as I stared into her sea-blue eyes.

"Yes, my lord," I answered him. "I believe it is possible."

"Oh, Merlin." Uther's face contracted with emotion. "I confess I know nothing of Ygraine beyond scurrilous hearsay, and yet this very void is a sweet nettle at my back, heating my blood, urging me on. She exists here"— he thumped his forehead with the heel of his hand—"in my mind, a perfect image. The perfect woman." His hand curled into a white fist. "And so though I sin I must have her. I must!"

I put my hand on the crown of his head. Like Ygraine, I could feel the royal bloodline, the cacophonous sweep of history as the Pendragons subdued the warring clans of Briton and forged an empire that even the indefatigable Saxons could not topple.

When I spoke, my voice possessed an odd echo. "So be it. Who am I, then, to stand in the way of so great a passion?"

That night, in the tent beside Uther's, I slept poorly. Possibly Elaine took that as the opportunity she sought to pay me a visit. She appeared first as a vision, insubstantial as smoke from a brazier. Her smile seemed tentative, but that might merely have been a figment of my imagination.

When her form became real, she said: "Have a care, Myrddin. I fear for your safety here amongst the Pendragon warhost. I smell deceit and betrayal and I like it not."

"Are you so much like your mother, then," I said, sitting up in my muslin cot, "to think so little of the humans?"

"It is not the humans I fear for, Myrddin. It is you."

"Do you care so much for me, then?"

"You know it not?" She seemed puzzled. "Did you not feel what I felt when we touched?"

I could not deny to myself what had happened between us, and yet I was possessed of a powerful trepidation of these women. I knew not what they planned or even of what mendacity they were capable. "Yes, I felt what you felt. But I am too little time in the world to understand the nature of all things, especially an emotion so profound."

"I understand this not. My spirit guides me and I follow it as willingly and avidly as a child."

"Then I fear for you as you do for me. Guard your spirit more carefully, Lady. It is more rare and precious than any gem I could name. Like a sword, it should be kept in its scabbard and not imprudently exposed."

She pulled her thick, cowled cloak close around her. "Now I have offended you."

"Not at all. And I do not say that I feel differently than you. But non-action allows the natural order of things to be revealed. It is my nature to lie hidden in the shadows, to watch and wait. At least for a time."

"Then time is what I shall give you," she said, becoming once again as transparent as haze. "And I shall mark well your words." What remained of her rose in a spiral, evaporating into the darkness at the top of the tent.

Unnerved by Elaine's appearance, I took my time settling back onto my cot. My heart had just slowed sufficiently for slumber when I heard Morgaine's voice whispering to me. "I know what you plan, Myrddin."

"How can you know my mind," I said, startled, "when I myself know it not?"

"Because I want the same thing." She sat close beside me on the edge of the cot. "You and I have much in common, Myrddin. More than I would have thought to first look at you. We both chafe to disobey Ygraine."

I confess I was taken aback, but sought to conceal my consternation in quick denial. "I fear in that you are mistaken, Lady."

She took no heed of my words, however, but leaned toward me and pressed her mouth against mine. In the dead of night she wore but a thin cotton shift, and I could feel the heat of her skin as if I had drawn near an armorer's kiln. Her lips were warm and moist and, after a very short time, I felt the dart of her tongue like the

graze of a wasp wing against my lips. Then she pulled
away and held my face cradled in the palms of her
hands. "You are not afraid of Ygraine, nor are you destined to be her cat's-paw," she whispered. "You have
your own ideas."

"I have no wish to—" But she put a hand across my
mouth, silencing in midstream my unconvincing protest.
In almost the same motion, she pushed me down onto
the rumpled blanket and spread her body over me like a
mist across the sea-edged moors. Through my body ran
a tremor of recognition and my mind flew back to the
compelling charge of energy I felt when I had gripped
Elaine's shoulder. Morgaine moved upon me and at once
I felt all the hillocks and secret valleys of her body. I
imagined myself standing on the edge of a swamp, being
pulled slowly and inexorably into its very heart. Her
shift parted magically, drenching us both in the scent of
her most intimate parts. At that moment all choice fled
me. I could do aught but partake of the sweetness of her
moist body. But I confess that while my ignited flesh
was lost inside her my mind was consumed by images of
Uther and Ygraine. Now I felt his yearning for her as if I
were myself the future king. Then, this too faded, to be
replaced by images of Elaine when we had first met and
touched, and then when she had come to me moments
ago.

The animal sounds of Morgaine grunting out her passion caused my thoughts to dissolve like base metal in
acid. I became acutely aware of our surroundings, and
casting my consciousness about the tent, I sensed an in-
voluntary movement in the darkest part of the far corner.
Someone spied upon us!

I lit the darkness with my consciousness enough for
me to make out the figure standing rigid as a block of
ice. It was Elaine! So she had not, as I had imagined, de-

parted. A dank coldness such as that I felt within doomed Tintagel overcame me. Now I wished only to push Morgaine off me, but she was as entwined upon me as if she were a strangler fig. While she worked vigorously to bring us both to completion I could do aught but watch Elaine's face as it became paler and paler. Just at the moment her sister cried out in ecstasy, Elaine turned her white face away. My own rationalization came back to flail me: non-action had proved as treacherous a course as its opposite. If this were the natural course of events, I wanted no part of them. Then my heart leapt in my breast. Perhaps all was not lost.

Elaine! I called to her in my mind. *It is you I love!*

Ah, Myrddin, you were right to fear for me. I should have kept my spirit sheathed. My heart quailed when I heard her reply echo dreadfully in my mind.

I was a fool to have sent you away.

As you said, it is your nature.

Elaine, for you I would cause the sun to burn at night. I would cause water to run uphill.

Even if you could accomplish the impossible, it is too late. It is too late for us all. More fool me to think anything could be changed. You have betrayed me with mine own sister. Our Fates are sealed. Now, surely, all of Ygraine's wishes will come true.

I saw her image begin to fade, and I closed my eyes and wept.

Morgaine of course mistook my tears for those of delight. "Ah, Myrddin, now that our desire has been brought to fruition," she whispered still atop me, "I propose an alliance. You and I will wed. Together, we will make a stand against Ygraine. You possess a power unknown to either of my sisters."

"Or to you, either, I take it," I said drily.

"Now you mock me."

"I do no such thing," I lied, at last carefully unwinding myself from her embrace. "I am simply feeling my way in the dark."

"Then let me light the candle for you. I will be your guide and you will be my strong staff. Together, we will gain more power than any of our kind has ever before conceived of possessing."

I confess that I was sorely tempted, for I saw in her unholy alliance a way for me to save Uther from the butcher's knife. But I knew that if I agreed I would be bound to Morgaine as I was now bound to Ygraine. A man with an unsupportable burden has little incentive to switch one boulder for another.

"You have given me much to ponder, Lady," I equivocated. "And you will agree that this alliance is not one to be lightly entered into." More than anything else now, I needed time to extricate myself from the webs these women were spinning, each in her own way and to her own ends.

Her eyes lit up the darkness. "While that may be true enough, when moving against Ygraine a swift lightning strike will serve us better than walking with cat's feet. We must work the element of surprise to our best advantage. If she comes to suspect anything amiss before we have begun we will surely be undone."

"How goes your labor, Myrddin?"

I had already discovered that Ygraine had her own spy in the Pendragon war camp, but it would have been foolish to give her an inkling of my knowledge. "I have demonstrated my powers to the brothers Pendragon, and as a consequence they have clasped me to their mailed bosoms."

She smiled her strange reptilian smile. "That sharp tongue of yours will make your repute, I will warrant."

Ygraine was the kind of woman who cherished repute to the detriment of her spirit. She prided herself on being upright and righteous, and was therefore neither.

We were in her vast chambers at the heart of Tintagel, which were deliberately kept dark and full of burning incense. Tallow tapers ringed the rooms, providing a multitude of small, glowing haloes that illuminated wooden chests, animal-skin carpets and hammock-like chairs. Atop one chest floated a miniature boat, low and sleek, with both oars and crimson canvas sail painted with a white egret in flight. The prow of the boat arched upward in a graceful swan's neck and ended in a female face. The whole was so intricately carved it was nothing short of exquisite.

While I drank in these surroundings, Ygraine leaned on the stone sill of a slitted window and peered down at the courtyard of the castle keep, where her husband, the man she plotted against, took his exercises with his most robust knights. "You have not yet drawn blood."

"It is true that Uther still lives, my lady."

"Then kill him swiftly," she snapped. "I do not intend to dally in being impregnated by Aurelius or in bringing the fetus to term. I can in weeks accomplish what it takes human women nine months to do. And with a lot less pain, I might add."

"I do not dally, my lady," I said.

"Good. Because you know not yet the insidiousness of their notions. One need look no further than their God, who lives only for vengeance. To say nothing of their Devil, who was once their God's sure right hand. Cast out for his sin, he lives only to thwart his former master. It is nasty business to be avoided at all costs. I do not want you infected with their zealousness."

"Have no worry, my lady," I said. "I merely await your help."

She turned away from her contemplation to gaze at me with her colorless eyes. "How, pray tell?"

"Gorlois must be seen outside the walls of Tintagel—leading a raiding party, possibly meant to probe the opposing army's current strength. That will certainly appeal to him. Word will filter back to the Pendragon kings and I shall use it to full advantage when, posing as your husband, I slay Uther."

The Lady Ygraine was the only person I ever met who looked evil when she smiled. Possibly I was the only one who saw it, for it is truth she captivated all the human men in her life. "A lie swaddled like an innocent babe in the cloak of truth. I like your mind, Myrddin," she said, that smile in full flower. "Yes, I like it well, indeed."

And so she worked her magic on Gorlois, who obeyed her in all matters great and small, so smitten with her was he. And he was doubly careful to make certain no other human was privy to this weakness; he was as obsessed with repute as was his wife.

The very next day he set out with a small band of knights on an expeditionary foray. With my connivance, it did not take long for Uther's men to bring back news of his movements. Uther ordered his scouts to shadow the band and to take careful note of all they surveyed. Aurelius of course wished to ambush them and murder Gorlois straight away, but Uther had other plans. He did not wish such a sweet, swift warrior's death for the duke of Cornwall. Rather, he wanted Gorlois alive to know that he had been cuckolded—and by whom. Only then, he told me, would he slay the duke. Of these inner plots he revealed nothing, not even to his beloved brother. Instead, he made a clever and logical argument for giving Gorlois what he was obviously seeking—a glimpse of the opposing army. But only a piece of it. Gorlois, thinking the army arrayed against him was far smaller than it actually was, would become overconfident and this would swiftly infect his entire force, making it that much easier to defeat. It was a clever plan, even Aurelius could see that, and he acquiesced with a minimum of debate.

I had now before me a thoroughly repellent choice. I could do aught but commit murder, that much was clear. But I knew that if I did precisely as Ygraine bid I could not live with myself. Murdering Uther would be akin to killing a part of myself. Slitting Aurelius's throat was not easy. The act weighs heavily on my conscience still. But I know that had both Aurelius and Uther led the triumphant army against Tintagel that autumn, disaster would have ensued. For both these men were born to rule; neither had the temperament to share the title of king. They would have torn each other limb from limb before they would have acquiesced to that. In the end, I could not change what Fate had decreed for them.

You see these hands, my girl. They are covered in blood, many times over. Well, that is my Fate and I have come to accept it. Most days, that is.

So then, I stood over Aurelius in deepest night. Outside the tent-flap, I could hear the soft chink of metal against metal as his guards exchanged a few whispered words. I could feel Uther's love for him as if it were a blanket that protected him. But that was not enough. Fate had dictated that Uther's love at this moment be turned aside. During the last of my preparations, I felt the presence of the Grail, as if some fragment of it existed inside Aurelius or Uther or both. But as for their God, he was far away. His face was turned in another direction entirely, allowing a curious darkness to form like the nexus of a violent storm. I held Aurelius's sword high above my head. I directed myself to feel about this human as Ygraine felt about all humankind. Failing in that, I almost angrily willed myself to feel nothing. Drawing the sword from its scabbard, I brought it down across his throat, stepping back as the fountain of blood gushed forth. Even so, some of it splashed across my lips and, before I had a moment's thought, I swallowed it convulsively. Now the very life force of the Pendragon was a part of me. It was a tangible sign of what I had known from the moment I had first seen Uther—that he and I were inextricably linked.

But now there was no time for contemplation. Making the proper incantations, I rushed out of the tent. The clouds had parted, doing my bidding, and by the light of the half-moon I slew one guard and wounded another, making certain he marked well the face of Gorlois, which I wore like a mask at a pageant, before I used another glamour to vanish into a camp newly roused to tragedy.

"I should murder you on the spot!" Ygraine, in a rage, was a most unlovely sight. "But I must ask myself whether you are merely stupid or dangerously willful."

"I am neither, my lady," I said in my meekest voice. "How was I to know that Aurelius fell asleep in his brother's tent while Uther, restless and sleepless, went on a night foray?"

"Can you not tell one Pendragon from another?"

"It was dark. In the tent, all the tapers were guttered."

"You are a wizard, Myrddin!" she burst out in exasperation. "You can see in the dark!"

"I was concentrating on the act I was about to commit, my lady. And if I may say so, Uther—"

"You may say nothing without my permission!" she cried. "I desire only silence from you while I devise the method and duration of your punishment!"

Her hands shook slightly as she turned away from me. We were again in her quarters. From the courtyard below

came the sounds of Gorlois's war machines gearing up
for what would no doubt be the decisive battle with the
Pendragon warhost. For a long time, she stood silent,
contemplating the miniature boat. Candlelight flickered
on her hair, making of it a Medusa's nest that seemed
alive and malignant. At length, she sighed, and in a voice
less steely, said, "What could you possibly tell me of
Uther that I already do not know?"

"My lady, he holds in his heart the desire to possess
the Holy Grail of Christ. When he confided this to me I
at once had a vision of this artifact. One day he will possess it; it will be given to him by one of his knights. You
already know that the Pendragon place in history is set.
Now you know that Uther is the chosen of his God." I
paused for a moment to see what effect my words might
have on her, but Ygraine's mood remained opaque to
me. "There is also this, my lady. When I brought him
here to Tintagel he marked you and immediately fell
hopelessly in love. He is on fire to take you to your marriage bed."

At this, Ygraine turned to face me. "Bring him here,
Myrddin," she said without preface or explanation of
what was in her mind. "Bring him now and if all goes
well I may yet grant you a reprieve."

I bowed and took my leave of her. In the Pendragon
war camp, Uther was inconsolable. "Bring me good
news, my wizard," he thundered when he saw me, "or
begone from my sight, for the foul and cowardly Duke
of Cornwall has taken from me that which is most dear."

I separated him from his retinue. "Now is the time for
us to fly to Tintagel, my lord. Ygraine awaits you—or
rather, the man she thinks is her husband."

"Too late for that." He ground his teeth in his rage.
"Ah, God, were it me who had been slain in his place! I
tell you, Merlin, all justice has fled this world. Surely

God has turned his face from the Pendragon cause. How could my brother be taken at the very moment of our greatest triumph?"

His words chilled me. "This battle will be bloody and you will triumph, my lord. This I have seen. But it is only the beginning of the Pendragon triumphs. Gather you now to yourself, otherwise your men, who look well to you, will lose heart, and you will fail them."

"Then help me, wizard. Aurelius's death has all but undone me."

My heart ached for him. The knowledge that I had caused him such profound pain diminished me in my own eyes. "My lord," I said, "I know what needs to be mended inside you. Toward that end, come you with me to Tintagel. Think, Uther. Now, on the eve of battle, you will have your revenge on Gorlois tonight, and tomorrow as well."

By the same means as before I brought Uther into the sanctuary of his mortal enemy where this time Ygraine awaited him, anointed with saffron oil, aphrodisiacal spices, and the glamours only she could devise. His despair made him more vulnerable, and he fell completely under her spell. He would, if she had but asked him, walked out the window and happily fallen to his death.

Ygraine enjoyed him—enjoyed him far more than I knew she would have the rough and unruly Aurelius. As I understood, he was a man she could, like a gobbet of prime mutton, thoroughly chew. And yet she chose to punish me still by compelling me to watch them as they coupled long and noisily into the night. All the while, in the keep's great knights' hall directly below, Gorlois caroused with his generals, prematurely celebrating their anticipated victory on the morrow.

At one point during my long vigil, Morgause came

and stood beside me. "Ygraine has a lovely sense of humor, does she not?" she whispered.

Only if one's idea of lovely is a nest full of adders, I thought. But I held my tongue, for I knew nothing of Morgause and, therefore, had no way of knowing whether she was more like Elaine or Morgaine.

"This world, it seems to me, is wasted on these humans," she said as her eyes avidly devoured the convulsions of the couple in bed. "They live their lives like blind men without an appreciation of beauty. No wonder they squander their energies on animal lusts, on slaughtering each other. In their moral and emotional squalor, what else is there to divert them?"

I closed my eyes for a moment—but for a moment only, for Ygraine would know and punish me further if she sensed I was disobeying her. It was becoming clear to me that none of the women, save Elaine, knew what it meant to love. For it seemed to me that if they possessed the capacity to love they could not so thoroughly vilify humans. They would have found, as I had, the good qualities among humankind, and begin to appreciate them for these qualities, some of which were lacking in us. Instead, they were all too eager to couple with these powerful men who they considered no better than the animals they ate for food and skinned for clothes. In their lust for sex, power, and dominance they were no different than humankind.

Anger filled me like an empty cup. A murderer I might be, but yet my conscience had not withered on the vine. "But if we do not care for them," I said, "who will?" As Morgause turned to look at me, I continued. "If we hate them as they hate themselves, if we seek ways to murder them as they murder themselves we are no better than they are."

Had she been Morgaine, her lips would have curled in

contempt. But she was not her sister. "I do not hate
them, Myrddin. But they are ignorant. They see not our
goddesses, who bring forth bounty upon the earth. It is
their sense of the holy that offends me. Uther Pendragon
puts himself above all other men. He sees his mission as
one sanctioned by God and woe betide any who gainsays
him."

"Have a care what you say," I told her. "After this
night I have seen that Ygraine carries a child of his lineage who will become king."

"I should have been carrying that child." Morgause
said nothing more, but she did not have to. I saw her poi-
sonous thoughts seeping through her pores like acid.

From the moment Arthur was born, Ygraine appeared to
have little use for him. Once she had determined that her
seed had taken root in the human infant, she gave him to
Morgause to raise. This came as no surprise. Ygraine
was not what one might call the maternal type. Besides,
she had more immediately pressing matters to attend to.
Uther, now comfortably installed in Tintagel, had had little difficulty in winning the allegiance of what was left
of Gorlois's army after the Pendragon warhost infiltrated
the castle. As for the duke, Uther had dispatched him
himself in Tintagel's crowded knights' hall where, only
hours before, Gorlois and his generals had made their ill-
timed celebration. For weeks afterward, the duke's severed head rode one of his own pikes in the courtyard of
Tintagel, a silent but telling reminder to those who
would oppose Uther's drive to unite the land.

Ygraine was busy preparing for her marriage to Uther
and, as well, scheming to unite Morgause with King Lot
of Orkney, the most powerful and dangerous of the vas-
sal kings now united under the Pendragon banner. I did
not like King Lot, nor did I trust him. I had early marked

him as the general in Gorlois's circle most eager to attack the mistakes of others in order to elevate his own power with the duke. It had not escaped my notice that of all the generals he had been the only one to refrain from the last celebration. This led me to believe that he had known something no one else in the duke's retinue did. If this were indeed the case, I determined that I needed to discover who had informed him of Uther's impending victory. Toward this end, I made myself useful to him, first in the most casual of ways then, as he sought out my counsel, in an ever more intimate fashion.

Lot was a born deceiver. In this, he was a perfect match for Morgause. Small and sallow, he had the fierce, beady eyes of a raven and an instinct to match. He was cautious enough to keep his emotions in check at all times. Often, he appeared inert and unresponsive, so it was easy for his contemporaries to make the mistake of discounting him. But when he judged the moment was right I had seen him strike at his enemies without mercy, exterminating them so quickly they had no time to retaliate.

Uther, busy consolidating his power, needed Lot. He could not afford to distrust him, so I did it for him. It did not take me long to gain Lot's trust, and the first thing he asked of me was to take Arthur. He claimed that Morgause had no great love for the child, which was true as far as it went. However, he could not conceal from me his intense desire to start his own family with her without the burden of an adopted child. And yet he bade me keep Arthur in chambers not far distant. This disturbed me, since it was my understanding that he bore no special love for Arthur himself. For six years did I comply, but then the child became too much for them. Feeling ill equipped to look after a contentious six-year-old myself, I sought out Elaine to ask for her assistance only to discover that without a word to her sisters or to me she had quit Tintagel. Ygraine, however, knew of her flight.

"She has made her mind to take the veil," Ygraine said when I found her in the gardens. She had split a peach, and the clear juices dripped from her fingertips. "She is gone not to Afalan, where mayhap she will heal, but to the priests of Christ the Redeemer." Tearing off a crescent of white flesh, she popped it into her mouth. "The problem with this fruit," she said, "is that the sugar rises only when the flesh is too overripe for me to enjoy." She contrived to watch me while she ate, periodically turning her head to spit the pulp into a sheared boxwood hedge. "Now I have lost Elaine to the god of humankind." Reaching the pit, she turned it slowly over in her sticky fingers. "Tell me, Myrddin, have you an idea why she would of a sudden take herself to the convent at Five Lanes?"

"I have not, my lady."

She gave me that smile. "Pity. I had it in mind that in this matter you could be of more use to me."

"I could take myself to the convent and interview her," I offered.

"Think you a satisfactory answer would be forthcoming?"

"Not for you, my lady," I said with a heavy heart. "Surely not for you."

As he had done with Gorlois, Lot made himself indispensable to Uther. He was always at his right hand, always Uther's staunchest supporter. Say this for him, he fought with vigor and acquitted himself with honor on the field of battle.

Late one night, when Arthur was in his ninth year, Ygraine summoned me to her chambers. Of all the candles ranged around the rooms only one was lit, casting her quarters in a thick gloom.

"They are going out, Myrddin," she said when I arrived. "Despite my best efforts evil times are almost upon us."

I made no answer, but took the one flame and went about the room, trying without success to light the other candles. "It is no use," she said. "They are my gazing crystals. The candles were made in Afalan by my own hand, using the rendered tallow of the unicorn. In them, the nature of the future takes shape and is made manifest to me. And now they have gone dark."

I turned to her and, holding the candle between us, said: "What can I do?"

"Look after Arthur," she said. "Whatever may occur you must keep him safe from harm." Her colorless eyes regarded me with unaccustomed candor. "We have had our differences, Myrddin. At times it seems as if we have worked at cross-purposes." She lifted a hand as I made to reply. "Oh, there is no use denying it. I confess I am impressed by your loyalty to Uther." She put a hand on my arm. "Now I charge you with his son's life." She took the lone lit candle from my hand. "But in this one thing, at least, we are of one mind: In Arthur does the future reside. *Our* future—us and humankind alike. If there is to be any peace between us and humankind Arthur will be its standard-bearer. And you must forever be at his side, protecting him, guiding him because there are forces arrayed against him. Dark forces you cannot begin to imagine." Her gaze grew fierce, and her fingers gripped me with a curious strength. "But he must never know. Such a heavy burden is too much for one man. Swear you will keep him ignorant of his Fate, no matter the temptation to do otherwise."

"This I swear to you, my lady," I said. "But you are his mother. You must also be at his side."

Ygraine turned away and briefly touched the curving hull of the miniature boat. "Who knows where I will be in five years—or even one." When she turned back to me she seemed calmer than I had ever seen her. "Go you now, my Myrddin. You have your own Fate to meet." When I was almost at the door, her voice stayed me but a moment longer. "Do not for an instant think I am ignorant of the heavy burden you yourself bear." I turned, startled, to look at her, but she had already vanished into the gloom of the chambers. Only the flame of the single candle she had placed by the side of the miniature boat was left to keep at bay the darkness.

I confess that during these three years I bethought me many time of flying forthwith to the convent where Elaine had sequestered herself. I had not the slightest doubt what had turned her mind away from the world. What had happened—or, more rightly, what had not happened—between us was never far from my thoughts. When I slept I dreamt of her—or of the Holy Grail. In either case, I would awake and pray that in murdering Aurelius I had not caused Christ's Chalice to be lost forever. I had slain Aurelius and had crushed underfoot Elaine's pure and simple feelings for me. What other sins was I fated to commit, I wondered in despair, before I shed this quasi-immortal coil?

That night I was awakened by Ygraine's scream. I rushed to the king's chambers to find Uther lying spread-eagled amid the rumpled bed linens. Ygraine and King Lot stood on either side of him, staring down, too paralyzed by the sight, it seemed, to take action. Brushing past them, I knelt over Uther. Not a spot of blood could I find anywhere; neither could I find a drop of breath left within him.

"Poisoned," Ygraine whispered hoarsely. "Murdered in his own bed."

"Who would take such vile and contemptible action?" Lot asked.

"Uther Pendragon had many enemies," Ygraine said.

"Yea, Lady," Lot replied as he made to withdraw his sword. "Tell me but which one and I myself will behead him without so much as an interview or a tribunal."

"They are *all* guilty," Ygraine cried. "Each and every one bears the stigma of his base murder."

"Then I will myself slay them all!" he shouted, stalking from the bed chamber.

"You heard him." Ygraine stared bleakly at me from across the corpse of her husband. "Now will the darkness come. Now will we be plunged into war most bloody."

"Ygraine, we both so close to him." I was wrung with emotion. "How could we have let this happen?"

"Marked you not my words? For all our powers, there are times when we are helpless against the horde of humankind. The weight of sheer numbers, Myrrdin! Uther had so many enemies."

She climbed upon the cold bed and took up Uther's lifeless hand in hers. She whispered to him for a moment, but when she raised her voice it was to me she spoke. "Look you now to Arthur, my Myrddin. Whosoever poisoned Uther will surely seek out his son to try to end forever the line of Pendragon."

Though I was reluctant to leave the fallen king, I yet heeded Ygraine's command and I took Arthur from his bed. Without saying a word to any one, I bundled him tightly in his bedclothes, and with him curled like a salamander in my arms we took our leave of Tintagel through the secret entrance. We rode in utmost haste through the windswept night to Five Lanes where, lathered and winded, my horse deposited us before the heavy oak-and-iron doors of the Convent of St. Angelus. Its moss-laden stone walls jutted skyward as if reaching for the very heavens themselves. The stones were massive and roughly cut, giving the structure an air of both excessive bulk and age. After an interminable time, the gates creaked open and we were admitted.

I confess the ancient Mother Superior, newly risen from her mean and narrow cot, liked not the look of me. With her keen cockerel's eyes she marked me as neither knight nor lord. But then she spied Arthur and knew we were seeking sanctuary.

She arranged for us a room as spare and abstemious as her sense of charity. But then I have found that such is the power of fear it closes even the minds closest to God. Of Elaine there was no sign. She had stayed for almost three years, the Mother Superior grudgingly gave up, but no less than six months ago she had stolen away without a word to anyone.

"To be truthful, her disappearance came as no surprise," the ancient one said. She was thin as a spike and bent like a fine ash bow. Coarse hairs of age pocked her lined face, but her hands were steady as she brewed strong black tea for us in her cramped study, and, as I have said, her eyes missed no detail. "She came to us in the dead of night, and she slipped away just the same." She poured the tea into sturdy mugs, offering me honey directly from a neat slice of comb. "In between, she applied herself to her devotions sporadically. Often, I would find her staring blankly out her window or sitting alone in the cloister when she should have been reading her office or on her knees praying for Christ's guidance." She took a judicious sip of tea and dropped a slice of comb into it. "From the first, it was clear to me that

she was troubled but, stubborn one that she was, she refused all counseling. It was my fervent hope that God
would heal whatever was amiss inside her, but I suppose
she had been wounded too deeply." Stirring the wine-
dark tea with a tiny bone spoon, she had the look of
someone who had lost the need for sleep.

"Have you any idea where she might have gone?" I
asked.

"We may assume it was not back home," she said
dryly.

"Yes. I have just come from there."

She shrugged. "Then I am afraid I cannot be of further
help." She stood up, indicating that whether or not I had
finished my tea the interview was at an end.

I knew there was room to barter here. Indeed, the ancient traded on information—what other currency would
a cleric use? So I said: "She was running from me. It
was a sin to reject her, and now that she has fled I must
find her."

"It is you she loves, eh, young man? Well, youthful
folly can be forgiven. I will pray for you both." She
made the sign of the cross over me, then seemed to lapse
into a state of deep contemplation. Even as I wondered
whether I had paid enough for what she knew she inhaled deeply of the steam coming from her mug and of a
sudden lifted a hand. "Wait. There was something . . ."
She walked across the stone floor of her chamber until
she stood before a carved wooden image of Christ on the
cross. "Let me see. What was it she said to me? It was in
a fit of pique, I believe. Finding her idle in the cloister
when she should have been in the chapel at vespers, I
had newly reprimanded her. Tears sprang to her eyes and
she said . . . What was it she said? . . . Ah, yes. 'You
treat me as if I were an animal in a cage. Worse than
that, for I am expected to forego sleep and sustenance in

order to see to my devotions.' 'As you will learn,' I told her, 'God will provide when you give yourself wholly to him.' But she was adamant in her rebelliousness: 'You want nothing more of me than to become your servant. You may as well consign me to Saltash Moor.'"

"I have never heard of Saltash Moor."

"It is seven leagues to the west."

"You believe Elaine has gone there? But why? Is there a special significance to that place?"

"Oh, yes." Possibly she was tired, after all. A tic had commenced to draw her right eye downward. "Saltash Moor has a long and unpleasant history in these parts." She paused for a moment, possibly to bring under control the muscle spasm. "Truth to tell, it was why this convent was founded here, for as the ancient tale is told Saltash is the special haunt of the Devil."

Leaving Arthur in the care of the ancient Mother Superior, I traveled over low and desolate terrain, my horse galloping due west. Do not think that I simply left Arthur at St. Angelus on his own. Before I left I spread a glamour over him so that none but the Mother Superior could see or hear him. On the remote chance our enemies came looking for him at St. Angelus, the nuns would truthfully say they knew aught of him and even the most rigorous search would not reveal him to those who meant him harm.

This glamour would last only seventy-two hours, which is why I made all haste to Saltash Moor. It seemed clear to me—as it had to the Mother Superior—that Elaine had come here to meet her end. Despair and self-loathing are the mortal enemies of coherent thought. That these venoms existed inside her was a forgone conclusion. I only hoped that I would arrive in time to save her from herself. The Mother Superior entertained the same hope. To that end, she drew from behind the image of the crucified Christ a sword of uncommon length and beauty, which she placed in my hands. A gleaming black stone capped its pommel and across its guard were etched gold runes from a language wholly unfamiliar to me.

"The nuns who built this convent a century ago discovered this weapon during their excavations," she explained. "It has been handed down from one Mother Superior to another with us knowing only the prophesy buried in the apocalyptic writing of the Apostles." She wrapped surprisingly strong fingers around mine. "If you go to do battle with the Devil the least I can do is give you the means to successfully defend yourself."

"These runes," I asked her. "Do you know their meaning?"

"Because the sword is, in a sense, alive the ancients gave it a name. The runes spell it out: *Caletuwlch.*"

I saw the ancient standing stones first, those craggy slabs whose lichen-covered crevasses hold secrets no one could ever plumb. They glowed with an ethereal light. In some other age even Ygraine could not imagine they had been sacred. As such, they were both beautiful and terrifying. The wind was freshening out of the west, bringing with it the brackish smell of the rolling moorland. The moon was full, riding in ghostly splendor high over my right shoulder, so that it seemed I was balanced on a beam of light, illuminating without color or texture the terrain ahead.

My mount drew up at the edge of the moor, snorting and stamping its hooves. I was obliged to use a glamour to calm it down after repeated digs at its flanks failed to goad it forward. Moonlight lay across the moor like hoarfrost. Not a tree, not a hillock could be found. A more blasted, desolate landscape one could not easily imagine. I had just bethought myself that from all I had heard of him this was, indeed, the perfect place for the Devil to inhabit when I heard a peal of hysterical laughter. I was chilled to my vitals even before I turned around, for I had already determined by the tenor of the voice that it was Elaine laughing like a lunatic.

I wheeled my mount around to see her walking across the moor. She was naked, her white skin glowing in the moonlight. By her side was a creature so hideous and misshapen that it could only be termed an abomination. If I can describe it aright it had the chest and shoulders of a leopard, the hindquarters of a lion, the hooves of a deer, and the head of a serpent. When it spied me its mouth gaped wide and the sounds of baying hounds rolled over the heaths and heathers.

"So you have come for me at last, Myrddin." Elaine's once beautiful voice was pitched so high and hysterical it became like nails being scraped over slate. "What a pity you have left it too late!" The creature beside her bayed again, setting off another round of unpleasant laughter.

"Not too late, Elaine," I said as I slid from my saddle. "You live and that is all that matters." I held out my hand as I advanced over the lichen toward her. "Now come. It is high time you left this place."

Her companion beast snapped at me, causing me to recoil in order to keep my hand from being severed from my wrist.

"Have a care! My child is a jealous guardian indeed!"

"Your child?" I goggled at her. Her skin was waxen and her eyes had an odd glazed cast. "What madness is this?"

"No madness." She grabbed the ruff of the abomination's neck. "I mated with the Devil and this is his issue.

Is it not exquisitely, deliriously beautiful?" She threw her head back and laughed loud and long. "Ah, what sweet moment this be, to see on your face etched the same pain that you caused me!"

Summoning my wits, I threw a glamour across the beast's eyes and while it was confused and blinded I slew it with the sword Caletuwlch. The abomination howled in rage and pain while gouts of black ichor pulsed from its wounds. Elaine's eyes grew wide in horror and then they rolled up in her head and she collapsed into my waiting arms.

Without a look backward at the spawn of the Devil, I ran to where my mount waited, but each time I appeared to near it, its image flickered and it was again as far away as it had been a moment before. Foul magic was at work on that moor, of that there can be no dispute. But making incantations, I swung Caletuwlch in an arc in front of me. The immediate effect was akin to a shaft of sunlight cutting a swath through a dense and impenetrable fog. Now I saw that, bedeviled, I had been running in a circle around my horse without ever coming any closer to it. Keeping the sword in front of me, I headed directly toward it. Behind me, I heard an unholy howling and surmised that the father had come upon the unseemly corpse of his offspring. With that, I draped Elaine's inert form over my mount's neck while I climbed into the saddle, wheeled it around, and put heels to its flanks. Unlike before, the horse was only too happy to obey me and we galloped long into the night.

I had planned to take her straightaway to the convent, but with each league I could feel the life seeping out of her like the strange and unpleasant ichor from her child. I made all the proper incantations, swaddling her in a glamour of healing. To no avail. Once, I thought I heard echoing that awful howling, but possibly it was only in my mind. Elaine was dying, of that I had no doubt. And I had no hope that the primitive ministrations of the Mother Superior would have any salubrious effect. I had never before felt so hopeless and alone. If Elaine died, I knew full well that a good part of me would perish with her. What then to do? Where to go? I racked my brain for an answer. And then I recalled something that Ygraine had said about her daughter: *She is gone not to Afalan, where mayhap she will heal. . . .*

Afalan! I headed east toward the great circular lake that girdled the hidden isle. All the rest of that night I rode and into the crimson-and-gold morning, with the sun in my eyes and the tears streaming down my cheeks. Toward twilight, we reached the lakeshore. By then, my steed was done in and I knew I had run out of time. Elaine was on the point of death. No blood seemed left within her. Her pulses barely registered beneath my fingertips and when I put my face against hers I could scarce detect a breath.

It was only now as I dismounted in the silty mud that the enormity of my foolishness washed over me. Even if time had not run out how in the world was I going to ferry her across the lake to Afalan itself? I cursed myself and, in a towering rage, unsheathed Caletuwlch.

I confess I may have had in mind to do myself in so that in death the two of us could at last be entwined. Possibly it was the thought of my own selfishness that stayed my hand—I had, after all, given my word to protect Arthur. In any event, the sword, unsheathed, rippled with power. That energy struck Elaine in the center of her breast so that she was wrenched away from me. She stumbled down the bank, pitching headfirst into the lake.

"No!" I cried, wading in after her. I scooped her up, brushing back hair streaming with water. The rest of her was still immersed and I saw to my astonishment a tiny blush inhabit her cheeks. Feverishly, I checked her pulses and found them stronger. I could see her breast rise and fall as the breath slowly returned to her.

Crying and laughing with relief, I picked her out of the water and began to wade back toward the shore. At once, the color fled her and her breathing faltered. For a moment, my will collapsed with the swift and inexplicable ebbing of her life force, and I fell to my knees. Elaine, immersed again in the lake, began to revive. The water was akin to a tonic for her. I had been right, after all, to bring her here within sight of her beloved Afalan.

So I kept her there, hour after hour, floating her so only her face was above the water's surface. Her pulses rose and steadied, as did her breathing. But she did not awaken. With a clutch of horror, I wondered whether too much damage had already been done her. But then my faith revived and I bethought me to push her all the way into the lake.

Unclothing myself completely, I swam out with her to the deep water and pulled her completely under. She went down vertically like a pillar being driven into the lake bottom. When she was too far below me, I could no longer hold on. Something was dragging her down. For an instant, I felt a flicker of fear that having come this far I would now lose her to the swift, cold currents of the lake. But then I saw that her eyes were open. She was staring up at me and nodding.

I let go.

Down and down she went, vanishing into the mysterious blue depths of the lake. I waited for her . . . And waited. At last, with the cold sapping my strength, I swam back to the shallows, where I retrieved Caletuwlch. It warmed me just to hold it in my hand. I gazed out at the lake where the mist rose in dense spirals, where brightly colored loons swam with their families

and bass leapt, catching small, skimming insects in their
open mouths before disappearing again beneath the
water's silvery skin. Overhead, the sky reflected the last
remains of the day, glowing like embers in a banked fire.

"Ah, Elaine," I whispered as a chain of snowy egrets
appeared from the mist. They circled a spot not far from
me and then vanished from whence they had come. A
moment later, I spied a soft purling of the water at that
spot. At first I thought a school of bass had found a feed-
ing ground, but then the purling deepened, widening
until the ripples reached my knees. At that precise moment, Elaine rose from the depths and beckoned to me.
As I waded toward her, I saw that her eyes were clear
and luminous.

"Elaine, you are alive. Remember you what happened?"

Life had returned to her cheeks and when she spoke
no residue of her previous hysteria remained. "Only as
one remembers a dream." She reached out her hands for
me. "But I do know I am alive because of your love for
me."

"Ah, Lady." I embraced her. "I wish only that you not
hate me."

"Hate you? Could I meet a love such with hatred?"

As she said, the immediate past was a dream. That
being so, it was better that her own words remained forgotten so that they might eventually crumble into ash.
"Turning you away was fraught with such pain. But my
obligation was to Uther and now to Arthur, his son. But
holding you close like this makes me tremble. Would
that I were not powerless to change."

"Oh, Myrddin, the love that is inside you rushes like a
river in spring thaw." She caressed my cheek. "Do not
wish for change. It is both your blessing and your curse
that you love the humans so. If the Pendragon line sur-

vives it will be because of you. And at last I understand
that their survival means life for all of us. Had we run
off together as I selfishly longed for, Arthur would be
cold and dead now, interred beside his father, and the
Pendragons would be no more than a footnote in history."

"Now that you have recovered fully in these life-
giving waters, come back with me. Together, we will
care for young Arthur, protecting him as we teach him."

She smiled. "Oh, I will play my role in Arthur's life.
But as for leaving the lake I cannot. It is my home now.
If I leave, I shall perish. Whatever happened to me after
I left St. Angelus had at least a lasting effect on my con-
stitution." Her smile deepened. "But you will come
here often, Myrddin, and each time you do I will rise
from the depths and we will be together as if for the first
time."

That unearthly howling echoed in my mind one last
time as she uttered these words, making me shudder.
"Take you now this sword," I said, thrusting it into her
hands and pressing her fingers as the Mother Superior's
fingers had pressed mine. "Caletuwlch will protect you
while you gather your strength and regain your power. In
time, I will come for the sword."

"It is not for you."

"No," I said. "It is for Arthur. I knew it the moment I
first used it. His will be a dark, tortuous path even when
he gains the Kingship. There will always be those who
will try to wrest it from him. His crown will never but lie
uneasy upon his head."

"I fear that before this is done we shall both shed tears
for him, Myrddin."

"But not yet. His time still lies before him," I told her
as I kissed her long and well. "Farewell, beloved. Heal
yourself here in the land that first nurtured you."

*   *   *

For four years did Lot, King of Orkney, carry out his
boast. He asked for and received from Ygraine the title
of regent, so that all would know he had the backing of
the Royal Court. Say this for him, he used his new title
to the full extent of its power. As regent, he brought to
the executioner's blade each king, liege lord, duke, and
knight about whom his spies unearthed even a breath of
treason. He posted rewards, encouraging even brother to
inform on brother. In tribunals the new regent had no interest whatsoever, for his heart appeared consumed with
taking his revenge on Uther's supposed murderer. And
yet as weeks turned to months, months to years and still
his war raged on unchecked it became clear that with
every enemy executed Lot himself grew in power and
influence. He took to wearing a cloak manufactured
from the beards of those he had himself dispatched, and
this cloak grew from hip-length to knee-length to a
length where it swept the ground as he walked. It made
him a terrifying sight, and even those he had not yet opposed grew to fear him.

Ygraine was anxious for Arthur to be coronated, as
the only direct heir to Uther Pendragon, but again and
again Lot dissuaded her. While any enemy of Uther remained, it was still too dangerous, he told her. Also,
while war still raged he remained unconvinced the North
Isle kings would follow the lead of a callow thirteen-
year-old, who had yet to be soundly tested in battle.

In this manner, four years passed, and then five. And
at last Lot returned in triumph to Tintagel. Usurping the
Pendragon throne, he crowned himself king.

The moment had come for Arthur's ascension and I
betook myself to reclaim Caletuwlch for him. But I was
in for a thoroughly unpleasant surprise. Elaine, rising
from the lake surrounding Afalan, embraced me in terror

for, she said, she had lately heard a terrible howling, even from the watery depths of her home.

"It draws nearer every day," she said, "and every day I grow more frightened."

I took her hand and tried to calm her. This was not easy for at that moment there was precious little serenity inside myself. The day I had dreaded was at hand. I knew that her abominable mate sought her still. I took from her Caletuwlch, and with the sword strapped to my side I set off once again for Saltash Moor.

I arrived in fog-bound twilight. A dank stench arose from the ground, as if the land all around were mortally ill, oozing dreadful toxins. The abominable beast that I had slain four years ago was where I had left it, unde-composed, silent in its pool of noxious ichor. It was as if here upon this moor no time had passed since last I stood here, rescuing Elaine from her infernal Fate.

At once I drew Caletuwlch and, holding it before me like a torch, advanced along the moor. Wherever I pro-ceeded, the unnatural fog recoiled as if it were a living thing. As I went, I listened, but there was no sound of birds nor of insects, and if the air moved at all, I dis-cerned no evidence of it. All was utter silence; the si-lence of the tomb.

Finding nothing, I turned back and when I came again upon the fallen beast I drove Caletuwlch point-first into its skull, twisting the blade as I did so. At once, I heard the familiar howling, so close at hand this time that the hairs at the nape of my neck stirred and I felt a nauseat-ing chill course through me.

"Who comes to defile my child?" The words seemed to come from everywhere at once.

"It is I, Myrddin. The one who in the first place slew this abomination."

For a time there was silence. Then into this void there

came a Darkness, but one such as I had never before experienced. It was at once complete and suffocating, as if it were sucking all the air out of the surrounding landscape. A sudden cold bloomed hoarfrost upon the heaths and heathers and it was all I could do to keep my teeth from chattering. I refrained from drawing my cloak close about me, not wanting him to see the extent to which I was vulnerable. Instead, I brandished Caletuwlch, and again I heard the unholy howling.

A great pressure came and went upon my eardrums and then I stood face to face with the Devil. How to describe the indescribable? If one puts fire and ice together the laws of what the modern-day world call physics dictate that the result is steam. But what if fire and ice could co-exist? Impossible, you say. And yet this is what was made manifest that evening on Saltash Moor. I suppose the sight was a metaphor, for in this entity everything remained unresolved. It was a living oxymoron—a being in which diametrically opposed forces co-existed in a repugnant stasis. I imagine it must be a painful existence, which I suppose is the point. Apart from the fire and ice the only other feature discernible to my eyes were a pair of wings—or, more accurately, the stubs. Horribly foreshortened, they had obviously been clipped or possibly burned off, for the stubs appeared blackened at their ends.

"Myrrdin," this Horror bellowed, "I know your end. I know everything about you."

"Then you know I will never allow you near the Lady Elaine."

There came a sound as of a massive herd of horses galloping across the moor. With a start, I realized that this dreadful noise was a kind of laugh. "I *will* have her if that is my wish."

"Then kill me now," I said.

"That accursed sword . . . I cannot."

"Then you will have her not."

"Recompense!" the Horror screeched. "I will have recompense for her life!"

"Take as you may," I said, "but know I will ever stand against you."

The column of fire-and-ice swirled upward, elongating into the night sky. "Antagonists!" it bellowed. "That is what I crave!"

"Then that is what you shall have!" I shouted into the maelstrom of its making.

"You cannot harm me. I wished to die, but that surcease is not within my purview. An irony: I can cause others to die, but cannot myself be so released. Instead, I subsist at God's insistence, for without me He becomes meaningless."

"Then we are at a stalemate," I said.

"A stalemate, no, not at all. For I have information vital to you. A truth long hidden, a dark and terrible secret you will appreciate." The fire-and-ice maelstrom grew in malevolence, and I had the impression the Horror was licking its chops. "These humans believe that they were born in the image of God, that they are his children, that a tiny piece of Him exists inside each and every one of them." The rumbling laughter came again, roiling my vitals. "A fatuous conceit. No, Myrddin, these people are *my* progeny. Yes, they are the offspring of an Angel, but one fallen from grace, yet no less important for that. I sinned, and they inherited my penchant for it. They blaspheme, murder, pillage, rape. They lust for power and hate their neighbors. They are prideful and intolerant."

My blood ran cold. "Not all of them."

"No body is perfect; that is the essence of my existence. Sin resides in them all, even the best of them. It is darkness made visible."

"You are Sin Incarnate," I said. "I reject all you have said for a base falsehood."

"Say what you may, Myrddin. You cannot refute the evidence of your eyes. Look around you! What do you see but war, murder, hatred, and betrayal. My words have only confirmed what was already in your heart. Your people were pure and sinless. Once. But you have since become infected by proximity to humankind. And now the final step in your doom: you have successfully procreated with the humans. Well, from my perspective that is delicious, indeed! Your purity has been compromised. Now you are no better than my own children. Are they not irresistible? Of course they are! They have dragged you down into the mire of their sin. You see how it is, Myrddin? I have no need to harm you, for you have done it all yourself! I can now sit back and watch events unfold. As you have no doubt surmised I am someone who can fully appreciate irony. And who better than I? For I *am* Irony."

The dreadful laughter rolled like a plague over the moor. "Your precious Arthur, who you are pledged to protect, is the very instrument of your downfall. Through him will come the end of your race. You see him as the future, but he is a false future—a dead-end for your race. Quite soon, the human traits will overwhelm whatever is pure and sinless in you. And then your kind will vanish like a puff of smoke!"

"I will see to it that never happens," I said boldly, ignorantly, stupidly.

"Oho, do you really think so?" I was obviously providing the Horror some amusement. "But, you see, it is already too late, Myrddin. While you tarry here jousting verbally with me Arthur has seduced King Lot's wife. It is why I brought you here in the first place, so he would have his chance to sin most grievously. Arthur knows Morgause not as his half-sister—you were most punctilious in keeping this knowledge from him. For his own good, you thought. Now it will be his ruin, for Morgause will bear him a son that is also his nephew. Ironic, is it not, that Arthur was born from deceit and his future nemesis is similarly born."

"I will make sure Arthur knows all that transpired here," I said.

"Will you then break so easily your pledge to the Lady Ygraine?"

"I can at least warn him about the child."

"You may warn him, but have it on good authority that it will ill avail you. This child will survive to slay Arthur and bring down the entire Pendragon line."

"Why tell me this?"

"I will have my recompense! It is the price you pay, Myrddin, for the life of the Lady Elaine."

Willing to take no more of this, I struck the Devil a mighty blow with Caletuwlch. At once, I felt a terrible wrenching, and a profound pain ran through me. The blade shuddered and quaked, but yet held together. Above me, the column swayed, divided like a river of smoke, only to re-establish itself. I dealt the Devil blow after blow, though the resultant agony built inside me. At last, I could take no more and I fell to my knees, the sword supporting me as my body trembled all over with my efforts.

When I arose from my stupor, I found myself alone upon Saltash Moor. The dead abomination had vanished, and even the echoes of the unholy howling that had haunted me since its death had ceased. Looking down, I discovered that I had thrust the sword into the heart of a granite boulder, and it was this base that had supported me at my weakest moment. I made to pull it out, but bethought me of a way for Arthur to prove his legitimacy to all the kings of the Isles. Even Lot the Usurper would not be able to long stand against the man who had pulled the sword Caletuwlch from the stone.

Because the sword was meant for Arthur he and he alone was able to draw it forth from its stone bed. In his tongue the Welsh Caletuwlch became corrupted to Excalibur. With it, he waged bloody war, defeating Lot the Usurper, the other rebel kings of England, the Saxons and, lastly, the warlords of the North Isles of Ireland and Scotland. As to Mordred, his son and nephew by Morgause, Arthur ordered him put upon a ship with all the royal children born that day—for because of my pledge to Ygraine I could, in my prophesy, tell him only that a child of royal parentage born on a specific date would be his undoing. But, in the end, the Devil had his way, for the ship foundered in a great storm, its splintered heart fetching up onto a reef where a handful of the children, including Mordred, survived. So indeed did Mordred return to the court years later and, as the Devil had predicted, slew Arthur.

By that time, Arthur's court was corrupt and unjust, riddled with jealousies, feuds, and betrayals most foul. In that, also, the Devil told the truth. It took but a space of several heartbeats for all the purity that had once existed in us to be overwhelmed by the venality of humankind. Luckily, Ygraine did not live long enough to see her dreams fall to ash.

Instead of protecting Arthur I confess that I abandoned him to his Fate. Had it been Uther, I could never have brought myself to it. I loved Uther unconditionally, as a father loves his son. But Arthur and I never had the same connection. As I say, he was born in deceit, and this was never far from my mind. It is true that Uther cuckolded Gorlois, but he truly loved Ygraine and I was not one to gainsay that love. For his part, Arthur seduced Morgause simply because he could. It was a whim, nothing more. So, you see, in the end it was more easy than not to vanish from the midst of the people I had grown to love too well, and who had disappointed me too profoundly. With Uther's passing, an era had ended. In Arthur's birth were already flowering the seeds of corruption, decay, and dissolution. He was meant to be the savior, but he was only a human being: venal, jealous, lecherous, selfish. But even had he not been all these things, it was too late for me. The knowledge of humankind's origin cut too deeply, and it was a wound that would not heal.

So it was that I withdrew to Afalan, where Elaine and I lived until the day she died. Now I am where I left her at the last—at the portal to death. It is indeed ironic, for these days the Devil, who I had not seen in many, many years, now visits me often. This is as close as he will ever come to the death he so desperately desires. How he envies me! How much pain he has caused me! He is, at the last, as I have said, a living oxymoron. In that sense he can never be fully understood, even for the likes of me.

Well, they are all dust now, every one for whom I had a care. It is truth that I loved the humans too much for their own good. I suppose I still see the good in them, though they be sinners all. But how they disappointed me! How bright was my love for Uther; how small and weak the flame is now.

And yet it has not yet quite died. Which is why in the first place I made this appointment with you. Now you know everything, and when I die you must carry the flame forward. As you have seen, it is a fragile thing, and at every step I have no doubt the Devil will seek to snuff it out. But you will not let that happen, will you? Here is all the help you will need. I have kept it all this time, simply for this moment.

No, it is not the sword Caletuwlch. In the end, that belonged to the Lady Elaine. She has taken it back with her to wherever she has gone. No, this is a simple chalice, but in it lies the future of the world.

You do not believe me? Well, you are young yet. In the following years will you find the truth of my words. Faith, you see, is as fragile as this candle flame. It may waver, but it must never be allowed to gutter out. Mine died at the moment I discovered mankind's origin, so I have been waiting all this time for another whose faith will not be broken by the truth.

Are you the one?

Tell me.

Tell me now, for the Devil approaches on soft cat's feet.

The Mouse's Soul

Nina Kiriki Hoffman

The dragon snaps me up and swallows me whole.
I make only a morsel for a mouth as huge as his,
And hours has he been hungry. This I learn
As in his gut I give up the ghost, and ghostly going,
I do not leave. Instead I enter
Into a hole where waits an emptiness of soul.
There I bide as in a crack between stones,
And peep out as possible. So I learn my new life:
Hidden I am in the dragon's head,
Able to use his eyes and see my surroundings.
The dragon hides in a hole that could hold
A hundred hundred mouse holes, holds instead a heap
Of glittering metal and stones
Impossible to eat except with eyes,
And in the corner, a maiden cowers.
Such I have seen before, but then
From a level lower than feet.
She screams not, only shrinks and fidgets,

Hiding behind hands as though
They could cover her completely.
In my belly I feel the grumble for grain,
Loud as a leopard's cry.
In my mind I taste a toasted hand,
Savor an imagined scent, fire and flesh
Alloyed into ambrosia. My mouth
Fills with water. Why wait?
I taste fire in my throat and on my tongue.
I lean and lurch, unsteady, unnerved
To find my feet scaled claws,
Each talon longer than the self I used to use.
At each step the ground shakes.
My stomach scrapes the stone below.
Measure me some meat! Only an arm
To start with, you can carry with one,
Live without other. Just an arm, a foot,
I pray you!
At last she screams and scampers, quick as liquid
Silver. Just so have I run, many a time,
From the shadow of something larger.
So many are more than mouse-size that
I eked out an eternity of rushing.
Hunger howls louder than halt or help.
Still, I slow my staggering stumble,
Recalling the push of panic, the taste
Of terror. The maiden slips behind
A stack of stricken armor, flawed and faulted,
Cracked and crushed by claws like mine.
The hard-shelled ones, the dragon thinks,
Taste best roasted in the shell, then winkled out.
Fire rumbles in my belly in response to ancient taste.
Then comes the clatter of worked and worn metal
Against rock to my rear. I raise my head.
What waits? What comes? What new thing

Nudges the senses, frets the fears?
It smells of grease and grime and goodness.
As I twist to take its measure,
A shaft of fire pierces my chest,
A pain sudden and staggering, shadowed by a second,
Then a third. I scream. My sound
Shakes stalactites, shatters stone.
Pain overpowers hunger, health, horror.
Have I not died once already this afternoon?
I spy the stinging thing that struck me,
See its sword slice air as it strides forward.
Not another knight! The dragon thinks.
Knights I have known only from
Rustling through the rushes below tables
Where they take repast. Casual crumbs
Cascade down to those who wait.
Though below table dogs dance and dart
More freely than mice, the smallest scraps
Sustain the souls in smallest frames.
I lift my claw to crush. Its talons darkly shine.
Forth darts the sword, and slashes
Through scale and skin and sinew.
I scream again. Poison from the earlier arrows
Has made a home in all my hollows,
Runs the roads my blood travels,
Saps my strength. I stagger, stumble,
Fall.

A short space only I have spent
Looking down on others,
And that eaten by hunger, inclined to impulse,
Averse to thought.
At the root, I think this scarce span
Better than those stretched seasons

Of hiding, hunger, dread, and dodging
When I sojourned small.

The maiden emerges from the mail,
Approaches me. So weak I am
I cannot lift a limb, jiggle my jaw, lower a lid.
She smells of summers, sun, sweat,
And sugars, enticing tastes my tongue's too tired
To track. From her gown she draws a kerchief.
"Dragon's blood," she whispers, dipping
Linen in my life.
Then, I know not how it happens,
I no longer linger in the dragon's husk
But blend with the blood to blot the cloth.
She folds the kerchief with blood inmost
And hides it again about her person.
In my nest against her skin, I feel her turn.
"Oh sir," she says, "God knows you have my gratitude."
"God knows," says the knight, "I was glad to give aid."
In my nest against her skin, I know
More than ever I should about the maiden's mind.
What she wants with dragon's blood
Is wickeder than anything ever a dragon did with it,
More frightening than all the fears in the life of a mouse
Who shivers every second of his life.
Here in blood I bide
And wait for what comes next.

ABOUT THE EDITOR

Since 1984, **Jennifer Roberson** has published twenty-one novels and edited three anthologies. Her primary genre is fantasy, including such series as the "Sword-Dancer" saga, the "Chronicles of the Cheysuli," and the historical fantasy *The Golden Key*, co-written with bestselling fantasy authors Melanie Rawn and Kate Elliott, which was nominated for the World Fantasy Award in 1997. She has also published three historical novels: *Lady of the Forest* and *Lady of Sherwood*, both featuring the Robin Hood legend; and *Lady of the Glen*, based on 17th-century Scotland's Massacre of Glencoe. Her short fiction has appeared in numerous anthologies, collections, and magazines. In addition to *Out of Avalon*, she has edited *Return to Avalon* and *Highwaymen: Robbers and Rogues*.

(The following constitutes an extension of the copyright page.)

Introduction by Jenniferf Roberson copyright © Jennifer Roberson, 2001.

"The Heart of the Hill" by Marion Zimmer Bradley and Diana L. Paxson copyright © Marion Zimmer Bradley and Diana L. Paxson, 2001.

"The Fourth Concealment of the Island of Britain" by Katharine Kerr copyright © Katharine Kerr, 2001.

"Prince of Exiles" by Rosemary Edghill copyright © Rosemary Edghill, 2001.

"The Secret Leaves" by Tricia Sullivan copyright © Tricia Sullivan, 2001.

"The Castellan" by Diana Gabaldon and Samuel Watkins copyright © Diana Gabaldon and Samuel Watkins, 2001.

"Lady of the Lake" by Michelle Sagara West copyright © Michelle Sagara West, 2001.

"The Mooncalfe" by David Farland copyright © David Farland, 2001.

"Avalonia" by Kristen Britain copyright © Kristen Britain, 2001.

"Finding the Grail" by Judith Tarr copyright © Judith Tarr, 2001.

"Me and Galahad" by Mike Resnick and Adrienne Gormley copyright © Mike Resnick and Adrienne Gormley, 2001.

"A Lesser Working" by Jennifer Roberson copyright © Jennifer Roberson, 2001.

"Grievous Wounds" by Laura Resnick copyright © Laura Resnick, 2001.

"Black Dogs" by Lorelei Shannon copyright © Lorelei Shannon, 2001.

"Marwysgafn (Deathbed Song)" by Eric Van Lustbader copyright © Eric Van Lustbader, 2001.

"The Mouse's Soul" by Nina Kiriki Hoffman copyright © Nina Kiriki Hoffman, 2001.

Look what we have for you to read next...

❏ **THE DARKEST ROAD: BOOK THREE** by Guy Gavriel Kay
In a world of extraordinary imagination, a final battle is
waged against a power of unimaginable proportions.

458338/$13.95

❏ **RESURRECTION** by Arwen Elys Dayton
In 2600 B.C., the first ship built by the Kinley race capable of
travelling faster than the speed of light, the *Champion*, is sent
to explore a tiny blue planet called Earth. But the *Champion's*
first mission would also be its last...

458346/$6.99

❏ **SILVER WOLF, BLACK FALCON** by Dennis L. McKiernan
The final novel in the bestselling world of Mithgar "blends lore
and prophecy with vivid battle scenes and emotional drama to
create a tale of high fantasy that should appeal to...fans of
epic fiction." (*Library Journal*)

458036/$6.99

Prices slightly higher in Canada

Payable by Visa, MC or AMEX only ($10.00 min.), No cash, checks or COD.
Shipping & handling: US/Can. $2.75 for one book, $1.00 for each add'l book;
Int'l $5.00 for one book, $1.00 for each add'l. Call (800) 788-6262 or
(201) 933-9292, fax (201) 896-8569 or mail your orders to:

Penguin Putnam Inc.
P.O. Box 12289, Dept. B
Newark, NJ 07101-5289
Please allow 4-6 weeks for delivery.
Foreign and Canadian delivery 6-8 weeks.

Bill my: ❏ Visa ❏ MasterCard ❏ Amex _____(expires)
Card# _____

Signature _____

Bill to:
Name _____
Address_____ City _____
State/ZIP _____ Daytime Phone # _____
Ship to:
Name_____ Book Total $ _____
Address _____ Applicable Sales Tax $_____
City _____ Postage & Handling $_____
State/ZIP _____ Total Amount Due $ _____

This offer subject to change without notice.   Ad # JanROC (9/00)

*Return to the world of **The Black Jewels**...*

❏ THE INVISIBLE RING

Anne Bishop   0-451-45802-8 / $6.99

In this darkly mesmerizing tale, from the world of **The Black Jewels**, a young Warlord, is auctioned as a pleasure slave by a notorious queen. He fears he will share the fate of her other slaves, but the Gray Lady may not be what she seems....

❏ TREACHERY AND TREASON

Edited by Laura Anne Gilman and Jennifer Heddle   0-451-45778-1 / $5.99

Celebrate the worst in human nature with this anthology that unveils the darker side of the soul. It includes tales of trickery, deceit, treachery, and betrayal by some of the best minds in science fiction, fantasy, and horror. Including: William C. Dietz, Dennis L. McKiernan and Irene Radford.

Prices slightly higher in Canada

Payable by Visa, MC or AMEX only ($10.00 min.), No cash, checks or COD.
Shipping & handling: US/Can. $2.75 for one book, $1.00 for each add'l book;
Int'l $5.00 for one book, $1.00 for each add'l. Call (800) 788-6262 or (201)
933-9292, fax (201) 896-8569 or mail your orders to:

Penguin Putnam Inc.   Bill my: ❏ Visa ❏ MasterCard ❏ Amex _____ (expires)
P.O. Box 12289, Dept. B
Newark, NJ 07101-5289   Card# _____
Please allow 4-6 weeks for delivery.
Foreign and Canadian delivery 6-8 weeks.   Signature _____
Bill to:
Name _____
Address _____ City _____
State/ZIP _____ Daytime Phone # _____
Ship to:
Name _____ Book Total $ _____
Address _____ Applicable Sales Tax $ _____
City _____ Postage & Handling $ _____
State/ZIP _____ Total Amount Due $ _____
This offer subject to change without notice.   Ad # Bish2 (9/00)

<u>Now in Hardcover!</u>

Return to the world of Mithgar!

Dennis L. McKiernan

SILVER WOLF, BLACK FALCON

Dennis L. McKiernan's newest epic takes you back to
Mithgar in a time of great peril—as an Elf and an
Impossible Child try to save this ravaged land from a
doom long ago prophesied....

"Once McKiernan's got you, he never lets you go."
—Jennifer Roberson

"McKiernan's narratives have heart and fire and drive."
—Katherine Kerr

❏ 0-451-45786-2/$23.95

Prices slightly higher in Canada

Payable by Visa, MC or AMEX only ($10.00 min.), No cash, checks or COD. Shipping & handling:
US/Can. $2.75 for one book, $1.00 for each add'l book; Int'l $5.00 for one book, $1.00 for each
add'l. Call (800) 788-6262 or (201) 933-9292, fax (201) 896-8569 or mail your orders to:

Penguin Putnam Inc.   Bill my: ❏ Visa ❏ MasterCard ❏ Amex _____ (expires)
P.O. Box 12289, Dept. B
Newark, NJ 07101-5289   Card# _____
Please allow 4-6 weeks for delivery.   Signature _____
Foreign and Canadian delivery 6-8 weeks.

Bill to:
Name _____
Address _____City _____
State/ZIP _____Daytime Phone # _____
Ship to:
Name _____Book Total $ _____
Address _____Applicable Sales Tax $ _____
City _____Postage & Handling $ _____
State/ZIP _____Total Amount Due $ _____
This offer subject to change without notice.   Ad # MCKN 2 (4/00)

PENGUIN PUTNAM INC.
Online

Your Internet gateway to a virtual environment with
hundreds of entertaining and enlightening books
from Penguin Putnam Inc.

*While you're there, get the latest buzz on
the best authors and books around—*

Tom Clancy, Patricia Cornwell, W.E.B. Griffin,
Nora Roberts, William Gibson, Robin Cook,
Brian Jacques, Catherine Coulter, Stephen King,
Jacquelyn Mitchard, and many more!

**Penguin Putnam Online is located at
http://www.penguinputnam.com**

PENGUIN PUTNAM NEWS

Every month you'll get an inside look at our upcom-
ing books and new features on our site. This is an
ongoing effort to provide you with the most
up-to-date information about
our books and authors.

**Subscribe to Penguin Putnam News at
http://www.penguinputnam.com/ClubPPI**